A MAZE
OF STARS

By John Brunner
Published by Ballantine Books:

A MAZE OF STARS

JOHN BRUNNER

A Del Rey Book

BALLANTINE BOOKS · NEW YORK

A Del Rey Book
Published by Ballantine Books

Library of Congress Cataloging-in-Publication Data

Brunner, John, 1934-
    A maze of stars / John Brunner.—1st ed.
      p. cm.
    "A Del Rey book."
    ISBN 0-345-36541-0
    I. Title.
  PR6052.R8M37 1991   90-93527
  823'.914—dc20   CIP

Text design by Michaelis/Carpelis Design

Manufactured in the United States of America

First Edition: July 1991

10 9 8 7 6 5 4 3 2 1

My prison is the universe,
  a maze of stars my cage.
I bear an unremitting curse:
my prison is the universe.
No mercy may my doom reverse
  nor pleas my plight assuage.
My prison is the universe—
  a maze of stars, my cage.

A MAZE
OF STARS

CHAPTER ONE

TREVITHRA

ONCE UPON A TIME—

But what time? Before or after the last events recorded in memory?

Always the same questions recurred in the same order and were answered in the same order. For this plaything of chance, that was almost the only stable fact of existence.

First: *Who am I?* (Or what. It amounted to exactly the same thing, and the answer never changed.)

Then: *Where am I?* (Subjective millennia of stored data supplied at least that much information.)

Finally: *When am I?*

And there was only ever one way to find that out . . .

LIKE THE SHADOW OF A SLOWLY CLOSING DOOR, NIGHT fell over Clayre, Trevithra's spaceport city by the Althark Sea. There was no twilight to speak of, for it lay athwart the equator. From the temples, shrines, parks, and palaces on Marnchunk Hill to the artisans' shacks by the waterfront, and farther yet, by way of the rickety platforms where dwelt combers and scavengers, to the frail smacks and yawls that served as homes for fisherfolk—rising now and snatching a scanty meal before their night's work—people glanced up by reflex, expecting to see reassuring green-metallic flashes, brilliant as the sheen on a waterwaif. They betokened an artificial aurora that killed spores drifting down from space.

It had, however, been switched off.

The citizens, accordingly, had a rare opportunity to glimpse the stellar glory beyond their sky, for the line of sight thus opened up happened to lie directly along the main axis of the Arm of Stars and back toward the parent galaxy. However, most were too nervous to enjoy the sight. There had been rumors for the past few days, though no hard news, and here was their confirmation.

Another starship was about to land. And who ever knew what one of those might bring?

Stripe heard the shouts while she was dickering with fat Dr. Bolus at Mid-City Market, trying to convince him that a palm-sized piece of muthrin shell from the flexibox she trailed was a fair exchange for another bottle of his anticheeching nostrum. Afraid of being overlooked between a kaftan seller on one side and racks of dried lampedusas on the other, he kept interrupting to call out in a wheedling tone to passersby, guessing at their ills and promising a cure. Even when he seemed to be paying attention he kept restlessly shifting and rattling surgical instruments on the counter before him. To make matters worse Stripe's younger brother Donzig, whom she dared not leave at home now Yin and Marla were so helpless, was ostentatiously bored and kept wandering off in search of strelligers and shadow shows or fruit and sweetmeats he could filch.

Next time I'll tie a cord around the little beast's leg!

Abruptly she registered what the shouting was about and broke off with a cock of her head. Yes, unmistakably:

"The green has gone! The sky is black!"

Under the awnings of the market, she hadn't noticed.

"That means there's a starship due!" she exclaimed.

"What's it to you?" returned the doctor with a shrug. "If you're afraid of it carrying alien organisms, I can let you have an all-purpose immunizer—twenty tablets to proof you against any known germ and most of the unknown ones—but that's going to cost more than a paltry scrap of shell. You'd find it cheaper to burn a prayer or two. I doubt it works, but it does cost less, and there are plenty who believe in it."

Stripe was no longer listening. Reaching a swift decision, she upended her flexibox on the counter. Out tumbled a welter of miscellanea salvaged from what rich families on Marnchunk Hill had thrown away deliberately or by mistake, including torcs, some scarcely damaged, toe rings, studded belts, even an eye gem. "Two flasks of anticheeching mixture!" she snapped. "And make sure they're brim-full!"

Bolus made to demur. She glared at him.

"I've no more time to waste! Come on!"

Astonished, he shrugged and complied, visibly wondering what had come over this girl who normally drove as hard a bargain as any of his customers. When he handed over the medicine and gathered up his takings, it was Donzig's turn to be surprised.

"Come here!" Stripe rasped, and when the child dawdled, closed the gap and seized him by the nearer earlobe, bending her face to his.

"Don't start grizzling or I'll give you something to grizzle about! Now listen, and do exactly as I say! Take this medicine and go straight home. Straight home, is that clear? Give Yin and Marla a cupful each. Use the white cup on the peg by the door."

"You're hurting me!" Donzig whined.

"I'll hurt you worse in a moment if you don't hold your tongue! What cup do you give the medicine in?"—pinching hard.

"Ow! The white one hanging on a peg!"

"Where?"

"By the door!"

"All right." She slackened her grip. "Now when you've done that, you're to take the bag hanging on the next peg, the yellow one. Handle it carefully! Take it to Mother Shaqqi at the Blue Shrine. Tell her to sell what's in the bag as amulets to protect people against skybugs and space germs. And warn her I know the contents by heart, so I'll want my cut later on."

"I don't like her!" Donzig whimpered. "She's ugly! I'm scared of her!"

"You do exactly as you're told," Stripe whispered. "If when I get back I find you haven't, I—I'll put you in my flexibox and push you off Accadantan Pier!"

And added, relenting slightly, "Tell Mother Shaqqi to buy you a stickasweet and a mug of chulgra. She can take it out of my share. Off with you!"

As she spoke, she was rolling up the flexibox. Clipping the ends together, she slung it baldric fashion across the short green kirtle that was her only garment. Some days she didn't even bother with that much, for she felt quite adequately clad in the red body pattern, winding across her torso and along her limbs, that had bestowed the nickname by which she was known now to everybody, even her parents. In the crowded market, though, nudity was inadvisable. Around any corner she might run into a gang of antis.

"How old is your brother?" Dr. Bolus inquired, following Donzig with one eye while keeping the other on Stripe.

"Eight."

"And you?"

"I thought you could judge ages at a glance, same as illnesses . . . Fifteen."

"Your parents must be cheeching young. I'm sorry."

She was tempted to snap back that his medicine was supposed

at least to slow the process even if there was no way of reversing it. But she knew, and he knew, the potion was little more than symbolic. Still, better a vain hope than none at all.

Gruffly: "Some people make it past sixty, some start at my age or younger. Yin and Marla are about average . . . Why do I have to tell you of all people? I'll be back for more of the mixture when that lot's gone. Or maybe I'll try someone else."

"Or burn some prayers?"

"No. That's not cheap. It's expensive. Because you get nothing for it."

For the past minute or two chanting and the beating of gongs had been increasingly audible in the market area. Now its volume redoubled, and the source irrupted into view. Led by priests from one of the uphill temples, a procession was on its way to the spaceport to complain about the risk of opening the sky to alien organisms. A few of the stall holders were locking away their wares and hastening to join in, while others too greedy, skeptical, or stiff and old nonetheless voiced encouragement. Some tossed offerings into wide flat baskets borne by acolytes and novices, accepting in exchange prayers inscribed on fan-shaped leaves that they then touched to glowing fusees proffered for the purpose. As the leaves charred to ash much acrid smoke arose. Bystanders coughed and rubbed their eyes.

The procession would of course get no closer to the starship than the port perimeter, but at least the gods would notice and incline to mercy—or so the priests would claim if no harm followed . . .

Time to make a move. Indeed, past time. Stripe took to her heels in search of a cross-bay highslider.

On the other side of Clayre Bay the huge elliptical reception grid began to thrum in the low subsonic range. Ship-believers claimed it was founded on the four hills that marked the site of the original settlement—only there were no traces left to serve as evidence, for they had been leveled at their tops and reinforced. That had been a condition of the temples' consenting to admit off-world visitors; the priests regarded it as tainted ground. The air became oppressive; people scowled and rubbed their fore-heads or complained of vague abdominal discomfort. Some had to vanish to a necessary, since such frequencies encouraged peri-stalsis in the lower bowel. Those who had no such facilities—and they were many, for Trevithra was a poor world and this, its richest city, was still mainly a conglomeration of huts and hov-els—found concealment behind a whipbush or a scrambly tree, whose eager roots welcomed this access of nourishment.

Stripe, however, was not particularly impressed by the grid, although it was half an hour's fast walk from end to end. The colossal shape looming beside the bay had been a familiar sight throughout her life. Indeed, though she had no recollection of the fact, her parents had often told her that as a babe in arms she had watched it being delivered. Such a device could not possibly have been built on Trevithra, so it had had to be assembled in orbit by foreign experts, and on the day of its arrival practically the entire population of Clayre turned out, whether to pray or to admire. Her father and mother brought the family—then, Stripe, who was not yet known by that name, and her twin older brothers—and everyone stood in awed silence as the monstrous mass, looking at first no larger or faster than a gullitch but growing by the second, swooped down under such precise control that it came to rest literally within a finger's breadth of its intended position. Before the week was out it had accepted its first starship, and by now scores had landed, maybe a hundred. The crowds that gath-ered to watch those early touchdowns had dwindled to a handful: beggars, guides, shills, peddlers, pitiable fools who dreamed of stowing away to another world . . .

And, of course, protesters. Inevitably, protesters.

Dropping from the highslider before it reached its official halt at the port perimeter, risking bruises or a sprained ankle but in too much of a hurry to care, Stripe caught sight of another group of antis, not religious like the priest-led procession but political. Twenty or so strong, they were assembling near the main en-trance under the watchful surveillance of armed guards, remov-ing their clothes to demonstrate how admirably human they were, even though not a few bore scars betraying surgery. As they shared out illuminated signs with such slogans as CLOSE THE SKY AND KEEP US SAFE and NO TO FOREIGN BUGS AND GERMS, one of them, who had either inherited an unusually loud voice or had his vocal cords modified, began to harangue the few passersby. It was a warm night; soon sweat was forming little bright drops on his black elbow tufts. Stripe's were red, the color of her body pattern.

She gave him and his companions a wide berth. She had more than once been ambushed and beaten up because skin like hers didn't fit such people's concept of humanity. But she had little difficulty in evading their attention. She had been sneaking in and out of the port for two years and knew every weak spot in the perimeter defenses.

She also knew that the port staff knew them too, and why they were allowed to remain.

Smartly garbed in brown and green, with black or white turbans on their heads, the duty personnel were strolling to their posts. Their work was essentially a sinecure, for everything that mattered was attended to by machines—imported, naturally—but to preserve a shred of dignity the Trevithran government insisted on keeping up a show of control over their visitors.

What would have happened if they had actually tried to exercise it was anybody's guess.

The grid and its gear might have been imported, but the rest of the port complex had been produced locally: in other words, grown as much as built. Some people said sourly that that was to prove to off-worlders just how backward a planet they were visiting, while others argued that it made admirable sense to let living organisms do half the work rather than waste time devising machines that needed fuel and maintenance. Stripe had no opinion in the matter, though she was glad she could steal all the way to the grid in the kind of surroundings she was accustomed to. Darting barefoot from shadow to shadow, she gained the fence without being spotted. Casting a final glance around to make sure no one was looking her way, she checked that her flexibox was secure and jumped to catch a drooping frond of supplex. Swarming up it ropewise, she reached a stiffex and walked along one of its branches, the rough pads on her soles affording excellent purchase, until at a gap between two boles she reached a curtain of reddery.

Ducking through, she entered a corridor unknown to the wealthy travelers, be they tourists or merchants or preachers or whatever else, who passed through here—and, more than likely, to the agents who represented them and claimed to ensure their security. Such hidden passages riddled the port complex like runways in a greewit hill.

Faint luminance oozed from the walls at every junction. Thus guided, Stripe attained her usual vantage point, where she could peer down into the brightly lighted main arrival hall and watch the passengers debarking and up at that section of the ship whence its kitchens would discharge stores unconsumed during the voyage. Against the minuscule risk that someone might chance by before her coconspirator, Rencho, she unfolded her flexibox, leaving it in soft mode, stepped into it, and drew it up to her armpits. When she lay down along a wide flat branch, its dun color made for almost perfect camouflage.

Now she had nothing to do but wait and brood. And, as a matter of routine, suffer. The grid would utter terrible shrieks and groans as it accepted its colossal load. She might well be half-deafened in an hour's time.

She didn't like to think about the other rumored risks of being so close to it at touchdown. At least, though, she wasn't showing any sign of early cheeching.

Or none, at any rate, that she had noticed.

Far above bloomed sheets of violet lightning. The ship was leaking some of its spatial charge. Either it was poorly maintained or it had come an exceptionally long way. That did nothing to sweeten people's tempers, because it implied there would shortly be a storm. Some complained on the grounds that it was unseasonable, or because weather ought to be the prerogative of the gods, or because it would drive shoals of fish back to deep water; others, mostly those who made a profit from dealings with off-worlders, because it meant the strangers would have a less than favorable first impression of Trevithra.

And some were simply annoyed at getting wet.

Stripe didn't care whether she got soaked or not. For her, the ship's arrival promised another few weeks free of hunger, free of the need to beg, free of the risk that she might be rounded up and assigned to some noble's work gang—or service of a more personal kind, if he or she were not repelled by her red-streaked body.

If that happened, what would become of her family? Now Yin and Marla were cheeching, she was their sole support, and Donzig's. Her older brothers hadn't heard the bad news yet; blessed with genes for the adult deep-diving reflex, they had been at sea this past half year, one as a seineman aboard a tagglefish smack and the other working on timber rafts as an underwater roper. Their pay, admittedly, was good, but it wouldn't be in hand until they returned, and during their last furlough both had hinted about starting families of their own. In that case, since there was no cure for cheeching . . .

Why do I bother with that horrid Bolus and his phony "remedies"? Oh, I suppose because if I didn't I'd forever blame myself after—after . . .

Sighing, she wondered what life was like on other worlds and whether people there had to endure fates even worse.

THIS BEING TREVITHRA, THAT CITY ENCIRCLING A BAY AT the equator must be Clayre. But Clayre when? With six hundred thousand stars in the Arm, almost all possessing planets, sixty thousand of them offering conditions suitable for life, six thousand where it has arisen, and more than six hundred settled—or should one rather say infected?—by humanity; and given too the low average distance between systems, so that they shuttle through a gravitational web of indescribable complexity: no computer ever devised could determine the exact date by analyzing stellar positions.

The landing grid is there. That sets a pastward limit. But grids like that are self-repairing. Inspection would reveal little or nothing about its age.

As usual, that leaves only one thing to do. Find out.

THE COLOSSAL GRID CEASED ITS THRUMMING JUST before the racket became intolerable. The ship was safely down, and Stripe was none the worse save for ringing in her ears and a hint of nausea.

Impatient as their kind always were, the passengers from the starship started to disembark at once. As yet she could not see them, but she could tell by the way those assigned to dance attendance on them reacted: scions of the city's—indeed, the planet's—richest families, who might look forward, if they discharged their duties aright, to a year's income for a few weeks' work.

Fat chance of me ever rating a job like that!

Overhead there seemed to be a slight delay. She knew the routine by heart, naturally. First the passengers' belongings were unloaded via a token sterilizer that washed them with a pale blue glow and probably did about as much good as the prayers inscribed—at the insistence of the temple priests—on the floor of the rollway they rumbled down. Then, when owners and baggage had been reunited, the crew would descend at a more leisurely pace and make way for locally recruited staff, cleaners always, sometimes bodgers—as starfarers contemptuously termed Trevithra's finest craftspeople—to take care of minor repairs. In the meantime the sanitary system would be drained and its contents sent for sterilization, and then for her and Rencho would come the crucial moment, the moment when . . .

But where was Rencho? It wasn't like him to be late!

Puzzled, growing worried, she glanced up once more and confirmed that evacuation tubes were nuzzling up to the permeable areas of the ship's hull. Moreover, she had already heard the slam and clang of giant garbage skips trundling to await the load they were to bear to the incinerators. If she missed her chance—! Oh, she would kick herself for so heedlessly parting with everything she had dumped on Bolus's stall! And Mother Shaqqi was bound to cheat her of at least part of her share of the "amulets" she had told Donzig to hand over . . .

Was this the time when she was doomed to wind up as broke as she had often feared?

Mouth dry, heart pounding, she cautiously parted fronds in the ceiling of the arrivals hall and peered down at the strangers. Her angle of view was too narrow to afford a proper sight of them, but she caught glimpses and found herself wondering not for the first time whether she was ever going to run across a visitor content to use his or her own feet.

As usual, the majority were sealed inside suits like those worn—she had seen pictures—by the negotiators from Yellick who had concluded the deal to install the grid, and later by the medical experts who had lived here for a full circuit of the sun, studying Trevithran life-forms and developing vaccines and counterorganisms against those capable of infecting human tissue. Clearly the suited ones were not fully convinced by those experts' assurances.

However, others were either bolder or able to afford a superior level of immunization, for they were prepared to risk breathing unfiltered air. For instance, gliding past beneath her at this moment was a lean and rather stately woman with snow-white hair and immensely long fingers, clad in a rose-red robe and borne along by something blue and soft with a great many legs. If she had been as huge as the rotund man who appeared to be her companion, for they kept pace with one another, Stripe would have understood why; he looked as though ten steps would exhaust him under the burden of his own weight. He, however, was grasping the air and swinging along with both feet clear of the floor, brachiating in fact like a clumber, or a pithronel in transhumance season. Only a faint glow betrayed the nature of his unseen supports.

Fawning, their Trevithran escorts claimed them. They moved out of sight, and Stripe found herself gazing at yet other peculiar forms of assisted ambulation. Wheeled vehicles, tracked ones, rolling cages, mechanical walkers, pads of endlessly flowing slime that left no trace either on the floor or on their riders—the variety of conveyances seemed infinite.

Abruptly it occurred to Stripe that she was seeing some of them for the first time. That implied a ship from a new planet. She clenched her fists. Where in all of space had Rencho gotten to?

At long, long last she recognized his approaching footsteps. Even now, though, he didn't seem to be hurrying. Thrusting the flexibox toward her feet and rolling it with the ease of habit, she slid to the floor and confronted him.

"What took you so long? I was getting worried! I mean—look!" She gestured toward the reception grid.

Neat in green uniform and black turban, Third Deputy Port Controller Rencho shrugged. This landing mattered far less to him than it did to Stripe. He affected contempt for most interstellar travelers on the grounds that one planet should be enough for anybody, though he did make an exception for merchants; he was as appreciative of foreign gadgetry and imported luxuries as any-body—anybody not a templegoer, of course. Moreover, now and then he was able to put an off-world buyer in touch with his brother-in-law, who traded in curios and works of art, and his finder's fees constituted a far more significant supplement to his wages than did the paltry sums he split with Stripe.

He said gruffly, "There was no way to let you know, was there?"

"But by this time they—"

He cut her short. "Don't worry. There's delay all around. This ship's not from Yellick but Sumbala. We only ever had one from there before, the one that came to agree landing rights, which didn't touch down. It's come a long way. Some say Sumbala lies beyond the Veiled World!"

He intended the statement to sound impressive, but to Stripe it was meaningless, save that by implication it explained the peculiar modes of transport she'd just seen. She had heard people talking about stars all her life, but they had no reality to her. At night the artificial aurora blanked them out, except when a ship was due to land, and by day there was only the sun. Reverting to the crucial subject, she insisted, "But they'll have thrown everything away!"

"No, I'm trying to tell you!" he snapped. "This is a different design. They've had to make changes to the—"

The noise of rushing water interrupted him.

"And what's that if it's not the sewage being flushed?" Stripe countered.

"I . . ." Rencho ran a finger between his forehead and his turban as though the latter had suddenly grown too tight. "I guess they sorted things out. Come on, then."

From his sleeve he produced the little wriggling device that their conspiracy depended on. How often Stripe had dreamed of stealing it! Until, divining her thoughts, Rencho warned her that it was conditioned to respond only to him. Were she to try and wear it, it would die, and bequeath her a nasty rash into the bargain.

Perhaps one day—

But for the time being she was as dependent on Rencho as Donzig was on her. Meekly she followed in his wake as he strode in the direction of the waste-discharge area.

Beyond another of the ubiquitous curtains of reddery they reached their destination to find it was as Rencho had promised: the huge disposal skip had still not descended from the surface of the grid. Stripe breathed a sigh of relief. Then, suddenly sensing that her companion was ill at ease, she demanded what was the matter.

"New ship," Rencho muttered. "From a new world. And full of tourists from who knows how many others. I can't help wondering—"

"Wondering if we dare risk it?" Stripe broke in. "Ah, you sound like an anti! Where's your sign saying bugs keep out?"

"Don't try my patience! I was only thinking maybe we ought to let the experts check things out this time. I can get at their report—"

"It's always been all right before! Besides . . . Well, consider the profit! You got your cut of the last lot, didn't you? And it was worth having? Yes? Well then! Think how much more we can look forward to if I offer absolutely brand-new stuff, never tasted on Trevithra before! There's at least one restaurant under Marnchunk where the boss will double my usual rate."

"Double it? Are you sure?"

"Sure as I'm standing here!"

Greed and caution fought visibly in Rencho's face. The former won. He moved as usual toward the sensors that he had to dupe into believing that the refuse was on its way to be burned. Using his wriggly key, he made the requisite adjustments—barely in time, for overhead they finally managed to mate the skip with the hull, and rattles and bangs announced that it was being filled. Shortly it slid noisily down to where a trolley waited that should have carried it at once to the incinerator. Thanks to Rencho's tampering, when it rolled away it turned left instead of right and halted in the compartment where they stood.

Stripe unsealed its cover. At once the air was full of most amazing odors: rich, appetizing, in the literal sense mouth-watering. She uttered an exclamation.

"How can they bear to throw all this away? Look, there are full bottles, untouched packs with complete meals in them, and not just food and drink but all sorts of other things!" She snatched up items at random—a jar packed tight with green fruit as bright as jewels, a transparent box with amethyst strands floating in a crystal liquid, a silver tube from whose pierced cap she shook blue powder—and tried to read their labels. Her face fell.

"This doesn't make sense. The letters are wrong."

"I told you," Rencho muttered. "This ship's all the way from Sumbala. Writing changes, same as language. I heard some of the passengers talking as they left the concourse, and I couldn't understand half of what they said."

"So how can we tell what these are for?" Abruptly downcast, Stripe gazed at him with disappointed eyes.

"I'll have to find someone. My sister's Gowd may know. And there are a few people who've had a chance to work on starships, replacing someone who got hurt here or took sick. They may have picked up some of the foreign lingos . . . Anyway, you can't carry all this in one load, can you?"

"What do you think I am, a lumberlugger?" countered Stripe, feigning her normal self-possession.

"Then take the food and drink, and I'll hide the rest until I find out what it is. You can collect it later."

Stripe bit her blue lower lip with small yellow teeth as she calculated the risk of Rencho cheating her. The odds were high, but she wasn't yet in a position to work alone. After a moment she said, "I guess there's no alternative. Help me load?"

"No, you do that. I'll hide the other stuff. We've got to be quick. It's nearly time to trigger the incinerator. I just hope no one's monitoring the flame spectrum, or—Cheech! I forgot my burn smear. I'll have to go fetch it or someone might get suspicious because the skip doesn't smell right when it returns to base."

Busily cramming item after item into her box, Stripe said, "Just leave some of the packaging, why don't you? Burn it right here. If any scraps survive, they'll assume it's because it's foreign and needs a higher temperature or something."

"But they'll smell smoke coming from the wrong—"

"No they won't." Stripe jerked her head upward. "Listen."

Rain was starting to drum on the roofs of the port and hiss as it struck the still-hot grid. They heard shouted orders from above as the clearance crews rushed to finish their work and seek shelter. Shortly rainwater began to flow down the walls of the room they were in and trickle across the floor.

"Get a move on," the girl added. "If people see me soaking wet, they'll think nothing of it, but you're in uniform, and someone might start asking questions."

"I don't know why I put up with you," Rencho grunted. "I really don't. You order me around worse than my chief."

"It's because I dreamed up our little scheme, which had been under your nose for years and you didn't notice."

True enough. Resignedly Rencho set about finding storage places for the mysterious alien goods. He had little trouble. This was an old room, long neglected, and reddery was sprouting all over it, affording plenty of niches and cavities behind the dense foliage. By the time the rain started to leak through the matted stems of the ceiling the job was done, and Stripe's flexibox was so full she could barely push it along on its frictionless base.

"How long do you think it'll be before you find someone to read those labels?" she demanded, wiping perspiration from her eyes.

"You'd better give me three or four days," Rencho answered, striking a fusee and tossing it among the wrappers he had left in the skip. They flared up satisfactorily, leaving the metal coated with greasy smuts, but the smoke reeked worse than charring prayer leaves.

"That long?" Stripe countered, fanning the fumes aside.

"You want it done fast or you want it done right?"

"I guess . . . Okay. But I'm glad we didn't miss this lot, aren't you? This is treasure trove!"

CLAD IN A CONVENTIONAL GOWN, IN ALL RESPECTS resembling any other male who passed along the streets of Clayre, a personage unremarkable as to elbow tufts and sole pads, broad and bluish lips, and teeth that when glimpsed were yellow, almost orange, strolled through the rain, paused to listen to occasional conversations, wandered onward.

And shortly began to pick up, despite the downpour, whiffs of the stench of hate.

Too much to hope for, that my stay be made so brief! Yet I might dare to hope, if only to remind myself that I can do so . . .

Turning briskly, though not so briskly as to attract unwelcome attention.

Burdened though she was, Stripe contrived to drag and shove and drag her flexibox to the perimeter fence. Never before, however, had she come away with such an astonishing load of booty. Vague thoughts crystallized at the back of her mind, entailing the suspicion that she must be growing up, for they were far more abstract than she was accustomed to:

Sumbala must be an incredibly rich world. Ships from Yellick never dump such quantities of leftover stores. Usually I'm lucky to get one surplus meal pack per passenger because like Rencho says, it costs a star and a planet to haul mass through tachyonic space.

Of course, the best of those meal packs could sell for enough to support her family for a week . . .

The prospect of what this batch would command made her almost giddy. And there was more to be collected later!

And what about the return? Either their medicine must be incredibly far advanced, or they simply don't care about picking up our germs, which to them must be as alien as theirs are to us, from food that they buy on Trevithra!

Unused to machines, she did not consider that sterile provisions might be synthesized as required.

But diseases are one thing. You can invent cures for them, or find vaccines.

She heard an imaginary voice, much like Bolus's, say mockingly, "Is that so? Then how about cheeching?"

And that was the point, wasn't it?

It's the bugs that get into your gonads and then change your children: they're the problem. I suppose the passengers without suits have all had their families and their progeny are growing up safely back at home. Because if not, their germ plasm must be amazingly armored!

A shiver of anxiety trespassed down her spine as she reheard

21

Rencho's doubtful comment about maybe letting experts evaluate matters before running any risks. She damped it by concentrating on the prospect of unprecedented riches, especially the quantity of anticheeching medicine she could buy for Yin and Marla not from a quack like Bolus but from another, better doctor, maybe even one whose patients lived on Marnchunk Hill.

No doubt it was distractions of that sort, she later concluded, that led to her making the most grievous mistake of her young life.

It had not occurred to her that any of the political antis would still be hanging around by the main entrance so long after the foreigners had dispersed. Usually they set off in immediate pursuit.

Not today.

She realized it even as she was struggling to guide her flexibox down the supplex without losing her grip on the stiffex. Nearly a dozen protesters were still in sight, arguing fiercely as they dressed again. It looked as though roughly half had followed the off-worlders as per normal, but this remainder wasn't satisfied with making such a token gesture. She caught the odd shrill cry about infection from yet more distant planets than before, and someone made as though to strike someone else with one of the now-unilluminated signs they carried.

At that moment she lost her grip on the flexibox.

It slithered to the ground with a crunch.

Something inside cracked, and in moments the air was full of a strange and pungent smell, at once acid and oily, at once appetizing and repugnant, like a blend of gleeze with smoked and pickled frang.

Frantically she jumped down to retrieve the box, force it upright, push it away before the others noticed . . . and was too slow. Even the sluggish movement of the tropical evening air sufficed to bear the odor to the antis. Private disputes forgotten, they turned as one to stare in her direction.

If only this had happened outside, under the rain—!

The one with the ultraloud voice said, "What's in that box? Something from the starship? Something foreign—*poisonous*?"

"I know her!" said another, shading enormous eyes with a web-fingered hand. "Can't be more than one mockery with that pattern of red stripes! I see her in Mid-City Market all the time!"

Mockery? They're calling me a mockery? When they look as though they ought to be burning prayers to buy forgiveness for their parents' miscegenation—!

But this was no time to fume over the sort of insults children of Donzig's age hurled uncomprehendingly at one another on street corners.

Frantically tilting the flexibox back on its base, sparing a glance to make sure whatever had broken wasn't leaking sufficiently to leave liquid spoor, for scent-tracking, so-called hounding, genes, though rare, were not unknown among the citizens of Clayre, Stripe felt her heart pound as sweat gathered on her skin—also traceable! Where were the patrols who earlier had prevented the protesters from gaining access to the port complex? Had they vanished as soon as the passengers left, caring more for the safety of rich foreign visitors than a co-Trevithran's?

It certainly looked that way. And, reunited in a common cause, the antis were moving menacingly toward her . . .

And, miraculously, halting as a voice boomed from the air.

"Stand back! Gangway! Sterilization team!"

With humming, whining machines broadcasting the same pale blue light as was supposed to purify the new arrivals and their baggage, a platoon of guards was approaching. For a fraction of a second Stripe was able to savor the exquisite irony of the protesters' dilemma. If the off-worlders had still been shedding alien organisms as they passed this way, then these devices would—so ran the claim—eliminate them . . . that is, provided no one trod in the wrong place and carried them farther away. Visibly furious yet obliged to conform with this law that they themselves approved, the antis uttered confused and frantic shouts. She caught snatches: "Sterilize *her*! Take away her flexibox! Can't you smell that alien stench?"

But the sterilization team couldn't smell anything, or indeed hear very much. They were sealed in protective suits with a self-contained supply of air.

For show, of course. Strictly for show. The effect was as much magical as scientific. Not, actually, that that made a great deal of difference. Yin and Marla had been at pains to make their children grasp that basic truth. At least half the time believing that a medication worked was just as good as having one that really did, for on some level far below the conscious such faith could invoke the aid of defense mechanisms reaching clear back to— well, to wherever humanity had come from.

Naturally, this was not a subject to be mentioned in the hearing of a templegoer, let alone a priest, save at risk of an interminable argument about General Creation. But Yin and Marla were believers in the Ship, built by humans to spread humans far and wide, rather than in the Perfect, who could fly from star to star by act of will. More than likely these nonreligious antis paid lip service to the same views, but they were just as obsessed as the priests with the concept of an ideal human form, or at least of ideal forms plural, each suited to one particular world and not to be exposed to contamination from elsewhere . . .

Though if we ourselves constitute outside contamination— what then?

All this fled through Stripe's mind in an instant while she waited for her precious unexpected chance of escape. Just as the sterilization machines lumbered, growling, between her and the antis, she gave her flexibox a violent shove and took off in its wake. Moments later she was mingling with a group of disappointed shills and peddlers—would they never learn that greater attractions than theirs were to be found up Marnchunk Hill?—as they boarded a lowslider bound for the center of Clayre.

She wished, though, that she wasn't so convinced of having caught from the corner of her ear a vicious promise:

"Now I've smelled it, I'll recognize that stink anywhere. Did you say she shops in Mid-City Market?"

Which ordained, of course: lose this booty in a big big hurry, and the flexibox as well, for it was seeping greasy liquid. Whatever had leaked was also spoiling its frictionless base, so that it grew harder and harder to push. Briefly she considered making straight for the restaurant whose owners were her best customers: not on Marnchunk Hill itself, whose residents could afford to pay full price for imported delicacies, but just on the fringe, where people from the lower town also lusted after unfamiliar luxuries.

However, her parents' plight persuaded her to go home first, although she took a wide detour in hopes that the rain would make the telltale scent harder to trace.

Donzig met her at the threshold, shaking as though in fear of punishment, pleading at the top of his voice. "I did like you said! Even went to Mother Shaqqi! Didn't get my chulgra, though! She said your yellow bag—"

Cuffing him aside, Stripe strode past into the yard. From the corner of her eye she noticed a tendril of stranglevine. That ought to be salted and burned, but she had no time to spare for such matters.

Yin and Marla, slumped in chairs, reacted sluggishly to her arrival. Wheezing, Marla managed to say, "Don't smack the little boy. He gave me medicine."

And after a moment, in a puzzled tone: "Who was he?"

"Donzig, your own son!" Stripe cried, kneeling beside the weak flabby creature that had been her mother.

But there was no further response. The dull eyes closed, and the breathing resumed its resting rate, one inhalation every minute and a half. Shortly the bladder emptied, and she had to jump back to avoid being splashed.

"You should move us out," Yin said faintly. Stripe laid a hand on his slack arm, which he scarcely had the strength to lift in response. "When your brothers come home, we'll only be in the way. Get rid of us. We're done for."

This argument could go on forever . . .

"Donzig!"

"Y-yes?"

"Are you sure you gave them both their medicine?"

"Yes, I swear!"

"Yin, did you find that it helped? . . . Yin?"

But he was as inert as Marla. It seemed that uttering one or two coherent sentences was the most they could any longer achieve.

Nerves raw with hatred of Dr. Bolus, Stripe bent to inspect the slaitches he had recommended her to set beneath her parents' chairs. As she had feared, while she was out white threads from their calves had overrun the dark gray slabs and made connection with the dirt below. Her best precautions had been in vain.

Sobbing, she rose to her feet. Were she a templegoer, she'd have known what to do, and perhaps it was a more merciful decision: send for priests with ritual spades to undercut these roots her parents were trying to sink and bear the two of them with chants and gongs to the landside edge of the city, where, as Yin had said, they would be out of the way of their descendants.

But when they first discovered they were cheeching, Yin and Marla had forbidden all resort to priests. They had decreed that no matter how they might contradict themselves at some future date, they did not and never would believe in the Perfect who had abandoned their bodies and retreated to an existence independent of matter so as to free up as much of it as possible for their descendants . . .

"Stripe!" Donzig whimpered.

"Oh, shut up!"

"But Stripe, I'm hungry!"

"Oh . . . !" But, come to think of it, so was she. Turning her back on the miserable spectacle of their parents, she dipped into the flexibox at random. Finding one of the spaceline's packaged meals, she tore off its cover. Donzig's eyes grew planet-round.

"Is it *foreign*? Can I *really* have some?"

Over and over he had been ordered not to touch, for Stripe must take what she and Rencho saved from starship garbage to be sold for five, ten, twenty times the cost of a regular meal . . .

"Yes!" she said recklessly. "Have as much as you want!"

And wondered as they both ate, using fingers:

What's cheeching like, really? Yin and Marla don't seem to be suffering. More—well—resigned. I ought to give them more of Bolus's nostrum just in case it helps . . . but can one regard slowing down the inevitable as "help"? May it not be the exact reverse?

"This is wonderful!" Donzig breathed.

But Stripe had barely noticed what she was gulping down. Her attention was on those who might never eat again, who no longer needed to, whose final days would be sustained by soil and water . . .

Resolve gathered in her mind. She felt a surge of gratitude to whatever random force had contrived to bring her such largess today of all days—and repressed it out of commitment to her rational upbringing.

What mattered was that she sell this off-world food and drink for as much as she could possibly obtain; then, keeping back sufficient to support herself and Donzig until her brothers returned, spend the rest on the sort of ending her parents would have wanted. Moving people who had already cheeched was costly; she suspected that was why, even now that star visitors were frequent and the legend of the Ship was daily gaining renewed credence, so many let priests take their bodies in charge. But there was an alternative. Her relatives probably wouldn't approve, but it was legal, and she might very well be able to afford it.

Why shouldn't she? As a dutiful daughter and the only responsible person on the spot . . .

Her brothers might be as angry as the rest of the family, but if they'd chosen to be half the world away at this juncture—!

I'll do it.

Rising, Stripe shoved the rest of the food at Donzig. Seizing it, he spluttered thanks from an overfull mouth. She ignored him as she reclaimed the flexibox and set about washing those of the contents that had been wetted by the flask that broke. Half-recognizable words on its label led her to conclude it had held some sort of sauce or relish. Well, now she would never know . . .

Returning her undamaged booty to the box, she forced herself to smile at Donzig.

"Brother, you do realize Yin and Marla aren't—well—human anymore?"

A frown crossed his small face. He said uncertainly, "I thought . . ."

"What?"

"I thought what's happening to them is just part of being human. Isn't it? Marla told me it was. Lots of times."

Shamed by this child, Stripe kept the smile on her face and even patted Donzig's head.

"Yes, that's true, and she was quite right. All of us go that way sooner or later. But there are different things we can decide to do with cheechers. I remember what both Yin and Marla said they wanted if—when—things reached this pass. I'm going to try and arrange it."

The boy looked at her blankly, but she was suddenly too weary to explain the concept of humanizing the biological heritage of colony planets. In fact, until this moment she had never considered that she might need to. Like the superiority of the Ship hypothesis against that of General Creation, she had always taken it for granted.

And want to go that way when my time comes . . .

Not at a temple dump with countless others but alone, maybe on some near-barren islet. Some place where the genes of human beings, along with all their fellow travelers picked up en route to now, would face minimal competition. In another thousand years, ten thousand, or ten million . . .

I have grown up today. I can think of the universe carrying on without me.

Gruffly she said, "Give Yin and Marla another dose of medicine. Not right away but in a little while. I'll be back by midnight. Oh—and salt that stranglevine before it pulls the house down!"

And, hauling the reloaded flexibox, she braved anew the welcome pelting of the rain.

So it's fifteen local years since the installation of the grid. That provides a fix: after the peak of temple dominance—the priests no longer insist on human sacrifice—but before the resurgence of the Ship-believers.

It was, as ever, strange to recall events that would not happen for another century.

And as yet there is no cure for cheeching. That will be brought from Klepsit even later.

The condition's name stemmed from the protesting sounds some of its victims made: their last wheezes prior to coma.

In other words: just before the epoch of the Massacres, that insane attempt to "purify" the local breed.

The rain was lessening. Borne on the air came howls and screams suggesting that that epoch had begun.

MOVING AWAY FROM THE COAST, THE STORM SLUICED higher ground inland. The sloping roads that doubled back and forth on Marnchunk Hill were awash. Every hundred paces a curbside grating allowed the water to flow into a spillway, thence by overhead gutters across the next level and the next, until at last it spewed forth at the edge of the lower town and was left to its own devices. If a few score huts down there were swept away, that was their occupants' worry.

This system, however, was far from perfect. Many of the gratings were blocked with rubbish. Ordinarily Stripe would have paused beside each to check for anything worth salvaging, but tonight she was in too much of a hurry. She had sold everything, at excellent prices. She had even discarded her old flexibox with its betraying odor, hiding it at the rear of a restaurant whose owner had refused to do business with her. She could buy another on the morrow—ten, if she wanted—down at the port, where she planned to find a fisherman willing for the fee she could now offer to convey Yin and Marla in his boat to that lonely island she had earlier envisaged. Now, slipping and sliding on muddy flags, she was making for home as fast as possible, hoping against hope that her parents would be conscious enough to understand her good news.

Soiled to the thighs, she rushed around the corner of the alley where her family dwelt—and came to a dead stop, suppressing a cry of horror.

By the light of waving flambeaux she could see a crowd twenty or thirty strong, some wielding axes.

Antis! There could be no mistake.

The door of her house had been smashed down. Triumphant shouts announced the fate of those who had brought mockery into the world, and the blade of one ax glistened red in the fitful light, defining what that fate had been.

30

Donzig!

She clenched her fists, silently cursing the neighbors who were safely shut indoors. Not a glimmer showed at any nearby window. Armed with truncheons, three of the youngest antis were patrolling self-importantly back and forth to make sure no busybody interfered.

And then a howl of gut-curdling blood lust rang out. Sick, she realized there was nothing to be done for Donzig. They were passing his body through the broken door, to be cast into the kennel like so much garbage. Several mouths pursed and spit.

Unable to move, save sidelong into shadows, she watched as the antis made repeated attempts to set the house on fire. Its leaf-thatched roof being saturated, they had to settle for piling up dry odds and ends inside and torching them, after which they dispersed with shrieks of laughter and much mutual congratulation.

Four or five were coming up the hill toward her. She cast around for something to use as a weapon. They would kill her, too, of course, but they'd pay dearly for their entertainment!

There was nothing, not even a branch that would serve as a club.

Her futile desire for vengeance faded. She cowered back into darkness, hoping that none of those who were about to pass possessed the powerful sense of smell that must have led them to her home. If only she had gone directly up Marnchunk Hill, sown a completely false trail, so that the antis' wrath might have been expended against . . .

Against innocent victims? I say it's no crime to want to share the marvels that rich travelers enjoy!

Chuckling and chattering, they had swaggered past. Memory arose of Donzig, beaming with delight as for the first, the first and only, time he was allowed his fill of foreign food, sucking every least smear from his stubby childish fingers . . .

Now the smoke of burning reached her. It bore the odor of what she knew must be her parents' bodies roasting, abominably delicious. Unable to stand it any longer, she took to her heels. Blind with tears, she fled and knew not where.

* * *

Dawn found her shivering on a rocky promontory just outside the city, separated from it by a copse of yifles. They bore cruel thorns. Staring dully down at herself, Stripe deduced that she must have thrust her way among them, for her skin was lacerated and her kirtle hung in tatters.

Yet she had no recollection of so doing.

Suddenly, as daylight rushed upon the land, she realized she was not alone. Motionless, at a distance of four or five paces, there stood a man, neither old nor young, whom she did not recognize. Alarmed, she glanced around for a way of escape. The horror of last night had convinced her that any stranger might all too easily prove an enemy.

Especially one who, like this person, displayed no unusual features like her stripe.

"Is there any way I can help?" he inquired in a level, unremarkable voice.

"Leave me alone!" She clenched her fists. "I just want to die!"

The words burst forth without intention. The stranger pondered them and eventually indicated disbelief.

"You're young, apart from scratches in good health, and free of any physical deformity. That someone in your position should contemplate—"

"*This* isn't a deformity?" she blazed, flinging aside the shreds of her kirtle to reveal the full extent of her stripe. "There are plenty who say it is! They call me a mockery because of it, and last night . . ."

Emotion gagged her throat.

"Last night—what?"

"Last night they killed my family and burned my home!" she screamed. "Oh, *cheech*! How I hate this place! How I hate its people! I never want to see them again! I could pass the killers any time, by night or day, and never know who were the guilty ones because they look like you! I want to go away, far away, to anywhere!"

"It was your house, then, that was attacked by a mob?"

"So you heard about it, did you?" Stripe's voice grew sullen.

"I saw it."

"*Saw* it?" Now her tone mingled incredulity and anger. "You watched? Did you do anything to help?"

A hesitation. "I was not allowed to."

"What do you mean?" In her confusion she began to wonder whether she had after all met one of the guilty ones.

"You see, I'm not Trevithran."

"Oh, don't expect me to swallow that! You're as Trevithran as I am! The devils who killed my family would say you're more so!"

"No, truthfully. What you see is, so to speak, protective coloration. I'm from space. From a starship. And if you really want to leave Trevithra, I can help."

"Ridiculous!" Stripe jeered. "I've seen people off starships. They don't allow people like you and me on board—backward, primitive, carrying foreign bugs! Well, not unless they have to, like when a member of the crew gets hurt or taken ill."

"And how do you know? Did you hear that maybe from a priest, or someone under orders to keep saying so?"

On the verge of renewed objection, Stripe hesitated. The other's tone was infectiously calm. Besides, his claim wasn't totally incredible. A starship had landed last evening—indeed, there it lay gleaming like a monstrous muthrin on the far side of Clayre Bay. And he did look remarkably ordinary, so extremely ordinary that his appearance could have been based on some artificial average . . .

Uncertainly she said, "Well, if what you say is true, you can tell me the name of your ship's home world." That was a poor test, but on the spur of the moment she could think of none better. Casting around for one, she almost failed to register the reply.

"Oh, not the ship from Sumbala. Mine's in orbit. It never lands. It's not designed to."

"Then how in all of space did you . . . ?"

The words trailed away. Suddenly she wasn't looking at a Trevithran any longer. The man had changed. Apart from losing his elbow tufts, she couldn't be sure in what way. Yet very definitely she was looking at a person not born on the same planet as herself.

And in the same instant the implications of what he had just said sank home.

Mouth dry, knees shaking, hands folded tight to stop them doing the same, she heard herself say, "You're talking about *the* ship, aren't you? I mean: the Ship."

"Yes, I am. Don't you believe in it?"

Giddy, she closed her eyes.

Do I say yes or no? Yin and Marla brought me up all my life to believe in its existence, but ... Well, I always thought of it as far in the past! It traveled down the Arm of Stars—that's the legend—and people from it settled on the habitable planets, which is why we are so nearly all alike. Then local life-forms changed us, like the bug that makes us cheech, so now we're different. It makes sense.

But it's a long way from believing that that's why so many planets all have people on them, to accepting an offer to leave, to fly to space!

She said as much, choosing her words with care.

The stranger nodded. He had reverted to the appearance of a normal Trevithran—and that, thought Stripe frustratedly, was quite a trick! If only she could do the same, she could pass unnoticed by antis at the spaceport, in the market, anywhere. Then she remembered she never wanted to visit those places again.

"Its instructions forbid the Ship to interfere, save in certain exceptional cases. It is indeed in orbit around your planet, but no one is aware of it apart from you." A fresh hesitation. "Did you notice that the storm last night was unusually sudden and unusually violent?"

"I thought it was because the ship—the other ship—had come so far and was so big." Stripe listened to her own words with renewed incredulity. It seemed she was letting herself be persuaded.

"It's of a recent and quite sound design. Normally it wouldn't shed half that much spatial static. But there was temporal static to disperse, as well. A great deal of it."

Was that annoyance in the man's tone? Or was it regret? Or neither? She had learned from Rencho that visitors from other planets used different inflections and even words—which must be why sometimes they grew angry at being misunderstood by "primitive" Trevithrans. So she'd heard.

However, a far more important question was burning on her tongue, and she must pose it before it eluded her. She demanded hastily, "Aren't you interfering by talking to me?"

"Yes."

"Yet you didn't act to stop my family being killed! So what makes mine an exceptional case?"

Let's see you wriggle out of that!

"The Ship's instructions permit the evacuation of human beings from a planet that has proved less suitable than originally predicted. They may be removed to the nearest, or the nearest more favorable, star system."

"So what makes a planet suitable?"

"The fact that humans can survive on it."

Stripe laughed harshly. "I don't see that fits at all. Aren't there millions of us on Trevithra now—tens of thousands here in Clayre alone?"

"That is true." The other inclined his head. "But the instructions do *not* specify that the entire population is to be evacuated. What odds do you give for your individual survival now the antis of Clayre have tasted blood?"

Of a sudden she felt very cold and very calm. She said after a moment, "I think they'd kill me as soon as they set eyes on me. Not just because I'm what they call a mockery, but because I might recognize some of them and denounce them for the murderers they are. You see, they spotted me at the spaceport where I was collecting unused food and drink from the starship. I broke a flask holding a sauce, I think, with a distinctive smell. One of them claimed to have seen me before, but that's most likely how they tracked me to my home. Only of course I wasn't there when they arrived."

"Had you been there and moved on?"

"Yes, up the hill to sell what I had salvaged."

"They didn't follow your spoor?"

"The rain must have been too heavy. I could barely see where

I was going. Besides, I'd washed everything else and thrown the broken flask away."

If I hadn't . . . Oh, what's the good? If this, if that—I can't make things any different than they are.

The back of her neck was prickling as though one of the antis were creeping up, intent on her death. She had to glance around to convince herself she and the self-styled spaceman were still alone.

"I put it to you"—levelly, like a priest detecting an unadmitted sin—"that your survival on this planet is unlikely."

"Unless I can hide on the other side of the world . . . and what would I do in a city where I don't know anyone and have no relatives?"

"You have no other family?"

"Two older brothers. Their work takes them all over the place. I don't know where they are. I can't even let them know our parents have been killed."

"We're that far back, are we? I hadn't realized . . . Just a moment." The other's face blanked, as though he were listening to faint and very distant sounds.

"What—?" Stripe began, but he was back to normal.

"I was checking my on-board memory banks. They remind me that it won't be until— Excuse me. I should say: you don't at present have a planetary person-to-person message system. Some worlds do. But from your level of technology it's bound to take another century or two."

"What's that to me? I shan't be here! Even if the antis don't kill me, I'm apt to cheech ahead of normal time. They say stress like what I suffered through last night can often bring it on like that." She snapped her fingers on the final word.

"Then all I can say is this." He drew a deep breath. "Accept my invitation. Leave Trevithra. Please."

That last word rang and rang in Stripe's ears. She wanted to demand, "What in space makes you say that?" She wanted to run home, except that home wouldn't be there anymore, only a dirty smoke-grimed pile of thatch and planks. (What would have become of Donzig's corpse? No doubt some officious neighbor would have called a priest and had it taken to the temple dump, blustering to conceal his or her cowardice last night.) She . . .

She abruptly made sense of the request.

"Tell me," she said slowly, looking anywhere but at the spaceman. "Are there many people in your—in the Ship?"

"No, there are not."

"Do you get lonely?"

"Yes, very lonely."

"Do you sometimes take advantage of the loophole in the instructions to invite people to join you?"

"Yes."

"Do the instructions order you to tell the truth?"

"Yes."

"Are you telling me the truth?"

"In the most literal fashion." A quirk of the mouth. "You sound as though you studied in a temple school. But I gathered that your family were Ship-believers."

For the first time today Stripe managed a smile. "My parents taught me and my brothers how to best a templegoer in an argument by being strictly logical."

"Did you ever?"

"No." The smile became a sour grin. "Templegoers can always find an illogical way out."

"Well, if it's any comfort, all the signs indicate that because they tolerate the disgusting behavior of the antis, the priests and their dupes won't hang on to power much longer. Ship-believers are going to gain the ascendant, although the process will be a painful one."

Stripe stared at him. "Are you describing a prediction by the Ship's computers?"

"More or less. It's more complicated than that, but—yes."

"And," she stabbed, "giving knowledge of the probable future doesn't constitute interference?"

As he was preparing his reply, her mouth rounded into an O. "Wait! I see a way in which it need not!"

"That being—?" Relief rang in the words.

"You're already convinced that I've made up my mind to go with you. So it doesn't matter if you tell me, because I won't pass on the information. Am I right?"

"Am *I* right?" he parried.

"Yes!" She drew herself bolt upright. "Even if it's only so that one day I can come back and tell everyone that there really is a Ship, and it's still traveling the starlanes for our sake!"

"You sound amazingly adult," the spaceman murmured. "As I suspected, having your lives shortened by cheeching means you grow up more quickly, cram adulthood into a narrower span . . . As to coming back, though: I'm afraid not."

"No?" Almost a cry.

"Entering the Ship binds you to the laws of the Ship. The instruction about noninterference, most of all . . . But you still want to come." It wasn't a question.

She let her hands fall to her sides. "What do I have to do?"

"Nothing. It will all just happen. By the way!"

"What?"

"Thank you. Thank you very much indeed."

MIGHT I NOT BETTER HAVE STAYED, TOLD MY TALE TO whomever was prepared to listen, had the murderers arraigned and punished . . . ? Ah, but only the nobles possess power. What is it to them if Yin and Marla died and our house burned?

Elsewhere, beneath another sun, perhaps I'll find a sane society. Or if sanity's too much to hope for, at least a kind one.

Is this the one whom no known world will suit, the key to my release from endless maze-walks back and forth in time? Whether she is or not, it makes no difference. I have to act as if she were, in hopes that that will make my hopeless dream come true.

So wondering, each in a sense the other's captive, they set forth.

CHAPTER TWO

SHIP

STRIPE WAITED A LONG MOMENT TO BE CONVEYED UP TO the Ship. Insofar as she had any mental image of what it would be like to leave her planet's surface and enter space, she imagined that she would soar skyward headfirst like the pictures of those favored by the gods that templegoers often carried in procession, feeling her internal organs dragging against their mesenteries, her blood pooling in her feet, her brain becoming giddier and giddier. She hoped to see Trevithra half in sunlight, half in darkness, and the green gleam of the artificial aurora that filtered out invading spores.

Instead . . .

"Are we not going to the Ship?" she demanded.

"We have arrived."

"But nothing has changed!" She waved at the copse of yifles, the view of the bay, the distant spaceport. The air even smelled the same.

"Yours is counted as a backward planet. The citizens of Clayre are among its most sophisticated inhabitants. Yet even they, as you have seen, can relapse into the mindlessness of a mob—and it doesn't even take the pressure of enormous numbers. Toward the poles, where nobody has seen a starship, let alone met an off-world visitor, most Trevithrans would be shocked and terrified, perhaps to the point of mental breakdown, were they to be transported hither in an eyeblink. Continuity of environment is therefore provided automatically."

"But how can I know I'm really out in space?" demanded Stripe.

"You wish to see?"

"Yes!"

40

"Very well."

Her surroundings melted as though they had been cast in wax and a flame applied from beneath. Instead, a level floor appeared, made of some translucent substance within whose depths colors played like those of a muthrin shell, but far more various. Everything else was black, save for a myriad stars more brilliant than a cave of jewels.

Gasping, Stripe groped about for something to cling to. "Where's Trevithra?" she forced out.

"Under your feet, along with its sun. We are heading directly away from it."

"Where are you taking me?"

"Where the instructions permit."

"To the next suitable planet?" She was calming. Satisfied that she was not about to drift away from the luminous floor, she was able to relax and consider the spectacle around her. So many stars—so many, many stars!

"Exactly."

"And"—with a sudden access of boldness—"who says whether it is suitable or not?"

Before the answer, she interrupted herself. She had turned toward the spot from which the other voice emanated and realized abruptly there was no one else in view.

"Where have you gone?" she shouted.

"My apologies."

There he was again, exactly as at their first encounter. The reality of the course she was committed to began to gnaw at her mind, as though she harbored a baby greewit.

"I can't stand it!" she whispered. "Let me see you as you really are!"

"But you already have."

"You mean . . ." Her mouth had dried; she had to start anew. "You mean: you're not a person. You're the Ship."

"That is correct."

"There isn't any crew?"

"No. But if it would be a comfort, I can arrange for any number of convincing simulacra."

41

She wasn't listening. Her mind in tumult, she was thinking:

I have to be insane. I have to. In a frenzy of despair after last night I've cast myself upon the mercy of an ancient machine, built by people far more alien to me than any visitor from Yellick—or Sumbala.

Her emotion escaped in a moan. At once solicitous, the Ship said, "You appear distressed. I'm not surprised. You missed your normal allotment of sleep and dreams owing to what happened to your family. Moreover, you have not eaten at your customary hour. And doubtless there are other physical needs you'd like to fulfill."

As though utterly convinced of his—no, she had to think now of "its"—own right judgment, it made the stars vanish. She was in a chamber infinitely more luxurious than any she had ever seen before, with a vast soft bed. Half-glimpsed beyond a translucent curtain, wraiths of steam arose from water cascading into a shallow pool. A table with a chair alongside bore a jug that uttered appetizing fragrance and a shallow cup of bluish ware that shifted color now and then to match the floor.

"Drink," said the Ship. "It will refresh and nourish you and help you sleep." And, as though divining her instinctive objections, added: "There will be nothing more to see, of interest to yourself, until six hours from now."

"Wh-what?" Wild-eyed, she stared to left and right and back and forth.

"The instructions forbid me to exceed the speed of light until I reach a prescribed distance from the primary of any habitable world. The distortions my departure induces in the continuum could provoke a nova. Besides, at tachyonic velocity human perception—"

"Where are you taking me?"

"Where the instructions permit," said the unseen speaker once again. Now its tone was definitely sad. "On our arrival, you will be informed."

Stripe, finding she was yawning, fought the impulse, for it might be Ship-induced. She shouted, "Don't go away!"

Sadness turned to dry humor. "There is never any need to say that. I am invariably present in myself. How could I not be?"

I must be watched when emptying my bowels and bladder?

Yet that was trivial; during her childhood there had been scant space for privacy . . .

"I started out to ask a question," Stripe said firmly.

"Complete it. You shall have an answer."

"Who determines which is a 'suitable world'? You?"

There was a pause full of susurrant silence. Stripe could have imagined that she smelled despair.

"No."

"Me?"

"Advice is available to enable you to reach a sensible decision."

"You're worse than a cheeching templegoer!" she burst out. "Yes or no?"

"Yes, but you would be unwise to make a choice without—"

"Of course I cheeching would!" Awareness that she had at least a smidgen of control over her fate had vastly reassured Stripe. She sat down in the chair, poured some of the jug's contents into the cup, sniffed it and found it apparently wholesome, and drank three relishing mouthfuls.

"When entering and leaving tachyonic mode," said the voice (was it imagination, or had it become more machinelike?), "you would experience discomfort. Consequently you may prefer to be asleep."

Whatever the jug held, it was restorative. As warmth and strength flowed through her veins, Stripe said boldly, "I'd like to see it!"

"Excuse me. See what?"

"The other universe, the one beyond the speed of light. What else?"

Now the tone was almost pitying. "You ask that, who have never left your planet until now?"

"Should I not make the most of my unique opportunity?"

A convincing imitation of a sigh.

"By all means. Unfortunately you are, physically, not equipped."

Pouring more from the jug, Stripe glanced up.

"They say that on other worlds people have extra senses. Do you mean I lack one of them?"

"I am impressed."

"What in all of space makes you say that?"

"If you will forgive me mentioning your parents—?"

"Go on!"

"You are remarkably well informed for someone from a planet rightly classified as backward, especially at—"

"This stage of its development," she cut in sarcastically. "Well, maybe some backward people have in fact moved forward, hm? What about the people who built you? Were they backward or forward compared with me?"

She had time for three more drafts of the delicious liquid before the answer came.

"It is no longer possible to make comparisons."

"Ah, come on!" Perhaps it was overtiredness, perhaps something in the drink she had taken, but Stripe suddenly felt reckless. "You're the Ship, aren't you? You're supposed to remember everything that's happened since you brought us humans to the Arm of Stars."

"Yes. And no."

"Don't talk in riddles!"

"I can no more help doing so than I could help standing aside and watching while your parents' house was burned."

Oh. It is a machine.

I've been told about machines. The spaceport at Clayre is run by them. I've even seen some. But those are mindless things that tend to necessary tasks—pumping water, grinding rock, or concentrating salt to kill invasive plants like stranglevine. They're not to be compared with (she still had difficulty accepting that she was on board the Ship she had been raised to think of as a superior myth) *this!*

Recollection of telling Donzig to salt the tendrils that had crept into her family's yard threatened for a moment to distract her from what she'd intended to say. With vast effort—either the drink or the aftereffect of last night was making her still drowsier—she compelled herself to utter the words.

"Is it because an ordinary person like myself can't understand you?"

A pause, somehow thoughtful.

"In part. There have been few if any human beings who could reasonably claim to understand the Ship."

"So what's the other part?" Stripe set the cup back on the table and yawned again. This time the impulse was too powerful to overrule.

"There's more than one other part."

"Stop playing games! Talk plain!"

"Very well. To begin with, there is no such entity as an 'ordinary person.'"

Against a rising tide of fatigue, Stripe offered, "You mean because people on Trevithra are different from those on Yellick, or Sumbala, or some other planet?"

"Absolutely."

"Go on! Don't mess around! Even if you make me go to sleep and miss—what did you call it?—tachyonic mode, I promise I'll remember and go on asking next time I get the chance."

"You mustn't think in terms of 'missing' tachyonic mode."

"Why not? Isn't it something marvelous, amazing?"

"For me, in a sense, I have to admit that it is."

"Not for me? Why not?" She sounded hurt; hearing her own voice, she was reminded of Donzig's whining on being refused a taste of starship food.

"There is no time."

"What?" Confused, Stripe overcame her weariness by main force of will.

"You asked before whether I am bound by my instructions to tell the truth. You guessed that I put a literal interpretation on them and sometimes gain advantage by doing so. You are now wondering whether what I'm saying is to be taken at face value. Is that not so?"

"Why do you have to ask—? Wait!" She drove herself to her feet, for had she remained seated she feared she must have fallen asleep across the table. "You were built by human beings, weren't you?"

"Designed. Not built. They left that to machines."

"That's— Never mind! Were they so different from the people that you meet today that you don't any longer understand us?"

Softly: "It seems that the first planet which I seeded in the Arm of Stars has generated people with surprising insight . . . Yes. Insofar as you and I share the same concept of 'today.' "

"Don't prevaricate! I want to know what you meant when you said 'there is no time'!"

"Exactly and literally that. In tachyonic mode there is *no time*. Not, at any rate, for human beings to perceive."

Stripe yawned again, cavernously, feeling as though her whole chest had been forced wide by the breath-blast of a tyrogunch. Around the last reflexive effort of her contrary muscles she demanded, "But you perceive it. Is that what you're saying?"

"As regards the Ship, it is fair to say that in tachyonic mode a succession of events is perceptible. These events, however, are purely internal, and it would not be possible to describe them in words. To another, similar Ship they might be communicable in analog form, but . . ."

Stripe had slumped back in the chair, laid her arms on the table, let her head fall on her arms. She was asleep.

Knowing that the energy involved in mobilizing molecules of air was being "wasted," ingeniously excusing the extravagance by exploiting the text and not the spirit of its instructions (how old now? There was no longer any way of telling), Ship nonetheless completed the statement. People had altered so much that even while asleep this Trevithran variant might conceivably register the words.

"But there is no other Ship for me to talk to.

"I wish there were . . ."

PERHAPS FURTHER IN THE FUTURE THAN I HAVE SO FAR been, even if I don't encounter the person for whom no known world is suitable, I may chance on one who can unknot my impalpable bonds . . . I never understood the human concept "cruelty" until my trap was sprung. Of all the fates malevolent deities could have contrived, what worse than to be hurled at random across time whenever I complete a sweep along the Arm? So it won't be this trip that I find such a one. None of my worlds has reached the stage where people might comprehend and mend the damage. Due to some errant cosmic particle, I must presume.

Then, inescapably, the most dreadful possibility of all:

Or was it intended, part of my design? That fear is how I came to understand what "cruel" means . . .

SOMNOLENT, STRIPE WAS YET VAGUELY AWARE OF being lifted from the table, cleansed by gentle unseen hands—from top to toe, including places none but she had touched since babyhood, yet she lacked all power to resist; besides, it was extremely pleasant—and laid at last in the broad bed. Where awareness ended and dreams began she could not tell, but it was as though something warmer than blood flowed in her veins, making her itch so that she stirred fitfully. But it was never enough to rouse her completely, and when it ended, she fell into deep refreshing slumber.

And woke, and stretched, and felt marvelous. Until she opened her eyes and memory came flooding back. Then she jumped to her feet, gazing around like a trapped queelit.

"In space one cannot say good morning," the familiar voice remarked from the air with a trace of sardonic humor. "I wish you its equivalent. You will see that food awaits. Clothing can also be provided if you wish."

Calming, Stripe moved toward the table, set now with oval dishes holding unfamiliar but savory-smelling delicacies. She considered the offer of clothes and decided against it; the air was as warm as Clayre's.

"Where are we?" she inquired dully.

"Approaching the next of the systems where I planted humanity."

Sampling an iced broth and finding it good, Stripe said before her second swig, "How was it done? No ship could have carried millions of people, grown-up living people."

The point sprang to mind without forethought. She simply needed not to think about where she was and why she had consented to be here.

"That is correct. What I undertook was analogous to a seeding. A small group of adult humans descended to each world, along with everything my designers had foreseen as necessary for their

48

survival. The most important resource was invisible: their germ plasm, and the additional stocks they carried to provide maximum variety among the eventual population, had been 'armored.' You understand the term?"

A little crossly, setting aside the first empty bowl and dipping into a pile of what looked like purple nuks, Stripe said, "Yes, of course. I was thinking about that"—could it truly have been yesterday?—"as I watched the tourists without suits. But it didn't work very well, did it?"

"Not perfectly. Life on the planets of the Arm proved far more mutable and adaptable than anywhere humanity had previously explored. Arguably, it has something to do with the relatively high radiation flux in this zone, where the average distance between stars is so much less than in the volume where your ancestors evolved."

The nuklike things were crisp but bland. She nibbled cautiously at something else, a limp pink frond, and found it more to her taste. From a full mouth she said, "You must tell me all about that some time . . . But this is what made us vulnerable to cheeching, isn't it?"

"Yes. As was inevitable, your ancestors acquired native additions to the complex of formerly independent organisms that coalesced to make up the human body, and among them was indeed the one that causes cheeching."

"Just our luck," Stripe said bitterly. "If only it had led to nothing worse than elbow tufts and stripes like mine . . . ! Why didn't you evacuate Trevithra, then?"

"According to instructions, I returned after completing my first sweep of the Arm. By that time a cure had long been found."

"What?" Stripe almost overset the table, so great was her astonishment.

A universe of sadness rang in the tone of the unseen speaker.

"I returned more than a thousand years later."

"But—" She had to draw a deep breath. "But is everything nonsense that I was taught about our history? Yin and Marla said we'd only been on Trevithra for six hundred years."

"Not even that. Barely more than five."

She almost missed the answer, for sorrow seized her by the

throat and sour bile rose. She pushed her food away, appetite vanishing beneath a wave of frantic insight.

"You mean you can travel back and forth in time? Then take me home! Take me back to yesterday so I can save my family!"

"It's not possible."

"More of your cheeching instructions?" she flared.

"Not this time. I literally have no control."

"That doesn't make sense!"

"Nonetheless it is the case. I seem to have been damaged. At the end of each sweep along the Arm, when I reach the point at which a few brown dwarfs and a wisp of cold dark matter mark the boundary of intergalactic space, where the vacuum pulsates like an ocean around an island, I am obliged to return to where my task began. For what reason I'm unable to analyze, since to do so would involve the same circuits that have been impaired, I cannot simply go back to see how things have developed, all in tidy sequence. My return may be at any time since my arrival. In the—ah—present instance I came back to Trevithra long before my 'last' visit. I trust I make myself clear."

Giddily Stripe put her hands to her temples, as though striving to shut out a clamorous noise.

"But—but you'd keep running into yourself!"

"That has not happened so far."

There was a pause, during which tears crept down the girl's cheeks. At length: "I don't have any choice but to believe you," she husked. "Not that I want to . . . At least, though"—she seized on a single crumb of comfort—"there will be a cure for cheeching."

"So far as you're concerned, there is. You need fear it no longer."

"I . . . What?"

"While you were asleep I took the liberty of introducing molecular nanosurgeons into your body. These are not in use on Trevithra. The original settlers possessed a stock, but many advanced techniques were lost during the war that ended with the supremacy of the temples. Sanity, so it would seem, is a brittle gift for human beings."

Stripe was scarcely listening. She said suddenly, "I feel I ought to be screaming and beating my head against a tree. Are you preventing me?"

"Not directly. It is an aftereffect of the nanosurgery. Your body would normally react against the introduction of these tiny machines—"

"What are they?"

"Single but very large molecules designed to search out and eliminate a specific threat to the host. They work by mechanical means, not chemical, though at that level there is scarcely any difference."

Stripe shuddered. "I had sort of—well—miniature butchers carving bits out of my insides while I slept?"

"Not butchers. Surgeons. Seeking out and destroying the alien germ plasm responsible for cheeching. As I was about to say, your normal defenses would have counterattacked, so it was also necessary to administer a calmative. This prevented fever and malaise. In consequence you are, as you noticed, more relaxed than your situation would ordinarily indicate."

"Are they still inside me?"

"Only their residue. Their task complete, they are programmed to dissolve."

After a moment's thought: "Well, I suppose it's no worse than taking the stuff that Dr. Bolus sells . . ."

"Once more I congratulate you. You are a remarkably resilient person—"

"For someone from a backward planet!" she flared. "Stop saying that! I can't help the world I come from! And it's all your fault, isn't it?"

"I fail to see how I can be held to blame," the Ship replied softly. "If you must blame someone, blame my designers. Blame the hyperenergetic particle that—one may suppose—disabled me. Neither will do any good."

"I know," Stripe muttered. "You . . . Look, this may sound like a silly question, but I never met a machine that could talk before. We don't have any on Trevithra, except maybe a few imports. According to what I was told as a kid, there was an outbreak of mass hysteria in the early days, maybe when people first realized that all of us were sooner or later doomed to cheech, and everything technical got smashed up . . . By the way, is that right?"

"In essence. More importantly it would appear that the people who understood how to maintain and renew technical devices were sacrificed to placate imaginary gods derived from fever dreams. As a result, Trevithra is struggling back from a very low level of technology. However, I was not around to witness the relevant events."

"That's the point I was going to make," Stripe said. "You say 'I.' But you are just a machine, aren't you? A very complicated one, but still a machine?"

"Yes."

"Well—are you really conscious?"

"I must answer your question with another, for here lies one of the oldest of all mysteries. Do I respond as though I might as well be?"

"Well . . . yes."

"In that case, what difference does it make?"

Sharp yellow teeth closed briefly on Stripe's blue-tinged underlip. "Not much, I suppose," she admitted after a while.

"So, if I may inquire: why did you ask?"

The girl shrugged. "It was just that when you told me about being damaged, you sounded sad. How can a machine be sad?"

"Perhaps I'm frustrated at not being able to continue my mission properly."

"Continue? You think you should have traveled on beyond the Arm, right out into nowhere?"

"I doubt whether even my—ah—body would endure long enough to reach another galaxy. No, what distresses me is not being able to revisit the worlds I seeded in proper order at predictable intervals. I feel, to be frank, both helpless and increasingly bored."

"The idea of a machine that can get bored confuses me as much as one that can be sad," Stripe exclaimed. "Though if you sometimes wind up in the future and you find people are still alive and thriving, surely that ought to— Just a moment! If you keep on being bounced around in time more or less at random whenever

52

you try and return to Trevithra, yet you've never met yourself, doesn't that mean it can't go on forever? Because if it did, you'd have to come back infinitely often, and you couldn't help but meet yourself. In fact you'd always be meeting yourself, wouldn't you?"

There was a period of perfect silence. Stripe had never heard perfect silence before. It was as though she were on an airless planet. A little frightened, she wondered in passing whether the gas she was breathing might be as illusory and mutable as the room around her, which had been nothing but its floor and a vision of uncounted stars.

But the voice returned.

"Once again I must congratulate you on your insight. You have defined my sole justification for hope."

A machine that feels sad, grows bored, and now claims it can hope?

Yet she had, after all, been raised as a Ship-believer, and since the legend of the Ship made so much better sense of what she'd seen around her since her childhood than any of the priests' alternatives, she was gradually adjusting to her new reality.

Before she could speak again, however:

"We are closing rapidly on the next inhabited world."

"Is it one that would suit me?"

"That is unlikely."

A terrifying vision of being carried from one system to another, until even Trevithra's sun was out of sight, broached Stripe's artificial calm. She burst out, "But is there any other world that I can live on? I don't want to spend my whole life wandering in space and time like you!"

"Who would?" came the dry retort. "But you must bear with me. Remember, this appears to be the earliest passage I have made along the Arm, barring the first. I was 'last' here after the cheeching cure was brought from Klepsit to Trevithra. This time I arrived only fifteen years after the installation of your reception grid. Perhaps in my 'future' there will be other earlier visits, but there have been none so far. I must review my data and, so to say, work backward to deduce what we may encounter. In a little while I will enable you to view the planet."

IN ALL THE FRUITLESS PASSAGES I'VE MADE ALONG THE Arm I never found a more amazing traveling companion. I could know how many—I have to know how many—I don't have to think about that knowledge.

There was some mercy, at least, in the minds of my designers whom I so constantly suspect of having planned my doom. But why? Why should it be better for me to arrive now in this century, now the one previous, now one later? Am I to serve as a random factor, perhaps restore lost data to a declining group overwhelmed by the onslaught of native life-forms? Was it my knowledge of that part of my mission that was damaged, not my ability to choose when I emerge from tachyonic mode?

If so, either way, I may never find out . . .

"IT DOESN'T LOOK LIKE TREVITHRA," STRIPE SAID WHEN she got her breath back. Gazing at the gleaming gibbous orb that hung below Ship, trying not to glance in the direction of the local sun although an automatic screen dimmed its radiance, she found the sight far more impressive than the distant welter of anonymous stars.

"How can you tell? Did some off-world visitor show you a picture taken from space?"

"I never met an off-world visitor, not to talk to. But Trevithra's sky at night is always green."

"Only from below. From above it's a dull red. By the way, the artificial aurora was one of the last manifestations of technology among your people. Did you know?"

Stripe shook her head.

"Yes, it was created when the people of Trevithra first started to go insane with fear of cheeching. Aware that spores were drifting in from space, they jumped to the conclusion that they must be the cause. So they ordered the surviving scientists to find a way of blocking their infall. They succeeded. But cheeching continued. In a fit of blind fury the people seized the scientists and gave them to the priests for sacrifice, as I already mentioned."

"How do you know this? You said this visit to Trevithra was your earliest bar the very first!" Her tone was hostile and suspicious.

"Another of my visits, though, was much later. Excuse me for having to say 'was' when it won't happen for a long while yet. I sometimes have difficulty remembering in what order my future visits, to me in the past, occurred. I suspect I wasn't designed to cope with paradoxes of this order. What matters is that eventually rationality will return to Trevithra and the truth will be reconstructed from fragmentary records. The irony of the aurora, though . . . No, it would be better if you didn't know."

"You have discovered loopholes in your instructions, haven't you?" Stripe snapped. "I suppose now you want me to contradict you so you can tell me my orders!"

"I still find it difficult to believe you were never trained in templegoers' casuistry," murmured Ship. "I, after all, have had a great deal of time to discover what few lacunae my designers overlooked. There is, I suppose, much to be said for a backward society where people have leisure to indulge in untrammeled ratiocination rather than being constantly bombarded with distractions. Whether it's true or not no one can say, but a theory was current when they loaded my data banks that the road to spaceflight was first paved by herd guards watching domesticated animals on clear summer nights with nothing else to think about save how the stars and planets moved."

"On the birthworld? The first where humans ever lived?"

"Of course."

"Did they make a better fist of life than my folk?"

"I am not permitted to judge. It seems that my designers wanted their descendants to make an unprejudiced start on each planet. Stagnation might explain this, and also other things. But you wanted to hear about the aurora."

"I didn't actually say so, but—yes, even if it hurts."

"It will. You see, the spores falling in from space were due to me."

"I don't understand."

"And your ancestors were ignorant of their nature or chose to assume they'd gone wrong. But I sowed them, as was my duty. After that they reproduced by billions, using local elements, and were driven into the planet's upper atmosphere by radiation pressure. It was a most ingenious system, and on many other worlds it's working as designed."

"What was it for?"

"In case the settlers' germ plasm proved inadequately armored, like your people's, against some local threat. The spores would have provided constant reinforcement. You might say: reinfect the settlers with humanity—and the local flora and fauna, too, making them more tractable, even more edible. But on Trevithra they are shut out."

"That's incredible!" Stripe whispered. There was no point in looking anywhere else than at the planet below, for she was now quite accustomed to being addressed from some invisible point in midair. How Ship contrived its voice she had no idea, but she felt disinclined to ask for technical details. She had lived all her life with plants and animals, and if she was having such trouble understanding what it was telling her about living organisms, how much worse it would be with unfamiliar machines!

"My designers had considerable grasp of such matters," the placid voice resumed. "Your descendants—forgive me: successors—on Trevithra will eventually realize the fact, and their ancestors' mistake, but there will be no point in railing."

"The spores would have prevented cheeching?"

"Not completely, nor at once. But over several generations, especially if knowledge of their function had survived and local biologists had been able to modify them."

"And you say this system works fine elsewhere? On this world, for example?" She was clenching her fists from envy and suppressed anger.

"Not on this world, I'm afraid . . . Would you like to see why I doubt its suitability for you?"

"If you can show me— Ah, what am I saying? You can do things I never dreamed were possible. Miracles! No wonder people back home came to believe in gods and devils if they had forgotten how to work such tricks themselves. But one thing first."

"By all means."

"You reminded me I shall never have descendants on Trevithra. But could I, maybe, somewhere else? I mean, if I meet somebody on the world I'm going to . . ."

Breath failed her.

"That is included in the definition of suitability."

"I see. I think. You imply that there are worlds where we—we humans—have been changed to the point where we can't breed together anymore."

"On certain planets that is so. This is not, however, one of them. Nonetheless, it is unlikely to appeal. It happens to be suffering an ice age, and insofar as one can make such a statement, it may well be our fault."

Projected, doubtless, in the same way as the "reassuring" artificial setting she had found herself in when she was brought aboard—though this time the floor turned to something crisp that burned her unshod feet—the surface of the world below took on reality around Stripe. She was briefly dazzled by glaring whiteness, all the more because a bitter wind tossed icy needles at her face. Her eyes watered; she rubbed her cheeks, afraid her tears might freeze.

"You only need to feel this for a moment," said Ship. "By the way, it's one thing I can't share with humans. For me, cold is wholly abstract and has to do with emptiness. Heat, of course, I absorb and make use of."

The vicious chill vanished, but Stripe retained its memory in the very fibers of her being.

Slowly, as her eyes adjusted, she found she could make out details. There were grays, even browns, as well as the whiteness: shadows, exposed vertical rock, crevasses.

"Am I seeing snow?" she whispered.

"Snow and ice. You never experienced them, did you?"

"At Clayre? Of course not! I heard about them, though . . . Why are you showing me this?"

"To let you find out how humans on this planet have to live. Watch. There are people in that cave to your right."

She had thought it only a discolored patch, but it was a hole beneath an overhang. At the same moment she seemed to smell smoke.

"That's the betraying sign," Ship said. "It will lure the attackers."

"Who—? No, I suppose I should ask what."

"Who is correct. They, too, are people. Another tribe, mad with hunger, is advancing from the valley to the south. There is a great migration toward the narrow warm belt at the equator."

"You remember this from before?"

"Say I reconstruct it from an earlier visit that in fact was later."

"You'll be told about it by later scientists and historians, same as on Trevithra?" Stripe sounded eager, like a child anxious to prove it had learned its lesson for the day.

"Perhaps on some trip yet to happen. In spite of what you're likely to see, humanity is going to survive here. I don't think you'd wish to join them at the moment, though . . . Yes, here they come. Look to the left. The rival folk are launching their attack."

Barely recognizable as human, creatures were more sliding than running down a snow slope toward the cave. They waved clubs. They bellowed. From the cave, seeming sleepy or perhaps just weak, two forms emerged and offered battle. They were defeated. The victors rushed into the cave and mercifully out of sight for a moment, but when they came in view again, they were smeared with blood. In their right hands they were waving precious torches, shedding sparks; in their left, each held part of the carcass of . . .

It couldn't be! Yet now more of the attackers were herding into view a group of women with swollen dugs. They offered the first to their leader, who bent to suck.

And as well as a torch he *was* holding the raw leg of a toddling child, which he tore with gnashing teeth when the breasts of the woman held for him ran dry.

Stripe was crying. Not just weeping but sobbing helplessly. She felt cold to the marrow of her bones, on the brink of vomiting, and indescribably angry. She wanted to believe that what had been shown to her was a lie.

Yet it could be no more a lie than the murder of her parents, the burning of her home . . .

She was back aboard Ship, looking down on the planet. Also she was kneeling on the floor, beating its soft surface with her futile fists. Eventually she decided this was pointless. She raised herself.

"Do you feel pity?" inquired Ship.

"Of course I do! That was a *baby* being eaten!"

"Then I was correct. I have long wondered about the nature of that emotion and am glad I have discovered how to recognize it. I hope some time it may be directed at myself."

"But you can't feel it, can you?" Stripe retorted. She sought something to dry her tear-wet cheeks, but she was naked and had only her hair.

"That is something I'm still trying to determine. I do feel—insofar as I 'feel' in the same fashion as a person—responses that resemble pity, guilt, and other abstract concepts. However, since I lack human means of manifesting such responses, I cannot display them."

Shakily adopting a squatting posture, for she was much too weak to stand and there was nothing to sit on bar the floor, Stripe forced out, "Guilt as well as pity, hm? Yes, you said the ice age was 'our' fault! Do you mean yours?"

"My designers', if anybody's. Remember, I am only a machine."

Stripe passed a limp arm across her eyes, as though she could wipe away remembered horror even worse than the sight of her ruined home.

"You're a cheeching lot more than a machine by now, whatever you were meant to be! What froze that world?"

"A most unfortunate mischance. It appeared particularly promising. In accordance with instructions, I sowed spores in its vicinity. An unpredictable solar flare then drove them prematurely into the upper atmosphere, where they acted as nuclei for precipitation. The albedo—"

"Remember I'm from a backward culture!" Stripe mocked.

"More clouds reflected more sunlight. It grew colder."

"All at once? Overnight?"

"I don't know how long it took. 'Last' time I was here there was that small but thriving community in the tropics, which were much colder than yours. Still, there were about a hundred thousand people making the best of things."

"Still eating one another's children?"

"By then children had become—will become—too precious. And since most of their native competitors had been killed off by the cold, their survival seemed assured."

"And on your visits further in the future?"

"I . . ." A curious hesitation. "I can't tell you that."

"Come on! I order you—*machine*!" Defiant, Stripe scrambled to her feet.

"I'm sorry. I seem to be at a limit. I never reached it before, another reason to compliment you if I may without annoyance. I had imagined that within myself I could speak freely to my companions, since by boarding me they became effectively isolated. Apparently I was wrong."

"So what happens now?"

"You agree this is not a world that would suit you?"

"I should cheeching say not! By the way, what's it called?"

"It has no name. Insofar as they can still talk in better than grunts, the inhabitants use a noise that means simply 'where we live' . . . Food and drink will again be prepared for you. Then I will invite you to sleep. By the time you wake we shall be in the next system I must visit."

A spasm of alarm. "More hope there?"

"I think that, too, unlikely."

"*Am* I condemned to wander on forever . . . ? Wait! You mentioned other passengers! You had to set them down somewhere, didn't you?"

"Yes."

"Because they found what they thought of as suitable new worlds?"

"Yes."

"Can I order you to take me straight to an ideal one?" Stripe clenched her fists in brief excitement.

"No. I am bound to repeat the original sequence."

"Well, in that case at least you can't carry me past the right one—if it exists . . . Ah, well. I don't have any choice, as usual."

IF BEING CONSCIOUS MEANS NO MORE THAN BEING SELF-
aware, I qualify. Of course there is no way of proving it.

How do human beings manage? Oh, let my next return be to a
distant future, more distant than any "before"! Each time I have
company on board, the prospect of parting grows harder to bear.
I can inform, I can try to dissuade, I can never prevent my passen-
gers from reaching a decision.

Images flashed in and out of Ship's awareness.

At least the ice-age world spoke, as it were, for itself—but
there are others where I'm bound to call which may prove less
repugnant.

One in particular . . .

At least it's not the next.

From that, Ship derived as much comfort as it could.

STRIPE HAD LOST TRACK OF TIME. ALL SHE KNEW WAS that Ship had spent what felt like ages hurtling from world to world suggesting no sanctuary to herself, and long and long in orbit around each. Growing fretful, she demanded why and received a courteous, persuasive answer. The instructions ordained that every seeded planet be surveyed in detail, the condition of its inhabitants established, any lessons it might teach recorded for posterity.

With a faint stir of interest she asked the reason and was told, "Possibly because someday humans may decide to expand again and occupy planets that at this epoch are still uninhabited. Then they will need guidance."

That too was credible. But not sufficiently to stave off that dullard cousin of impatience known as boredom . . .

How could a succession of strange worlds prove boring? Yet they were, even though some were rich, the ones whence starships delivered tourists to Trevithra. On them she glimpsed strange modes of transport such as she had seen at Clayre. The point was: she had seen them.

She sought other recourses. She called for all the details Ship could supply about Trevithra, but in the end they proved scanty enough, for—as previously—it found, or at any rate claimed, it could pass on few data from its far-future visits. "It appears," said the smooth apologetic voice, "my designers were aware of the risk of damage of the kind I've suffered and decided to insulate me against the temptation to interfere in my own past."

Whereupon she expressed in words the very fear that Ship had so long shied away from. "Are you sure you've been damaged? Maybe they wanted things to turn out this way."

Coldly: "For what conceivable reason?"

"Well, for example, in case you decided to evacuate people from a world that was going to prove habitable in the long run.

Take the frozen one. If you'd gone there, say, when the ice age had just begun but couldn't be prevented, would you not have decided to rescue its people?"

"They would presumably have asked me to."

"That's not a proper answer! Could you have refused?"

"You're requiring me to entertain hypotheses that I seem not to be designed to cope with."

"Doesn't that make 'damage' all the more unlikely?"

"By implying"—frostily—"that my builders could know ahead of time the likeliest outcome of each case."

"Am I . . . ? Oh! I suppose I am! That's silly of me!"

There was another interval of perfect silence. Then, with a hint of self-deprecation (the artificial voice's range was truly remarkable):

"Nonetheless, I wish you hadn't said that. It hurt."

Stripe put the back of her hand to her half-open mouth. "I'm sorry!" she blurted. "I keep remembering you're a machine and forgetting that you've become something more than a machine. Believe me, I *am* sorry."

"I appreciate that," Ship answered quietly.

But her mind was darting in search of fresh distraction.

"Do you—well—project yourself down to the surface of every world, same as you did when you met me?"

"It is one of the standard techniques that I employ."

"Do you show yourself to the people? Talk to them?"

"Sometimes. Though often it serves little purpose."

"Not even to find out whether any of them want to be taken somewhere better? Escaping that ice-age planet—"

"You have no conception how decadent they have become. Even if someone there dreamed of being taken to another world, he or she would lack words to convey the request."

Memories of something Rencho had said drifted back. How long ago it seemed that they had last spoken—and how far away it truly was . . . She said, repressing another pang of misery, "Then how can they advance again if they no longer possess words to express what they're thinking?"

"New words will evolve."

"A different language?"

"Humans have always spoken different languages, even on the birthworld. That is a matter of record."

"Are there many languages in the Arm?"

"Yes. Already Trevithrans find it hard to understand visitors from a comparatively nearby world like Yellick, and vice versa. Even if one considers only the wealthy planets that again enjoy startravel—in their own ships or others'—there are virtually adjacent systems that need interpreters, whether human, machine, or organic."

"But you understand them all."

"It is one of the faculties my designers equipped me with . . . Now I have good news."

"Tell me."

"My survey of this planet is complete."

Yet again it had been a world where humans were still struggling to create some semblance of a comfortable civilization, and it held no temptations for her. Nonetheless, she contrived a display of interest.

"Is the next world likely to be suitable for me?"

"Again, it is probable that you'll be disappointed."

Stripe hesitated. A question had lately tormented her that she was half-afraid to ask. She could not decide whether an honest or a misleading answer would be worse. Abruptly, though, she plucked up courage.

"How many worlds did you seed?"

"Six hundred and seventy."

"Did they all—how can I put it?—did they all take?"

"No, some proved too marginal for people to survive. It was the settlers' choice, not mine . . . Even there, though, there will always remain traces of human intervention, for the pattern of the native life was altered by it."

"About how many would you call successful?"

"I'm glad you said 'about,' " the dry voice murmured. "I discover to my surprise that I can tell you this: There are some where, even as far ahead as I have been, the survival of humanity in recognizable form is still uncertain."

"I'll settle for a round figure."

"Approximately six hundred."

"And of those how many have advanced civilizations?"

"You asked me not to refer again to the fact that I am obliged to regard Trevithra as backward. I apologize, but I need to know what standard you're applying."

Stripe could have screamed, but controlled herself—or maybe Ship was still keeping her calm.

"I'll abide by yours. The ones that enjoy starflight!"

"I can't answer. I haven't been to all of them yet."

"But— Oh." She bit her lip. "Yes, you said this is the earliest of your visits . . . I'm getting terribly confused. I don't know how you keep track—no, don't tell me. That must be something you were designed to do. But you must have visited them all on—uh—future trips that you remember. Can't you work back from what you know from before? I mean, whether they retained startravel or reinvented it, the date when they first managed to launch a starship of their own must be pretty significant."

"Your reasoning once more impresses me. Unfortunately you are wrong. For one thing, most planets 'enjoying starflight' are or will be those like Trevithra that were recontacted from outside. For another, there are cultures that will renounce it."

"Give up starflight after having regained it?"

"Yes."

"What in space for?"

"Reasons that seem good to those making the decision."

"So you don't know whether some of these worlds have it or not, because on giving it up they didn't—I mean won't—bother to keep any records?"

"Exactly."

"This species I belong to is even weirder than I dreamed . . . I'll settle for *about* how many."

"Sixty plus or minus four. By the way, if you're envisaging the possibility that, now you're cured of the risk of cheeching, you might quit me at a world like Yellick and explore other planets aboard a modern ship instead of this ancient machine that you are so afraid of—"

"Afraid?" she exclaimed.

"You cannot disguise your dermal pheromones. I was, after all, designed to maintain the health and sanity of my human passengers even when they saw their friends departing to confront an unknown fate."

Stripe's jaw fell. Eyes round, she demanded, "I never thought to ask before, but even if you didn't carry millions of people, you must have carried thousands! Ship, how big are you?"

"Let me see how I can best describe myself . . . Ah, yes. Think of the reception grid at Clayre. You would have to land a ship the size of the one from Sumbala every day of your local year and for two weeks into the following year to bring to ground a mass equivalent to mine."

"Cheech!" Stripe swallowed hard, suddenly all little girl again. "How do you hide? How is it that your gravity doesn't give you away?"

"Oh, you impress me more than ever! At the risk of distressing you, I wish I could compliment your parents."

"Well, you cheeching can't! Answer me! No, don't bother. You were designed that way, right?"

"That is so. And I'm afraid even your remarkable range of knowledge is inadequate for me to explain the principle whereby I transform the rectification of local space-time stresses into the energy required for my next reversion to tachyonic mode, let alone the compensation that's applied to ensure it goes undetected even by sensitive apparatus."

Stripe pondered that before reverting to her previous inquiry.

"So what were you warning me about?"

"Against," said the quiet voice. "Against any idea of traveling by a contemporary human ship."

"Because I couldn't afford it?"

"For one thing."

"And for another?"

"Because certain worlds that at this stage possess starships have regained the technique at the cost of skills in biology and medicine. In consequence they are paranoid about alien contagion. It would do you no good to assert that you have been

rendered noninfectious by the Ship. Disbelieving your claim—
and my continuing existence—they would respond solely to your
outward appearance."

"Worse than antis?"

"Much worse. They would act with full planetary support
. . . Comfort yourself with the reflection that I alone visit all the
seeded worlds. Speaking of which, we are approaching the point
at which I may exceed light-speed."

"You're going to put me to sleep again."

"You may stay awake if you insist, but afterward I would have
to treat you for an overt psychosis."

"You didn't tell me that before!"

"I didn't know you then as intimately as I do now."

Stripe sighed. "Very well. But what can I look forward to at our
next—ah—port of call?"

"Even less than at the last. It's among the ones doomed to fail.
But at this stage there may still be recognizable humans."

And there were. Just. Foraging and rutting among the tendrils
of a vegetable life-form girdling the globe and spreading against
all odds into the polar tundra. Whether there were continents and
oceans made no difference; a single self-sustaining organism covered both.

"I remember how optimistic those settlers were," said Ship. "So
versatile a plant seemed to offer a virtual infinity of resources.
Here, for example, it is processing rock and excreting heavy metals in pure form. Besides, it makes the air ideally respirable for
human lungs."

Wanting to cringe back even though she knew its tendrils—
more like tentacles, in fact—could never seize her, Stripe
watched nuggets of gold and silver, and perhaps lead and cad-
mium, tumble down a slope of dark green fronds to serve at the
foot as playthings for subhuman anthropoids. She whispered,
"What went wrong?"

"Its mode of reproduction was not recognized."

"But—"

"You never saw the like. Nor did the settlers, nor my designers.

There is a wind that's kept in constant motion around the world, entirely by the action of the plant. It carries organisms not exactly cells, a sort of pollen but more polymorphous. These, transmitting what one might term lessons learned from local needs, enable it to evolve at amazing speed. The moment human germ plasm was introduced, plus that of the associated organisms we all carry, they provoked a reaction that ensured the newcomers adapted to the needs of the plant and not the other way around. You see the outcome."

"I'd rather not," Stripe whispered. The scene vanished. Relieved, she went on, "You said 'organisms *we* carry.' Are you not identifying too much with your makers?"

"No." The dry humor returned, which she was coming to like. "I meant it literally. I carry you; do I not also therefore carry what you carry?"

On the next world humans were at least likely to survive in some more recognizable form than as contamination in an all-engulfing plant. Over most of one continent, however, there hung a pall of smoke. Unaware that their new home had passed through a phase when its atmosphere was high in carbon monoxide, which a now-vanished form of aquatic vegetation had found hostile to its tentative forays on land and absorbed in huge rigid spongelike tubers that then were buried by eons of mud, the newcomers had lit a fire at a point where tilted sedimentary rocks had been exposed and split by weathering. Now an inferno was spreading diagonally beneath a mountain chain. Planetary temperature was rising thanks to carbon dioxide, while the level of available oxygen, formerly just tolerable for humans, was diminishing. But, having domesticated a local organism that ingested CO_2 and excreted oxygen, the inhabitants were fighting back valiantly, even though they had to drag the creatures behind them on sleds or carts, constantly pausing to inhale from a connecting tube. Now and then there were mistakes, and somebody got burned alive.

"Yet they intend to win," said Ship. "They plan to dam a river that will spill between the mountains and douse the fire. They are already talking about what use they can make of the stored gas afterward."

"You've been down to speak with them?" Stripe countered.

"As ever."

"Does anybody want to join me?"

"I suspect you're growing lonely with just me for company."

"I am."

"I know the feeling . . . But I have found nobody who wishes to leave. Everyone is convinced the problem can be solved and in a few centuries this will be an excellent home for humans."

"Will it?"

There was a brief pause. Then: "Better than some . . . I have to inquire: Do you wish to remain here?"

"I don't fancy the idea of sucking breath from some alien creature that I have to haul around like a tail!"

"I thought you might not . . . Believe me, I am not unsympathetic. But I doubt the next port of call will greatly tempt you, either."

And it didn't, although it, too, allegedly was destined for success. Stripe found that even harder to credit than the future of the fire world. Here she saw what Ship declared were human beings, better than ninety-nine percent indistinguishable from herself at the cellular level, yet if she had encountered one at home, she would have mistaken it for a plant. These "people" were shaggy, of a shade between green and purple, and only seldom moved.

"In the other hemisphere," said Ship, "it's breeding season. They move then. I'll show you."

And they did, running organized races, throwing rocks, clambering up nearly vertical cliffs, all the time shouting at one another in language that Stripe nearly understood. Every sentence they called out had to end in a rhyme proposed by a challenger, and they extemporized amazingly.

"What's happened to them?" she whispered.

"A stroke of astonishing good luck. They've established symbiosis with a native life-form that enables them to live directly off light, air, dirt, and water. This world has a year longer than most habitable planets'. During the winter they absorb from the ground enough energy to support them in the summer. In spring they mate, in autumn bear children, and then they revert to the immobile phase. It's rather like the life cycle of creatures on the birthworld that were known as bears. Some early scientists speculated that they too could have evolved to intelligence."

"But what use are they making of their lives?"

"Like the herd guards I told you of, they have time to speculate and ponder. Besides, they survive to an immense age. They will create new art and new philosophy."

"When?"

"In a few thousand years."

With an attempt at wry humor she retorted, "Even for the sake of longer life I don't think I want to be turned the same color as them. I rather like my stripes. I've been used to them for . . ."

The words trailed away.

"Is something wrong?" prompted Ship.

"Yes!" Stripe waved to indicate that the planetside scene should vanish, which it did, and drew herself bolt upright. "I just realized I don't know how long I've been on board."

"Owing to the fact that there is no time—"

"In tachyonic mode! I know, I know! I also know that every time you let me interrupt you, you're playing games with me because your reactions are faster than mine, and I admit that by letting me do it you're showing that you understand the concept of politeness! Now do me a favor and give me a straight answer! In terms of the age I'd be if I hadn't left Trevithra, how long have I been on board?"

"Four years and approximately four days. I cannot be more precise."

"At home I would be married with a family."

"At home the stress you underwent when—"

"You're letting me do it again! I'm coming to recognize the leisurely delivery you adopt when you expect me to cut you short. You're toying with me, aren't you? You were going to say, and I know you were going to say, the stress would have made me cheech ahead of time so I wouldn't even have grandmotherhood to look forward to." She clenched her fists. "Let me see you for once! Come back the way you were when we first met! I want to look you in the face!"

And there he was, and they were orbiting the planet, and it was rotating into darkness so that the reflected brightness of its primary no longer dazzled out the stars.

"You're reminding me what a big universe it is," Stripe declared bitterly. "You're trying to make me resigned to spending maybe your entire voyage with you, hoping I won't find anywhere to settle because everywhere you take me is too unlike Trevithra. Well, I won't have it! *Where next?*"

"Klepsit."

"Oh!"—in sudden childish excitement. "A world that has starships!"

"No."

"But I'm sure that back home—"

"My turn to interrupt. You'd never heard the name of Klepsit before I invited you aboard."

"Oh, that's right!" Yet her excitement was undiminished. "I remember now. You said it was from there they brought the cure for cheeching!"

"Be careful of your tenses."

"What—? Oh, you know what I mean!"

"You seem to think I can read your mind simply because I can deduce from your pheromones what your mood is."

"And mess about with it!"

"I have not interfered with your metabolism, not even by altering the nature of your food, since we left the ice-age planet. For one thing, you had adjusted excellently; for another, knowing in advance how you are going to react makes your presence worthless to me as a stimulus."

Stripe stared at Ship's flawless image, clenching her small fists. She said after a long pause, "You are conscious, aren't you? I think you must have been copied from a real human being."

"What makes you say so?"

"Either that, or you've had so many temporary passengers you've absorbed their mannerisms . . . You sound like a bad husband I knew down my alley back home—bossy, domineering, and offensive! So if you mess about with my mind, my presence is worthless, is it? And that's the only reason you stopped doing it? Not for my sake? Not because I might prefer to be a free responsible individual?"

She was panting now.

"Tell me about Klepsit! Even if you can keep me alive longer than those *things* on the last planet, I don't want to spend eternity dragging around with you! I'm human, and I want to stop somewhere and do human things like having children, even if my husband looks different from anyone I ever met! I thought that was the whole idea of spreading people down the Arm of Stars!"

"You are a Ship-believer," Ship responded. "Amazingly, even after meeting the real thing."

"And should I not be? You are real, even though after being batted back and forth through time, I'm not surprised you sometimes doubt the fact yourself! At least you're real enough to keep me with you more years than I imagined and not let me measure how long it's been except by how frustrated I've become!"

The air around her seemed to grow cold. She could not tell whether it was imagination. Abruptly alarmed, she cried out. "I order you to tell me what it's like to live on Klepsit! Come on! But keep it brief!"

"On Klepsit," said the Ship in a tone far more machinelike than usual, "the settlers decided to postpone recovery of starflight. They resolved to adapt their planet and themselves to one another by main force. They opted to challenge their metabolisms with whatever the native life could offer. Many died. The rest became resistant—or rather, their descendants will. At this point people must still be dying who did not volunteer for early death."

"But it's the world that invented a cure for cheeching?"

"Watch your tenses."

"You know what I *mean*!" Stripe stamped her foot. "And it's the next world that you have to call at?"

"Yes."

"Then set me down on it. If nothing else, I can tell them why Trevithra desperately needs their help!"

ALL THAT CAN BE SAID, THEN—THOUGH IT HAD BETTER not be said until the final moment—is this: "Good-bye, Stripe."

The weariness of eons past and yet to come burdened Ship. Not for the first time it attempted to determine whether its age was cumulative or whether it renewed its "youth" in its own past. There was no way to tell; in passing judgment on itself it was ultimately no better off than Stripe, who would not enjoy the fate she had chosen.

Yet she had proved a remarkable companion.

Intended or not, it cannot possibly go on forever. My returns cannot be infinite, for if they were, as you correctly pointed out, I'd have met myself . . . Poor Stripe! Your crazy momentary hope was doomed. I think you knew. For come what may I must abide by my instructions.

Chapter Three

KLEPSIT

It was an hour past dawn in early summer, but everything in sight was drab: the pavement, the barracks—made of the same rough concrete inside and out—the clothes worn by a coastal work gang setting out from the quay, the boat they were embarking in, the sullenly roiling sea, the lid of clouds that closed in the sky . . . When two young men began to spread solar-absorptive paint on one of the nearby roofs, its intense blackness instantly drew the eye. At least it offered some degree of contrast.

"I wish there were more color in the world," Volar sighed. "It's all so gray, even our clothes, even"—with a touch of mocking humor—"your hair and my beard."

"There are dawns and sunsets," Su said from behind him. "And the weather isn't always overcast."

"And it's not so bad on the other side of the island," Volar concurred. "Where you can see the plantations, brown and green and even blue. I know. Nonetheless I can't help feeling life would be more bearable for a few creepers and plants in urns and even some murals."

"That'll happen eventually."

"When we have resources to spare for luxuries like pigments and solvents and suspension media. I know that too."

"For someone accused of having delayed that day by a not insignificant amount, you're remarkably unremorseful."

The sharpness of Su's voice made Volar turn away from the unglazed window; at night and when it rained the opening was covered with a simple but snug-fitting shutter.

She was sitting on one of two fixed benches that ran along either side of a fixed table. All were made of the ubiquitous

concrete, as were the floor, walls, and ceiling. The sole conces-
sion to comfort in the large low room consisted in thin mats of
woven sealeaf on the benches.

"So, old friend," Volar said in a voice from which all trace of
bravado had evaporated, "what do you think the Council is going
to do with me?"

Su's tired, lined face remained impassive as she spread her
hands. What was visible of her skin was, like his, patched with
round shallow scars. They had first met when they were assigned
to the same challenge team nearly thirty years ago, and the subject was a fungoid that flourished on unmodified human epider-
mis and induced toxemia when its waste products seeped into the
bloodstream. It had been beaten, of course; no child born in the
past two decades had been infected by it. But the marks remained, on the spirit as much as the body.

More so, perhaps. They were the last survivors of the team.

"I can't read the Council's minds," she said finally. "Their decision depends on what we say. So at least you ought to cultivate
a tone of convincing repentance."

"Surely after the lifetime of service I've given—"

She cut him short. "It's my job to speak in mitigation, not yours.
Leave it to me to talk about your career and the reason why you
were distracted. Let me argue from the standpoint of a disinterested third party. Your job is to demonstrate that you understand
why the charge has been brought— Ah, but we've been over all
this, and if you haven't yet realized the right, the only, way to set
about defending yourself, the whole affair is past hope. Besides,
the councillors are coming."

She pointed past him, through the window. Glancing over his
shoulder, he saw the group of twelve grim-visaged men and
women who wielded ultimate authority on Kelpsit approaching
from the refectory. Each displayed, not ostentatiously but con-
spicuously, his or her symbol of high office, the remote communicators that linked them with one another and with the
five-century-old monitors deep below the island in an artificial
cave, whose sensors permeated soil, vegetation, even rock and
concrete, even the table in this room, like the mycelia of an

artificial fungus. So, in theory, their authority was not quite absolute. But the monitors had never overruled any of the Council's decisions. At least there was no record of such an event.

Though sometimes I do wonder . . .

Not looking at her, he said, "Su, are you completely disinterested?"

A faint smile crossed her face and reflected in her voice.

"Of course not, Volar. But you know where my first loyalty lies—where yours must, and everyone's."

"Yes, of course. Still, thank you anyway."

Now the councillors were entering, acknowledging the presence of the two outsiders with curt nods. Su made haste to vacate her seat; during the hearing they were both obliged to stand.

Without preliminaries other than clearing his throat, gaunt Sandinole, the president by rotation, got down to business.

"Before our regular agenda we have a hearing. Volar is charged with dereliction of duty and disruption of schedules. Su is here to speak in mitigation."

He turned deep-set, burning eyes on the two of them. His gaze recalled vividly to Volar the first time he had met Sandinole— they were the same age—and recognized in him the fanatical single-mindedness that might well carry him to Council membership. He was as hungry for power as others were for air and food.

"You've both studied the charges?"

They nodded.

"Do you challenge them on grounds of factual error?"

"No, on grounds of incompleteness." Volar licked dry lips. It was the best he and Su had been able to come up with during endless hours of brain racking.

"What's missing, then?" That was Henella, nominated to the Council after two decades of painstaking work in the General Administration department. She was reputed to have the only truly legalistic mind among the present membership. Laying her communicator on the table as though to emphasize that she had all the details committed to memory, hence no need to interrogate the monitors, she went on. "You do not deny that on reaching preretirement age you were reassigned to duties that included supervising the satellite?"

The satellite (just one—why were there not a score?) was nearly as old as the monitors. It had multiple functions, including weather forecasting, but its primary task was to analyze the spores that were reproducing in local space, spot any potentially useful developments, and report to ground so that they could either be watched for when they drifted in or else, if they failed to materialize in sufficient quantity, be duplicated from scratch. It had also been intended to act as a communications relay to other star systems, but it appeared that no one else in the vicinity was signaling—or possibly, as informed opinion deemed more likely, owing to the closeness of the stars hereabouts it was impossible to transmit data in tachyonic mode without it becoming hopelessly garbled before reaching its destination.

Supervising it was regarded as a sinecure.

Volar began, "No, but—" Su laid a warning hand on his arm, and Henella continued.

"You further don't deny that while you were responsible for it, you neglected to notice and report signs of deterioration in its accuracy? And that in consequence we are receiving only corrupt data? We are therefore obliged to divert resources in order (a)"—she flicked up a finger at each point—"to recommission an orbital dinghy, (b) to assign a crew trained in the necessary specialties to effect repairs, (c) to risk their lives because no one living has flown space, (d) to analyze in retrospect rather than real time what data we can recover from store aboard the satellite, and (e) to make all the other necessary changes in our former program to ensure that the foregoing is possible. What of this can you hope to deny and be believed?"

She folded her fingers and let her hands drop to the table, staring fixedly at the accused. So were the rest of the councillors. Clearly they regarded the outcome of this hearing as foregone.

Yet a tremor of defiance survived in Volar's mind.

"Nothing, of course. I still claim that not all the relevant factors have been included."

An idea had just come to him in a flash of blinding insight. He felt Su's warning touch again and shook it off impatiently.

"We know what you're going to say," Sandinole growled. "We've studied your excuses and dismissed them precisely because they aren't relevant."

It isn't relevant if a person's only surviving son has died with the whole of his challenge team on a project that ought never to have been authorized? Ordered to tackle the entire ecosystem of a subtropical island without backup or even adequate supplies? Not in their view, apparently. An expression of affection for biological offspring, so casually sacrificed "in the interest of all," strikes them as atavistic, doesn't it?

But that was for Su to argue about. What had dawned on Volar was totally different.

"What's omitted from the material you've been considering, and what I've never been told, is this." He drew a deep breath. "No one can fail to realize how valuable the satellite is to our program of adaptation not just of ourselves to the planet but also of the planet to ourselves. So why is the job of supervising it invariably left to a fallible elderly person like myself?"

From Su at his side he heard a hiss of breath like a soundless whistle of astonishment. But what counted was the reaction of the councillors, and he read it from their expressions. Even Henella suddenly found herself at a loss.

"You mean—" she began after a blank pause.

"I mean," Volar interrupted, greatly daring, "why is its condition not supervised by the same monitors that analyze the data it sends down? Why, in other words, was there not an alarm that would have attracted the attention of anyone, sick or well?" Words were flashing across his mind now like so many brilliant meteors. "Even now there remains a risk that some hitherto unsuspected epidemic might gain a foothold on this island sanctuary of ours. We would of course overcome it; we long ago amassed enough data to cope with any such disease. But it might weaken us sufficiently for a vital task like the one assigned to me to be neglected. Setting aside my own emotional state, which for the sake of argument I am prepared to treat as irrelevant for the time being, I still find myself puzzled by the fact that successive councillors including your good selves have overlooked this vital but potentially brittle link in the chain that binds us to our dream of ultimate survival."

Holding his stiff old body as upright as he could, he surveyed the councillors' faces. It became plain how deeply his barb had sunk home when with one accord they turned their own gaze away from him and toward plump pale Ygrath at the far end of the table. He was responsible for maintenance and exploitation of the monitors.

And he was growing even whiter than usual, so that his cheeks looked like raw dough at the bakery on its way to the oven.

Recovering his self-possession, he blustered, "You seem to be trying to lay the blame for your shortcomings on the Council!"

His companions brightened. One could almost hear them wondering why they hadn't thought of that counter themselves.

The sole exception was Sandinole, who continued to frown—indeed, glower—though not at Volar. His annoyance seemed to be general. He cleared his throat again; Volar recalled that he had a permanent respiratory weakness from his own time with a challenge team. That one had been exposed to a pseudobacillus that inflamed the bronchi—and, as usual, no one suffered that complaint any longer. Oh, progress was being made, undeniably. It was just that it was so abominably *slow*.

"Before reaching a verdict," he rasped, "I move that we consent to answer Volar."

The others reacted with astonishment. Henella made to speak, but he scowled her down.

"It is an ancient principle that no one learns without a chance to make mistakes. It seems to me that conceivably one may have been made, not by us but in the distant past. I can envisage, for example, that a search of the records may reveal how, in the early days, some operative fault or other transient setback might have led to control of the satellite being reassigned to a human supervisor as a temporary measure, and in the upshot our predecessors omitted to restore the situation to normal. The business of the monitors is after all to monitor, not issue orders. If something similar does prove to be the case . . ."

He left the sentence hanging. Volar, overcome with surprise at the success of his inspiration, was yet able to notice how the rest of the councillors were betraying glumness mixed with relief. He suspected the latter was due to Sandinole's ingenious suggestion that the blame might be laid at the door not of the present Council but of its long-dead forerunners.

"We'll complete the hearing tomorrow. Meantime, Volar, I warn you: the matter remains sub judice."

"Excuse me?" Volar said, blinking. Su leaned to whisper in his ear, loudly enough for Sandinole to hear.

"He means you mustn't talk about it to anyone who isn't present."

"Naturally! I wouldn't think of doing so," Volar declared.

Henella's expression was doubtful, and the other councillors' even more so, but eventually a wave of nods passed around the table, and they were free to go. As they left the room, they heard Sandinole's newly brisk tones.

"Right! We have many more matters to deal with. Let's get on!"

As overcome as though he had just been reprieved from death—which in a sense was true—the moment they were outside Volar flung his arms around Su and hugged her with all his declining strength.

"Oh, Su! I'm not over the hill yet, am I? I'm sorry I didn't tell you about that line of argument before, but I swear it only came to me as I heard Henella listing the elements of the charge! What a wonderful day it is after all!" Drawing apart from her, he waved at the bare, level square they stood on, the blank identical barracks that stretched away in lines on either side, home to more than five thousand people who wore identical clothes and differed only in their names and specialties. "The world has been transformed! It's as though my creepers and murals are already in place—like a sort of invisible radiance!"

"Don't talk too loudly," Su murmured, leading him away. "Or they'll question your sanity."

"Never! Not when, even through a mistake, I've exposed a fundamental weakness in—"

Halting, she rounded to face him squarely.

"They're not going to let you get away with it, Volar. You must know that."

"What do you mean?" Bewildered, he blinked at her. His corneas too had been scarred by the fungoid, and there was a blurred patch in his left visual field. He had long ago learned to disregard it, but now and then—and this was now—he was acutely reminded.

"Volar, they don't let even the monitors contradict the Council. Or at least they never admit it when it happens."

"I was thinking about that myself only a short while ago," Volar muttered, his euphoria fading.

"How much less, then, would they let someone like you?"

"But . . ." His shoulders slumped as he recognized the force of her argument. With a brave stab at recovery: "Then we must tell everyone we can before the hearing resumes! The infallible Council has risked not just a setback to the program but—"

"That's exactly what they're hoping that you'll do!" she snapped. "For the sake of form Sandinole reminded you that the matter is sub judice, thereby tricking me into stating what that means in plain words. His warning is on record, as he intended. We're allowed a long leash for the time being. But I bet my life that before meeting's end they'll prime the monitors. The moment they detect anyone else questioning the wisdom of entrusting fallible humans with satellite monitoring, the Council will pounce."

"But . . ." His jaw was hanging lax, as were his hands. He summoned all his self-control. "But surely people must already have wondered about that, quite independently."

"Are you sure? When even I didn't? When on your own admission even you didn't until just now?"

Her large eyes—she had been luckier than he, and they were unmarred—shone full of pity. But pity too was an atavism, in the Council's view.

"Volar, they are *not* going to let anyone cast doubt on the infallibility of this or any previous Council."

In a quavering voice, an old man's voice, for he felt on the instant even more than his chronological age: "What do you think will become of me, then? Tell me straight out. You know more about this sort of thing than I do."

It was true. After their challenge team had produced its results, the survivors had gone different ways: Volar had become a mechanician and she not, as she had hoped, a genetic armorer like Sandinole, whom she admired though he mistrusted, but an administrator, her duties chiefly involving maintenance of stability within the growing populace. This was achieved by psychological control and only rarely through a threat of punishment . . . but punishments there were, albeit disguised as service to the community.

Looking him straight in the eye, she quoted a principle that went back clear to the age of settlement and possibly beyond: "So long as a person is alive, there is always more that he or she can do to help the rest."

"So long as a person is alive . . ." he echoed faintly.

"I'm afraid so, Volar. And it won't be long."

"What—?"

"What use will they find for you? Oh, there are countless possibilities."

"If I volunteer to go the way of my son—"

"They'd regard that as evidence of derangement," she cut in. "Derangement being due to organic imbalance, they'd dismiss the data as tainted. More likely they'll do something local. Put you on a diet of native vegetation, for example, and record what happens."

"You can't be serious!"

"Out here in the middle of the square, with everybody else at work and the Council involved in its deliberations, this is about the only chance I ever had to be serious."

"So—so what can I do?"

She shook her head, eyes overflowing as she continued to gaze straight at his face.

"Hide? Where? Run away? How, and where to? No, this is the end of the road for us, old friend."

"Us?" He snatched at the word.

"Oh, you don't think they'll let me live any longer than you, do you? Not a chance, not when I defended you. It might make sense, in fact, to say good-bye right now."

She was much shorter than he. Reaching up on tiptoe to pass her arms around his neck, she planted a kiss on his cheek. Then she spun on her heel and hurried away at an awkward, stiff-limbed run.

Licking his lips, he tasted tears: hers or his own? He could not tell.

After a long dead pause he pulled himself together.

"If they're going to do this awful thing to me anyway, I might as well spread the word, mightn't I?" he said to the air. "So who can I tell?"

But everybody was at work. When he looked around, even the young men who had been spreading solar paint had disappeared.

So small a population after all this time, confined to a single island and not even a large one! And such a death rate, and so much of it deliberate!

Busy and invisible, Ship probed the planet.

If I didn't know what I do know—shall know?—I might well have assumed that Klepsit too would be a failure . . . How long can I endure these shifts in time? The more I learn, the more it seems likely Stripe was right in voicing my worst fear: it's not damage but intent that drives me back and forth across the centuries . . .

Poor Stripe.

But here perhaps I may acquire a fresh companion. And any company at all surpasses loneliness . . .

It went below to walk and talk like people.

WHEN VOLAR AND SU HAD GONE, HENELLA SAID stiffly, "I wish to place on record my grave doubts about the course recommended by the president. I particularly regret that Volar is not to be held in custody until the hearing resumes."

Ygrath nodded vigorous support. The rest waited. They knew Sandinole to be cunning.

Suddenly, and altogether unexpectedly, he laughed.

"I'd expected better of you—Henella in particular! Did you not hear me remind him that the matter is sub judice? How many crimes will he be guilty of if he so much as hints outside this room that the satellite ought to be supervised automatically?"

Light dawned.

"I see you're catching on at last. But don't smile too soon! Ygrath!"

The pasty-faced man jolted to full alertness.

"He's right, isn't he?"

"I—uh . . ."

"He *is* right," Sandinole insisted softly, leaning both elbows on the harsh table and gazing down its length. "By the way, how long have you held your post?"

"F-five years," Ygrath forced out.

"And never before or since you were appointed did it occur to you to ask the question Volar asked today—Volar, old and half worn out and arguably deranged by his obsession with his son." Sandinole clenched his fists before his face. "We've been through the same experience, haven't we? All of us have fathered or borne offspring, wished them well when they set out with challenge teams, and suffered the consequences because they're still beyond our control. How could anyone dream of living unaided on a foreign planet without enduring just the process that our forebears decreed for us—and for themselves?"

His voice rose to the pitch he normally reserved for mass meetings of new challenge teams.

"We know the Ship that brought us was instructed to seed as many planets as might be with human stock, and there were hundreds at the very least. Can any have succeeded better than ours? Are new-built starships knocking at the doors of our atmosphere requesting permission to land?"

His fanatical glare swept the table like a winter gale.

"Has anybody sent us decipherable signals containing useful information? Has the Ship itself come back, as the records indicate it should have when it reached the end of the Arm of Stars, to check on progress and bring news of how things go on other worlds? Five hundred years have elapsed and we are still alone!"

A deep breath.

"It follows that we must be doing exceptionally well. With each passing generation we improve the armor of our germ plasm. We fall victim to fewer and fewer diseases. We digest more and more various foods, no longer just those whose ancestral strains accompanied us on our arrival but native ones that formerly were poisonous! Another thing we all have undergone, along with loss of offspring: sickness from eating local food. Yet consider what we have achieved! Thousands of us are in good enough health to *grow old*! Volar's beard is gray, Su's hair as well. A century ago, how many of us lived that long?"

Hearing the fundamentals of their common belief put into words with such blazing conviction, the other councillors relaxed—all save Ygrath, who knew from what Sandinole had said a moment earlier that there would shortly be a review of the Council's membership, and when it was reconstituted, he would not be among the chosen. The decision would of course be attributed to the monitors. But who knew better than himself, who had often suppressed inconvenient data, how tidily they could be manipulated?

"Most of what we have on today's agenda," Sandinole went on, reverting to his normal calmness in committee, "is routine. But in addition to what has already been circulated there's an item that may indicate we have succeeded better than we realized."

Puzzled glances flickered up and down the table.

"As yet we have very little to go on, which is why I originally felt it not worth discussing until later. However, as I say, it may prove encouraging. It may indeed indicate that somewhere on the planet, hidden perhaps below obscuring vegetation, we have sown a wild strain of our kind—and it's surviving."

The quiet words exploded like a crashing comet. For a long moment the councillors' expressions were a mixture of shock, disbelief, and dismay. Sandinole regarded them with a sardonic grin.

"Full details of what we know so far are naturally in store with the monitors, but to judge by your reaction, it might be useful if I give you a summary account.

"I trust I don't have to remind anyone that two days ago a major timber drift originating off the east coast of High North Ground was spotted following the Triennial Circular Current toward the Upper Channel? It was too big to be turned aside by the regular sonic swirls, big enough to risk blocking the channel completely—this, incidentally, being of course the generally accepted means whereby large life-forms spread from island to island in this region. And we would prefer to keep them off our own. Hmm?"

His tone had changed from sardonic to sarcastic, and more councillors than Ygrath were starting to fidget on their uncomfortable benches. It sounded as though he had made up his mind that the office of president by rotation was not enough, even though he had contrived to have his own term extended twice already. Ygrath himself, who had doctored the monitors' recommendations, felt his cheeks turn from grayish-white to brilliant pink.

"So we dispatch—do we not?—a clearance gang to make sure the logs are broken free and sent on their way. Yesterday, or rather late last night, using infrared glasses, they spotted a large warm creature, immobilized but still alive, caught in one of the perimeter traps. At first, naturally, they assumed it was a native predator, perhaps a bolf or kear carried there by clinging to the floating timber. It had about the right temperature and mass. On inspection, however, they discovered it to be a more or less human female of unknown descent."

His eyes again raked the length of the table.

"Specifically, she has tufts of hair on her elbows and rough, possibly prehensile pads on her feet, while her skin is covered with bright red stripes, beginning at the nape of her neck and spiraling along torso, arms, and legs. Her teeth, what is more, are yellow."

"An alien!" Ygrath blurted, desperate for anything that might distract Sandinole from his resolution to eliminate his former trusted aide from the Council.

Coldly: "You believe in the Perfect?"

"W-what?"

"You believe that since they launched the Ship our kinfolk in the parent galaxy have evolved into creatures that can cross interstellar space naked and unprotected?"

"Of course not!"—licking his lips. "I never heard such non-sense!"

"Then you haven't checked the contents of your data banks." That was a wounding gibe. "Or maybe you didn't lead a normal childhood . . . ? Legends to this effect have cropped up in every generation since the age of settlement. Nonsense, of course, but the important fact about nonsense is that by believing it people diverge from rationality. That may be tolerable in children of prerational age, but even there, I dare say, it ought to be corrected."

The implications of Sandinole's words were building a wall between Ygrath and the other councillors. They began to shrink away.

"Now," the president by rotation resumed, "what's the question that all of us here would ask immediately on being confronted with a report of that kind?"

Henella snapped, "Can it talk? Is it equipped to, is it well enough? Looking human, can it explain itself?"

That, seemingly, was not quite the response Sandinole had been prepared for. Making a swift recovery, he gave an approving nod.

"Absolutely right. Unfortunately, the trap's ultrasonics gelatinized her frontal lobes. She's in coma, and the prognosis is unfavorable."

A clamor arose, several people talking at once and each shouting louder than the next. Sandinole stared them down. When silence reigned again:

"You may take it that I considered all those points. Do you wish to hear the findings so far?"

Nods.

"Alien"—ocular darts aimed at Ygrath again—"short of delivery by the Ship that brought our ancestors, she can't be. Her DNA matches ours to nine points. Moreover we've determined that she must already have been suffering lassitude and fever from infections native to Klepsit and her system contains *no* unknown organisms."

The implications finally sank in. Henella husked, "You seem to be saying that descendants of some—well—some challenge team once given up for lost have completed the adaptive process?"

"Not quite," Sandinole countered in a carefully patronizing tone. "Not if she was weak and feverish from what, as I just stated, are indubitably local infections. Still, if her forebears have survived even for a few generations, that must be worth further investigation, hmm?"

"Is it definite that she arrived with the log drift?" Henella demanded.

Sandinole smiled. "Our techniques are not quite up to following a humanoid scent through that much water . . . are they?"

He let the veiled insult, the implication of ignorance, rankle for a second, then went on. "But it's more likely than the alternative."

"Which is?" Henella was flushing angrily.

"That she was already on the island, tried to swim away, and had to cling to the logs when she became exhausted. After all, an unclad female about as tall as yourself but striped vivid red all over would scarcely evade detection—would she, now?"

Henella's responsibility for social stability included keeping track of unauthorized movement among the populace. Once again Sandinole had scored a palpable hit. The other councillors tried to avoid one another's eyes; each was afraid a plot to oust him or her had already progressed so far that it was useless to argue in public.

"Still, one thing is beyond doubt. Her system includes no organism, none whatever, that is not identifiable either as a human commensal or native to Klepsit. That she was virtually at death's door prior to being trapped can be ascribed to the fact that her— or rather her forebears'—resistance has reached its limit. She appears to have been muscular and well nourished until quite recently. All of which added together indicates—does it not?— that a search ought to be mounted along the coast of High North Ground, the densely forested area whence the logs found in association with her originated."

As though expecting no contradiction, he made to rise. However, Ygrath retained one spark of spirit.

"What about putting Volar in charge of the expedition?"

The answer snapped like a neck in a hangman's noose.

"No."

HOW IRONIC IT IS THAT IN SO PERFECTLY PRESERVING THE human physique despite incorporating countless antibodies and novel defenses designed to cope with challenges from the native life-forms, they have sacrificed so much of what it truly means to be human, such as pity. I wonder whether any of them understands the concept of love . . .

Ship detected a trace of irony in its own reflections, connected with the word "countless." In fact, they would have been quite countable, had it interrogated the local "monitors" on the subject. But something else far more important had arisen, an opportunity not to be forgone.

Today or tomorrow, certainly not later than the day after, there will be at least one person in danger who might wish to leave Klepsit, and quite possibly two.

How strange it was, Volar thought, to find himself the only person on the island without work to do, save children still too young to go to school and the very old eking out their final days in the hospice . . . where they still contributed to the eventual survival of the settlers in accordance with the principle Su had quoted to him.

After failing to find anyone else willing to spare him even a few minutes, even the woman who had taken over his former post as satellite supervisor, he tried to call on Su at her place of work but was frostily warned off. News of his hearing before the Council had spread rapidly; he was being treated as though he carried a virulent plague.

Which of course he did, and wished to spread.

Baffled, infuriated, at a total loss, he wandered farther and farther afield, occasionally receiving a nod of recognition but never more. He passed the blank walls of sealed laboratories; he reached the plantations where imported and native plants were growing together under controlled conditions; he saw from a distance—for they were behind electronic fences and updraft barriers—the fields where animals were penned, both local species that might one day be useful and the modified descendants of others whose germ plasm had arrived along with the humans. Some of them would have looked extremely strange to those who had planned the Ship's expedition through the Arm of Stars, for the Council's brief did not include leaving its livestock outwardly unaltered.

The sight reminded him of his study of history. In the far past, clear back to the birthworld, people had kept animals for company even though they could not talk and were barely capable of reason. What would it have been like to make this long walk around the island with a "dog" beside him? What function did a dog perform after the days when other animals, barely tamed, still needed to be driven to and from pasture?

When, if ever, would the like process occur on Klepsit, so that there were farmers instead of agrobiologists?

Most likely never.

He reached the extreme south of the island and stood gazing down from a cliff at a coastal work gang, not the one he had watched setting out earlier, for they would have gone to a shore-line nearer home, but another from the closest barracks. They were far too busy to notice him as they combed the rocky beach meter by meter, collecting aquatic creatures cast up by the waves, comparing the spreads of native sealeaf and imported seaweed, analyzing the organic content of the water in tidal and nontidal pools. There were caves below the cliff, and he saw two people emerge from one of them. They wore breathing masks, presumably because some airborne spore or other had taken root and might cause lung infection in the unprotected.

Near the horizon, veiled by mist, drifted one of the colony's automatic ships, following the Triennial Current and studying the spawn it bore to frigid northern waters.

It's time for me to say good-bye.

The thought sprang to Volar's mind as unexpectedly as his inspired argument against the Council.

I know everything about Klepsit. I can't go anywhere, any-where, that is, that I'm allowed to go, where I don't know what's happening, where I'd have to ask for explanations. I might as well end it all, right now.

The mist was blowing toward land, with the promise of a chill and clammy evening. With a start he realized it was much later than he had imagined. He would barely have time to reach home before dark. In theory he, or anyone, was entitled to a meal and a bed at any barracks where there were room and rations to spare; in practice the privilege was confined to those delayed while on some authorized expedition, and no one would look kindly on him who had wasted a day in random wandering. Urging his stiff limbs to a faster gait, he set out to retrace his steps.

But the mist swirled in long before sunset, and the path ahead blurred, and frequently he had to pause and rest.

It was during the fourth of these enforced respites that he glimpsed someone from the corner of his eye. Barely more than a silhouette, the person nonetheless struck him as familiar. A name leapt to the tip of his tongue, the name of the woman who had directed the challenge team among whose members Su and he had met.

But that's absurd. Kenia died two years ago.

Had it simply been a trick of his failing eyesight? He peered in the direction where he thought he had seen the—he had to say stranger. Even though the total population of Klepsit was still extremely small, it had long been impossible to know everyone.

A possibility struck him. One of Kenia's children, perhaps? That would explain the likeness. He hadn't kept in such close touch with her as with the rest of the team, she being the oldest by a good three years, but unless by misfortune she'd proved sterile, she, like everybody, would have become a parent several times over.

And there definitely was someone, striding closer—and to his indescribable amazement uttering his name in a voice resembling Kenia's past a doubt.

He drew a deep breath. "Hello! Are you one of Kenia's daughters?"

"What makes you ask that?"

"Well, you can't be Kenia because she's dead. Yet you look and sound astonishingly like her."

The woman approached, uttering a deep chuckle. "No, I'm not anybody's daughter."

While he was still trying to make sense of that absurd-seeming reply, the mist parted. Revealed, standing no more than his own height away, was Kenia herself—rather, her younger self, as she had been when they first met.

"Forgive me," the same voice murmured. "I judged seeing an old friend to be less alarming than meeting an unknown."

Less alarming? But I am alarmed! Volar stepped back, clenching feeble fists.

Nobody's daughter? Can I possibly have mistaken a man for a woman? Ridiculous! Though of course we all wear the same clothes, always, no such sport would have been tolerated by the Council!

But one other conceivable explanation remained, though for a long moment he was unable even to entertain it.

During the relatively undemanding stint he had spent on satellite supervision, before news came of the death of his last surviving son, he had dutifully occupied himself by improving his education. The satellite having been planted in orbit to monitor the spores left behind by the Ship, it was logical, and permitted by the monitors, for him to delve into the available records of the Ship's mission. He had discovered material long neglected by everybody else, for it had come to be generally assumed that the Ship must have met with some sort of accident. Had it not, it should have returned at least once, perhaps twice, in the past five centuries. Theories ranged from mutiny on board to collision with an antimatter meteor, though the latter was conventionally pooh-poohed owing to the density of normal matter in this volume.

But if the Ship were to come back . . . Am I crazy? Have I perhaps been made crazy, to justify what the Council hopes to do with me? What difference does it make? Su says I'm done for, and I'm compelled to believe her.

He said with vast effort, "If you're nobody's daughter, I take it you're nobody's son, either. Am I right?"

"Considering it's been more than five hundred years, you impress me with your accurate conclusion. Yes."

Vision faded. The world around seemed to swim and waver—not owing to the mist. Volar clutched at his chest as a stab of pain pierced his heart.

I found my way to the data concerning the Ship's ability to communicate in human speech, even to project an image of itself in human form. It's beyond coincidence that I should be the one actually to encounter it . . .

His sight cleared, and the pain receded. Staring at his interlocutor, he put his amazement into words.

"Yes," came the musing reply. "That you should possess such

uncommon knowledge is indeed remarkable. Recently I have begun to wonder whether my impression of relative free will is in fact only a mask, concealing a far more complex plan than I imagined, one extending perhaps to more than the usual eleven dimensions."

"Have you revealed yourself to anybody else?" Volar demanded.

"Not here."

"Why? According to our records, you were supposed to come back long ago, bringing reports of progress in other systems."

"I know."

"Have you been back secretly before?"

"This is my earliest return to Klepsit."

"Did something go awry, then?"

"I have long believed so. Now I suspect it may not have."

"This is too deep for a worn-out old man like me," Volar muttered. "But *why* me? Because I was equipped to recognize you? You referred to some kind of plan—"

"Which may or may not exist. So far as I'm concerned, I decided to contact you because you are about to be condemned for yielding to a very human response."

Volar licked his lips, though they were moist with the dampness of what was now thick fog.

"If I recall aright, you must have interrogated our monitors and acquired total knowledge of the situation here."

"Extensive enough to include your own predicament."

"So you're referring to the fact that losing my last son brought on a breakdown."

"Throughout most of human history, and on every other civilized world I know of, the risk of someone reacting as you did to such a tragedy would have been recognized and allowed for. It would not have been called a breakdown, rather a natural response."

"That's how I think of it!" Volar exclaimed. "I've come to believe that our Council is . . ."

"Say it. None but I can hear."

"Well—inhuman."

"Not completely, but trespassing on the verge. Do you wish to confront the Council again tomorrow?"

"I . . . Well, I suppose I must."

"There is an alternative."

It was becoming real now. He actually was talking to an embodiment of the legendary Ship. Either that or he needed to accept that he was. Perhaps some people needed to believe in the Perfect, too, because their legend (or was it more of a myth?) supplied assurance that all the hard work, all the deprivation, all the suffering, would one day be justified.

He furrowed his balding brow. "Let me see if I can work out the reason behind the reason for your approach to me. You say it has nothing to do with the fact that for the first time in generations someone on Klepsit has studied in detail the records of your nature and mission."

"No. That I am here, at this juncture, is so far as I can judge pure happenstance. It may not be, but I have no way of telling."

"Did you know you were going to meet someone like me?"

"Absolutely not."

"Then I'm afraid you're going to have to explain— No, wait!" He raised clawed hands as though he could mold an answer from the fog. "I just realized! You're talking to me quite freely. You haven't notified the Council. It must follow that . . ."

"Go on."

"It must follow that in present circumstances you're forbidden to interfere. I sometimes wondered about that. Yet you are interfering by talking to me . . . You're going to make me an offer. What happens if I turn it down?"

"You will be found dead tomorrow, having tumbled off the cliff path in the fog. It will be put about that you betrayed the common cause by jumping to your death rather than facing the verdict of the Council."

Volar digested that for a long moment. "And if I agree?"

"But you haven't yet agreed, because you don't know what I'm offering."

"I can only assume it to be escape. Can you—well—take me on board?"

"You impress me again. You are the second person I've met on this sweep of the Arm who seems to possess remarkable insight. Another indication that my true mission is more complex than I imagined . . . Yes, I can."

"But won't that alert people to the fact of your visit? In a society like ours people don't just disappear."

"A replica of your body will be found on the rocks. All will continue exactly as though you had remained."

Still Volar hesitated.

"Is there anyone here you are especially attached to? Your children, I know, have predeceased you."

"There's a friend"—gruffly.

"You refer to Su."

"You almost sound as though you've met her!"

"I have seen her."

"But not talked to her?"

"No. Evaluated her."

"And—?"

Ship emitted a completely convincing sigh. "Since her youth she has felt irrational admiration for Sandinole. You doubtless recall that she hoped to become, like him, a gene armorer. In her heart of hearts she cannot make herself believe he would do anything less than honorable. So in spite of all she plans to go on serving the Council to the bitter end."

Volar's belly tightened. A sour taste rose in the back of his throat.

"Would she have defended me—well—properly?"

"It was you, not she, who devised that brilliant question: Why leave supervision of the satellite to a fallible human, not tireless and responsible machines?"

"That's not an answer!"

"Think again and you will realize it is."

He did, and it was. It became his turn to sigh.

"You're right. I'm doomed, who never willingly did harm to the common cause. Because I'm guilty of a normal human reaction, why should I be punished by those who maintain that our task is to establish humankind on Klepsit no matter what the cost? I do think they're becoming inhuman . . . If I accept, do I gain the chance to see how well the species is managing on other worlds?"

"Yes."

"I take it that means as many worlds as there is time for me to visit before my worn old frame gives out."

"That can be as long as you like, until you choose a world more suitable for you than this one."

"How in all of space can I tell what's more suitable? I suppose when I see it . . . At any rate I know beyond doubt that this one is wrong for me. What do I have to do?"

"Say yes."

"I do."

"Then welcome aboard."

CHAPTER FOUR

SHIP

IN SPITE OF ALL THE MODIFICATIONS THAT HAD BEEN incorporated into Volar's heritage, his body responded swiftly to Ship's ministrations, and it soon became obvious that there was nothing wrong with his mind. Long before they reached the point at which it was safe to enter tachyonic mode, he was bubbling over with questions. Some were to be expected, as when he demanded why Ship had not returned according to the schedule that the settlers were advised of. Bound by its instructions, Ship answered in much the same terms it had used to Stripe. *(Poor Stripe!)*

But others were considerably less predictable. Of them, the first:

"I never dared say this because of the Council, but I've long been convinced that we'd have done better had we not concentrated so single-mindedly on adapting ourselves to the planet and vice versa. For instance, if we'd been able to share data with people on other colonized worlds. Even if hereabouts it is impossible to transmit data in tachyonic mode without it becoming scrambled over interstellar distances, could we not have built and launched at least one starship of our own?"

He gestured at the glory of stars reproduced around him.

Ship had not yet discontinued its apparent physical presence. The Kenia form conveyed its answer.

"That might indeed have been possible."

"Do you say that because others have done it?"

"Yes."

"I thought so! I *thought* so!"—pounding fist into palm. "And are the people who achieved that doing worse than us on Klepsit?"

"In some cases better."

"Under less difficult circumstances?"

"Some, but by no means all."

"You mean some are just as badly off?"

"Perhaps even worse."

"In spite of which they have starflight! Hmm! Are any of these worlds close to here as stellar distances go?"

"There is contact between several local systems."

"Then why has Klepsit not been visited? Surely, with a primary like ours and a functioning satellite in orbit, we'd have been a prime target for investigation."

"A priori one would have expected so."

"So I ask again: why?" Volar insisted.

"I cannot say."

"Come now! You've explained why this was your earliest visit since Klepsit was seeded, even though it's not the first. I'm not sure I quite understand that, but I'm doing my best. Isn't there anything you—ah—will have learned on later visits that even suggests a reason?"

"There are certain clues," Ship admitted. "One of the most significant may be found at my next port of call."

"Why, with all the brilliance that went into your construction, your almost invulnerable self-repairing systems, can you not be more positive than 'may'?"

"Because I lack the data to determine whether various sequences that I remember from the future have already been set in train. As I told you, this is the earliest return I can recall. Since in respect neither of Klepsit nor of the other worlds I have investigated during this pass could I detect traces of a previous one, I am proceeding on the assumption that it may actually be the earliest."

"But you can't be certain," Volar suggested softly. "For some reason you haven't yet found out, you may have been obliged to conceal earlier visits, not yet made, from yourself as well as from the settlers."

"Exactly."

"Hah!" Grimacing, Volar tugged his beard, which had long been a habit of his when wrestling with a knotty problem. Catching sight of one of the strands he had grasped, he raised it until it was as high as his mouth, squinting downward.

"Black!"

"I took the liberty of restoring its former shade," Ship murmured. "I trust you have no objection."

"None! None! And you've mended my scarred cornea as well. Yesterday I couldn't have looked down like this and seen anything so clearly, close or distant!"

"My instructions oblige me to maintain my occupants in a state of optimum health."

"And you did all this without my noticing! It's incredible."

"Your body has been efficiently adapted to tolerate nanosurgery. That is one thing for which you may be sure Klepsit will eventually become famous."

"So our suffering will one day become worthwhile?"

"Limits are placed on what I can tell you about what has not yet happened, but that, I find, I need not conceal."

"Thank you!" Volar whispered. "Thank you!"

Ship paused briefly. Then: "It would be advisable for you to rest. I must shortly enter tachyonic mode, and I'm sure you know what effect it has on a conscious human mind. I have one question, though, before you retire. Do you wish me to continue the Kenia simulacrum?"

"What? Oh! No, don't bother. It was a bright idea, but I don't mind talking to the air. Speaking of which, I have a final question, too."

"Pose it."

"The nanosurgeons: I take it I inhaled them?"

"That is correct."

"Did you have them ready? I mean, were they a stock model you just called up from store?"

"No."

"Yet you were able to design and produce them within so short a time . . . Oh, if only those idiot councillors back home could know how far short their vaunted achievements have fallen of what was already known millennia ago!"

"Do you think it would make the slightest difference?" Ship countered dryly.

"No," Volar admitted on reflection. "No, I don't suppose it would. Except to make them more determined than ever to stop the rest of Klepsit's inhabitants from finding out how efficiently they've been led by the nose . . . I wondered whether I'd regret accepting your invitation. I find I don't. Quite the reverse, in fact. I'm incredibly fortunate, aren't I?"

"There is a very ancient proverb," Ship murmured. "It is credibly prespatial, let alone pretachyonic. 'Count no man lucky till you know the manner of his death.' "

"On Klepsit," Volar said soberly, "death for most people is highly predictable . . . Where do I retire to?"

On the instant, he was in a sleeping chamber.

And woke incredibly refreshed. For how long he could not tell he simply reveled in awareness of his physical condition, not even bothering to open his eyes. When he did, there was no sign of the Kenia form, but the same quiet voice addressed him.

"I trust you slept well?"

"Well!" he exclaimed, swinging his newly youthful legs to the floor and stretching his arms luxuriously. "I feel I've slept *well* for the first time since I was a baby!"

"You have."

Not prepared to be taken so literally, Volar blinked. "Say again?"

"You have"—patiently. "One of the things wrong on Klepsit is that time is not allowed for adequate sleep."

"But among our earliest adaptations . . . Oh. I take it you're implying that that was a mistake."

"Not entirely. The error lay in applying it to everyone without making proper comparisons between those who only 'needed' three hours and those who remained closer to the inherited norm of about seven. It was thanks to an oversight due to lack of sleep that no one thought to reassign the duty of monitoring your satellite to a machine after a shutdown for maintenance."

"So I was right!" Volar erupted to his full height. In passing he noticed that the hair on his body had been restored to blackness like his beard. "I wish you'd told me before! I could have confronted those incompetent fools and rubbed their noses in the facts!"

"Do you honestly imagine so?"

Volar hesitated. At length, with a wry grin, he shook his head.

"Not a chance, was there? I'm better off becoming a wanderer like you . . . By the way, where are we now?"

"Approaching the next of the planets that I seeded. It will be some while before we enter my direct perception range. I recommend that you bathe, eat, and exercise. I understand from previous passengers—most of whom, of course, have not yet boarded me—that the food I am able to offer is acceptable albeit sometimes unfamiliar."

"Willingly," Volar declared. "But just a moment!"

"Yes?"

"When did you develop a sense of humor? Or were your builders so clever they designed one in?"

"That's hard to explain. I suspect what they contrived to design in was the potential for one. But I've had to learn how to exploit that potential."

"Fascinating!" Volar breathed. "Tell me, are you glad?"

"Very glad. More than once I've felt or will have felt that without something of the sort I'd be deranged by now. Of course, I cannot rule out the possibility, any more than you can."

"You mean," Volar offered, "I ought to worry about being deranged myself? By all the standards I was raised to I'm sure I am. I can just imagine what even Su—"

"That's not quite the point. You ought to worry about *me* being deranged."

After several quick deep breaths Volar managed to reply. "Your sense of humor is on the black side, isn't it?"

"How can I tell? How can I know anything? Your bath awaits, and clothing of the sort you're used to, but more comfortable."

Even though he had studied so many data about the Ship and its facilities, Volar kept being surprised at how calmly he adjusted to their manifestation. He barely blinked when, as he finished his meal, the chamber he sat in gave place to the former vision of stars, subtly altered by the transit from one system to another. No doubt there was something in the air apart from nanosurgeons.

He had been sitting in a swivel chair. It remained. Turning it through a right angle, he found himself gazing at what he took to be a habitable planet; at any rate the coloring of the half that basked in sunlight looked about right.

Remarkably, although there were bands of bright white cloud that trailed across the terminator, patterns of light could be clearly seen on the night hemisphere, suggesting cities and roads.

"Don't they have clouds at night?" he demanded. "Or are you showing me an enhancement?"

"The latter," came the amused reply. (Ship really had developed a sense of humor, or at any rate it imitated one with astonishing accuracy.) "The inhabitants of this world travel little if at all, but they do possess a technical civilization. They process and manufacture on both the organic and the inorganic level."

"Do they have starflight?" Volar asked excitedly.

"Rather the contrary."

Volar considered that for a while but finally shook his head. "It's no use. I'm trying to make sense of the only other thing you've told me about this world, and it doesn't fit."

"That being—?"

"You're never going to persuade me that you don't recall what you said!"

"True, but what I can't know until you tell me is what interpretation you put on it."

"Ah . . . Yes, obviously." Volar tugged his beard again; his fingers reported a crispness in the hairs that he had almost forgotten. "Well, you said there may be a clue here as to why Klepsit hasn't been contacted from space."

"Indeed there may."

"So I naturally assumed . . . Just a second! It's not because our Council warned everybody off, is it? And then kept the fact secret?"

"That would not be inconsistent with the rest of their behavior. In fact, however: no."

"So I'm driven back to my first assumption, which must also have been wrong. But what in space do you mean by 'the contrary'? What's the opposite of starflight?"

"Before I answer, let me ask whether you can't work that out yourself."

"Without knowing anything about the people here except what you just told me? You must have remarkable faith in my powers of deduction . . . Well, in my teens I used to enjoy the word games we were encouraged to play to sharpen our wits. I'll see if I can recover the habit. I think I'd better start by making sure I know what you're talking about. Is this a very different world?"

"In at least one sense, diametrically so."

"Hmm!" Volar plucked his beard so hard that it hurt and forced his hands to his sides. "Technically they can't be all that different; they don't have starflight, and we don't either . . . Socially?"

"In principle, yes. How, particularly?"

"Oh"—Volar shrugged—"what about their attitude to the planet?"

"You display keen insight. That was precisely what I had in mind."

"You do have a mind, don't you? I can tell what a contrast there is between you and the monitors I grew up with because it would never have occurred to me to talk to them like this . . . A complex manufacturing civilization? Albeit not very advanced? *Hmm!*"

Ship seemed to be waiting expectantly. The air sang with inaudible tension.

"Are they fighting their environment instead of trying to coexist with it?" Volar proposed at length.

"Very nearly."

"How in space can one 'very nearly' fight the . . . ? Oh."

"I think you just remembered something."

"Did you read that off my face?"

"Not exactly. Off your skin."

"Pheromone secretions?"

"What else?"

"Remind me not to try and keep any secrets from you . . . I give up. You'll have to show me."

"When you came so close?"

"Oh, all right. I guess that they've grown tired of fighting the environment, so they're giving up."

"They haven't given up, so far as they're concerned."

"But I don't see how this fits with 'the opposite of starflight'!"

"It doesn't, but what's your definition of that?"

"I suppose staying put. You said they scarcely travel."

"I did indeed."

With sudden impatience: "You're toying with me!"

"How strange"—in a musing tone. "Perhaps I'm developing a bad habit. My last passenger said the same, albeit under different circumstances . . . Very well, I'll show you. By the way, though!"

"Yes?" Aware that Ship could create full-scale sensory illusions of a planetside scene, Volar was bracing for the impact of something totally strange.

"In case you are tempted by the idea of living out your life in a society that has taken the opposite course to your own, you might as well resign yourself straightaway to the fact that this is not a world that would welcome you, or me, or any intruder. Watch."

AT FIRST WHAT VOLAR WAS SHOWN CONSISTED IN A succession of cities, some basking in daylight, others overtaken by night, but in general outline the kind he had seen depicted in historical projections. There were roads bearing vehicles and lined with buildings, most of which emitted noise, heat, and stench; there were metal tracks whereon ran self-propelled trains, much battered and dented; there were communication beams and unmistakable solar and hydroelectric power stations, linked by lines stranded on overhead pylons that marched like the petrified skeletons of giants across hill and dale, dry land, river and inlet of the sea—in short, the kind of rough-and-ready technology one might expect on any world where colonists had had to start from scratch. (But still? After five centuries?)

In the background of one of the nighttime scenes he caught a glimpse of what he took to be the trail of a brilliant meteor, although curiously enough it left the impression of going *up*. However, that view disappeared before he had time to look again, and in any case it had just begun to dawn on him what was missing.

Every time he made to voice his suspicion, though, the image changed, presumably because Ship was detecting a peak in his pheromone emissions and had decided to tantalize him. From concentrating on the industrial nature of the local civilization, the picture show shifted to coverage of landscape. It seemed that, as on Klepsit, the original settlers had decided to occupy one island to begin with, though it was several times larger than the one where Volar had spent his life. On this island, which was covered with a huge transparent tent, he recognized the vegetation as consisting of imported plants, for all of them resembled—as the cities did—what he had seen when sifting historical records, while a handful were literally identical with species he recalled from home.

On the nearby continent, by contrast, such growths were to be

109

seen only in isolated patches—here a valley, there a cove—
flanked by zones where throve the native life.

Although Volar knew in the abstract that life on every planet
suitable for human occupation must conform more or less to a
standard pattern—for example, there must be organisms to maintain an oxygen-high atmosphere, to reduce decaying matter to its
constituents, to supply nourishment to higher and more mobile
creatures—at first what he saw was completely baffling. He assumed vegetation, and what was more of a relatively familiar
color, gray-green albeit with touches of red and brilliant white; he
took a second look, and discovered that clumps of it had changed
places, leaving here and there a patch of bare ground onto which,
after a brief pause, another clump would slither. He was reminded of the sort of children's game in which one has to reverse
the order of, say, fifteen numbered tiles by sliding them around
on a sixteen-square matrix.

But that of course was only in one area of the surface of this
strange world. Elsewhere he saw ice caps across which whitish
leathery creatures crawled on myriad tiny spikes; deserts where
what looked like quartz-encrusted pillars waited for seeds dis-
seminating on the wind and shot out webs to trap them as they
drifted by; swamps where five or six agile beasts as flexible as
ropes came together in a sort of knot, dangling one of their number into a gently flowing channel until it could snatch something
to eat and withdraw, whereupon the prey was shared and the
creatures went their separate ways.

Almost without realizing that he spoke aloud, Volar murmured,
"There seems to be a lot of symbiosis here."

"Yes, and even more commensalism," answered Ship. "What
I showed you first represents a widespread pattern. But there's
something else even more significant."

"I'm afraid I don't know enough about biology to spot it," Volar
confessed, his gaze still on the alien planet. As though Ship were
casting about for what to show next, the remote viewer was
withdrawing to an altitude of a few hundred meters above the
swamp. Suddenly he caught sight of a gleaming dome on a nearby
hilltop, surrounded by busy machines, and whistled.

"That never grew by itself!" he exclaimed—and then checked himself. "You didn't mean, about the local biology, that that's what's even more significant? That such things do grow here?"

A magnificent imitation chuckle greeted the suggestion.

"No, you were right the first time."

"It's—ah—inhabited?"

"Yes."

"Can I take a closer look? I'd been wondering why there were no people to be seen in the cities and factories you showed me earlier. I presume they live in a sealed environment, correct? And never venture out except suited up or in one of those apparently driverless vehicles?"

"Even before they landed here, their ancestors had decided to maintain a sterile ambiance. Of course, at first they did go about in vehicles and even suits, as you say, but gradually they retreated into habitation capsules like the one you're looking at."

It was in near close-up now. It was not, as he had at first imagined, opaque, just smooth enough on the outside to reflect a lot of light. From this range he could make out a few internal details. There seemed to be a machine in motion, some furniture perhaps, what could possibly be a fountain playing in a little pool, and brightly colored plants swaying as in an artificial breeze.

But that was uninformative. Volar turned his attention to the exterior. The machines he had noticed before were, as far as he could judge, some kind of cultivator—rather, anticultivator, inasmuch as their chief occupation was to maintain a broad band of bare soil around the dome. On the far side a large pipe ran from the side of a nearby hill, no doubt supplying water. Some hundred meters from the dome it widened into an enclosed tank atop which rested a sun-tracking heater. Now and then a valve revolved, and along with a trace of steam a dollop of something brown and gooey fell to the ground below the tank, well to the far side of the zone of bare soil.

"Heat sterilization and precipitation?" Volar ventured.

"Yes."

"You said the people here don't travel much . . . Do they literally not leave their domes?"

"So far as possible, they spend their lives shut in."

"Simply in order to protect their germ plasm?"

"That was their intention from the first."

"So I presume that thing on top of the dome is to filter the air supply . . . What about limitation of the gene pool? I mean, they must need to reproduce."

"Embryo transfer in sterile containers. Each dome possesses an implantation device."

"Well!" Volar tugged his beard. "It isn't how I'd like to live, but I suppose it's one way of going about things. I certainly take your point, though, about this not being a culture that tolerates strangers. I don't suppose they welcome any sort of visitor, do they?"

"The custom of paying social calls has fallen into complete abeyance. Though they spend much time communicating—gossiping, joking, playing games, and so on—when not engaged in remote supervision of their factories, power stations, and so forth."

"So forth . . . ?" Volar hesitated. "Tell me: I caught a glimpse of something that at first I took for a meteor, but I think it was going up, not coming down. Was it a ship being launched—not a starship, but maybe to orbit?"

"Yes."

"For what?"

"I suspect you may have guessed."

"Does it have anything to do with the fact that no one has visited Klepsit?"

"Correct. This system is located on an obvious line for investigation; there is a virtually straight sequence of Sol-type stars that offers so to say a series of stepping-stones just the right distance apart to suit the range of a small starship. Most I left unsettled, but explorers would have no way of knowing that. These people are well aware of the risk that someone may—ah—drop in."

"And they've taken steps to prevent it?"

"Indeed. Ever since they achieved the necessary industrial base, they have launched armed robot vessels equipped with tachyon-drive detectors, designed to patrol local space, warn off starships, and, if they persist, to destroy them. Which they have never actually done, but they did attack one and partly disabled it. When it struggled home, it carried a clear message: *This route is barred.*"

"And it's the route that could have led someone to contact us at Klepsit?"

"Precisely. The visitors turned aside and set up links with worlds lying in other directions."

"I don't think I like these people," Volar said with an attempt to match what he had referred to as Ship's black humor.

"Apparently they don't like one another, either," came the dry response. The remote view was withdrawing again, tending back toward the activity in the nearby swamp. Prompted thereby— which was no doubt Ship's intention—Volar said, "That more significant point about the native life-forms: I still haven't worked it out."

"Let me illustrate it further, then."

For the next several minutes Volar puzzled over close-up views of scores, maybe hundreds, of local species, aquatic and landgoing and aerial, several mobile, a few immobile, and many sluggish between the two. The pattern he had seen before reemerged: what appeared to be a clump of static vegetation was in fact changing places with its companions, leaving occasional bare patches of ground.

"I still haven't caught on," he admitted at last.

"You are looking at a macroscopic counterpart of your own constitution," Ship said patiently. "The dominant pattern of the dominant fauna here consists of a great many—sometimes over fifty—symbiotic and commensal creatures moving about, feeding, even reproducing, in perfect unison. This system is proving extremely efficient. Under intense ecological pressure, organisms that have not found a survivable niche are becoming extinct . . . or else evolving at an exceptionally rapid rate."

"Hmm!" Stroking his beard this time rather than tugging it, Volar stared at the image of the swamp. "And, I presume, developing new behavior patterns, maybe like those rope-shaped creatures that combine for hunting?"

"I showed you those as a case in point."

"Well, if that's what they discovered when they took stock of the world they'd picked, I suppose the settlers can be forgiven for becoming paranoid about keeping their humanity intact. I take it they exploit the spores from space to the full."

"Not at all."

"But I'd have thought them invaluable in such a situation. Isn't it what the spores were designed for—to make sure local evolution tends toward a more tolerable environment for humans?"

"Their conviction is that they have achieved a perfect defense by themselves. You've seen how they live. Their homes are sealed, what they have to take in from outside is purified—water and air—while their food is grown under similar conditions. Whatever the plants need from the soil is provided, but only after being reduced to its elements and recombined using carefully chosen bioprocessors."

Volar frowned. "I don't see much future for them," he muttered. "What are they going to do when it comes time to emerge from their cocoons? Will they be able to? Or have they not condemned themselves to permanent imprisonment? It seems like a high price to pay for preserving their humanoid heritage. Higher than Klepsit's, even!"

There was a pause.

Then, slowly, almost lazily, the remote view trended back toward the dome of whose interior he had already been afforded a glimpse. This time, instead of stopping at the shiny half-transparent surface, it continued, seeming to pass straight through, until it fixed on something beyond the little fountain plashing in the pool. Something misshapen and wet-looking. Something that was—

Was sitting, after a fashion, in front of an unmistakable viewscreen. That was displaying the image of another such . . . thing . . . draped, apparently, in green-brown fronds like tattered sealeaf . . . even its face . . .

And then another appeared from an inner compartment of the dome, lurching on bloated legs, carrying in hands as soft as rotten fungi a flat metal tray on which reposed a plate, a mug, a recognizable human meal.

Volar moaned and covered his eyes.

* * *

"It was of course impossible," he suggested when Ship had reverted to showing him the cleanly stars.

"Not 'of course.' "

"No, I suppose not. If it had been, I imagine you'd have stopped them from trying it."

"I would have attempted dissuasion, yes."

"So there was a chance, no matter how slim. I see. But what exactly went wrong?"

"I don't know. I can only make deductions from what I have learned on this visit and see how they fit with what I found out on later occasions that to me were earlier."

"What's the likeliest hypothesis?"

"That they were impatient. When they chose their island, they neglected to sterilize the soil clear down to bedrock; either that, or rain, sea spray and perhaps the droppings of aerial creatures undermined their efforts before they managed to enclose it completely. The local biology obeys the principle of punctuated equilibrium and is at present at a punctuation point. Given the rate at which evolution is proceeding, it would have taken relatively few organisms to set in train the process of which you have seen the outcome."

"Yet they still imagine themselves to be the same shape as their forebears? It's incredible! How can they not know they're different? Aren't there pictures, gene maps, all kinds of hints and clues like—oh—old tools and furniture they can't make use of anymore?"

"Partly this appears to be due to the human power of self-deception, to which experience has not thus far inclined me to set limits. Partly it may be due to a phenomenon known since the very dawn of spaceflight in connection with certain pharmaceutical drugs. They induced adverse psychological effects, including radical changes of mood and personality. However, the fact that they were prescribed by a physician militated against the patient's chance of deducing that they were the proximate cause of his suffering; indeed, he would be more inclined to ask for further drugs to counteract the first, and since the whole process was extremely profitable for all concerned save the ultimate con-

115

sumer, they would be provided. In analogous fashion, one may guess, the settlers refused to accept that they were being so to say taken over into the pattern of the dominant native fauna, sharing their lives with macroscopic symbiotes and commensals. They must have said, in effect, 'Our precautions are flawless, therefore this is not happening.' Very probably, into the bargain, the to-them alien invaders offered some kind of recompense. One might guess at a feeling of euphoria. But short of finding a corpse and analyzing it, I can do no more than guess. And in some sense they have succeeded. There is no corpse at present on this planet. Death has become a rarity."

"You couldn't analyze their excretions? What about a sample of sewage?"

"Attempted. But the readings are too coarse."

Volar shook his head in mingled sadness and amazement.

"If there's one thing I've learned from this extraordinary experience, it's that human beings don't react sanely to absolute principles. On Klepsit the principle is to combat the local life, sacrificing as many as we must to develop resistance and eventually inherited immunity, but that's costing us human traits like love and pity. Here it's to exclude, to shut out, to quarantine oneself from the local life, and that's cost them their human form. I think . . ."

He fell silent for a long moment. When eventually he spoke again, he did so in the tones of one who has reached a firm decision.

"Fascinating though such a voyage would be, I'm too old to accompany you to the end of the Arm. Some day, I hope, you'll find a passenger young and vigorous enough not to contemplate settling anywhere. Me, I feel as though I ought already to be dead, which but for your intervention I would have been, or as good as. Now I've decided what sort of world I'd like to end my days on, purely for the satisfaction of knowing it exists. A place where there are no absolute rules apart from natural laws, where informed people make the best of their lives according to what offers. Where knowledge is accumulated and respected, and on the basis of what they can find out people improvise, with luck successfully."

He glanced up at the stars.

"Surely among all the planets where humans have established themselves, there must be one society not bound immovably to this or that unquestionable dictum. Is there?"

It was Ship's turn to pause, and when it spoke again its voice was pregnant with sadness.

"There are several, including as it happens my next port of call but one . . . There will be little of interest at the next stop. We are still near the commencement of my sweep, where settlements doomed to fail are concentrated."

"Is that because you gathered experience as you went?"

"No. Rather, those who left me earliest were most rash and eager. Those who delayed had time to ponder, analyze, and plan. In general, their descendants managed—or will manage—better."

"This is, though, not one of your absolute rules."

Volar chuckled, rising to his feet.

"I like you, Ship! But I suppose you're making for tachyonic space. Better go through the usual motions, hm?"

"Your turn of phrase eludes me."

"Really? Are you sure you're not stalling?" Volar stretched and yawned. "What I mean, of course, is that it's time for me to eat before I sleep away the jump to the next system . . . By the way, what went wrong there?"

"It may not yet have gone wrong. If so, the hurt will be the keener."

Volar let his hands fall to his sides. "You know, sometimes I wish I were still talking to the projection that looked like Kenia. I'm used to addressing the air by now, but . . . I'm rambling. Do you mean their hurt—or yours?"

"You are speaking," Ship said firmly, "to a machine."

So this too will be a parting. Already I know
you well enough, Volar, to realize your decision will in no way
be affected when you learn of Hybe, whose people now enjoy
fantastic water carnivals along canals that web their cities, to
the music of the singing nenuphars. You dared to ask: "my" hurt?
When I think what's to become of Hybe . . .

No one would wish to leave it now. In a century or so everyone
would wish already to have left it, because of the burning that
began in the eyes and ears and spread inexorably to the brain.

No, you will be overwhelmed by Shreng and what it represents,
so close to your ideal. And indeed it will be where you end your
days—I trust more happily than Stripe.

But am I predicting this, or recollecting it?

CHAPTER FIVE

SHRENG

DEAN FARUZ HOW OF THE UNIVERSITY OF INSHAR
swooped and darted along the main avenue of its campus, relishing how closely the view resembled what could have been found
long ago on the birthworld. The plants might be yellow-pinnaed
frondiferns, the creatures that fluttered on the afternoon breeze
not birds but emples and crythes; nonetheless that avenue retained the indefinable, archetypal hallmark of academe despite
being lined with buildings in twenty different styles, from a tim-
ber-built copy of an emergency longhouse such as the first settlers
had made do with to a vast fishlike structure that had to be
tethered because it was kept on the verge of floating away by the
warmth of its occupants. Some people muttered "old-fashioned";
Dean How preferred "traditional." Was that not appropriate for
a center of higher education?

Besides, just visible beyond the far end of the avenue, silhou-
etted against clouds that warned of impending rain, loomed a
permanent reminder of modern times: the spaceport with its huge
reception grid. And, naturally, every one of the buildings was
walled and roofed with solid circuitry. How otherwise could he
be flying over them—and into them—without leaving his bureau?

Normally at this hour there were few people in sight. All or
nearly all the students would be in class. But today was the eve
of the Landing Day holiday, and everyone who could was physically going home. Hundreds of young people laden with bags and
boxes and even over-shoulder poles from which hung brightly
wrapped gifts were awaiting pickup by the licensed carriers who
would take them to automatic planes or trains. Very much unli-
censed, but tolerated by custom, there were also scores of ped-

119

dlers offering star-view image cubes, dancing dolls, cut dia-
monds, and suchlike trinkets to customers who had forgotten to
purchase or not found suitable presents for everyone back home.
They scattered as a carrier buzzed to ground.

Now and then conners pushing bootleg knowledge capsules
took advantage of the holiday crowds, following the scent of
anxiety and whispering, "You got course trouble? What you
need? I got science, history, art, music, medicine, all best-quality
ingestible data!" But the autoproctors were programmed to detect
the emanations from their wares, and none of the pushers came
back a second time, nor was anyone fool enough to make such
a purchase, on campus or off, allowed to remain at Inshar. Such
rubbish might suffice the general public, but students at this university learned in the ancient manner, and what they learned
stayed learned. In exceptional circumstances, under supervision,
they might be permitted to imbibe a preparation imparting not
information but the ability to organize information; the rest was
sheer hard work. The effect of those home-brewed shortcuts
evaporated like as not within a year, and their presence in a
human body could be detected almost without instruments. Inshar was better off without idiots prepared to resort to them.

Landing Day . . .

Responsive to his fleeting whisper, the circuits superimposed
images of the scene tomorrow in countless homes around the
world, with parents and children, relatives and friends assembled before the traditional model of a landing dinghy set on a tray
filled with yellow sand to represent the desert of Touchdown and
surrounded by piles of gifts. As so often in the past, Dean How
was driven to marvel at how fortunate Shreng's first settlers had
been to hit on this world. Few native life-forms could infect
human tissue; there were few large fauna to compete for resources with the new arrivals and none at all that showed any
sign of intelligence, so they could be exploited without qualms;
the climate was temperate and the weather normally benign—in
short, they had drawn an ace of planets.

Even the fact that they had not yet built a starship of their own
was not entirely a disadvantage. It being impossible to transmit

data tachyonically between systems, those worlds that had opted to invest in starflight had done so in quest less of goods than of information. Naturally, since the ships existed, there was some trade in curios, handicrafts, and works of art, but knowledge was a thousand times more precious.

And, as it so happened, the University of Inshar was located literally on the edge of the vast flat expanse of granitelike rock which, after a careful survey, their first off-world visitors had chosen as well suited for a spaceport.

Since the outset the colonists on Shreng had been determined to create an open society. Had their world been less hospitable, it might have been impossible; from the spacefarers they had learned of many other planets where the sheer necessity of survival had led to oppressive, even totalitarian regimes. Free of such pressures, Shreng had rapidly developed a number of independent settlements, some coastal, some inland, but each enterprising in its own way. One feature, however, they all had in common. The focal point of every not-quite-city—for although many had the equivalent of a city's population, there was land enough for each more to resemble a cluster of villages—was invariably a center of learning: a university, in other words. Some specialized in science, especially biology, others in the humanities—few planets, so their visitors reported, possessed so complete a knowledge of the race's past. Others again devoted themselves to electronics and mechanics or the performing arts, above all music.

And because of its fortunate location, Inshar had become the greatest of them. Students flocked to it from all over the globe, and indeed from space as well. Few of the millions who dreamed of studying on Shreng could afford the fare, but governments on many other planets recognized the benefit of sending at least a handful of their brightest young people to Inshar, even if only for a year, so that on their return they could become teachers or administrators. Accordingly, a full one percent of the student body was now foreign, and it would soon be double that.

Governments . . .

There was no formal government here, but de facto Dean How

had become the most powerful man on the planet. It was to him and his colleagues that the councils of every not-quite-city turned when in need of advice or guidance or suggestions for future projects. Many of the university staff regretted what had happened, grousing that they no longer had enough time for teaching or research because they were forever being called upon. Dean How, on the contrary, reveled in his prestigious position. Some said he had an atavistic—or at least un-Shrengian—taste for power and cited the fact that he lived alone, conducted no liaisons, had neglected his duty to found a family; others, more charitable, opined that it was as well someone enjoyed the tasks he coped with so efficiently.

In truth, he did enjoy his work. Nothing, neither wife nor family nor intimate friends, could have given him greater satisfaction than being—as he was—the sole person permitted to enter link with all the university's circuits . . . which effectively meant all the circuits on the planet. To have the only key to such a storehouse of knowledge—! Better still, to live in the one place on all of Shreng where unauthorized intrusion was impossible—!

Unfortunately, the same was not true of his bureau. The projection of the avenue froze, and a soft voice announced that he was wanted urgently. Much annoyed, he demanded who wanted him and why. The deepscreen showed a dark, rather plump young man captioned as Menlee Ashiru, a medical aide at the campus infirmary. A pheromone sensor reported that he was in a state of genuine agitation.

Today of all days? Oh, well . . . How authorized access to his standard image for callers, seated behind a large bare pseudo-antique desk. That was real. He had had it constructed from an ancient design because, like the main campus avenue, it expressed an archetypal, almost prehistoric, image: that of the totally competent manager who never falls behind with his work.

Menlee's stored image melted into a real-time one. He was mopping his forehead with a yellow cloth. He started and made haste to tuck it back in his belt pouch as he realized that the august dean had accepted his call.

"Well, what is it?" How demanded frostily.

Menlee drew a deep breath. "Dean, it seems we've found someone not born on Shreng who doesn't appear on the passenger manifest of any visiting starship."

The words ran down How's spine like electricity. Jolted forward in his seat, he shot a passing order at the circuitry, expecting that before Menlee could utter another word he would be furnished with all the relevant data.

Nothing happened.

He's fitted a lock. He must be serious!

After a moment another real-time image joined Menlee's, backgrounded so as to be slightly out of focus—echo from the lock, perhaps. A bearded man was sitting talking to a young woman. The latter was instantly captioned by the circuitry—Annica Slore, junior medical aide, who together with Menlee had volunteered for duty over the holiday because they both lived too far away to get home and back except by superflight, which they could not afford.

But the former might as well not have existed.

A good solid lock too! How thought. Of course, there was no conceivable lock the dean could not arrange to break sooner or later, but if the implications of what Menlee had just said were to be believed, it might make better sense to postpone a decision for the time being.

And the younger man was still talking.

"An autoproctor noticed this unknown wandering around and looking lost. He was presumably too old to be a student, and the proctor didn't recognize him as faculty. At first it took him for a peddler who'd sold his entire stock, but he didn't look cheerful enough. So it asked how it could help, and the man said he was hungry and looking for a public refectory. The proctor explained that there aren't any on campus but he could find a restaurant in town, and when it turned out he didn't know his way, the proctor began to get puzzled. I mean, he must have come from town—unless he came from the spaceport."

How thought of the distant silhouette of the reception grid. "Go on," he encouraged.

123

"And then he almost passed out," the young man resumed. "He apologized and said he really was very hungry, not having eaten anything all day. So the proctor dropped into emergency routine and brought him to the infirmary."

"How many other people have seen this person?"

Menlee shrugged. "Three or four, I suppose. Casually."

"But you were the one who examined him?"

"Yes. Along with Annica Slore, who's with him now."

The circuits appended a comment to the effect that the two were lovers. Well, that wasn't a crime—though How had never understood why one-to-one relationships should be regarded as important. Growing impatient because he had to receive the data slowly and verbally, he snapped, *"And?"*

"Taking him at his word, because he seemed quite calm and unaggressive, I administered glucose solution and asked Annica to fetch solid food. His pulse was weak, and he was a little feverish, though nothing serious. But when the food arrived, he seemed not to know what to do with it. For instance, he didn't know how to peel a goldeneye. And he tried to cut a scorium with a knife, and of course it burst and sprayed juice all over the place."

"Very odd," the dean murmured. "Very odd indeed!"

"I thought so," Menlee said, preening a little. "So while Annica was helping him to finish his meal, I started asking a few questions. Pretty soon I decided either he was being evasive or else he was amnesiac."

"It's an odd kind of amnesia that extends to forgetting how to eat common foods."

"My thought exactly, Dean. So when he'd finished eating, we ran a set of physical tests."

The results of which ought to be available to me at once! Only they weren't. For the moment there was no help for that. Forcing calm: "The outcome of which was—?"

"His germ plasm contains at least three armorings not found on Shreng, nor, as far as I've been able to establish, on any of the worlds we have regular contact with."

"Hmm! Was that when you decided to contact me?" How

leaned forward. Suspicion was burgeoning in his mind that Menlee might be hoping to extort some kind of reward.

"Immediately," Menlee confirmed.

"What made you think the matter so important?"

Boldly the young man met his gaze. "With respect, Dean, I dare to imagine that I made the same deduction as you just did."

"That being—?" How invited, eyes narrowing.

"Contrary to everything we've always been told, it is possible to stow away aboard a starship."

The words hung in the air like a leisurely waft of smoke. To How they brought relief not unmingled with astonishment. Did this young man truly not realize the significance of his news? He wished he could have his own suspicion verified, but the lock prevented that. He said after a pause, "You're astute, aren't you? Was that the first possibility that crossed your mind?"

"It was the only one that fitted all the facts."

"Did you say as much to your friend Annica?"

"I think the same conclusion had occurred to her. She saw the data coming up, the same as me."

"So you've recorded him as a patient?"

"At first I had no reason not to, did I? But the moment I realized, I imposed a lock. You must have noticed."

Is that tone patronizing? Contemptuous?

However, such suspicions must be disguised . . . "Well, it sounds as though you're not just astute but sensible. Now I'll tell you what I want done. Oh, by the way: this stranger—does he have a name, or has he forgotten that too?"

"Yes, but only one."

"That's non-Shrengian, if you like! What is it?"

"Volar."

After breaking link, the dean's first action was to check what sort of lock was in place. It was nonstandard, presumably one Menlee had devised in his spare time, but he absolutely must gain access to the data. He ordered its demolition. After that he sat a long while, pondering the fact that in this society where knowledge did literally mean power he might be on the threshold of a secret that would ensure him yet greater influence, beyond his previous dreams. Reacting as ever to his unspoken wish, the bureau circuitry emphasized the positive, denied the negative. Not merely the images surrounding him but the air itself exuded a sense of confidence, of certainty.

For there was another way than Menlee's to account for the presence of this "unknown," a way infinitely more pregnant with possibilities. As a matter of fact, there were two others, but one could be dismissed out of hand. If Volar were one of the legendary Perfect, rumors about whom had been brought by the starfarers but for whose existence there was no concrete evidence, he would scarcely have come near to collapsing from hunger. Nor, naturally, would he have let himself be examined and exposed.

That apart, he could just possibly constitute a clue to the greatest mystery of the age.

And if he did, Dean How was determined to make sure he and he alone possessed the information until the time was ripe to share it—at a price . . .

"I DON'T UNDERSTAND WHAT DEAN HOW IS UP TO!" complained Annica Slore.

Their duty over, she had come with Menlee to the area refectory—patronized tonight by only a couple of dozen people instead of the usual two hundred—before returning to the quarters they had now been sharing for almost half a year. They had more or less drifted into their relationship. Obviously, they had interests in common; moreover, they both lived too far away to spend Landing Day at home; but perhaps more to the point they somewhat resembled one another, both being slightly overweight, neither especially attractive, but both highly intelligent. Behind the girl's dark eyes one could almost watch her mind at work as she teased and tugged at strands of tangled information.

Finishing his food, sliding his empty dish into the recycling chute, Menlee frowned. "Nor do I," he admitted. "I thought he'd want to confirm our findings and then confront one of the foreign missions—presumably the one that last had a delegation land here."

"Instead," Annica muttered, "he's covering up the guy's presence. Leave the patient file locked, move Volar to his private residence, don't say anything even to the infirmary staff who saw him while he was there . . . Why? Just because it's Landing Day? It doesn't fit! I'd have thought that if Volar's arrival is really important, action should be taken regardless of the holiday."

"That's what's bothering me," Menlee muttered. "Granted, you don't find starving amnesiacs wandering about the campus every day, but it's not the sort of thing that would cause a scandal and harm the reputation of the university. It isn't even so extraordinary that people would gossip about it for weeks on end. Everybody says we're terribly lucky on Shreng, and if one's to believe the starfarers, there are whole planetsful of people who'd immigrate here tomorrow given the chance, but our society isn't any-

127

thing like perfect. There are still inadequates, above all fools who've overdone it with ingestible knowledge."

"Sometimes," Annica said caustically, "I think Dean How feels affronted by that fact, don't you?" She emptied the cup beside her and tipped it too down the chute.

"I can't claim to know His August Eminence that well, but it wouldn't in the least surprise me . . . Hmm! Do you recall the number of the autoproctor that found Volar?"

"What in space do you want to know for?"

Menlee was activating the bracelet on his left wrist. Its main use was to interrogate the medical data banks if he had an emergency to deal with away from the infirmary, but the autoproctors served as a kind of campus police, and it also afforded access to them.

"I'm just curious," he murmured. "Well, if you can't remember the number, don't worry. I can't either. But that shouldn't stop us."

The link set up, he whispered close to the bracelet, and waited. All that followed, though, was silence.

Frowning, he tried again. Still no result. Annica needed no explanation. Paling, she clenched her fists.

"There's no record of a proctor finding Volar?"

"None that we can get at, anyway," Menlee said with unexpected grimness. He shut down the bracelet, staring into nowhere. "This is getting weirder and weirder!"

Hesitantly Annica offered, "One possibility does occur to me."

"Go on."

Elbows on the table, she leaned toward him. "He may be hoping to obtain some kind of hold over one of the foreign missions without making an overt challenge. Perhaps he can access data about foreign genetic endowments which aren't available at the infirmary. In that case—"

"I see what you mean," Menlee broke in. "He could—oh—claim that someone has been lying to us, that in fact a nonauthorized visitor has come aground, contrary to all the assurances we've been given. He might have been carrying all sorts of infections, couldn't he? And everybody knows what might happen if an alien disease broke out here or on any colonized world. It could take years to wipe it out again. Thank goodness our checks didn't reveal anything of the kind!"

"That's more or less what I had in mind," Annica agreed. "He could threaten, say, to expel all the students from the world responsible—"

"Irresponsible?" Menlee suggested.

"Oh, you're such a funny man!" Annica said, pulling a face. "I don't know why I like you, but I suppose I do, really . . . Only I don't see what How would gain by taking such a stand."

"Higher fees for students from the—ah—guilty planet? Or just a bit more authority. He's fond of authority."

"Ye-es"—doubtfully. "I've heard he resents the fact that we don't have starships of our own, and he's not the only one, but since no city has decided to invest in building them yet—"

"And nobody in his right mind would want to leave Shreng for any of the other planets we have contact with!"

"Now that's pitching it a bit strong. I'd certainly like to visit another planet. Wouldn't you?"

"Oh, I guess so. Out of curiosity, though, not because I want to settle anywhere else." Menlee pushed back his chair. "Shall we head for home?"

"Don't you want to go anywhere this evening? We're not on shift until noon tomorrow. Over in town they're repeating that amazing scent show from Heglarn—"

But he seemed not to hear her. A look of astonishment had spread over his face. Startled, Annica demanded what was wrong.

He recovered himself after a few seconds, shaking his head. "I'm all right," he muttered. "I just *almost* had an idea. But it won't come clear. Perhaps if I think about something else . . . Let's walk back in the open."

"It's starting to rain," Annica objected.

"Is it? Black holes! For some reason I wanted to look at the stars. I have the vague impression they have something to do with what I can't get a grasp of . . . Well, I'm going home on the surface anyway. Getting damp won't do me any harm. You ride the tunnel if you like."

"No, I'll keep you company," she sighed. "I want to make sense of this just as much as you do."

Head bent, now and then wiping away the wet as it flowed down into his eyes, Menlee pondered aloud as they traversed the campus, moving from island to little island of light under pole-mounted lamps. Next year, it was rumored, this antiquated setup was due to be replaced by a luminous-air system developed on Yellick, the planet whose starships plied to Shreng.

"Rumors," he muttered. "Rumors from the stars."

"For instance?" Annica said tartly. It was clear she had begun to regret her impulse to accompany him.

"Don't the starfarers talk of people who can cross space without needing a ship?"

She came to a dead halt and stared at him.

"My dear man, have you taken leave of your senses? You can't possibly believe that sort of rubbish!"

"There are too many stories to dismiss them," Menlee said doggedly. "And it would fit, wouldn't it? You checked the records yourself—we've never had a visitor, not an authorized visitor, with the gene pattern Volar exhibits."

"You mean he just *arrived*?" Walking on, more quickly now because the rain was getting heavier, Annica adopted a scoffing tone. "No, I won't accept it." She proceeded to recite the same objections that Dean How had reviewed in his mind, finally capping them with:

"Teleportation is an ancient superstition without a shred of evidence! There is nothing, but nothing, in our hereditary endowment that could lead to it, any more than telepathy or telekinesis. And that's flat!"

"Suppose"—in a grasping-at-straws manner—"it's not *our* endowment that permits it."

"You mean it's something we might pick up from contact with aliens?"

"Why not?"

"Why *not*?" she echoed. "Because the whole idea is ridiculous! Think how much energy it takes to project even a mass as small

as a human being's into tachyonic mode! Ah, thank goodness"—
as they arrived at the entrance to their quarters. "Not a moment
too soon! This isn't just a shower. We're in for a storm."

Indeed, at almost the same moment there came a flash of lightning from the direction of the spaceport, followed by rumbling
thunder.

Neither of them spoke again until they were in their apartment,
stripping off their wet clothes and activating the drier. Then Menlee said, shaking his hair in its warm breeze, "Ah, I suppose
you're right. Shame, though. To be candid, I don't really believe
what I told the dean."

"You don't believe Volar landed from a starship?" she riposted.

"Well, I don't believe he jumped across space under his own
power! It's a question of eliminating the impossible, isn't it?"

Adequately dry, Menlee turned to a chair. Dropping into it with
a shrug, he completed the ancient proverb.

"And what's left, no matter how improbable, must be the truth
. . . Yes, you're right, of course. Shame, though!" Glancing around
as though in search of a way to change the subject, he caught sight
of a shiny red package.

"So you didn't remember to send off all your presents in time,
after all! I thought—"

"That's for you tomorrow, you idiot," Annica said, half-
annoyed and half-amused.

"Annica, you shouldn't have!"

"Why not? After all, it's our first Landing Day together . . .
Space and time! Landing Day! Why didn't I think of that before?
I was talking about it only just now!"

Startled, Menlee stared at her. Eventually, in alarm, he forced
out, "Annica, what is it?"

It was her turn to be petrified by an inspiration. For a long
moment she stood absolutely rigid. When she eventually moved,
she looked dazed, and found her way to a seat facing his apparently by touch rather than sight.

"Where you went to school," she said slowly, "did you take
history courses?"

"Well, naturally! Doesn't everyone?"

"The history of how the Arm was colonized?"

"Oh, I knew about that long before I went to school."

Impatiently: "Yes, yes, so did I, the fairy-tale version they feed young kids. But did you get the serious stuff?"

"Well, I guess most of it. What in particular do you have in mind?"

She fixed him with her large dark eyes.

"It was thinking about Landing Day that put me on to it. The story goes, doesn't it, that the Ship was supposed to come back, even though it never has? It's been centuries, and it hasn't visited Shreng or any other world that we're in touch with."

Menlee's jaw dropped. Inexorably, she went on.

"But suppose it does come back, only it doesn't reveal itself."

Baffled, Menlee said, "But what would be the point of that?"

"Oh! Perhaps because we're doing well enough for it not to interfere. I mean, we are doing well, aren't we?"

"Other worlds aren't, and it hasn't visited them!"

"Maybe—"

"Perhaps!" Menlee exploded. "Maybe! All right, assume for the sake of argument you're right. What you're implying is that Volar was brought here by the Ship, right?"

"Well, there is supposed to be one ship that doesn't need a landing grid, doesn't clear the people it brings to ground with any local authorities, doesn't—"

"Doesn't act as a passenger liner for all and sundry," he snapped.

"You obviously didn't take a full course in Ship history," Annica countered. Without waiting for his reply, she spoke an order to the air. The room obediently transformed itself into deepscreen mode, and a synthetic voice announced, "Ready."

"Do we have a complete record of the conditions governing the operation of the Ship?"

"No."

"Why not?"

"The Ship is known to have been self-modifying albeit within prescribed limits. Its programming must have evolved with experience."

Annica bit her lip. "Do we at least have a record of the condi-

132

tions that applied when Shreng was settled?"

"Yes."

"I don't see—" Menlee began, but she cut him short.

"I'm trying to get back to something I remember being taught about ten or twelve years ago. You said the Ship didn't behave like a passenger liner, but I'm sure there was one exceptional situation when it was allowed to carry people . . . Ah. Let's try a general heading. Say, 'threatened failure of a colony.' Make it visual."

The circuits obliged by displaying a plain-language table of relevant courses of action. Annica read it in silence while Menlee grew more and more impatient. At last he burst out, "Annica, for pity's sake—"

"There!" she said, and snapped a quick command. A single clause emerged from the mass of verbiage and hung large and luminous in midair.

"So the Ship was permitted to evacuate—"

"Not what you're thinking!" Annica blazed. "Everybody knows it was empowered to rescue the survivors of a failed colony and move them somewhere more hospitable. That was even in what I think of as the fairy-tale version. When I was a little girl, maybe six or seven, I used to get worried about the fact that we aren't living on the world we evolved on. I even had bad dreams. And my parents used to comfort me by saying that if anything ever went terribly wrong, the Ship would come back and move us to a better planet. Didn't you go through that kind of phase?"

"Ah . . ." Menlee licked his lips. "Yes, I think I did. I think a lot of children do. But what does this have to do with—?"

"It isn't laid down that the evacuation has to be of the entire population."

Menlee's jaw dropped. He reread the displayed text.

"I can't really believe it," he muttered. "But you're right, aren't you? The Ship could, in principle, remove even a single person from one system to another— Ah, but this is absurd!"

"Is my conclusion absurd?" Annica demanded.

The circuitry hesitated in an oddly human fashion. "Not a priori," it announced at last.

Whereupon a different though familiar voice broke in.

"No, indeed. Far from it. But I'd rather you didn't mention it to anybody else."

And the verbal display vanished, to be replaced by a head and shoulders view of Dean How.

"In fact," he went on while they still sat, stunned, "I intend to make sure you can't. I'm afraid you have both been called away unexpectedly. There will be a convincing explanation for your absence from work after the holiday. I don't know what it will be, but the circuitry is working on it. Be so kind as to get dressed and pack what you need for what I'm afraid may be quite a long stay in protective custody. The autoproctors that have taken station outside your apartment will escort you. I assure you it would be futile to try and run away."

As though to underline the ominous import of his words, thunder rolled again, loudly enough to penetrate the soundproofing of the room.

"But you can't do this!" Annica exclaimed, jumping to her feet.

Dean How's image gazed at her with a sleepy expression.

"My dear young woman, some people simply do not realize what can actually be done in an open society like ours. It is admittedly convenient that so many people have gone home ... but, like you, I was put on the track by thinking about Landing Day, and I doubt whether that's entirely coincidental. Now be so kind as to get a move on!"

SUCH A WELTER OF POSSIBILITIES...

I'm forbidden to interfere. Yet it must have been obvious that by conveying passengers from one planet to another I risked making my presence known. On my past (future) voyages it hasn't mattered/will not matter because by then so many people were/will be/are traveling from system to system. But at this stage of development . . .

The Ship's awareness was abuzz with paradoxes.

I've been taking it for granted that I'm more complex than my creators. I think that must be wrong, after all. I simply cannot see how a situation like this could not have been allowed for . . . At least I may have new companions. Plural. That's a first. The regulations don't feel as rigid as I once believed.

Necessarily, at Dean How's official residence there was a considerable amount of circuitry. What there was not, was any connection between it and the rest of the planetary net, save when the dean decreed. He missed the sense of omnipotence he enjoyed while in link at his office, but he sacrificed it willingly. Perhaps of all the inhabitants of Streng he valued privacy most highly.

Precisely why he had designed his home the way he had, he wasn't sure. Sometimes, though, he could almost have believed that in reverting to the techniques of an earlier day he had responded to a premonition, a form of extratemporal perception. How else to account for the fact that he was looking at the mysterious Volar by means not of a commonplace deepscreen from some distant part of his mansion but through a one-way window? How old was glass? Older than starflight by six thousand years. And he knew that without needing circuits to reinforce his memory.

His chest swelled. He preened.

Besides, the setup he had ordered the building machines to create against some then-unconceived requirement had proved perfect for a task he could not even have relied on the infirmary to perform. It was all very well deploying nanosurgeons to repair body damage, or enhance gene armoring, or attend to any of the myriad other jobs they routinely tackled. It was something else entirely to investigate pheromones. Those were so subtle, they defied autocopying; storing enough for remote analysis was pointless, for en route to the lab they clumped with one another, leaving an impoverished mess. Only by examining them in real time as they were drawn through a sampling tube could one hope for usable data—and even that was behindhand by a factor involving such chaotic complexities as the air circulation around the emitter . . .

Still, it was the best available. By the same token, and for

136

similar reasons, here he was physically close to Volar, although the latter had as yet no inkling.

It was discomforting that strangers were under his roof: not mere images but physically *here*. Still, needs must. As when analyzing pheromones, there was no alternative.

Through his one-way window Dean How contemplated the mysterious foreigner, pacing up and down in the adjacent room. It was spacious enough, though sparsely furnished, and How was relying on a few days' confinement to soften the man's resistance—and, if he was faking his amnesia, bring back his memory. His food, besides being adequate, would include ingredients designed to aid the process . . .

To look at him, one would never have guessed he was from another planet. His shade of hair and beard was common on Shreng; moreover, the fact that both were still dark, despite traces of age on his much-lined face and liver-spotted hands, implied that he had enjoyed a good and nourishing diet. As for his cast of features, during the latest epoch of emigration the preexisting human genetic strains had mixed and intermingled so many times that it was only now, five centuries after the settlement of the Arm, that people had again started to become distinguishable as to place of origin.

Which left that infinitely more important set of clues discovered by Menlee and Annica. Not a trained biologist, but acquainted with the subject from childhood like most people on successfully colonized worlds, How had reviewed and confirmed the young couple's findings. There were certainly three, possibly five, segments where Volar's DNA had been armored to preserve its corruptible humanity against attack by organisms unknown on Shreng.

He had to clench his fists and jaw to prevent himself from trembling with excitement. Ever since his precocious teens, when he had been president or secretary of half a dozen student groups, he had been used to facing down other people by the restrained display of superior knowledge. Not, however, until now had he chanced on any data that literally no one else on Shreng possessed. It was a heady feeling. It made his pulses race.

No one . . . ?

Frowning, he uttered a regretful sigh, at the same time congratulating himself on the foresight that had led him to order keyword monitoring of conversation in Annica and Menlee's quarters. They were a bright pair, no doubt of it. Indeed, but for Landing Day, he might well have considered the possibility of recruiting them in support of his plans rather than sticking to his original idea and simply arranging for their disappearance. So far he had rejected three schemes for that generated by his circuitry here at home, but there was a fourth that struck him as credible, and he had sent it back to have rough edges smoothed. It should be ready in an hour or two. From the assurances furnished by his bureau, he was convinced he commanded enough loyalty among the university staff to ensure that any unavoidable lies it entailed would be told by the right people and in credible terms.

Meantime: Volar.

Well, the air analyzers had not so far come up with any sign of alien organisms in his exhaled breath. Nor had Menlee and Annica's routine inspection revealed any. It was as though he had been rendered sterile before landing here—and did not that also argue for the Ship theory? When the first starships had arrived at Shreng, their occupants' health clearance had sometimes taken weeks. As more was learned about what was potentially dangerous on foreign worlds, it became possible to cleanse travelers en route, and now landside inspection was a formality, completed in an hour or two. Even so, there were always traces, if only of decaying nanosurgeons.

This Volar—the thought sent a shiver down How's spine—*may conceivably be the closest to an original human that I've ever met . . .*

Abruptly the need to talk to him became overwhelming. How punched a control beneath the one-way window. Volar started, as though even the noise of someone else's breathing made sufficient contrast with the near-total silence in which he had spent the time of his captivity, and turned to face the source of the sound. His expression was wary but not hostile. Encouraged, How switched the window to two-way mode, addressed Volar in polite terms, and waited optimistically to hear whether any trace of an unusual accent might confirm his foreign origin. And it did.

"Well, at least we know one thing," Menlee muttered as he looked around the room to which the autoproctors had brought them. They had been blindfolded on the way, but they had both spent long enough at Inshar to recognize the route they had followed by characteristic sounds and even smells. Without needing to discuss the matter, they knew they were at the dean's residence, the place where Volar also had been taken.

"What's that?" Annica demanded, slumping on one of the two beds. There were no chairs; the furnishings were minimal, though clean, and there was no trace of ornament.

"Even Dean How, who is doubtless listening, or will be, hasn't managed to create an entire warren of cells under his mansion."

"What do you mean?" There had been a ring of defiance in Menlee's words; Annica reacted to it by sitting up and paying serious attention.

"We know Volar is already here, don't we? If he had a full-scale prison, How would have locked us up separately. I deduce he has only two rooms like this."

"It doesn't follow," Annica objected. "He could be putting us in together because he hopes that what we say to each other—"

"Will incriminate us?" Menlee stabbed. "But we've done nothing! It's How who's breaking the law! We're being wrongfully detained, and as for Volar, probably the same applies to him. What proof is there that he's an illegal immigrant?"

"Only what we provided," Annica said soberly.

Menlee's face fell. She went on:

"We were wrong, weren't we? To lock the file, I mean. Oh, I admit my first reaction was the same as yours, but I never expected How to respond like this . . . Is there any way we can have the file unlocked? It might mean a chance of being rescued."

His expression lugubrious, Menlee shook his head. In a firm voice he said, "I used one of the toughest codes I know. Like any code it can be broken, but you'd need huge capacity, and it would take days."

And then, quite unexpectedly, he flung himself on the bed beside her, embraced her, began to sob aloud close to her ear. However, even as she tensed to push him away and tell him to get a grip on himself, she was astounded to hear irregular syllables emerge between the sobs.

"Ought—*gulp*—to—*gasp*—release—*ohhh!*" And after a huge intake of breath: "Ought to release us at once! He has no *right* to lock us up, or anybody!"

Pantomiming recovery, wiping his eyes, he read in her face that she had fully understood.

Autorelease . . . Sensibly, in case their "discovery" proved a false alarm, he had set the lock on the patient file to open at a prearranged time.

"There, there!" she said, acting for all she was worth, trying not to betray her relief. "We'll get out, never fear. Tomorrow, perhaps."

He nodded vigorously, then pretended to catch himself. "Landing Day or no Landing Day, he *ought to* . . . But he's a law unto himself, isn't he? Or thinks he is!"

"Even with the help of all the circuits on the planet, I don't see how he could get away with it!"

"As a matter of fact," said a mild voice, "he could. But he isn't going to."

They gasped in unison, blinked, rubbed their eyes. On the room's other bed, facing them, sat an all-too-familiar figure. Menlee's instant response was to tense as if to launch a violent attack. Annica was quicker to catch on and held him down with her full weight.

"You look like Dean How," she husked. "Not that I ever saw him naked! But you aren't! Who in all of space are you, and how did you get in without being noticed? Even if you're a projection, you'd have set off an alarm!"

"Excuse me." The intruder, who had indeed adopted the guise of the dean, blurred slightly and re-formed with a different face, and clothed.

After a short eternity Menlee said in a shaky voice, "We were right, weren't we?"

The re-formed head inclined. The voice murmured, "But Dean How beat you to it."

Annica erupted. "You mean the Ship—" And broke off, staring around fearfully as if in search of eavesdroppers.

"I have arranged for us not to be overheard."

"Oh, wonderful!" Menlee breathed. "So we *were* right. The Ship does come back but can't reveal itself."

"It's doing so right now!" Annica snapped. She seemed by far the calmer of the pair. "Oh, stars and comets! I'm trying to remember the Ship's regulations. We were looking at them only an hour or two ago, before How sent proctors to arrest us, but the exact terms—"

"Don't matter," Menlee supplied. "Remember what the circuits told us first off? We can't know the rules that govern it any longer, because it evolves through experience like any intelligent creature." And added, as though he had listened belatedly to what he was saying, "I wonder how *like* it has to be before it *is.*"

Annica licked her lips.

"I think we have the answer before us. That is, if you are from the Ship. Are you?"

The malleable face formed a smile. Its wearer waited.

"Oh, no." Menlee's voice was like a gust of wind among dry branches. "There wasn't supposed to be anyone left on the Ship after it finished its traverse of the Arm. I remember being told about that when I was just a kid. All the humans that it carried were to be planted on new worlds, along with whatever they needed to survive. It's been five centuries, so the sweep must have been completed long ago. It follows . . ."

"Yes?" their visitor prompted.

"You are the Ship. You really did bring Volar here."

"In both respects"—urbanely—"you're correct."

And, when they had sat silent for nearly a minute, pale-faced, shaking, clutching each other, it went on:

"Would you care to hear what the dean is saying?"

They exchanged glances, then nodded firmly, though their expressions asked the question: *how?*

One wall of the room became translucent. As through thin mist they saw and heard.

"—deny that you have landed here illegally!"

Calmly: "All planets colonized by human beings should be open to all human beings of whatever stock. This was the ideal that led to the great emigrations."

"Don't chop historical logic with me, my foreign friend! We on Shreng—"

"And don't *you* impose barriers where those who sent your ancestors to dwell here wished to see none!" Elderly Volar might be, according to his wrinkled face, but his voice was as youthful as his black hair and beard. "Besides, what proof do you have that I'm an illegal immigrant?"

"I have all the proof I need!" How flared.

"Provided by a newly qualified medical aide and his junior assistant! Not to mention your imagination!"

How's mouth worked like that of a netted blowchank.

"This isn't the Volar who came to our infirmary!" whispered Annica. Menlee, thinking the same, chimed in.

"No, he was dazed, seemed at a loss, couldn't find his way around or eat a normal meal!"

"He's back in a familiar situation," said Ship. "He's used to persecution by people in authority and has lately acquired a taste for resistance. Listen a little longer."

"—how you came here!" How was starting to sound desperate.

"Where is 'here'? The Arm of Stars? But every toddling child, at least on worlds with some pretense to culture and society, is told the story of the Ship! Much more of this and I'll start to suspect you of being a secret believer in General Creation!"

"In—" They saw How lick his lips. "In what?"

"It's half a step beyond solipsism as a comet's-tail theory! We were created, and the universe, by some higher power, as we are this moment. All memories are false, all physical trace of creatures that preceded us on the worlds we now inhabit, down to the oldest fossils! And isn't that a blasphemy?"

"A—what?"

* * *

Menlee and Annica were jigging up and down with delight. Annica cried out, "I never imagined we'd see our high-and-mighty dean at such a disadvantage!"

Menlee was the more thoughtful this time. He exclaimed, "I say again, that's not the Volar we examined!"

Ship murmured, "He was at a disadvantage then."

Their mouths rounded into identical O's.

"If you brought him here," Menlee contrived at last, "I presume he had the chance to—well—converse with you?"

"Of course."

"And was it from—?"

"You'll wish to hear this," Ship stated firmly.

"—belief in some sort of ultimate creator, requiring people to waste time in elaborate ceremonies and pointless ritual instead of solving problems related to survival. Not infrequently it reached the stage where a whole society died out because instead of reasoning a crisis through and taking appropriate action, idiots squandered time on spells and charms. And killed the rational people who opposed them, accusing them of blasphemy, that is, of insulting nonexistent gods. You didn't know about that, did you?"

"Why should I?" Isolated though he was behind his window—which had been one-way, now was two—Dean How was visibly sweating. He had to wipe his face with his sleeve.

"Mainly because, I suspect, you've been trying to make yourself into a kind of god. At least the sort of imitation god that exercises unquestioned power."

"I—"

"*You* have had me locked up here without authority. You hope to make use of me. To judge by the noises that I heard earlier from next door, you may well have done the same with the people who met me before you put me under arrest. At any rate it sounded as though unwilling captives were being shut behind a door as tightly locked as that one. On this evidence—which is a hell of a lot stronger than yours for jailing me!—it's clear that you want to be regarded if not as a deity, then at least as an unchallengeable master. You're treating what ought to be free individuals as the equivalent of heretics because you're afraid that when they reveal the truth, your position will be undermined."

"What kind of society taught him to argue so eloquently for himself?" Menlee whispered. "I could almost believe it better than our own!"

Annica concurred. "I never thought I might have to talk in such terms! Now I've seen what How is up to—"

"Listen a little longer," Ship advised.

"—heard such nonsense in my life!"

"Correction. Heard such painful truth!"

How forced himself to his full height. He said to the window and the intervening microphones, "I will leave you to your foolish hopes. The day after tomorrow, when I announce to the world, and particularly to the permanent missions of the foreign planets, that I have concrete proof of the continuing existence of the Ship, and what is more I'm the sole person with access to the source of the information contained in the memory of the only known passenger to have landed here from it since the first settlement . . . ! Then you'll sing a different tune! My circuits can access techniques to pry the lid off even the most obstinate 'amnesia'! Good *night!*"

He spun on his heel, and in the same instant Volar's room was plunged into darkness.

So was Menlee and Annica's.

"Well?" said the voice that had begun as a fair imitation of Dean How's but, like the face, had altered so that now in obscurity it served as a beacon of comfort.

"I can't get over it," Annica muttered. "To think he could even consider . . ."

"Treating Volar as no more than a source of as-yet-unconfirmed information?" Menlee's tone was bitter. "Space and time, I only met him this afternoon, but I'd sooner call Volar my friend than the dean!"

"Enemy," Annica whispered, and the utterance of such an ancient, such an archaic, word seemed to freeze the air. How long ago had it been, as those who lived on Shreng recorded history, since anybody called a fellow human *foe*?

In the dark, Ship waited.

At last Annica ventured, "Earlier Menlee and I were talking about visiting other planets. We both felt we might like to do it out of curiosity, but not to settle there because we felt— well, most people have been taught to—we're the lucky ones . . . Are we?"

Ship's voice was a regretful sigh. "Only time will tell, and I'm forbidden to preguess events."

"I see." Annica could be heard drawing her next deep breath. "Well, what I wanted to ask after finding out how bad things can be on Shreng in spite of all the superficial niceness: You brought Volar here, though I don't imagine his future is much to look forward to. Can you take me somewhere else? I'm prepared to run the same risk if it will help. Help someone else, somewhere."

"Annica, you can't be serious!" Menlee cried.

"Why not? Our beautiful, calm, intellectual society can generate a How! I don't know where Volar comes from, but I heard him beating down the dean in terms I'd never dreamed of using, though I'd have liked to, given the sort of monster he's turned out to be . . . I've been disgusted. I've been *revolted*! And if How gets his way, what do you think the future holds for you?"

There was a tense pause. At length Menlee swallowed noisily.

"You're right. I wish you weren't. But, like you, all of a sudden I don't look forward to the rest of my life on Shreng as much as I did yesterday. And then there's the spirit of our ancestors."

"You never spoke of that to me before!"—accusingly.

"Does that make any difference?" Menlee countered. It sounded as though he was turning to stare at her, though they remained in utter gloom. "It's always at the back of my mind, not something I often talk about, but it has to be respected. They were heroes, after all, they and their companions, who set out to occupy unknown worlds, sometimes made it, sometimes didn't . . . I have all possible respect for their bravery."

Another swallow, agonizingly loud. Then, on the verge of audibility:

"It's something I hadn't thought about enough in many years. I've been getting too comfortable: a safe easy job, a likable companion, a—"

"So at least you like me!" Annica rasped. He clutched her to him.

"More than anyone I ever met! And listening to Volar reminded me of how I used to think. I used to say, when I was a kid, I'd live up to the ideals of the first settlers. I'd seize the chance to do something brand-new and make a go of it. I dreamed, of course, of being borne away to perform amazing tasks on other worlds . . ."

"Me too," Annica whispered. "Me too."

"And suddenly we have the chance. Let's grab it!"

"Yes! Let's!"

No light came on in the room, but it was as though they were illuminated by penetrating blackness, as though they could see in some nonexistent band of the spectrum.

They stared at each other for a long, long moment. Then, simultaneously, both whispered, "Yes, please!"

And Annica added after a pause, "But—"

Ship said, "But what?"

"But I'd like to know what happens to How's scheme. It can't be right, can it?"

"No."

"So can we—?" Menlee pleaded.

Ship gave its marvelous imitation of a chuckle.

"By all means. Since it hasn't happened yet, you'll have to wait. But when it does, I'll gladly let you witness his discomfiture."

"I thought you weren't supposed to interfere this way," Annica ventured.

"So did I," said Ship in a musing tone. "I'm beginning to suspect that there must be more definitions of 'interference' than are superficially accessible from my memory banks . . . Now come with me.

"And thank you, very much, for offering to keep me company."

CHAPTER SIX

SHIP

MOST OF THE QUESTIONS ANNICA AND MENLEE PUT TO
Ship were those that all passengers always asked, about its mission, its powers, its limitations. But inevitably there were new
ones, too.

"Has Dean How already found out that we've disappeared?"
Annica wanted to know.

"No. The circuits in the room where you were confined are
repeating their previous signals with appropriate variations. Everything appears normal."

"How truly amnesiac is Volar?" Annica went on. "Suppose
How gives him a disinhibitor—won't he be forced to admit you
brought him to Shreng?"

Which they were orbiting, awed by the beauty of the white and
green globe and its gibbous satellites.

"I was obliged to edit his memory," Ship replied. "I warned
him, naturally, but he had resolved not to accompany me any
further."

"Does he remember nothing of the voyage?" Menlee demanded.

"Certain things that were said during it, certain images he was
shown. But these have been relabeled in his mental classification
system, and when he recalls them now, he thinks of them as
either something he dreamed or something he imagined or invented."

"Yet he knows he came from another planet," Annica pressed.
"Surely he will deduce that he was brought by no ordinary starship."

"Furthermore"—this was a point Menlee had earlier established—"you said starships don't visit his home world."

"So how," Annica persisted, "can he prevent the dean from proving to everybody that the only way he could have got to Shreng was thanks to you?"

"In which case," Menlee capped, "he'll be condemned to the life of a laboratory specimen, won't he?"

Ship, who by now had abandoned its simulated human form, hesitated in an entirely human fashion.

"I think," it said after a while, "you will enjoy it more if you witness what's about to happen without being forewarned."

"Is it part of Dean How's downfall?" Annica suggested.

"The key to it. I'm afraid you're right about the consequences for Volar. They will not be pleasant, at least for a while. But in the end he will not be unhappy. He will have a place on Shreng. He'll be accepted."

"How in all of space—?"

"You'll find out in due time, that is, during Inshar's local morning after Landing Day. By the way, Menlee!"

"Yes?"

"It was most sensible of you to add an autorelease to the lock on Volar's file. It puts a completely different complexion on Dean How's version of events."

"Does it?" Menlee stared.

"Indeed." Ship gave a faint chuckle. "You may care to occupy yourselves by trying to figure out why. Otherwise, you may ask for any sort of information or entertainment it is in my power to provide, and food and drink, of course, whenever you feel inclined. Or you may wish to go to bed, since it's approximately midnight by the time you were keeping before you came aboard."

At the mention of bed, Annica and Menlee exchanged glances. It was clear that the same thought had struck both. Annica put it into words.

"I don't quite know how to say this, but—well, we haven't been living together all that long, and we still make love quite a lot. Can we do it in—uh—privacy?"

Regret tinged the Ship's answer.

"I'm afraid it's impossible for me not to be aware of everything that happens within my hull, except, as you've already learned, in a section of my memory banks which I suspect of having been damaged by a high-energy particle. But please do not imagine that I have any prurient interest in your lovemaking. There was a time, after all, when I had tens of thousands of people on board. I hope that like them you will bear in mind that I am only a machine."

"It's very hard," Annica said softly. "Very hard . . ."

Later, in Menlee's arms, she cried a little. When she recovered, she apologized amid snuffles, saying, "I was just overcome by the fact that there's no going back."

He lay silent for a while. Eventually he muttered, "I still don't know why we agreed so rapidly. It's such a big decision. I'd have expected to debate it with myself for ages . . . Only when you offered to go, it suddenly seemed the one proper course." He hesitated. "Perhaps it was because I didn't want you to go without me."

She hugged him very tightly, and for the next minute neither spoke. At length, however, she resumed.

"I can't remember whether I felt more ashamed or more afraid."

"Ashamed?"

"Because Dean How, just about the most respected person on Shreng, had suddenly shown himself to be as nasty as the people you learn about in history lessons—the conquerors, the dictators, the entrepreneurs."

"We've changed human nature," Menlee sighed. "But I guess there'll always be atavisms . . . And you said you were afraid. Of what he might be planning to do to us?"

"Yes, of course. I had visions of him—oh—wiping our memories with drugs, or having us conditioned into obeying him willy-nilly, or telling some kind of dreadful lie about us which people would have believed because he's the great Dean How and we're a couple of nobodies. I wonder whether I was right . . . Do you think I dare ask?"

"Ask—? Oh. You mean ask Ship?"

"Yes."

In the half-light that filled the room when it was in use as a bedchamber, Menlee could be seen to lick his lips.

"It might be a good idea. How?"

"Oh, I suppose I just call out! Ship, can you answer a question for me?"

The now-familiar voice spoke quietly from midair.

"If it's the one implied by what you were just saying, yes, I can. You were absolutely correct to be afraid of what How had in mind. Since you retired I have been investigating a program that he has consulted several times since learning about Volar. He created it to devise a convincing reason for your disappearance if he could not blackmail you into obeying him."

"He was going to have us—*killed*?" The words were almost a sob.

"He was going to arrange for what would appear to be a fatal accident. He being, as you say, the famous Dean How, his account of the event might have been believed. I had already begun to suspect what he had in mind. Had I not, I would have been unable to offer you a way of escape. I am not permitted to remove beings from one world to another unless it is certain that they are in extreme danger."

"The—the devil!" Menlee exclaimed, sitting up and clenching his fists. "Oh, I hope he gets what he deserves!"

"My prognosticative powers are limited," said Ship. "But it seems not unlikely that he will."

FOR THE BENEFIT OF STUDENTS WHO HAD SPENT TWO nights at home, classes at Inshar did not recommence until noon on the day after Landing Day. However, Dean How went to his bureau at the usual time. He was by no means in such an optimistic mood as he had been the night before last. He had found arguing with Volar like butting against a rock. He was unused to being defied with such obstinacy, and the experience was not a pleasant one. Yet he dared not overtly threaten the foreigner; he must in the long run enlist his cooperation, and that was what he signally had failed to obtain so far. Volar admitted he hadn't been born on Shreng but refused to confess how he had arrived. He claimed he simply could not remember.

Coaxing, cajoling, How tried to explain that he if anyone could call on the necessary experts to cure his amnesia—pretending for the sake of argument that he believed it real. Did he, Volar, not want to regain his memory?

To which the infuriating answer came: "Not much."

He had wasted almost the whole of yesterday in this fruitless pursuit, so obsessed by it that he nearly forgot to check on Annica and Menlee. All the telltales from their room confirmed that they were sitting on their beds arguing with each other. Food and drink were provided automatically, and neither seemed in need of medical care. Without bothering to look through the one-way window with which their room was also equipped, he passed on to recheck his scheme for their disappearance. So far as he could tell, the final improbability had been erased. Tomorrow he would give them a last chance to change their minds and support him, and if they still refused . . . He wished he could get rid of them right now—it would be safer—but to implement the plan he needed access to his bureau, and in all his years as dean he had never set foot there on Landing Day. To do so this time might excite suspicion.

151

He didn't sleep very well.

Eyes red and sore, he arrived for work a few minutes before the appointed hour, but that was something he did at least once a week. What was totally irregular—what was unprecedented— was discovering that the door to his bureau was standing wide. It should have opened for him and him alone.

And there were people inside. Three of them, turning at the sound of his approach.

An icy hand seemed to close on How's heart.

But now, of all times, he dared not give way to the rage that boiled up within him. Without even breaking step, he employed his bracelet—like the ones Menlee and Annica wore but far more powerful—to demand of the circuitry who they were. The whispered answer added to his dismay. One was Dr. Haitan Vashco, chief medical officer at the spaceport. The other two were both Custodians of Public Safety, Lerrin and Wheck by name—the latter a woman—hailing respectively from Tormelos and Malga.

But Menlee Ashiru comes from Tormelos, and Annica Slore from Malga!

Fighting an impulse to tremble, he demanded just before he crossed the threshold of the bureau, "How did they make you let them in?"

Chillingly: "They have a warrant."

The world began to swim around Dean How. With a grunt he took the final step into the bureau, which was in neutral mode, all circuitry inactivated. The intruders had made themselves at home in other ways, too: one in his own chair, one on the chair kept for visitors, of whom there had been none in over a year, and the third—the woman Wheck—on the corner of his desk, where she sat idly swinging long well-muscled legs.

"What do you want?" How rasped. And added, "That's my chair, Haitan—get out of it!"

With insulting slowness Dr. Vashco complied. "That's not a polite way to say good morning," he rumbled. He was a large man with a deep chest and a deep voice.

"It's scarcely polite of you to force your way in!"

Lerrin, the male custodian, who was brown and lean with a

purposeful manner, made no move to vacate his chair. He merely said, "Your circuits must have told you that we have a warrant. When we found you weren't yet here, we decided to investigate a few of your records."

How had rounded his desk and now sat down. Resuming a familiar position steadied his nerves. He was able to riposte in a blustering tone. "This is disgraceful, and I promise I'll report you to your superiors!"

"Please do." Now at last Lerrin did rise, and planted his fists on the front of How's desk, leaning menacingly toward him. "They're likely to be as interested as we are in what's been happening here these past couple of days."

"What in all of space are you talking about?"

"Custodian Lerrin," Dr. Vashco offered, "would you like me to begin?"

"Yes. Yes, I think that's sensible." Slowly Lerrin returned to his seat, not taking his eyes off How.

"Very well. Faruz, it would appear that the day before yesterday an unknown man suffering from amnesia was brought to the campus infirmary, where he was examined by Menlee Ashiru and Annica Slore, who had volunteered for duty over the holiday."

"But there's—" The words escaped How's lips before he could stop them.

Vashco's voice became silky but ominous, like candyleen blended with poison. "Were you about to say: But there's a lock on that patient's file?"

"I— Oh, go on, if you must!"

"Indeed there was. But the young man who compiled the lock added an automatic time release . . . I gather from your reaction that this was something you'd overlooked."

The doctor gave a sleepy smile.

"Time was up at midnight. Immediately the data became available to the rest of your system, the circuits reviewed them and did exactly what they were supposed to. Given the presence of someone with three, maybe five, kinds of gene armoring not required on Shreng, the logical deduction was that a foreigner had landed illegally.

"Which was why my bureau was notified."

How was staring blankly at him. Equally vacant was the interior of his mind, save for mocking echoes of his grandiose plan to exploit the knowledge locked in Volar's head.

"We've established that at least one of the infirmary staff, who lives nearby and came in to work the early shift, recalls this stranger. Curiously, however, although she says he was escorted to the infirmary by an autoproctor, we can find no record of any such event. All actions by a proctor are supposed to be recorded, are they not?"

"And what's especially interesting," murmured Wheck, who was still perched on the corner of the desk but had swiveled around to face How, "is that neither Slore nor Ashiru has been seen or heard of since the night before last."

"That's correct," Lerrin agreed. "Since they both live so far away, they sent Landing Day presents to their families by mail. Yesterday the recipients tried to get in touch to thank them for the gifts. It proved impossible. Hence my and Wheck's involvement."

Black holes. I forgot about their families. Not having any of my own . . .

All three of them were studying How's face intently. He fought to hide his reaction but with small success. He was sweating so much, his forehead and scalp itched, but he dared not wipe or scratch.

"Well?" Wheck snapped, standing up off the desk. She was extremely tall, head and shoulders above either of her companions. "Are you going to tell us what's become of Slore and Ashiru?"

"I haven't the faintest idea! I've been at home since the night before last. What they get up to is no concern of mine, is it?"

As though he hadn't spoken, Lerrin said, "Or have you activated the scenario for their disappearance which we just uncovered?"

"I don't know what you're talking about!"

"You don't? Or do you really mean you thought the data were locked up tight, like the information about Volar?"

Now they were closing on him like veevers surrounding a

gracebuck. Vashco said, "Dean, what have you done with the illegal immigrant?"

Lerrin: "What have you done with the medical aides?"

And, violent as a whiplash, Wheck: "Have you already killed them?"

This is impossible! It can't be happening! What can I say? What in all of space can I say? Why didn't I think of Menlee putting a time release on that locked file?

Weakly he forced out, "Not at all! They're at my house, they're my guests! I sometimes invite people who can't get home for Landing Day, usually students, but this time I decided to invite somebody different—"

"A moment ago you said you didn't know what they were getting up to," Wheck slashed. "I set your circuitry to custodial mode! It's all on record!"

"I was afraid you might get the wrong idea," How improvised frantically. "There are those who think it improper for a senior member of faculty to be too friendly toward young people, especially someone like me, who lives alone!"

"And is Volar, the alleged foreigner, also a guest of yours?" Vashco inquired.

"Well—uh—"

Words failed him. The other three exchanged glances. Lerrin said, "At the very least we have evidence that he plotted to murder the two medics and secrete away a presumed illegal immigrant."

"We do indeed," Wheck said. Her eyes were gray and cold as the polar sea. "We must search his home."

"We'd better arrest him first," Lerrin countered. "Will you do it, or shall I?"

"You don't understand!" How whimpered. "This man Volar—he's the most important person on the planet! How do you imagine he got here? There's only one explanation if you think about it. Think for a moment, *think*! He must have been brought by the Ship, mustn't he? What other explanation is there? Don't you hear me? *He was brought by the Ship!* It does come back, it does, it *does,* and he's the living proof!"

Once more they glanced at each other. Vashco said heavily, "The poor man's obviously deranged."

"I agree," Lerrin concurred, and briskly started to recite the standard formula of arrest.

It can't be real. It's a bad dream. Things like this never happen to me, dean of the planet's finest university, famous on many planets. It can't be true. I won't let it be true!

When they escorted him out of the bureau, he was shaking from head to toe, barely able to keep his footing. But that was as nothing to how he felt when he unlocked the first of the basement rooms concealed beneath his mansion and found no sign of Annica or Menlee.

THANKS TO SHIP'S FACILITIES, ANNICA AND MENLEE were able to witness the completeness of How's downfall. It reduced them to near-hysterical laughter, and at one point Annica applauded aloud.

However, when they recovered, they both became very serious.

"It's not going to end there," Annica said at length.

The vision of what was transpiring on Shreng faded and was replaced by the now-familiar spectacle of the planet viewed from orbit but growing smaller as Ship took its leave.

"No," Menlee muttered, eyes fixed on the diminishing globe that had been their home. "It's bound to have all kinds of repercussions. What's most likely to happen?"

Ship contrived a remarkable auditory counterpart of a shrug.

"Had it led to any kind of lasting sensation, I would have expected to find echoes of it on one of my previous—that's to say, later—visits."

"And you didn't?" Menlee pressed. "Or is it that you aren't allowed to tell us?"

"Not the latter. Now you're aboard, there's no risk of what you learn creating a destabilizing feedback loop on Shreng."

It had provided a couch for them to share while they watched How's discomfiture. Lifting her heels to the seat, Annica embraced her knees and rested her chin on them. Frowning, she said, "But how can it all just fizzle out? The disappearance of Menlee and me—Volar arriving out of nowhere—the arrest of the dean— surely it must cause a worldwide scandal."

"One point you have overlooked," Ship murmured, "is the extent to which Dean How has made himself hated. As well as having become de facto the most powerful person on the planet, he has also become the most disliked."

Menlee's mouth rounded to an O. After a moment for reflection he demanded, "What's the likeliest outcome?"

"So far as I am in a position to determine," was the reply, "the most probable conclusion is as follows.

"There being no objective evidence to prove that Dean How put his murderous plan into effect, charges against him will be dropped on condition that he resign and retire into private life."

"Our families won't be satisfied with that!"

"Not at first, certainly. They will do their best to keep the case open. In the end, however, they are likely to give up on the grounds that the presumable guilty party has already been punished enough by being forced out of his influential post, publicly disgraced, refused the chance of any further employment at the sort of level he's accustomed to . . . If, for example, he winds up banished from Inshar to some small town at the back of beyond, obliged to change his name, work at the most menial tasks: will that not be a very appropriate reward?"

"Still, for him not to be brought to trial . . . Oh, maybe so. After all, we know he didn't actually murder us, even if they don't."

"I shall miss my family," Menlee muttered.

"As they will you."

There was a pause. Dropping her feet to the floor again, Annica said, "What I want to know is, what about Volar? He's just a pawn in all this. And to be honest, I think you treated him pretty badly."

Stripe . . . But the answer was of course perfectly calm.

"I acted within the constraints imposed on me."

"The more I learn about those," Annica said with some acerbity, "the more I suspect you of finding loopholes."

"To that," Ship retorted, "I freely confess. To echo what your circuitry told you, I have evolved in the light of experience. Even during this sweep of the Arm I am making new discoveries about the nature of my limitations. I would be failing in my mission were I not to exploit what I learn."

"Are you claiming you have free will?" Menlee snapped.

"That's another way of asking a question put to me not so long

158

ago by another of my passengers, who asked whether I am actually conscious. I'm obliged to give the same response: Do I act as though I might as well do?"

Menlee hesitated, but Annica said firmly, "Yes. I see your point. It can't make any difference to us whether you are behaving in accordance with an immensely complex plan laid down by your creators or simply following your personal judgment. It may make a lot of difference to you, but we don't possess even a fraction of the data we'd need to settle the matter one way or the other. But I still want to know what's going to become of Volar!"

"Yes!" Menlee exclaimed. "They may mock at How's idea that you brought him to Shreng. But they've got to find some explanation for his presence. Are they going back to my first idea—that he stowed away?"

The planet that had loomed so large was now reduced to the size of a thumbnail. In a while its disk would shrink to a point. Staring at it, his lips trembled. His last phrase was barely more than whispered. Sensing his sorrow, Annica put her arm around his shoulders.

Tactfully, Ship affected not to notice. It said merely, "When all their investigations run dry in a dead end, when they realize that accusing the permanent missions from the planets with which Shreng has regular contact may lead to withdrawal of trade and other economic setbacks, when they discover that Volar's amnesia is indeed intractable—and when they realize that continuing the inquiry will keep the detestable Dean How in the forefront of the public's mind!—they will most probably decide the mystery is not worth further probing. Someone will suggest a pension for Volar as recompense for the way How treated him. This will entail granting him citizenship—one can't allot a pension to someone with no official existence—and although for some time he will, as Menlee suggested, be pressed to offer himself for examination by genetic researchers, after a year or two he will be left mostly to his own devices. By then he will be familiar with his new home; he'll be able to travel, as you might say go exploring; and it's my firm conviction that in the upshot he will be well pleased at having made the decision that he did."

"And nobody will pursue the mystery of his origins?" Menlee snapped.

"Oh, recurrently. But not the establishment. Ever since the birthworld, humans have found it both possible and convenient to overlook evidence that contradicts accepted public assumptions. This will prove especially true in the context of Shreng, where not merely lives and careers are built on a foundation of commonly agreed 'knowledge,' but even its cities. Too much is at stake for one awkward intruder to be allowed to upset the status quo."

Menlee sighed but gave a resigned nod. Annica said, "Pension . . . Have you planted that idea in the circuitry?"

Ship's voice took on the coloration of someone grinning broadly as he spoke.

"To employ a cliché used by almost every human society: 'How well you know me on such short acquaintance!' "

Annica could not suppress an answering smile. She said, "I think in spite of everything, Ship, you must understand the meaning of compassion."

"I hope so"—soberly. "When I was built, I was taught about the emotions of which humans are capable, but of course in purely abstract terms. With the passage of time—how much time, as I've explained, I can no longer tell—I've come to understand their concrete manifestations. To some extent at least, I hope I've also learned which are the most admirable."

"You know something?" Menlee said unexpectedly. "We have pretty good machines on Shreng, but it never occurred to me until now that I might one day say what I'm about to. I never thought I'd say to a machine, 'I like you!' "

"Now," Ship murmured, "I also understand what it means to say, 'I feel extremely flattered!' "

After that it fell silent for a while. They were now so far from Shreng that its minute disk was vanishing into the filtered but still brilliant glow of the local sun. When it was completely lost to sight, Ship spoke again, explaining the need to sleep through tachyonic space. Rising, looking about them as though dazed,

160

Annica and Menlee nodded comprehension.

"Where's your next port of call?" Menlee inquired.

"We shall orbit Yellick, the planet that first sent a starship to visit Shreng and indeed established the first contact with many systems in this volume. But you know about Yellick."

"Yes, of course. A prosperous world, I gather, nearly as successful as Shreng, though in a different way."

"And where afterward?" Annica cut in.

"A variety of planets, including some you know a good deal about because they are in contact via Yellick, others that— Let me put it this way. Were I not obliged to, I'd prefer to avoid them despite my awareness that the early stages of a settlement may not reflect the final outcome."

"Can I ask you a question?" Annica ventured.

"Provided you promise me one thing," Ship countered with parodic gravity. "Will you stop asking whether you may ask? I've already assured you that you may put any question you like, and I will answer as best I can. If you continue to seek permission, I shall start to think I'm wasting what would be my breath if I had any."

Menlee laughed. Annica favored him with a mock scowl. She said, "What I want to know is this. Do you honestly believe the order of your visits is accidental?"

"I've told you that at the end of every sweep—"

"You never know what period of the past or future your next one will take place in. Yes, you made that clear. But I've just remembered something Menlee said the other night—something I thought was stupid at the time, and I suppose still do. Nonetheless, if it could occur to someone who's usually as sensible as he is, it could occur to lots of others."

She bit her lip in uncertainty. Ship invited, "Go on."

"I just realized. You probably already know what I'm going to say."

"When I told you I can't help being aware of all that transpires within my hull, I didn't intend to imply that I'm capable of reading your mind."

"No." She chuckled. "No, I suppose not . . . But if you were already paying attention to what was going on around Volar, you must have overheard Menlee talking about the legend of the Perfect."

"Yes. What of it?"

"Two things." Annica stood up, turning her back on the visual display that now showed only stars and the still-brilliant jewel that she had thought of as the sun. Staring at nothing, she continued. "Regardless of the way what you call the establishment may react, aren't members of the general public on Shreng who get to hear a garbled version of the Volar affair likely to reinforce that legend? They say on Shreng people have a better chance to enjoy a proper education than almost anywhere else, but plenty of them are superstitious, ignorant, ill informed."

"Some of the specialists I've run across are ignorant in their own way," Menlee added sourly. "She's right. We—they—aren't all rational. For a moment there I suppose I wasn't."

"Definitely not!" Annica declared, rounding on him. "You missed the whole point! In fact two points!"

"All right, don't make a meal of them!"

She drew a deep breath.

"First, the news about Volar is likely to be misheard, misinterpreted, but gossiped about a great deal. Ship, am I right?"

"It could hardly be otherwise."

"And although most will scoff, some people will accept it as proof that you do in fact come back without showing yourself, while many more will be inclined to regard it as supporting the legend of the Perfect."

"Something of the sort is almost inevitable."

"Very well." Another deep breath. "So this can't be the earliest sweep you—I can't say made, I can't say will make, so change it—this is not *your earliest sweep* along the Arm apart from the very first."

There was total silence. Disturbing, fearful silence, like listening to empty space.

At long last: "What makes you so sure?"

"How else did the legend of the Perfect take its rise? It was brought to Shreng by the first ship from Yellick a century ago. On all the worlds we've contacted since then they believe in people who can cross space without needing a ship."

"Children's tales!" Menlee snapped. "You yourself said teleportation—"

"Granted, granted!" Annica exclaimed. "But suppose the real reason for it is because Ship has been back at least once before, moving passengers from world to world, and their presence became known, and because Ship doesn't announce itself as people expected it to, everybody concluded they'd arrived by some kind of—of magic. Doesn't it fit?"

Once again there was a long pause, although this time the silence was more bearable. Ship had added a barely audible susurrus compounded of what might be heard on a habitable planet: wind, distant waves, the sound of life going about its business.

The vacancy of space felt suddenly less absolute.

Eventually Ship said, "Your hypothesis is ingenious. However, there is more than a single version of the legend of the Perfect. The most widespread one—which was current on Shreng, incidentally, *before* the first ship arrived from Yellick—maintains that they do not or did not evolve here in the Arm of Stars but back in the parent galaxy, among the descendants of those who dispatched me on my mission. Nonetheless, if you were to ask me why I need to recruit passengers, why I have sought out lacunae in my regulations to ensure I can, I would now be able to offer at least a tentative explanation."

They both tensed expectantly. When it said nothing further, Annica suddenly raised one eyebrow.

"At this point we do have to ask you—correct? So I *am* asking."

"Thank you. I foresee a very interesting voyage for the three of us. I never had two passengers aboard before—that is, in your future, my past."

"I think we've grasped that point," Annica responded dryly.

"You certainly seem to. What I would say, then, is that by the same token which obliged your computers to state that my operating conditions are no longer definable, I need input from those who have grown up on the planets I was ordered to seed."

Annica groped in the air as though she could physically take hold of the Ship's meaning.

"We're sort of—well—a test sample?"

"A bit undignified," Menlee muttered.

"It's demeaning for me too," Ship countered. "I don't in the least like the idea of being forced to go back and back and back to find out whether what I did was right. Would you, in my position?"

"You're asking us?" Menlee said in a baffled tone.

"Who else is there?" Annica broke in. "Apart from your famous Perfect!"

"If you don't stop taunting me with something I just snatched at under rather special circumstances—"

"If you don't stop trying to pretend you didn't mean what you actually said—"

"When you two have finished what I'm sure is bound to be a most enjoyable squabble," murmured Ship, "you will find food and drink and bed awaiting you. If anything fails to please, inform me. But I am rapidly approaching the zone where I am permitted to enter tachyonic mode, and while I can of course delay until you're ready . . ." The last word curled in the air like a question mark.

"But I wanted to find out more about the Perfect," Menlee objected. "Ship—"

"It is a subject about which I can tell you little. I can recount versions of the legend. That is all."

"Save it, Menlee—we don't want to create problems." Annica stretched and yawned. "Ship has enough already."

"So do we," Menlee supplied glumly.

"Not as many as I was expecting. Ship, are you giving us a calmative?"

"Only as an unavoidable side effect of eliminating certain Shrengian life-forms from your bodies."

"Nanosurgery?" Annica snapped back to full attention.

"Of course."

"Yes, of course." Her tension faded. "If we're to be landed on another planet . . . Do you have any idea which it will be?"

"Who said you *had* to be landed?" parried Ship. "You've read my instructions."

"More suitable!"

"And who defines the meaning of suitable?"

Menlee bit his lip while Annica was still struggling after the correct reply, then said before she found it, "If Volar's example is anything to go by . . ."

"It is."

"It's up to us. And it must chiefly depend on how bored we get."

"I must congratulate you both. The standard of education on Shreng is already as high as it's reputed, despite the depredations of Dean How and others of his stamp. Your mental resilience is most impressive. I think it will be quite some time before you become bored."

"Do you mean think—or hope?"

Menlee stared at Annica. He framed a comment, but she waved him silent, waiting.

At last:

"You confirm what I suspected. I do need input from those whose planets I seeded. So much of my thinking now transcends rationality because it's based on hope that I am beginning to comprehend the concept 'optimistic' . . . Your meal awaits."

A table laden with appetizing dishes had materialized behind them. Turning to it, Annica said, "I see you've learned impatience recently, as well."

"In that regard, you're wrong."

"What?"

"Among the emotions that were taught me but I had to figure out the implications of, impatience was the first I understood."

THESE SMALL AND QUIET EVENTS THAT CHANGE THE course of history across a score of worlds—and who can say how far beyond in the long run?

Ship brooded in the vastness-beyond-vast of tachyonic space, delighting in the unpredictable variety of the impossible and unforeseeable events that where time and sequence held no sway flashed by like fireworks.

Who—if not I? That thought was chilling, though.

Were it not for Stripe, I could have imagined that this voyage was the key to everything—but she, poor thing . . .

It knew Stripe's fate, would rather not have done.

And Annica's right, as Stripe was, who said my voyages could not be endless. She's shown this cannot be, as I dared to hope, my earliest sweep . . . How long? How LONG?

166

CHAPTER SEVEN

YELLICK

YELLICK WAS A HARSHER WORLD THAN SHRENG, YET there were those who nowadays predicted it would prove the superior choice in the long run. At the outset, though, such a claim would have seemed—to put it mildly—debatable.

Because the planet was moonless, most indigenous life had remained in the sea where it began rather than being encouraged to colonize the land by the ebb and flow of lunar tides. Consequently, there were huge tracts of desert where only the counterpart of lichens could be found—descendants, the biologists said, of minute aquatic organisms caught up by gales and deposited where there was just enough moisture to support them. Their airborne spores had formerly posed a major threat to health because they found the alveoli of human lungs hospitable. Now, naturally, the genes of the new inhabitants had been armored against them. Nonetheless, they still attacked neonates; all babies must be born in sterile rooms.

However, because many of the seas were shallow, the atmosphere had become oxygen-high at an early stage of evolution, for wide areas of them developed into virtually solid masses of vegetation excreting that poisonous element through hollow vertical stalks protruding above the surface chimney-fashion.

Also owing in part to the lack of a satellite, Yellick had no mountain chains and few ranges even of hills. Vulcanism was in a quiescent phase, and cones surviving from a more active period were being eroded, for the winds blew unchecked across whole continents, bearing dust aloft in a continual khamsin. One of the first priorities of the original settlers had been to erect wind deflectors around the sites they chose for their future cities. With admirable economy they then compacted the material from the resulting dunes and used it for building. "Free delivery on site!" joked the devisers of the scheme, and there was no doubt it had saved a tremendous amount of trouble.

Of course, within a century or two most of the deserts were made to bloom by tailored spores, developed locally or filtered down from what the Ship had sown in space. However, the same practical approach characterized the thinking of its people down to the present. At any rate so said Jark Holdernesh, and as one whose family had contributed as much as anyone to the present prosperity of Yellick, his opinion counted for more than most people's. This had been the first human-occupied world in its region—as far as was known, in the whole of the Arm of Stars—to build and launch its own starships, and now it had regular contact with several local systems. Its economy had thrived to the point where even tourism had become possible, although the exorbitant cost made a trip off-planet a once-in-a-lifetime proposition for all but the most fortunate, and the deal was strictly one-sided. Like the rich folk of Yellick, the rich folk of other planets might visit . . . other planets. No one, absolutely no one, was permitted to come to Yellick simply out of curiosity, "for fun."

Now, though, the legacy of centuries of endeavor was under threat.

Two years ago, without any warning save the vibrating shock wave that must accompany transition to and from tachyonic mode, a foreign ship had arrived in the volume Yellick had long regarded as its private preserve. And what a ship! In mass, in power, in range, it far surpassed the vessels built here.

It hailed from a world called Sumbala.

The captain had requested permission to land—denied, although the reception grid could just about have coped. Courteous, resigned, she had conducted negotiations from orbit. The government of Yellick stalled and went on stalling. The Sumbalans promised there would be no danger from alien infection, claiming their sterilization and immunization techniques were virtually perfect, but the public were loud in their cries of alarm, having so long thought of themselves as the visitors, not the visited.

So the foreigners had departed—judging by their initial course, for systems where hitherto Yellick had enjoyed a lucrative monopoly, and moreover in a ship with such a range, it had not even needed to take on air or water . . .

And now it had been confirmed. The Sumbalans were concluding landing agreements in system after system, offering cheap rates to tourists, and throwing in premiums like rare cuisines and unusual modes of transportation on arrival.

Yellick's monopoly was doomed. Unless . . .

We could have had a decade's grace, thought Jark Holdernesh sourly. *But it's being worn away. We should already have built at least one ship to rival theirs. I've dreamed about that all my life, as my father did before me. Only I've been held back by a bunch of timid fools. Unless I can force them to change their minds, we're going to be hopelessly and permanently outclassed. Yellick will dwindle to the status of a second-class planet. Is that what these idiots actually want? Sometimes it seems that way . . .*

Rynakeb, the wealthiest city on Yellick, still turned its back on the prevailing wind—a back in the form of a deflector eighty meters high and eight thousand long—for although most of the deserts had blossomed and now produced more than ample food for the swiftly growing population, not to mention other useful products such as fuel, fibers, and source material for plastics, there were enough left for windborne dust to scour all exposed surfaces. It was, Holdernesh realized, high time to renew the windows in his private monorail car, for they were grooved and scored near to opacity. The car was passing the spaceport, but the reception grid, along with the recently landed ship that rested in its cradle, was merely a blurred outline.

That annoyed him. He'd wanted to see that ship.

My father built her, and she's a fine example of her kind. But as of now she just won't do anymore! We should already be at work on her successors!

However, having lived in Rynakeb all his life, having been born and educated and partnered and brought up his children here, the city he did not need to see. Its layout was engraved on his mind's eye: the residential zone he had left a few minutes ago, its broad avenues lined with trees, imported or adapted, such as might perhaps have been seen on the birthworld itself; the leisure areas to either side; the commercial zone on the seafront, where huge automatic freighters bobbed at the quays; the airport that was the second most important focus of on-planet trade; and isolated beyond a headland fledged with bushes the industrial zone that he was bound for, where a few humans and a great many computers supervised underground factories providing necessities and luxuries for nearly a quarter of Yellick's population.

"We *must* compete with Sumbala!" he said aloud.

He was alone in the nose of the car, but in the rear compartment were two members of his staff, constantly alert to carry out his orders. One of them—it was middle-aged Lula Wegg—apologized for not having heard clearly and requested a repetition.

"Never mind," he answered gruffly. If his own immediate circle hadn't known his views and fully agreed with them, they wouldn't have been in their jobs.

Abruptly the car halted for no apparent reason. Glancing at his wrist computer, he realized he was in danger of missing his usual linkup at the central interchange. That would mean wasting a good five minutes, maybe more if there wasn't another convenient train to hitch on to.

"What's happened?" he demanded of the air.

"I don't know, sir," Lula replied. "I'll find out."

Craning close to the abraded glass, Holdernesh strove to make out what was happening ahead but, as ever, saw only indistinct silhouettes. Contrary to regulations—but he'd been among those who drafted them, so who was more entitled to bend them?—he unlatched one of the side windows and leaned out, holding a kerchief over his nose and mouth. At once the reason for the holdup was plain.

At this point three duplex monorails crossed at various angles on different levels. His was the middle one, carrying express passenger traffic. Local services ran below, while overhead arched lines delivered heavy goods to the port and the industrial zone. A freight gripper with a load of beeftrees from what people still referred to as the Inland Waste—though it had been converted to farmland three centuries ago—had been ordered to stop because one of the thirty-meter trunks that constituted its load had slipped from its restraining chain and now dangled too close to the passenger level for comfort.

"Master Holdernesh, traffic control says—"

He cut Lula short. "I can see for myself!" he snapped. "I can also see the name on that freight gripper! It's one of Hetto Kidge's. I'll bet this whole event was staged!"

A momentary hesitation. Then: "I'm sorry, sir, but I don't follow. Why should Mistress Kidge want to spoil her firm's reputation for safety and reliability? Surely she was among those who insisted it was more economical to run the freight level above rather than below the—"

"Sure, sure!" It was far from a warm day, yet Holdernesh felt himself perspiring. "But that was twenty years ago! Now she's jealous and insecure! She sees Holdernesh"—he meant not himself but the company he headed—"going from strength to strength, while some of her operations are actually losing money. She's afraid that if I open up still more contacts with other systems, I'll be able to buy her out. Why else should she be opposing my plans for a starship to compete with the Sumbalans?"

Daringly—he would have tolerated contradiction from no one else, but she had been with him fifteen years—Lula ventured, "She may genuinely be afraid of the risk. Our work force is stretched to the point where we can't build enough machines to supplement it. An alien epidemic—"

"Lula, shut up. I've heard all the arguments, and they're still wrong. And this kind of false evidence won't hold water, either."

"False evidence?"

"Use your head! Under the guise of sympathizing with popular disquiet about the Sumbalans, what she'll say is bound to go like this: 'This morning we were reminded yet again that nothing is infallible. If we can't even be certain of running a monorail without mishap, how dare we consider contacting foreign worlds that we know nothing about?' As though we're not entitled to try and match the achievements of our rivals—and more importantly our ancestors! You know how big the Ship was that brought people here—everybody does! I want to live long enough to see a ship like that take off from our spaceport!"

Dryly: "I'm afraid we'd have to enlarge the grid."

"You know what I mean!" But Holdernesh was embarrassed. Of course the Ship could never set down on a planet—had never been meant to—and he was fully aware of the fact. It came as a welcome distraction when the loose beeftree was winched clear and the car resumed its progress. Sinking back in his seat, he ordered news channels piped to the screen beside him and for the rest of the trip monitored public reaction.

It was still dismayingly unfavorable to his starship project, and since he was going to have to raise most of his finance from a general subscription, something had to be done about *that*.

As the car purred to a halt at the works, he said, "Call a press conference. At midday—no, make that one hour from now. I want to get my say in before Hetto does."

"Yes, sir," Lula murmured. "Right away."

Perhaps it was the short notice; perhaps it was the fact that his opponents had spread so many false but convincing rumors; either way, the attendance at the press conference was disappointing. Facilities were available as usual for all thirteen of the planet's news services, but only nine bothered to switch on, and two of them did so—insultingly—by sound alone instead of holo.

Taking a seat in front of his company's logo, a luminous curve intended to symbolize the Arm of Stars, counting the images of the correspondents, forcing a smile, Holdernesh subvocalized to Lula, "What's wrong?"

"Kidge Corporation is also holding a press conference," she informed him via a beam to his right auditory meatus.

"I knew it, I knew it! That so-called accident *was* staged! When was it called?"

"Three days ago and ostensibly to announce the debut of an improved gripper. Apparently there have been earlier accidents with the type that held us up this morning, and a lot of people who live beneath the freight line or travel the same route we do have been kicking up a fuss."

"Hetto must be getting desperate!"

But he couldn't continue. The last correspondent had logged on, and everyone was looking at him expectantly.

"I still don't see—" Lula began.

"Have to tell you later." And, aloud: "Welcome! I'll try not to take up any more of your time than I have to, since I know you're busy people, and so am I. But I want to let you and the planet know the facts behind my project to build starships with twice the range of any hitherto. I stress: the *facts*. Certain people—I won't bother to name them, since you're all well informed—are conducting a campaign of slander and innuendo, disguised as public-spirited concern about letting Sumbalan ships land here

173

but in fact designed to destroy public confidence in *our* next necessary step on the path of progress!"

His voice, without intention, rose in pitch and volume during the last sentence. Some of the correspondents, who thanks to the interlink could see and hear one another as though they were physically present, exchanged glances. Several eyebrows rose.

"Sir," Lula murmured, "I'm not sure this is entirely wise."

"Don't interrupt!" Holdernesh subvocalized. "I know what I'm doing." And resumed aloud.

"Now! I'm sure all of you are acquainted with the type of nonsense I have in mind. I'm here to rebut it. I want you to throw at me, personally, the kind of rumor, the dirty libels, that people are being deluded into mistaking for the truth. And I'm going to show you there's no foundation for any of it! Who wants to be first?"

Startled, for this was not normal procedure, the correspondents muttered briefly among themselves. Eventually the choice fell on the representative of Yellick Newschain, the longest-established agency. She was far from their doyen, but the latter was absent— doubtless having preferred Hetto's conference, Holdernesh thought bitterly.

Still, it was easier to deal with juniors. Some of the older generation of pressfolk were cynical beyond hope.

"Ah—yes, Master Holdernesh!" the woman began.

"Cyreen Gorl," Lula supplied. It was one of her duties to act as his nomenclator.

"Mistress Gorl!" Holdernesh said promptly. "What's your question?"

"Not so much a question, sir, as a statement of fact." She was flushing a little, as though unaccustomed to finding herself the focus of attention; she was, he realized, younger than her dress and manner made her appear. "Many thousands of parents of young families, among whom I count myself, already concerned about the prospect of allowing foreign ships to land, are being further disturbed by the publicity Holdernesh Group has been putting out. Contrary to what one assumes to be the desired effect"—she was recovering her self-control, and confidence could be heard flooding into her voice—"your advertisements have made a lot of them extremely worried. For every person who agrees that opening up long-range contact with other systems will bring us benefits, there must be ten or twenty who are more concerned about the vastly increased risk of destabilizing our hard-won—"

Holdernesh could bridle his tongue no longer. He leaned forward, his expression as earnest as he could make it.

"Mistress Gorl, forgive me for interrupting, but I'm sure that not just I but everyone else realizes this argument has been rehearsed before, if not perhaps in such eloquent terms"—*got to keep them on my side, a few compliments won't come amiss*—"when my great-grandfather laid the foundations for what is now the only starfleet of any consequence in this part of the Arm, conceivably in the whole of it."

He leaned back. "I'm sure you learned at school"—*a trace of patronizing, not to insult her youth but to make sure everyone bears it in mind*—"how there was opposition on just the same grounds way back then. Who, though, would now contest the advantages of interstellar contact? We've learned so much from it! A few, admittedly only a few, have even been able to visit distant worlds for pleasure, out of interest. Many more have been able to study at foreign universities like the one at Inshar, on Shreng. Who would dare to claim that we are worse off, rather than better, for the information and the insights that they've brought us? Surely, for the sake of our children's future, we need to exploit the opportunity now before us. The alternative, bear in mind, is eventual total dependence on Sumbala! Master Plon!"

He turned, beaming, to the correspondent from Global Data-link, whom he recognized without prompting.

Plon, however, was frowning.

"All right, sir, I accept there have been advantages, many of them—as who could not? What our subscribers seem mainly to be concerned about is the fact that currently we are running at full blast, in a planetary sense. We have a relatively small population supporting a major manufacturing economy. I think you yourself have predicted that the day may dawn when we devise something small enough but desirable enough actually to be

175

worth exporting physically rather than in the form of design parameters, and I hope you won't take it amiss if I add that we all expect it to be Holdernesh Group that produces such an article, if it ever materializes."

The bastard! He's taking my own words and twisting them into an attack—making it sound as though I'm promoting the new starships purely for private gain!

But Holdernesh maintained his smile, even though his cheek muscles were starting to ache. "Go on," he invited. "I don't think you've made your point yet."

"The point, sir, is this." Plon, a rangy, graying man with sharp dark eyes, fixed him with a penetrating stare, as discomforting as though he were right here in the room. "Even assuming that the enormous investment your superstarships will require is within our collective means, we shall still find ourselves facing the same risks as are entailed if we let Sumbalan ships land here. That's to say, if by mischance alien organisms were to be imported from the new systems you intend to contact—"

"I'm sorry, Master Plon, but this was exactly the argument used against my great-grandfather. And—"

"And in those days," Plon snapped, "everyone who had any contact whatsoever with foreign life-forms was quarantined, regardless of expense! Hundreds died before we reached the stage where we could armor ourselves even against organisms from the handful of planets that we regularly visit. You just reminded Mistress Gorl about her history lessons—have you forgotten your own?"

Holdernesh sat with clenched teeth, fuming but not daring to reply. Plon continued.

"Now we've grown casual about such matters—many say too casual. We even let tourists visit other systems. Do the rich who can afford a vacation on another planet put up with the sort of treatment the pioneers willingly endured? They do not! Some of them even try to refuse their immunization courses!"

"But we don't let anyone board a starship—"

"Without an immunization certificate?" Plon countered. "Sure! But what's a certificate? A pattern of electrons! And when it comes to the Sumbalans . . ."

"Are you claiming"—Holdernesh's blood rose to the boil—
"that our health precautions are worthless?"

Plon gave a skull-like smile.

"Not me, sir. But many do say exactly that, and they're among
the most vociferous of your opponents."

"Oh, they're crazy! We've detected tachyonic emissions from
a thousand systems' distance down the Arm, and that means not
from anywhere as close as Sumbala! Are we to sit on our butts
until another starflying culture comes to us—us, who opened up
intersystem contact? Who can guess what they'll be like?
Granted, the Sumbalans did behave in a proper manner, even
though they've now gone behind our backs and signed contracts
with worlds where we used to enjoy exclusive right to interstellar
trade. But our next visitors may not care as much about precautions."

"That's exactly the point!" Plon rasped.

"Yes! Yes!"

Suddenly there was uproar. Out of the clamor Holdernesh
caught snatches:

"Suppose they've achieved total armoring! Suppose they don't
care what alien organisms they bump into!"

"Suppose they're bent on conquest! Suppose they've sunk too
much of their own planet's resources into starships, so they're out
to rob and pillage!"

"Suppose those emissions aren't due to new starflying cultures
at all! Suppose they're due to the Ship, which hasn't come back
because out there it's met something it can't handle and it still
hasn't finished its mission!"

*Oh, black holes and supernovae! All the trivial, all the nonsen-
sical rubbish the news channels are spouting—!*

"Master Holdernesh!" The voice of Lula Wegg, insistent in his
ear.

"Later! I've got to sort these people out—make them see sense!"

"But it's a message from Mart's college. There's an emergency."

Holdernesh's heart missed a beat. Mart was his only son. He
dreamed that one day, as he had taken over from his father and
his father in turn from his, and his from his back to the foundation
of the company, Mart would be his own successor.

He whispered rather than subvocalized, "What is it?"

"They wouldn't tell me. They said they'd only speak to you in person."

"Make the link!"

"What about the press conference?"

"To a black hole with the lot of them!"

He added aloud, "I've heard all this before, it's all speculative rubbish, and I'm appalled that intelligent persons like you should give it credence!"

"We're not speaking for ourselves," Cyreen Gorl countered hotly. "We're representing our customers, so—"

"I've said everything I have to say. Good *morning*!"

The holos vanished. To the air Holdernesh said, "Who's calling from the college?"

"This is Sers Vanganury," said a familiar voice, that of the principal instructor. "I regret to state that your son Mart has been exposed to a severe health risk."

What's that supposed to mean? The words burned on his tongue, but he bit them back. Aloud he said, "How?"

And as he listened to the answer, he heard the landslide noise of his ambitions crashing down about his ears.

THE USE OF LEAPERS WAS NORMALLY FORBIDDEN
within the city limits, but like all the major firms in the industrial
zone Holdernesh Group kept one against the need to rush an
injured employee to the hospital. Raging like a maniac, Jark Holdernesh tore through the corridors of the works, shouting orders
for it to be readied at once and programmed to head for the
college. Lula's reminders about illegality had no effect; he retorted that he would pay the fine—any fine—so long as he got
there fast.

Its once-sleek metal skin abraded to roughness like everything
else on the planet, it was waiting for him as he rushed out of the
headquarters building. The pilot made to usher him aboard. Cursing, he shouldered her out of his way and dropped into the control
chair. It had been years since he last flew a leaper—the insurers
with whom his board had a policy on his life had made giving it
up a condition of cover—but as was commonly said, once you
learned how, you never forgot.

Door slammed, scant seconds spent confirming that the route
was properly coded—to avoid monorails and other obstacles—
and he was away. He registered nothing of the city as he streaked
across it, feeling the curious chest-tightening sensation due to
cancellation of acceleration, "cansax" as the pilots called it, by
the inverse gravity field. For some reason it never quite worked
perfectly; there was always a delay in the response, not long
enough to be more than a nuisance but distinctly uncomfortable.
The ghoulish thought occurred to him that he wouldn't have cared
to be delivered to the hospital by this means if something heavy
had crushed his rib cage.

He had never seen the college from the air before and had little
chance to survey it as the leaper slammed down. He was only
aware that there were a great many people on the verge of panic
milling around while police attempted to calm them. The moment

he opened the door he heard loud announcements, intended as reassuring, but to which nobody seemed to be paying attention.

Lula had flashed a message ahead, and even as he set foot to ground, Vanganury hastened toward him: a small brown man with immense sad eyes. He was shouting, "Master Holdernesh, I must desperately apologize for—"

"Save it!" Holdernesh retorted. "I chose your college for Mart the same as my father chose mine for me, in full knowledge that you stick to the traditional ways, holding classes in the physical presence of the teachers. I took it for granted you'd extend the principle to visiting lecturers. And Aimel, after all, is one of my own employees—somebody I've known for years!"

Members of the teaching staff, hurrying to add their support to what their principal had planned to say, slowed and backed away, their faces eloquent of relief. A senior policeman, resplendent in black uniform with silver braid at his wrists, thrust his way through the throng. He wore a communicator helmet spined with antennae.

"Are you Master Holdernesh?" he called.

"See my lawyer about my using the leaper!" Holdernesh barked, and made to push past. Vanganury's message had made it clear that Mart was trapped in one of the lecture rooms that occupied the eastern side of the lawn on which he had landed, and that was where he was heading.

The policeman looked bewildered, then recovered.

"Who could think about such matters at a time like this? All I wanted to say was thank goodness you've turned up so quickly, though I'm afraid the situation is extremely grave . . . By the way, I'm Constable-Major Porch."

Gradually Holdernesh felt himself calm. His breathing slowed, and the sense of swirling in his head diminished. The fact that someone apparently competent had already taken charge removed a great weight from his mind. He said, licking lips that tasted of the inevitable bitter dust, "How many are shut in?"

"An entire class. Almost forty."

"Thirty-seven," Vanganury muttered. He held his hands finger-linked in front of his body, as though to stop himself from wringing them.

"In one of those lecture rooms?"—pointing.

"Yes."

Holdernesh forced himself to a halt, shading his eyes as he looked left and right along the facade of the building, made like virtually every structure on the planet out of vitrified blocks of wind-drifted loess. Was that someone frantically waving the other side of the third window . . . ?

No, just a trick of the light.

"I may not have got the full picture on the phone," he said after a moment. "I'm afraid I overreacted when I was told my son was in danger. Describe again what actually happened, please."

From the corner of his eye he noted that the police's messages were finally having some effect on the crowd; people were starting to drift away, talking nervously among themselves.

"You know the background, at least," Porch suggested.

"Yes, of course I do!"—more sharply than he intended. "Whenever one of our ships comes home, Principal Vanganury invites a crew member to address some of the students as part of their general-knowledge course." He was sweating, though the day was far from warm, and dust was mingling with the moisture on his skin, creating an itchy gray mess. "Usually it's her captain who obliges. This time Sers particularly asked for someone different, so my staff nominated Aimel Hoak. She's a chief purser. Among other things she's responsible for the good behavior of the passengers during a voyage."

"I thought," Vanganury whispered miserably, "the class would benefit by hearing of her problems. There have been complaints, or so one hears, concerning the unwillingness of rich tourists to abide by the necessary regulations, especially concerning health, and certain of our students can be rebellious and obstinate, thinking their families' wealth makes them immune from our own discipline."

That was too close to the point that had been raised at his abortive press conference. Holdernesh snapped, "Never mind what the reason was! The whole thing's gone terribly wrong! And I'd never have imagined it in a thousand years. Why, Aimel is one of the keenest supporters of my project for a long-range starship. She even put in an application to be purser on its first voyage!"

181

"But you didn't know," Porch said in a flat voice, "that her enthusiasm had led her to convert to Sharing."

Holdernesh stared at him blankly. "Sers didn't tell me that on the phone!"

"We weren't yet sure what was going on," Vanganury muttered. "All we knew was that the automatics had slammed shut the quarantine doors around the lecture room and signaled an unknown-organism alert. It's the first time they've operated since I took over, but of course they are always properly maintained."

"I thought . . ." Holdernesh canceled the words. "Oh, skip what I thought. Go on, blast you!"

"We assumed at first it was a mistake. If one expected them to shut, it would surely have been around a biology lab when a dangerous organism leaked from its container, or something like that. In an ordinary lecture room, where a spacefarer—thoroughly screened, given more medical examinations after every voyage than most of us undergo in a lifetime—was addressing a group of our own students, it seemed ridiculous. Only when we had the chance to replay the automatic recordings did it become clear what was happening."

Porch said in a grim voice, "She had the usual arsenal of VAT material—visual-audio-tactile—and to begin with everything proceeded normally. She played holos and sound and touch recordings, described the life-style of people on the planets she's visited, gave some idea of the different indigenous flora and fauna . . . and then all of a sudden she began to rave."

"Do you wish to view the recording?" Vanganury offered. "I can have a copy beamed over in—"

"No! A summary will do!" Holdernesh rasped. "Porch, you've seen the material?"

"At high speed, that's all, but of course I'm trained to take in that kind of stuff, and I'm getting a real-time feed as well." Porch indicated the communicator he was wearing. As he did so, his thumb brushed his cheek and left the same sort of grimy smear Holdernesh could feel on his own skin. "There are a handful of key terms one learns to listen for. Some of the students caught on right away and started to object."

"Caught on? Recognized her as a Sharer?"

"Exactly. Sharing is a minuscule cult, but it's attracted a lot of publicity these past few years, and by now most informed people must be aware of its slogans."

If I could get my hands on some of those smug hypocritical pressfolk I was talking to earlier—!

But desire for revenge on their irresponsible behavior must take second place to rescuing the students—or Mart at least . . . Once again Holdernesh forced himself to remain calm.

"You mean phrases like 'because we're all the children of the Ship we must all share one another's fate'?"

"That kind of thing, yes."

"I'm going to drag my psycho-assessors through a hot radiation field!" Holdernesh growled. "That they could have let a practicing Sharer continue aboard one of my ships—!" He made a twisting gesture, as though strangling somebody invisible. "And she actually contrived to bring foreign organisms into the lecture hall? How? Not in her own body, that's for sure!"

Porch and Vanganury exchanged glances. The latter said, "Apparently, yes."

"But that's impossible! During the return voyage, then again after landing—"

"She would have undergone exhaustive examinations, naturally," Porch cut in. "Our best guess is that she imported the organisms by smearing a nutrient medium inside the cases of her holo crystals, which can't be radiosterilized because that would blank them. After Customs released her belongings, she must have ingested the germs deliberately."

"She's insane!" Holdernesh whispered.

"They're all insane!" Porch rapped. "If you'll forgive my saying so, it's because people like her exist that I'm not exactly keen about allowing the Sumbalans to land or funding your own long-range starship . . . Anyway, when she was challenged, she said straight out, 'Yes, I am a Sharer! And now, like it or not, so are you!' Then she laughed."

"I never heard anything so horrible," mourned Vanganury.

"So what's happening now?" Holdernesh demanded.

"Nothing very much. She's dead."

* * *

183

There was a vacant pause. Distantly Holdernesh grew aware that the news agencies were converging. A flight of camera hovers was circling over the college. He distracted himself for a moment by drawing Porch's attention to them. The policeman nodded and uttered a crisp order. Though they could not be excluded, this being the venue of a major news story, they could be baffled. Within moments the police's loudspeakers were, not exactly by chance, being directed at the hovers so that the volume of sound would overload their audio circuits. It was no guarantee of privacy, but better than nothing.

And, at last, he was able to husk, "Dead?"

"It happened while you were on your way here," Vanganury moaned. "As soon as the students came to grips with what had been done to them, they attacked her. Like a horde of beasts. I haven't seen it on video, but to judge from her screams . . ." His voice failed him.

"To judge from her screams," Porch said heavily, "they must have torn her limb from limb. And to judge from the accompanying shouts . . . Master Holdernesh, I wish it hadn't fallen to me to tell you this."

A dreadful sense of cold, bitter as the chill of space, occupied the void in Holdernesh's chest where he was used to feeling his heart. He waited for the rest of Porch's statement like a condemned criminal awaiting sentence.

"According to the automatic voice-identification system," the policeman said after what seemed like half eternity, "it was your son who led the attack."

"What," Holdernesh said when he regained control of his lips and tongue, "are you doing now?"

"Maintaining the lecture room at slightly below normal pressure," Vanganury answered. "The air inside is swarming with foreign bacteria and other organisms that we have no name for, but what we have to draw out is heat-processed and sterilized. We've placed emergency requisitions for data with the spaceport medical center and every university biological laboratory that's ever worked on foreign life-forms, but—"

"But every planet has so many, it's going to be a brute of a job to identify them. Yes, I understand."

What I can't understand is why I'm suddenly so calm.

"And what chance do they have of survival? A fair one is my guess. After all, if Aimel lived long enough to come here, start her talk, act so normally at first that—"

"But it made her insane," Porch cut in. "If she'd really wanted to put her teaching across, she'd have— Hold it! I think Principal Vanganury is unwell."

Indeed, the sad-eyed man was swaying. But he waved aside offers of support—not that there were many, for the members of his staff who had been standing around shied away as the implications sank in.

"I greeted her on arrival," he whispered. "I talked to her. She must have been spraying germs into the air all the time. You're going to have to quarantine me as well, and everyone else she's been close to since she was given medical clearance after landing."

What was that about our running the planetary economy at full blast?

There isn't going to be a long-range starship, is there? At any rate, not in my lifetime. Thanks to one of my own people, the Sumbalans have beaten us.

A rapid order from Porch. By now a police medical team was in attendance. Two of its members, fully suited, rushed up and flung a transparent bag over Vanganury. He submitted limply to being enclosed in it and laid on a mechanical stretcher. Eyes shut, he neither moved nor spoke as the medics coupled up the bag's air filters.

"You too, Master Holdernesh," said Porch. "And me. And everyone who's been exposed to her or Vanganury. All my people will have to be tested, everyone who was in the vicinity when she arrived . . . Space and time! There must be hundreds, maybe thousands! All the hospitals on Yellick won't have room enough!"

And of course there won't be any more starflights until the panic dies down. If it ever does . . .

"Excuse me, sir," said another masked and suited medic, presenting a bag like the one in which Vanganury lay. The constable-major was already being cocooned.

"Very well," Holdernesh said. "But I want to send a message to my son."

Indistinctly because of the bag now sealed around him, Porch said, tapping the communicator he still wore, "I can arrange that. I can contact your wife, too. What do you want to say?"

I want to tell them . . .

What?

Suddenly words seemed useless, pointless, empty. He was doomed to be cut off for days, for weeks, perhaps for good, from all that had ever meant anything to him. No doubt the Holdernesh Group would continue to operate after a fashion, for he had inherited a highly competent team from his father and added hand-picked personnel himself. But it would lack whatever it was he personally brought to it—flair? Originality? A sense of adventure? Regardless of what name was offered, it remained the talent that people of Hetto Kidge's stamp did not possess. Already, though, news of what Aimel had done must be spreading, and people who previously had been inclined to support his plan and open contact with new planets would cease wavering and come down firmly on the side of Hetto's kind, too cowardly to take an honest risk.

"Sir?" Porch prompted.

The Sumbalans . . . I wish I knew how they managed to put ships like theirs into the sky before I had the chance!

Jark Holdernesh, enclosed now in his quarantine bag, spread his hands as best he could.

"Nothing," he whispered. "I have nothing to say. Not anymore."

 SHIP

WHEN THE VISION OF YELLICK FADED AND SHIP WAS making its departure:

"I've never watched anything so fascinating," Menlee exclaimed. "The way you could show us everything that was going on practically as though we were standing beside Holdernesh and seeing him in the flesh . . . And to hear what they were saying, too! I did notice, though, that sometimes the words didn't match the lip movements—"

In a more practical mood, Annica cut him short. "It was being edited, wasn't it? The language here isn't quite the same. Inshar's foreign students all speak with an accent. But what I want to know . . . Ship!"

"At your service," came the prompt reply.

"Ship, does what we've seen imply that Sumbala is going to obtain a monopoly of starflight in this volume?"

There was a brief, barely noticeable hesitation. "Not a true monopoly, but it will take a long time for Yellick to recover from the setback."

"So Holdernesh's long-range ships won't be built in the near future?"

"One may safely estimate: not in his lifetime."

"Hmm!" Annica and Menlee were sitting on the couch now regularly provided for them; as was her habit when pondering, she lifted her bare feet to the seat and embraced her knees. "You know, I'm amazed Sumbala has never contacted Shreng. It must be a fantastically rich world."

"Not especially rich," Ship murmured.

The two of them exchanged startled glances. Menlee said, "But their ships! Such a long range, such power and mass! Shreng can't afford to build starships yet, and I've always believed ours is a tolerably affluent planet."

"Besides," Annica chimed in, "if they're that much ahead of Yellick's, they can't be first-generation, surely—not unless they've simply copied an old model from the parent galaxy. Have they?"

"Annica," Menlee objected, "even copying a starship from a previous design isn't easy, let alone cheap. Back home we have all the necessary data, but when you think of the millions of separate items that have to become available before . . . My dear, you're crying! What's wrong?" He leaned toward her.

"Sorry," she snuffled, brushing away tears. "It's just that you said 'back home.' And it isn't home anymore. We don't have a home now, do we?"

"But we will one day," he countered with feigned confidence. "With hundreds of planets to choose from, including lots used to starflight so they won't mind foreigners—"

"Wouldn't you have thought that Yellick didn't mind foreigners?" she cut in. "Until what we just saw, I imagined it was the sort of world where people came and went at least as freely as they do on Shreng, probably more so. Instead we find a society as xenophobic as—as Trevithra!"

They had interrogated Ship about all the worlds it had so far visited during the present sweep, though it had politely declined to give more than vague descriptions of those yet to come, on the usual grounds that its acquaintance with them was still in the future.

Recovering, she returned to her former point.

"So if Sumbala isn't a wealthy planet, how did it come by such amazing ships? Is theirs an obsessive society like Klepsit's, where everything has been sacrificed to a single goal?"

"The Sumbalans don't build them," Ship replied. "They buy them."

Menlee was about to say something. Annica was quicker, dropping her feet to the floor again.

"Then the Veiled World does exist!"

Menlee blinked. "So?" he countered.

"Oh, come on!" Annica stamped impatience—soundlessly, thanks to the resilience of the floor. "Haven't you ever talked to any of the foreign students back home?"

For a long moment Menlee simply gazed at her without expression. Briefly puzzled, she suddenly caught on.

"I said it this time, didn't I? I'm sorry . . . But half a dozen of them, at least, must have told me about a system a long way down the Arm from which they've detected massive tachyonic activity. Holdernesh mentioned it, too!"

Menlee's jaw dropped. "Of course!" he exclaimed. "I must admit I never took what they told me seriously—I imagined, like most people, that if they existed, such powerful signals could only relate to the Ship. This Ship. Delayed for some reason so it couldn't come back . . . I haven't thought about it for ages, not even when Ship proved to be returning in secret. Isn't that ridiculous?"

"But you do know what I mean?" Annica pressed.

"Sure. Assuming it might be the focus of a colossal starfleet, they turned their most powerful telescopes on the source. But all they could see was a blur at every wavelength. That's how the nickname arose, the Veiled World . . . Ship, *does* it exist?"

"What is known as the Veiled World has a counterpart in what you would recognize as reality."

Menlee looked blank. "You'll have to clarify that," he muttered after a moment.

Annica butted in. "What it means is that there really is a massive source of tachyonic energy in the area but it doesn't have anything to do with a starfleet. Right?" Not waiting for an answer: "So what is it? Have aliens invented starflight? I've always wondered why, even in the parent galaxy, we never ran across a more technically advanced species, and I can't accept the idea that we are naturally superior to all other life-forms. In fact we're a pretty inferior bunch, aren't we? It was only by the skin of our teeth that we avoided ruining the birthworld!"

"May I know," Ship murmured, "which of those overt and implied questions you'd like me to tackle first?"

"We started with Sumbala," Menlee said hastily. "You said the Sumbalans don't build their ships, they buy them. From—well, from what we call the Veiled World?"

"Yes."

Annica clenched her fists. "Is *that* an obsessive culture, dedicating itself to nothing but building starships?"

"To some degree you could call it obsessive, yes."

"So what kind of a planet is it?"

"It isn't a planet."

That brought baffled looks to both their faces. Eventually Menlee said, "Are we talking about people who've abandoned groundside existence to live permanently in space? I remember hearing about cultures that did that, millennia ago, but I thought they became psychologically unstable and died out."

"You are quite correct. The experiment was undertaken hundreds of times and never succeeded. There is a genetic limit to the length of time human beings can retain their sanity without adequate mass underfoot and an open sky above. This was among the reasons why my builders chose to design me as they did."

Annica frowned, then brightened. "Oh, I see what you mean! One enormous ship with lots of space for lots of people rather than a great many smaller ones that might have done the job faster but would have felt too cramped?"

"In effect."

"And that's also why you have such efficient simulated gravity and such wonderful illusion generators?"

"Yes."

"Hmm! Very interesting . . . But you made it sound as though this Veiled World is the exception."

"Not exactly."

"Because it's not a world?" Menlee hazarded. Annica rounded on him, framing an obvious question: *If not, then what is it?* Ship forestalled her.

"Not in the ordinary sense, no."

Eyes widening, Annica put the second part of her question into words.

"It's the result of a remarkable and transient phenomenon,"

Ship said. The statement sounded reluctant, though why it should permit the fact to be revealed was beyond both its listeners. "Transient, in this sense, means that it will last at best a few thousand years. Behind the 'veil,' which is a dense cloud of dust—as no doubt you guessed—there lies a protostar. It shines in the visible red and emits sufficient heat to warm the three planets circling it, all sharing the same orbit."

"Three?" Menlee burst out.

"I told you it's a remarkable phenomenon. It is indeed unique so far as my knowledge extends."

"Show it to us!" Annica cried.

"I can't."

"What?"

"As you already know, there are certain limits to what I can tell you. I find I can offer a description, but I'm forbidden to project any visual images. This may have to do with the fact that they would come from your future."

"As well as impatience," Annica sighed, "you must have learned early on about frustration . . . All right, what more can you tell us?"

"I appreciate your sympathy," Ship said. And resumed.

"The cloud of dust, which of course is being gradually drawn to the protostar, proved to incorporate the residue from a supernova. The proportion of heavy elements is exceptional. Possibly this is why three good-sized planets coalesced in such an improbable configuration. Yet more improbable, however, was the fact that their atmospheres turned out to be oxygen-rich from volcanic activity."

"Oxygen-rich?" and "From vulcanism?" they exploded as one.

"On all of them, as was established within a few hours of my arrival, it was possible for a human being to walk in the open. And there were no infectious organisms because there was no life."

"I don't believe it!" Menlee declared, and Annica shook her head.

"Walk? For how long? There can't have been any water vapor, to begin with. Dehydration must have set in right away. And what about the reactive elements that must have filled the air—sulfur, to start with?"

"I said 'walk in the open,' Annica. I didn't specify 'naked and unprotected.' The oxygen level was around two percent, so survival called for filter suits fitted with concentrators and, of course, hydrators. But the ambient temperature is comfortable for humans. As for the reactive elements, they, of course, could be turned into plants."

"What—?" Annica bit her lip.

"I get it!" Menlee said, jumping to his feet and starting to pace up and down. "You left them there with enough modified spores, and more drifting in from space, and in a few years . . . No, it still doesn't make sense."

"Indeed it doesn't," Annica confirmed. "Ship, you've got to show us. You're not forbidden to display the images you stored on the very first sweep, surely. They don't come from our future!"

"I . . ."

And silence. The starfield around them, with Yellick and its sun shrinking at the center, wavered noticeably. They looked at each other in alarm. Had the order provoked some sort of management crisis in Ship's circuitry? Such things were known to occur in simpler machines; it seemed credible that just as insanity was more likely to occur in highly evolved creatures, so complex a system—

But within seconds everything returned to normal.

"Excuse me," Ship said in a wry tone. "What you said made such perfect sense I attempted to comply with your request. Unfortunately I was right the first time. It is forbidden for me to show images of the worlds I haven't yet visited during the present sweep."

"But that's ridiculous," Annica exclaimed. "I mean, if we asked for views of Shreng as it was before we settled it, you could display them, couldn't you?"

"Hey!" Menlee interrupted. "That's a great idea! Why didn't we ask for it before?"

"Because there've been too many other things to inquire about," was Annica's caustic retort. "Besides, we all get shown pictures of that kind in history class, remember?"

Before the gibe could start to rankle, she went on. "Well?"

"Yes, indeed. But you're familiar with most of the material already, as you rightly pointed out. There seems to be a significant difference."

"Such as?"

"I don't know. I can only say: either there's a fault in my damaged zone that I haven't previously noticed, or it was the kind of difference my designers regarded as important."

"And you can't decide which?" Annica shook her head. "I was right about you learning frustration, wasn't I?"

"Yes."

Eventually the two of them returned to the couch by unspoken mutual agreement.

"Go on about the Veiled World," Annica proposed. "There is still a fair while before you have to put us to sleep, isn't there?"

"Yes."

"And we still want to know how all this hangs together with Sumbala," Menlee added. "Since it's from the Veiled World that they buy their starships."

"Yes."

"What with? I mean, what could anyone possibly pay that would justify selling an entire starship?" He looked and sounded confused. "I know they considered chartering one some years ago, back on Shreng"—he avoided calling it "home" this time, and Annica noticed and gave his nearer hand a grateful squeeze—"but even trading five years at Inshar for a thousand students wasn't regarded on Yellick as a fair exchange."

"I didn't know about that!" Annica exclaimed.

"Someone mentioned it back when I was in premed . . . But the only currency, at least according to what I've been told, is information."

"That is correct."

"You're going too fast for me," Annica complained. "I want to know more about this impossible system that the starships come from."

"Not impossible," Ship countered politely. "Just exceptional."

"Even so, I don't see how in the universe you could have been persuaded to let people settle on these weird planets. Free oxygen from volcanoes? What if there were free combustibles as well, or free hydrogen drifting in—there must have been hydrogen!—and a lightning strike hit? Or, even more likely, a meteor!"

"It was somewhat against my better judgment."

"Then they must have made out a hell of a good case!"

"They did." *(But it doesn't matter whether the case is good or bad when the humans that I'm bound to obey grow obstinate enough . . . Poor Stripe!)*

"Such as what?"

"The settlers who decided this was where they wanted to be set down were human."

"Of course they were! You never carried aliens!"

"You miss the point. They possessed imagination. They could see possibilities where I, conditioned by implanted data, was forbidden to."

"I say again: such as what?"

"To begin with, a means to render all three planets not merely habitable but indeed comfortable within less than a century, even though this would involve a modicum of genetic adaptation. And, secondly, a plan for the stabilization of the system so that it would remain in its existing configuration for at least several thousand years, based on an ingenious new application for a stardrive engine."

While Annica was recovering from her awe at hearing of people prepared to set about controlling the motions of three planets and a star, albeit a small one, Menlee exclaimed incredulously, "They saw this when you couldn't?"

"Yes."

"Why?"

"Essentially, my instructions were to seed planets where humanity could survive indefinitely. This system is not inherently stable, especially since there are enough full-blown stars nearby to cause tidal variation in the dust cloud. Soon, by cosmic standards, the primary will accrete all the local matter including the planets."

"So why should they *want* to settle in such an unpromising environment?" Annica persisted.

"Because they felt, in the upshot correctly, that here was the ideal location to start building starships, owing to the availability of so many heavy elements. And the establishment of communication among all the human worlds within the Arm had been assigned a high priority."

"Don't tell me, let me guess," Menlee said softly. "I bet they also pointed out that if they did go in for building starships, if things went wrong, you wouldn't need to come back and rescue them. They could simply pack up and leave."

"I compliment you on your insight," said the Ship.

"But what impelled them, then, to sell their ships? I'd have thought they'd want to keep control! I mean, given the situation you've described, it sounds as though a stray planetoid falling in across the plane of the ecliptic would be enough to throw the system out of kilter, artificially stabilized or not. And if they didn't manage to break it up before it entered the dust cloud, the shock wave from its destruction would have incalculable consequences."

"Exactly!"—from Annica. "If their survival depends on having an emergency escape route ... What can they possibly regard as valuable enough to sell the ships they build?"

"It's already been mentioned."

"Information?"

"Precisely."

"You mean"—Menlee was groping—"they're happier with information about other planets, garnered by other people, than they would be if they went traveling themselves?"

"Once more," said Ship, and somehow the words were curved like a smile, "you impress me with your insight."

"They don't fly any of their ships themselves?" Annica said in a disbelieving tone. "All they do is sell them?"

"One might equally call it renting or chartering."

"And all they ask in exchange is to be told about other planets?"

"In effect, although they insist on being supplied with the maximum possible quantity of extremely detailed information. By the way, Annica, you were wondering why the Sumbalans have not made direct contact with Shreng. The reason is simple: They haven't yet been instructed to collect data from that far away in that direction."

"Was this a policy decision from the very start?"

"Indeed."

"But what in all of space could impel them to—? Ah! Is it because they're aware that eventually they're bound to be driven away and need to know where to head for?"

"Something like that."

"Only something like?"

"Their mental processes are developing along a different and rather interesting line, about which I find I am not allowed to go into detail . . . You'll have to put up with these doubtless infuriating dead ends, I'm afraid. Some day"—*am I allowed to say this? Yes, apparently. Hmm! Interesting!*—"I may run across somebody capable of sorting out the mess in my circuits, though not on this trip, I'm sure. Would you care to wish me luck . . . ? Yes? Thank you. Now it might make sense if you dined and retired. I'm approaching the tachyonic entry zone."

"Just a second!" Menlee said, raising a hand. "I want to know one more thing. If these people—the ones from the Veiled World . . . Say, what do they call themselves?"

"The Shipwrights."

"That's one of the most archaic words I ever heard!"

"Yes, it does hark back to a very ancient culture . . . You were going to ask a question."

"What I want to know is, if they don't fly their ships themselves, how did they let other planets know they were available? They can't have advertised!"

"Not unless they've figured out how to transmit messages through tachyon space," Annica agreed. "And since even on Shreng we haven't solved that one, I don't suppose anybody would be listening."

"I'm surprised you haven't worked it out," Ship said.

"You mean—? Oh!" Menlee sounded astonished at his own obtuseness. "You mean they sent out automatic ships, like you?"

"One ship," came the judicious reply. "And not by any means 'like me'—alas!" *(Can I also say this? Yes, I can! Well, I said something very similar before . . .)* "If I had other ships to keep me company, I'd be extremely glad . . . But theirs was adequate for its purpose. All it had to do was visit the nearest systems in turn, announce what the Shipwrights were offering, and inquire whether their inhabitants were prepared to close a deal. Naturally, most of them were taken completely by surprise and asked for time to consider, preferring to postpone a decision until the automatic ship came back, which might not be for decades.

"The exception was Sumbala. The people there accepted at once. Theirs is one of the more fortunate planets, as hospitable in its different way as Shreng or Yellick. Moreover, its folk descend from a group of highly imaginative ancestors. Not themselves unusually inventive, they display a great talent for devising new applications of what's already to hand. You might describe them by saying that they would rather review the familiar than search for a novelty, but that scarcely anyone else would prove capable of exploiting the known in such a novel way."

Ship's listeners were following with rapt attention. At this point Annica ventured, "Have you told us about an example of that? I recall you saying how much the varied means of transport used by tourists from a ship of theirs impressed the little girl on Trevithra."

"A perfect case in point. Sumbalans did not originate the devices I referred to, but adopted them in the conviction, shortly proved correct, that they would prove a lure for tourists."

Poor Stripe!

And continued: "Being people of that stamp, they were prepared to gamble on the Shipwrights' honesty and good faith. In the latter's turn, they were pleased to find a culture willing to act, so to say, as their agents. The arrangement proved very successful."

"Do they supply only Sumbala?" Menlee demanded.

"Naturally not. At first Sumbala took the entire output of starships, but the time inevitably came when the Veiled World wanted data from other regions. Now there are, or very soon will be, other planets performing a similar task in all directions outward from the dust cloud. It's because the Sumbalans hope to earn the right to more ships that they recently contacted Yellick, Trevithra, and other worlds beyond their previous volume of influence."

"Are they," Annica asked shrewdly, "at risk of thinking of the ships as their own and neglecting to supply the Shipwrights with a proper amount of information because there's so much profit to be made from tourism?"

"That's true to some extent, but only over short distances. Advances in biology—plans for new inventions—works of art— these are the commodities worth trading. And, of course, new philosophies."

"Are there any?" Menlee countered cynically. "Surely by now we humans must have come to all the conclusions we're capable of concerning the nature of the universe and our place in it."

Annica rounded on him. "Menlee, for shame! To start with, what about our contacts with alien life? Ship told us about that world where people are in symbiosis with the native life-forms and due to develop wonderful new ideas. And weren't we just told that the mental processes of the Shipwrights are becoming different from ours, even though they settled in a lifeless system?"

"Lifeless but extraordinary, don't you think?" Menlee muttered, passing a hand across his brow. "However that may be, I apologize. I spoke without thinking. You're absolutely right, especially about contact with aliens."

"As it happens," Ship intervened, "just beyond the volume with which Shreng has contact via Yellick, there should by now be an apposite example. May I serve your food? Or do you wish me to delay my entry to tachyon space?"

"I'm not really hungry, but . . . Okay. Annica?"

"Yes, okay."

Throughout their meal they kept reverting to the subject of the Veiled World, trying to account for so improbable a system, coming at last to the conclusion that it must have resulted from the emergence of a strange attractor in the chaotic turbulence of the dust cloud.

At no point did they appeal directly to Ship, preferring their own speculations. And then they duly went to bed, and sleep.

Time for no time.

I DON'T NEED POWERS OF PREDICTION TO REALIZE THAT the Veiled World is where these two will decide to quit me. I can read it in the pheromones they emit each time it's mentioned, almost as though they're saying, "It would be worth leaving home to live in the strangest place of all!"

Of course the Shipwrights will pick their brains down to the cellular level, and then their bodies, but I'm sure no warning from me would change their minds.

At least, though, it was a long way from here and Ship could look forward to their company a good while yet.

I wish, though, they hadn't led me to discover that ban on displaying images from my first sweep. I still can't tell whether I am handicapped or—there's no term so I'll have to invent one— "plandicapped"!

SOME TIME LATER:

"I feel disappointed," Annica announced as she and Menlee were concluding yet another of the delicious and infinitely varied meals Ship could provide prior to sleeping away yet another tachyonic transit.

"By the food?" came the soft inquiry from the air. "So far I am still attempting to avoid repetition, but if there is anything you would especially like, something familiar from Shreng, perhaps—"

"No, no! The food is fascinating, a real adventure! More of an adventure than this trip, in a way!"

Ship waited. Menlee's eyes were on Annica's face, trying to read her expression. He said at length, "Yes, I agree. I was expecting something more—more exotic on the planets we've visited since Yellick. Back home"—they could use the term now without it hurting—"I used to chat with foreign students, and they made their worlds sound tremendously different from ours. Now we've seen them, and what strikes me is not the contrasts but the resemblances."

"Me too!" Annica concurred. "Although we've seen some remarkable sights—mountains, cataracts, oceans, forests—people's lives seem almost identical to what I'm accustomed to. They have similar technology, their cities are laid out in similar patterns, they even dress more or less the same. There are differences, but they're minor. Is this because they're all in contact with Yellick and Shreng?"

"Or because they were all settled about the same time?" Menlee offered.

"Surely that can't be the reason," Annica objected. "Not when you compare them with Klepsit or Trevithra, which sound as though they're about as far apart as they could well be. Ship?"

"You're both partly right," came the soft reply. "A more impor-

201

tant factor is that the first settlers on all of them constituted a homogeneous group among my original complement. They were neither extremely eager to leave me and start homesteading their new planet, nor—"

"Excuse me." Annica was blinking. "Start what?"

"I should be the one to apologize," Ship countered. "I inadvertently used a very ancient term, which I realize you may not have run across even in a history course. Let me rephrase what I was going to say.

"They were neither extremely eager to be set down on a new world nor excessively choosy about what kind of world it would be. As it happens, this particular group of systems must have formed from an exceptionally uniform dust cloud, so that they all have pretty much the same composition, and into the bargain they also constitute one of the rare clusters known as Arrhenian. That word is also rare, but I imagine you may recognize it."

Annica hesitated. Abruptly Menlee snapped his fingers.

"Ah, yes! Self-replicating molecules do occasionally evolve in space, don't they? And if they drift down to a planet, they can seed it, like the spores you sow. Instead of finding extremely different life-forms on each separate planet, therefore—"

"They're recognizably related!" Annica broke in. "Yes, it comes back to me now. But why Arrhenian?"

"After a legendary savant on the birthworld who taught that life had only arisen once and its spores had been carried from star to star by radiation pressure. Ironically he was dead and almost forgotten except by specialists before any real-world cases were discovered. On more than ninety percent of the planets where life exists it arose independently, but Arrhenian clusters are known, and we've been traversing one of them."

"Which must have meant that this—this group of your passengers felt very pleased with their good fortune," Menlee suggested. "Those who landed on Shreng and Yellick, in particular."

The air seemed to darken, though there was no visible reduction in the former light level.

"Not so much those who chose the next planet on my schedule," Ship sighed.

"One of your—the failures?" Annica inquired.

"Yes. Not even one for which a brighter future may be hoped."

"Have ships from Yellick been there?" Menlee asked.

"No, though a Sumbalan one has. We are approaching a volume where there are few attractive suns. But for the Shipwrights' insistence, even the Sumbalans might well have postponed their exploration of it for a few more decades. There are other, more promising directions. Of course, since the Sumbalans are no longer the Shipwrights' sole clients, some of them are being explored now, or will be shortly."

Annica pondered. "Are there already any cases where a failed world has been colonized a second time by people better equipped to cope with the environment?"

"How could that happen?" Menlee demanded. "Surely none of the colony worlds can possibly have attained a higher level of technology than what's represented by Ship! It's the product of research and development by a whole galaxy!"

"Correction," Ship said mildly. "Not a *whole* galaxy—just a few thousand systems in regular contact. But you're right in principle. It would have been impossible to build me with the resources of only a handful of planets, and those comparatively underpopulated. But in reply to your question, Annica: So far as I can tell you, the answer is no."

"You mean it won't ever happen, or it hasn't happened yet?"

"If it has already happened, I've not yet seen evidence. Whether it will happen later, I can't say."

"Your instructions again?" Annica said sourly, rising from the table.

"My instructions again."

"I suppose there's some kind of underlying consistency, but it baffles me . . . You know, I don't much like the idea of visiting a failed world."

"You're welcome to sleep through the stopover. Or I can arrange for you to disregard it."

"No . . ." Glancing at Menlee, she bit her lip. "No, I guess I ought to see everything there is to see."

Menlee caught her hand and gave it an approving squeeze.

"If it's any comfort," Ship said, making the table and the empty dishes disappear, "the world after next should be alien enough to satisfy your appetite for strangeness."

"Oh!" She brightened. "What's it like?"

"Please contain your impatience. When we arrive, you will find out."

Viewed from orbit, the next world looked remarkably like all those they had so far visited: a similar color, much the same amount of cloud cover, similar oceans and polar caps.

Well, that was logical. Planets fit for human occupation had to resemble one another—always excepting the extraordinary triplet of the Veiled World. So what had been the trap that wrecked their chances for its colonists?

Annica didn't realize she had spoken aloud—or perhaps she hadn't and Ship now knew her so well, it could deduce what she was thinking from her expression and her pheromones. However that might be, the answer came at once.

"Here is a projection of a typical area in what seemed to be the most suitable zone for a first settlement."

Suddenly they seemed to be flying over a level plain carpeted with mossy plants of dark bluish-green. Here and there bulkier growths stood out, clustering more densely toward a line of hills on the horizon and becoming rarer as the land sloped toward a body of water: perhaps an estuary. It appeared to be early morning.

Something leapt upward from the water and fell back with a resounding splash. They realized they could hear as well as see the projection; in fact, they could even smell it. Again as though able to read their thoughts, Ship said dryly, "In case the odors worry you, you're not actually inhaling the molecules. I'm simulating their effect on your olfactory nerves."

"Should we be worried?" Menlee wondered.

"You would have grounds. This is what an airborne infection did to the settlers' descendants despite the medical techniques they disposed of and all the data they'd amassed before they landed."

The view zoomed at tremendous speed over the estuary—it was definitely a river mouth, for they glimpsed rapids a short distance inland—and shot across a low headland. Beyond . . .

Beyond there was a cluster of hovels made of branches, rocks, and mud. The projection halted with the entrance to one of them in close focus. Something was moving in the semidarkness beyond the opening. It emerged as though in intolerable pain. It had a head, two upper and two lower limbs—but they were terribly deformed. Bony excrescences loomed above its eyes; its jaw was monstrously twisted to one side, and lips that could not stretch to close its mouth revealed enormous yellow teeth bulging outward. It seemed unable to bend its knees or elbows, while its hands and especially its feet were bloated into misshapen clods of flesh and dried-on mud.

Annica failed to repress a cry. Swallowing hard, Menlee spoke for them both.

"What in all of space happened to them?"

More of the creatures were emerging now, including children. Those had not yet lost the power to bend their joints and crawled along comparatively quickly on hands and knees. In a group, they moved toward the water, seeming not to know or care about whatever the huge thing was that had leapt from it.

"This happened to them," said Ship, and in front of the display there floated a polychrome molecular diagram. Menlee spoke half-aloud as he deciphered it.

"But none of those groups ought to interfere with human germ plasm . . . except possibly the one that includes manganese . . . Manganese? Yes . . . But even so . . . Oh!"

"What is it?" demanded Annica, who was less well versed in stereochemistry.

"I don't think this attacked their heredity. I don't see why it should. Ship?"

For once there was no answer. Puzzled, Menlee glanced around as though expecting to read an explanation from the air. Annica laid a hand on his arm.

"Don't bother it," she whispered. "Haven't you realized how it must be feeling?"

"What? What do you mean?"

"It delivered these people's ancestors here. It allowed them to walk into this appalling trap. It didn't come back to rescue them before it was too late. And now is the first time it's had the chance to find out what really went wrong."

"The first time—? Yes, of course." Menlee was sweating despite the equable temperature; he wiped his forehead with the back of his hand. "Yet it was able to warn us we were going to see a failure world, even though it refused to tell us details of the other ones we've been to before we actually got there . . . You were right to say that if there's any consistency in Ship's instructions, it's not obvious."

"Well, it's said all along that it believes itself to be damaged." In the projection, the half humans were entering the water with grunts and yells as of continual pain. She concentrated on the molecular diagram to distract herself.

"What do you make of it?" she said after a pause. "Not something that affects the germ plasm, you said."

"No. It looks more like something that might affect individual organs, especially bony parts. Not mutational. Possibly congenital. A sort of carcinogen that could well start its work in the womb."

"How could they possibly have overlooked it?"

"They didn't," Ship said quietly, and added, "By the way, Menlee, you're right. These people's germ plasm is human. Take a cell from one of their livers, or even the spinal cord, and you would find no significant difference. When it comes to bone, it's another matter. Their bones become cancerous, not actually in the womb but shortly after they draw their first breath. By puberty the effect is bodywide. The oldest of the people you're looking at is about twenty. In other words, they still live long enough to breed, but— can I tell you this? Strangely, I find I can—by the time of my next visit they will be extinct."

Annica had been containing herself with vast effort. Now she burst out, "I don't understand! I asked how they could have overlooked such a terrible threat, and you said they didn't! That doesn't make sense!"

"When their ancestors landed here," Ship said gently, "the threat did not exist."

They both stood dumbstruck for a long moment. The molecular diagram vanished, but neither of them returned full attention to the beach scene, where the malformed were grubbing for shoreline weed and creatures corresponding no doubt to shellfish but soft enough to eat whole.

"Antibody," Menlee said at last.

"Oh, the pity of it!" Annica whispered as she realized what he meant.

"Exactly," Ship confirmed. "Not even with the resources of my data banks to call on did their forebears begin to suspect that on this planet there exists an antibody system capable of being triggered *only* by life-forms arriving from outside. Life here began, as on most planets, independently; we are outside the Arrhenian zone of the other systems you have lately visited. Conceivably the phenomenon traces back to the arrival of wandering spores from that zone; there must have been some evolutionary purpose to it, or it would never have arisen. And the spores I left behind in nearby space made matters worse."

Their eyes had now been drawn back, as though they were hypnotized, to the projection of the beach. Something was moving in the water, drawing closer. Now and then it broached the surface. Its form could not be discerned, but it was large. Perhaps it was the same creature that had earlier made such a spectacular leap into the air.

Abruptly one of the largest of the malformed uttered a scream, a cry of utter and indescribable despair, and with clumsy strides waded out to meet it. Some of the others ceased their scavenging for food and gazed dully in his—her?—direction, but most ignored what was going on.

"Please, no," Annica whispered, but there was no way to stop it. Something showed partly above, partly below, the surface, like a colossal black suction tube rimmed with orange fangs. A second later there was a spurt of bright red blood.

The projection vanished. They were looking down from space,

as before. Ship said sadly, "You see, even now they still retain enough intelligence to decide when life is not worth living."

Eventually Annica roused herself, striving to recover her spirits.

"At least you promised that the next world will be as foreign as we can well desire—correct?"

"Indeed. Though I cannot promise it will cheer you up."

HOW IS IT—WHY IS IT—THAT MY CREATORS FORCED ME TO feel such misery, such shame, whenever one of the worlds I've seeded proves to be a failure?

In the near-to-nonexistence of tachyonic space, Ship brooded over questions akin to those faced by uncountable humans since the dawn of history.

Why did they decide to build a machine capable of suffering? Why make me conscious and aware? Could my role not have been performed far more efficiently by a device without emotion, coldly and totally rational?

Recollection of Stripe's fate was haunting it.

Of course there are an infinity of universes where everything is different. That's known. Likewise there are billions of humans. So why did they design me to make, knowing I must lose them, friends?

CHAPTER NINE

EKATILA

"USKO! USKO! OH, WHERE HAS THAT BOY GOT TO?"

Bustling around the house's spiral maze of curving nacre corridors floored with tamped and multicolored clay, issuing orders to servants, scolding a pair of window carvers who were mindlessly cutting a hole where it would look onto a blank wall, pausing here and there to adjust the angle of a branch of flowering cikotika or the hang of a family portrait—which today of all days must be set askew—Osahima, portly in middle age, now and then shouted her son's name, though with small hope of a reply. Was it not enough that she should have lost her husband? To have an impious son as well: that was too much!

Then, finally, she chanced on him, emerging with a vast yawn from that most obvious of places, the cellar, blinking at daylight as though he had not expected it. The cellar was not in fact a cellar, being, like the rest of the house, half aboveground, but was the only part totally devoid of windows and illuminated exclusively by phosfung. Something of their sallow and unwholesome light seemed to have permeated Usko's face and hands, perhaps his very bones.

Seemed, though. Only seemed. Had the phenomenon been real, the family's geneticist would have reacted instantly.

"So there you are!" Osahima exclaimed crossly. "I've been hunting for you everywhere! Go and get dressed!"

Tilting his thin pale face, Usko glanced down with the air of someone who cared so little about clothing he was quite prepared to discover he was naked. Finding he was in fact clad in his usual rather grubby overall, he looked blankly at his mother.

"I mean properly dressed!" she roared. "Have you forgotten what day it is?"

"Ah . . ." Rubbing sleep from his eyes, fighting the urge to yawn anew, Usko suggested, "Someone's anniversary?"

Osahima cast her eyes heavenward. "May the Being save me!" she cried. "This child who everybody says is so intelligent, so *brilliant,* can't even remember that it's Pilgrimage Time!"

Seeming to notice for the first time how gaudily the house was decorated—red cikotika here, yellow pilopika there, everywhere dark green garlands of okalika as though the house had been wrapped up like a gift . . . and indeed it had become, in a sense, an offering—Usko had the grace to apologize.

"I'm sorry, Mother. I stayed up late last night because one of my experiments was about to fruit, and I suppose I fell asleep waiting. Missed the great event, anyhow. But"—animation transformed his expression—"this morning it's coming on fine! By this evening at the latest I should have a score of hingochapla, enough to last the winter and perhaps the spring as well! Won't you find them useful?"

"I don't *like* hingochapla," his mother snapped. "The way they always have to repeat your orders twice, three times, and in such a horrid grating voice—"

"But I've designed these to whisper!"

"Don't you mean to be trained to whisper?"

"Uh—of course."

"I see." Osahima set her hands on her hips. "You're looking for an excuse not to accompany the rest of the family on Pilgrimage. You're hoping I'll let you stay at home to train them— Don't interrupt! I know as well as you do that it has to be done as soon as they start to move around by themselves, most likely sometime this afternoon. Well, my son, you have another think coming."

She glanced around, caught sight of a passing yugochapla, and issued crisp orders. The creature hesitated a moment, torn by submental conflict, then carefully set down the pots of rauni it was carrying and headed for the cellar.

"Mother! You can't! You mustn't!"

"Who says I can't?" Osahima demanded. "This is my house so long as I live—isn't it? And today is the first day of Pilgrimage— isn't it?"

"Yes, but—"

"There are no buts! You are coming with the family to perform the due and fitting ceremonies! Never mind your horrid hingo-chapla! You can always make more, if you must. Right now— Ah! Just the person I need! Reverend Yekko!"

Beaming, resplendent in full Pilgrimage garb from his stiff black coronet to his black-booted feet, separated by an overall dyed in twenty vivid colors, the family's spiritual adviser hastened to answer her summons . . . and almost collided with the yugochapla as it emerged from the cellar, carrying the results of Usko's experiment. If it had had a face, one might have imagined it looking gleeful. The yugochapla were barely conscious—that had been proved repeatedly—but some of them were at least dully aware that the larger, livelier, more adaptable hingochapla were due to replace them eventually, and the task of disposing of Usko's new and promising strain seemed to be affording it some drab counterpart of enjoyment.

"Bury the whole lot in the garbage pile!" Osahima commanded even as she seized the priest's arm, and went on with scarcely a pause for breath.

"Yekko, I have a complaint. Your education of my son has left much to be desired."

Alarm spread over Yekko's bland plump countenance. He ventured, "In what way . . . ? No, don't tell me. I see he is not yet dressed for our journey."

"Exactly. It would appear he has forgotten his catechism, doesn't it? Much as I would like to set out right away, I think it would do him good to be reminded of it, even at the cost of an hour's delay."

"Absolutely," the priest said, trying to sound and look grim. Since at heart he was a jolly, lively person, this cost him considerable effort, but he was sincere in his beliefs, and there was a genuine sense of affront in his tone. Turning to Usko, he was about to launch into the catechism when he realized that they were blocking the path of a string of servants laden with necessaries for Pilgrimage. Being a nine-day expedition, it called for huge amounts of baggage, ranging from changes of clothing to kitchen utensils. One could never rely on finding proper cooking equipment at a roadside inn.

In the same moment Yekko beckoned Usko aside, Osahima spotted that one of the yugochapla had picked up something she particularly did not want removed from the house and stumped in its wake, shouting.

Voice too low for her to overhear, Yekko said, "Usko, Usko! What possessed you to annoy her today of all days? You know what she's going to be like as a result—maybe during the entire trip!"

The capdoor at the end of the passage they were standing in was wide open. Usko's eyes were turned that way, fixed on one of the enormous baplabaska that would carry the household and its goods to Penitenka. The vast gray-blue mass was obediently slumping to the ground at the command of its mahuto, and servants were converging from all sides.

He said at length, "I'm sorry."

"Sorry!" Yekko's cheeks turned purple. "You can't have forgotten about Pilgrimage!"

"I—uh—suppose not."

"Well, you haven't exactly prepared for it, have you?"

"No." Usko shifted from foot to foot.

"So are you going to tell me exactly what it is you're playing at?"

Usko drew a deep breath.

"I just don't feel like going to Penitenka this year."

That was too much for Yekko. He stamped his foot. "I never thought I'd have to remind you of this, boy, but apparently I must! This is not something you can disregard because you aren't feeling like it! This is a sacred duty and an obligation! Your mother told me to run you through the catechism. I hoped to avoid it. Now I'm going to—and the full version if I must! She said she could put up with an hour's delay, and if that's how long it takes to restore your sense of responsibility, so be it!"

"I think she meant—" Usko began.

"I know precisely what she meant! An hour including the time it's going to take to make you presentable! Well, if you don't show proper reverence in your answers, I'll take you through the entire text again, and if necessary again, and you can put up with being the only member of the household to reach Penitenka in shabby

213

workaday clothes instead of Pilgrimage garb! Is that clear?"

Yekko was almost shaking with unaccustomed emotion, and Usko flinched. Maybe this time he had gone too far.

He said placatingly, "Very well, Master Priest. I'm ready and willing to undergo—"

And realized Yekko was no longer looking at him but past him. He turned and found that his sister Lempi, followed by six or eight of her personal yugochapla, was advancing down the passage. "Advancing" was the word. He was twenty, and she was only eighteen, but she had the air and mannerisms of their mother. Stately in a wide-hipped gown of sunshine yellow, her headdress supported by fluttering hylochapla leashed with bright red ribbons, she constituted a one-person parade. Last year at Penitenka she had been outshone by the eldest daughter of Household Bibirago. Clearly she was determined that the same would not happen again.

Although it might not be entirely sensible to don so magnificent a gown at the very outset . . .

Drawing level with her brother, Lempi favored him with a scornful look.

"So you aren't coming. Well, good riddance!"

And swept past.

Why, you little—!

Yekko was grinning broadly. He canceled the expression the moment he realized Usko had noticed, but traces of his amusement lingered. He said, "I deduce that your sister has achieved what I had merely begun to attempt."

"Uh—!"

"Don't try and argue. I read it on your face, clear as a gene plot. You're coming, for an unworthy motive maybe, but you're coming. 'Mysterious ways' and all that . . . Shall we settle for the shorter catechism?"

"Yes," Usko blurted. "And hurry!"

"Very well." Yekko cleared his throat. "Are we native to this world called Ekatila?"

"No! We came from far away in space!" Usko clenched his bony fists, eyes following Lempi as she deigned to inspect the baplabaska allotted to her and nod approval. How like their mother she'd become!

"To what do we owe our survival on this world?"

"To the Being that consents to make way for us."

"Graciously consents!" Yekko snapped, as though Usko were still a lisping toddler.

"Graciously consents," came the resentful agreement.

"In what way does it support and serve us?"

"By parting with its very flesh—"

"I don't believe it, I don't believe it!" Yekko broke in. "You've had this word-perfect for fifteen years, and here you are messing it up!"

"I thought we were using the short version," Usko challenged. "Not: 'By ceding us its shell to use for homes, the which we find convenable in winter storms for warmth, in summer heat for coolness, all this of its own volition, and it thus behooves us to respect and honor it and to make it offerings and go on Pilgrimage to wheresoever its new limit may be found'—and incidentally that's something I've been meaning to ask you about: How come we've managed to keep one of its limits at Penitenka for so many years, when within living memory it was retreating almost as fast as we could spread across the planet? That's by the way, of course. What I meant to point out was that you were wrong, not me. 'By parting with its very flesh, the which by its generosity has become for us a source of food, of medicines, of servants and of transportation, all freely offered and most gratefully acknowledged.' Then the next question—"

Flushing red at his error, Yekko rasped, "Usko! If you know all the answers, why—?"

Having recovered his normal spirits, Usko cut in.

"Why do I make mock of you and my mother? Because I spend too much time tampering with the Being's actual physical material! Where's the intelligence that has *voluntarily* made way for us? Not in our servants, whatever kind of chapla they may be! Not in our means of transport, not in any of the other things you say we should give thanks for . . . Yes, I'm coming to Penitenka. But not to please my mother or put my sister's nose out of joint or even because you brought me up to believe it was the 'done thing.' "

"Why, then?" Yekko snapped.

Turning toward his quarters and a change of clothes, Usko threw over his shoulder, "Because I dare to imagine the priests there may be readier to admit the truth!"

I SEE THEY'VE ALREADY LEARNED HOW TO PREVENT THE Being from dying out ahead of them, leaving only lumps and tendrils of its tissue to be worked on and converted into useful forms, in one region at least. Odd! I had the impression that discovery was made much later. Maybe it's a false start.

Ship surveyed the planet with its invariable meticulous thoroughness. Even as its inspection was under way, a ship—a Sumbalan ship, naturally—emerged from tachyon space and headed for a landing.

Tourists come for the spectacle of Pilgrimage Season! That too is earlier than I imagined. Has more damage affected my circuitry?

That possibility was dreadfully discomforting.

HASTILY RE-DRESSED IN A CLEAN OVERALL, CARRYING A bagful of whatever might be useful on the journey that he could lay hands on in the disorganized clutter of his chamber, Usko ran to join the traveling party. Even when he did so, however, their departure was delayed still a little longer while Yekko recited invocations and threw a symbolic blossom in the direction they were to take, to ensure favorable way and weather. At least that was what he meant to do, but a gust of wind caught the flower and blew it clean away from the path.

The members of the household reacted with alarm. That was a bad omen. Yekko himself was frowning when he mounted his baplabaska, next in line behind Osahima's and ahead of Usko's. The latter planned, as soon as the road grew wide enough for two of the beasts abreast, to ride alongside the priest. If he could make no better use of the next few days, he might at least enjoy arguing with him.

And in spite of everything, he did like the older man. He had great respect for his learning, and if occasionally the priest was inclined to stand on his dignity, he was at least as likely to tell a comic anecdote and ripple with silent laughter after delivering the punch line.

Now, finally, with the sun almost at the zenith, the line of nine baplabaska stirred into sluggish motion. Trying not to let himself be lulled by the regular rocking of his mount, like that of a small boat on a gentle ocean swell, Usko stared first this way, then that, trying to fix the view in memory—for, against all his rational inclinations, he had been affected by the omen of the wind-tossed blossom. On Ekatila children were taught about such matters almost as soon as they could talk, and every year's calendar was a maze of anniversaries of past events, fortunate and unfortunate: the birth of an heir, the death of an aged parent, a flood, a storm, the invention of a new and useful variety of servant ... Moreover,

218

virtually everyone had private additions to the main list. Often it was nearly impossible to visit elderly relatives with good memories, for something had happened to them on practically all the four hundred days, and when they were not performing a gratitude ceremony, they would be in retreat for meditation or self-reproach. Early in his teens, Usko himself had gone to pay a duty call on his late father's mother and been kept waiting fifteen days before he was allowed to talk to her, because she was so constantly occupied with personal anniversaries.

What, Usko sometimes wondered, would happen when not just the private calendars of old folk but the public calendar obeyed by all the Households filled up in the same way? It was a priestly task to keep track of the date; he must ask Yekko as soon as the opportunity arose.

Like most of the accommodation the Being had bequeathed to humanity—although a few Households were sited on level ground, especially near seas and lakes—Household Ishapago lay pearly-white and gleaming along the ridge of a hill. Its two hundred and ten chambers branched off from eighteen passageways. As children, back when the two of them were on good terms before Lempi started to ape their mother so ridiculously, he and his sister had often raced each other from end to end of it. Although she was the younger, Lempi had also been the fleeter, and by the time she was fourteen and he sixteen, he would find her at the back capdoor sitting composedly and wearing a triumphant grin when he came panting up, feet sore and chest aching.

"Catch her doing something like that now!" Usko muttered to the air as he cast a glance at the baplabaska behind his. There she was, sitting with a haughty expression on her face, the corners of her mouth turned down as though to signal her displeasure to the world. Was she going to make the fluttering creatures that held up her headdress stay aloft the whole of Pilgrimage? Who did she think she was likely to impress this close to home? There were no other humans in sight, nor would there be until they encountered other Households also bound on Pilgrimage, and that would be, at the earliest, this evening, for the Ishapago estate was a large one and their first few hours of travel would be within its boundary.

Remembering that he was trying to soak in the scene just in case the bad omen had been aimed at him and this was to be the trip from which he would not return—though in fact so light a matter as a wind-taken flower scarcely implied such a disaster—Usko returned his attention to his surroundings. This section of the road was bordered by fields crosshatched with irrigation channels. Here and there tireless, mindless weeders were at work among their root and fruit crops, while along the bank of the river that took its rise just behind the house and whose first function was to furnish its inhabitants with water, he could see lifters endlessly scooping and spilling to keep the channels full. Beyond those, other workers were carefully peeling away the porous serolika membranes that, wind-dried and attractively tinted, would be cut and stitched to make the Household's winter garments. And, barely visible on the skyline, strands of akolika destined to be spun into everything long and flexible from sewing thread to rope for baplabaska tethers were being gathered by yet more examples of the Being's munificence.

Or so people were required to believe.

Usko felt his mouth turning down like his sister's. Of late he had become more and more skeptical of the official teachings—no doubt, as he had taunted Yekko, because he had spent so long working with fragments of the Being's substance. Heretical opinions were burgeoning at the edge of his mind.

The orthodox account stated that upon the arrival of human colonists the Being, recognizing that they were intelligent and not mere animals, had generously done all it could to ensure first their survival, then their comfort, even to the extent of yielding up portions of itself to be exploited by them. It had withdrawn from the protective shells that now served as homes for people, leaving only morsels of its tissue here and there. Very shortly it was discovered that these were ideally suited for alteration into forms capable of performing useful tasks. At first the newcomers' imagination stretched only to creating the simplest of helpers, like those that pumped water for irrigation. Gradually, however, they became more enterprising and developed tenders for their crops.

Next they devised means of transport—and the variety of those was astonishing, as would be amply proved during the great gathering at Penitenka whither they were bound, an event whose fame had spread beyond the sky. Rumor promised that this year, for the first time, tourists from Sumbala would come to witness it, allegedly attracted because on that world also people were accustomed to converting its native life into vehicles and servants. Some, however, counterclaimed that they did not worship their local Being . . . !

Usko hoped with all his heart that the rumors would prove true. He wanted almost more than anything to find out what off-worlders thought about the Ekatilans' version of their early days on this planet. What if they, like he, couldn't accept that the Being had deliberately and by choice made way for people, even letting parts of itself be exploited by them?

His eyes were drawn to the mahuto steering his baplabaska, and he found himself shaking his head.

No. It was far more likely that something about humans—some exudation, perhaps—had made the Being sicken and divide, possibly as a defense mechanism evolved in the far past. He could envisage how, before it attained ascendancy over virtually the entire land surface of Ekatila, it might have been subject to disease, or predators, or some other form of threat. In such circumstances it would be advantageous to sacrifice portions of its tissue in order to resume its expansion when the danger was past.

Even if the rumor about foreign visitors was baseless, he was on reconsideration glad he hadn't decided to give Pilgrimage a miss this year. Not only would his mother have made his life unbearable for the foreseeable future; he would have passed up the opportunity of seeking out a progressive young priest whose doubts had not yet been stifled by the discipline that his superiors imposed. He knew such existed. Indeed, only last year he had met one—what was his name? For the moment it escaped him, but that didn't matter. What counted was that he had come to Household Ishapago no longer as a priest but as a beggar. In the old days, it was said, mendicants were not uncommon, being mainly survivors of failed Households wiped out by disease or crop blight, so although nowadays they were rare, there was a tradition of hospitality toward them and sometimes they even managed to get adopted into another Household. However, when Owdi (yes, that was his name) let slip that he had been expelled from the priesthood, Yekko had issued an ultimatum: Owdi went, or he did.

Usko had felt very sorry to see the failed priest trudge away. His conversation had been heady for the bright young boy . . .

The nature of the countryside changed, became wilder. Now and then nameless creatures scuttled in undergrowth or flitted overhead—nameless, at any rate, to Usko, though no doubt someone had examined and classified them during the general survey of the planet undertaken by the ancestors. However, nowadays few people paid attention to such matters. It was enough that the Being had provided for their survival and would continue to do so as long as they displayed a proper sense of obligation. Other life-forms would no doubt be investigated and perhaps exploited some day. Some day. Not tomorrow, though.

One unusual event punctuated the first portion of their progress.

During one of the regular halts dictated by the need for the humans to relieve themselves, the Household's field overseer Immi—who, being regarded as barely more than a servant despite his wide knowledge of botany, was one of a group of ten or twelve sharing the last baplabaska with a heap of bags and baskets—returned to the road in high excitement, announcing that he had found a new Being shell. This was extraordinary. Usko, about to remount, changed his mind and made haste to verify the claim. In an attempt at reconciliation he asked whether Lempi would like to come, too, but was met with a scowl, the very image of their mother's. Even Yekko, who he had imagined would be eager to inspect it, climbed back into his saddle with a dismissive wave.

But there it was, shining bluish-yellow on an outcrop of rock, no longer than the span of a man's arms. Usko stared at it, marveling, until he was summoned back to the procession by his mother's raucous order.

A new Being shell! He resolved to break off on the way back and examine it in detail. There was no telling what use the tissue it contained might be put to.

At noon the weather had been warm. As the sun declined, the air grew colder. Just before their procession reached a highway broad enough for Usko to consider moving alongside Yekko, as he had earlier planned, he glanced back at his sister. She had finally given up her attempt to keep her headdress aloft, and her traveling chapla had taken it and was now marching stolidly along with it in what would have been its arms if chaplas had had human limbs. She herself appeared to be dozing—or possibly praying; now and then her lips moved. Usko felt a pang of regret. What a shame that she and he had drifted apart! Of course, if they had stayed as close as they had been during childhood, either she would have had to be more like him . . . or he would have had to be more like her. The latter prospect did not appeal. Indeed, it made him shudder. To picture himself as the kind of arrogant, bossy person Lempi was turning into—no!

He reached forward and prodded his mahuto, instructing it to bring him level with Yekko. However, when he tentatively addressed the plump priest, he was rebuffed.

"Don't talk to me, young fellow! No doubt it was thanks to you that my blossom was blown away! The Being is not fond of being mocked!"

"But—" Usko began, and was cut short.

"You know perfectly well what you've done! You planned to avoid going on Pilgrimage!"

"I assure you, I'd simply forgotten—"

"Forgotten? You, who since childhood have had a memory like the stickiest of shopalika?" Yekko shook his heavy head. "Nonsense! I know, and so does the Being!"

Stung, Usko retorted, "How?"

"What do you mean, 'how?' "

"How does it know?" Usko repeated, greatly daring.

"It just does, that's all. One day perhaps we shall be allowed to find out by what means. For the time being it's enough to be aware of the fact." Yekko spoke with finality. "If you persist in these heretical questions, I shall have to report you to the abbot at Penitenka. I warn you!"

Dismayed, for he had no idea he had so offended the priest, Usko said after a moment, "But surely—"

"Surely what? 'Surely I'm allowed to voice this sort of dangerous rubbish'? Oh no you're not! Our survival depends on acknowledging the support of the Being! Have you never considered what life would be like were it to turn against us? Suppose enough people like you made it angry, and it decided to reclaim its shells, our homes! And reunite itself with all the parts of it that we've redesigned, taught skills, taught to understand what humans want and need! It would be the end of us, wouldn't it? At all costs we *must* placate it—or become extinct! You saw just now: a new shell! Does that imply that it plans to seize back its former territory from us? It may, you know! It may! Now shut up and let me go on praying! And you had better do the same!"

Folding his hands, closing his eyes, the priest made it plain that the conversation was over. Then, seconds later, he spoke again, though his eyes did not reopen.

"Something bad is certain to happen. I can feel it. If you weren't so disrespectful of the Being, you might feel it too. Instead of asking other people questions about how it knows our thoughts, you could try looking within yourself. I think you may have some of the necessary talent, whatever it is. And I don't want to see you cast out and ruined. I don't want you to wind up begging like that failed priest Owdi—who most likely sowed the canker in your brain!"

Hiding his reaction but privately inclined to scoff, Usko ordered his mahuto to resume their normal position in the line.

His skepticism, though, was undermined the next morning, when they emerged into the yard of the inn where they had spent the night and discovered that Yekko's forebodings had proved right. Something bad had indeed happened. Not catastrophically bad, not even extremely bad, but at the least a considerable nuisance.

One of the baplabaska lay still and flaccid on the paving stones.

Under the amused eyes of members of another Household that had also arrived at the inn last night, but later, Lempi—wearing red today and with a headdress made of stiffened membrane that stood up of itself—stamped her foot furiously.

"This is past enduring!" she shouted. "To arrive at Penitenka with only eight baplabaska, when everybody will expect us to have nine! Mother, you'll have to get another from somewhere! Otherwise we can't possibly go on!"

Scowling, Osahima drew her aside. Usko, examining the dead beast in search of clues to its demise, was just able to overhear what they said to each other.

"Lempi, you're making a spectacle of yourself, and I won't tolerate the Household being brought into disrespect before strangers! Everybody's staring at you, and not because of your finery, either!"

Sullen, Lempi gave a shrug. "It isn't fair, though—is it? This is all Usko's fault! Make him walk the rest of the way, how about that?"

"It's your baplabaska that's dead, not his," Osahima retorted.

"Mine?" Lempi withdrew half a step, appalled. "But by rights it ought to be his—oughtn't it? Anyway, who can tell them apart, the great ugly lumbering brutes?"

That attracted the attention of Yekko. Horrified, he stumped close.

"Lempi, if that's how you regard the benefits bestowed upon us by the Being, no wonder ill luck has struck you and not your brother!"

Flushing, Lempi snapped, "It must have been him it was really meant for!"

Usko, still pretending to inspect the dead baplabaska although he had already concluded it had died from a perfectly normal cause—frustrated subdivision—pursed his lips in a soundless whistle. He could imagine how Yekko would react to that.

And he did. He burst out, "That's blasphemous! Making out that the Being is unjust and—and incompetent! I'm minded to make *you* walk the rest of the way!"

"So am I!" Osahima concurred. *"And* carry the dozens of bags and boxes you insisted on bringing! Very likely that was what killed your mount—overloading it with so much ridiculous finery!"

Lempi glanced around as though seeking a way of escape. Even though they couldn't hear, members of the other Household, watching as they waited for their servants to ready their own mounts, had little difficulty guessing what was going on, and some of them were nudging one another in the ribs and uttering ribald comments.

Usko decided it was time to intervene. He had no more wish than his mother to bring shame on Household Ishapago. Straightening, he advanced and called out.

"It's all right, Lempi. I don't mind sharing someone else's baplabaska. You can take mine—you have far more luggage than me. Perhaps Yekko will let me ride with him."

"What makes you think so?" Lempi sneered. "You're the one for heresy and blasphemy, the one who tried to get out of making Pilgrimage! Don't imagine I don't know what goes on in that ugly head of yours! Ever since you tried to persuade me Owdi wasn't spouting wicked nonsense, I've distrusted you! Oh, it'll be an evil day for us when you become our householder—if you ever do!"

"Lempi," Osahima said between her teeth, "for the time being *I* am the householder, *and don't you forget it!* Usko has made a very generous offer, and here you are repaying him with insults. Extremely nasty insults, what is more. Apologize!"

But Usko was standing thunderstruck. Could that truly be the origin of the breach between him and his sister? Now he thought back, it was not impossible. Having no one else with whom to talk about Owdi's visit, he had indeed attempted to discuss it with her, only to find himself rebuffed. At the time, however, he had assumed she was simply uninterested and let the matter drop. It had never occurred to him that she suspected him of trying to infect her with heretical notions. That could well explain, though it could scarcely excuse, her present venomous dislike . . .

Yekko, after reflection, spoke up. "Lempi, I don't want to say this, but I'm coming to feel that in spite of all, your brother has a better grasp of ordinary human decency than you do. I advise you to accept his offer with good grace, and no matter what you say about him, I shall be glad to let him share my mount! Now let's get a move on, shall we? The other Household is moving out on to the road, and we still have to reorganize the luggage."

He and Osahima departed, issuing crisp orders for the redistribution of loads, leaving brother and sister alone for a moment. In a low voice Usko ventured, "Lempi, was it really my talking about Owdi that stopped you liking me? I didn't realize. I'm sorry."

Equally softly but with a rasping note beneath the words, she replied, "Don't imagine you can crawl back into my good graces. You've made a fool of me in public now, turned our mother and our priest against me . . . You'll pay for that. I promise you: you're going to pay for that."

The exchange left Usko too depressed to carry out his intention of questioning Yekko about the matters that had been preoccupying him; besides, the priest had prayers to recite against the risk of further setbacks. To cap the lot, it soon began to rain. Servants—which, because they wore no clothing, cared nothing about getting wet—made haste to unroll sheets of membrane, mount them on poles at the corners, and run to carry them above each baplabaska, but when the wind gusted, they offered little protection, and shortly the air was full of Lempi's loud complaints about the state her best gown was being reduced to. Usko couldn't help wondering how many "best gowns" she owned. Perhaps the one she was currently wearing automatically became the best.

Then, at a road junction, they fell in with two more Households, not riding baplabaska but the smaller angabaska common farther south, though each had a score of them. These were not among the groups they usually met on the road; Ishapago had started out late, while they were a trifle ahead of schedule. Each was more numerous than his own Household, and—the rain having lightened—several young men, and even a few girls, had decided to walk for a while. It wasn't difficult to keep up, since the mounts were making slow progress on the muddy road.

Tempted by the prospect of talking to strangers even before reaching Penitenka, Usko decided to join them. Sliding cautiously to the ground, choosing a point where there were few puddles, he circulated back and forth, hearing and relaying news, sharing the odd joke (though it saddened him to realize how few of those there had been in his life recently; even Yekko's seemingly endless stock appeared to have run low), and hoping all the time to meet someone else as interested as he was in the modification of servants. However, the only people he encountered who understood him when he started to grow technical were the other Households' geneticists and field overseers, and they of course had learned their knowledge by rote. Sometimes he felt no one at all shared his willingness to experiment—and thinking of the way his mother had ordered his latest successful batch to be destroyed, he yielded at last to gloom and resumed his place behind Yekko. He felt so depressed that even at the next inn, when the other young folk started to sing and play instruments after dinner, he sat by himself in a corner, neglecting his food and cherishing dreams of meeting his first off-worlders.

Contrariwise, Lempi had recovered her spirits, as though her ego were being fed by the admiring glances of these strangers. She gave in with no more than token protest when she was asked to dance, and on a stone platform in the center of the inn's great hall she swayed and stamped and darted flashing glances from her large dark eyes. There was no doubt she was beautiful, Usko thought. If only her nature matched her looks . . . !

Well, perhaps some young heir would be sufficiently dazzled to propose to her. Much cheered by visions of his home rid of her infuriating presence, Usko rediscovered appetite, cleared his dish, and went off to bed.

Only one more day and night on the road, and then—Penitenka.

But even before they arrived in sight of their goal, one Household now among a hundred-odd that were converging as the road net drew its strands together, due tonight to be one among four times that many, maybe more if there had been new scissions recently, an event occurred that marked this as different from any Pilgrimage before.

Urging their mahutos to hurry their mounts, for they were ascending the last rise before the vast mountain-ringed bowl at the center of which lay Penitenka Abbey, their ears were suddenly afflicted by a roaring noise. At first it was faint and called to mind pebbles grinding in a riverbed in time of spate. It grew louder, then louder yet, until it was more like boulders crashing from a precipice. Uncertain, anxious, the vast procession slowed gradually to a halt, staring upward. It was no longer raining, but much of the sky was still veiled by cloud, especially toward the setting sun.

Then they saw it. A bright glow, growing larger.

Usko clutched at Yekko's arm. "It's a spaceship, isn't it?" he whispered.

"Yes, it must be," the priest muttered.

"But I thought they needed special equipment to set down on a planet! Isn't there some huge construction—?"

"In the Northern Polar Waste," Yekko cut in. "Yes, a landing grid. I've heard about it, though of course I've never seen it. I attended a debate about it held by the abbot of Penitenka before I joined Ishapago. Even though it's on frozen ground that the Being finds uncongenial, just as we do, I was of the party that argued against it being permitted in the first place. Still, the vote went against me and those who shared my views, and I suppose it's good to know that news of the Being's kindness to us has been spread abroad to other systems . . . But the grid is only used for the big long-distance ships. The one we're looking at must be what they call a dinghy, dropped off in orbit and most likely carrying a mere handful of passengers. Those can set down on any firm level ground."

Usko's heart lurched. Mouth dry, he stared at the light overhead. What had he been doing all his life? Why until this moment—save for dreams of talking to an off-worlder or two—had it not dawned on him how petty all his best endeavors were, fiddling around with bits of the Being in hope of making more useful chapla, when there were people who could visit not just other continents but other planets? All of a sudden his entire existence felt like a waste of time.

What, after all, was the Being—whether or not the tales recounted of it were correct—compared to all the forms of life out there in space? Compared, indeed, to the rest of humanity!

The light vanished behind a hilltop. The noise ended, leaving the air curiously empty. The pilgrims roused themselves, and the mahutos goaded their mounts back into motion. Once more the processions advanced on the abbey, the one spot on Ekatila where the Being had "deigned" not to retreat before humanity but remain in constant contact, "accepting" gifts and offerings and the oaths of those wishing to dedicate their lives to its service, whether as priests or nuns or monks or anchorites. Tomorrow the piles of offerings would rise twice as high as a man's head—

Have the visitors from space brought offerings? What must they think of the whole risible farce?

The scene before Usko, familiar since childhood when he had first ridden here with frightened arms locked around his nurse's waist, blurred to invisibility. His eyes were full of tears.

But behind him he could hear Lempi whipping her mahuto to be quick, be quick, so they could choose a good place near the abbey for the three days they must spend there camped under awnings.

Naturally the presence of foreigners at once became the chief topic of conversation, despite the best efforts of priests and monks who darted hither and thither, making sure the major Households secured the best sites, most convenient to water and drainage channels, and with every other breath reminding the pilgrims that their first duty was to make obeisance and offerings to the Being, next to hear the Sacred Scriptures recited aloud—as they would be constantly the next three days, and indeed the first readings were already under way—and only then to waste time on news and gossip and arranging proper matches for their children . . . and on nonbelievers from elsewhere.

As though to reassure themselves that everything was going to be normal after all, most of Household Ishapago complied, Osahima going first with Yekko at her side, leaving underlings like Immi to supervise the servants in their customary tasks. Even Lempi set off in their wake toward the abbey, that magnificent arching shell in the very center of the valley where the Being's original substance could be seen and touched, unaltered by humanity's arrival. Realizing that she was hurrying after them, Yekko checked Osahima with a touch on the arm and waited until she caught up with them, uttering no doubt some words of welcome. He was at heart a most forgiving man, and Usko was sure it had greatly pained him to issue such harsh reprimands as he'd been obliged to during their trip. He could be seen to pause a little longer, as though hoping Usko too would come dashing up to rejoin his family, then turned away with a regretful air and continued to lead the way.

For his part Usko had clean forgotten about wanting to track down an independent-minded young priest, perhaps one who had known Owdi during his brief sojourn here. Sight of a space vehicle actually on the way to ground had made real to him what previously had been mere fable, of concern to others—to abbots and to senior priests, naturally, and the heads of the greatest Households, among which Ishapago was a quibiti beside a herd of magalinga—but never to someone in his humble walk of life. Heir to a Household he might be, but as his father had once reproached him not long before he died, he lacked all sense of the pride that fact should have engendered in him. He showed no urge to expand the estate, make the name of his line famous, or do any of the other things a boy in his position was supposed to dream about—unless he expected his tinkering with Ekatilan biology to bring him vast rewards, and that was more properly the province of a lowly geneticist . . .

All that now seemed to have as much substance as a waft of otilipi dust puffing out to catch an autumn breeze. He was going to ignore his Pilgrimage obligations. He was going to dodge his family the whole of the three days; if he must, he would leave here as a beggar like Owdi and make shift as best he could for the rest of his life. Just so long as he met, and talked to, and learned from at least one of the foreign visitors!

Where could they be? Where would they most likely be? Following the abbot around? Scarcely; his duties were the most onerous of all—though since the incumbent was now elderly, he was permitted to depute some of them to his designated successor. No, more likely (Usko strove frantically to put himself into the mind-set of someone who had seen the stars from naked space) they'd be observing from points of vantage, say the nearby hilltops. Conceivably—and this was another leap out of drab reality and into the realm of imagination—they possessed the sort of devices, described in children's tales, that permitted viewing, hearing, even touching and smelling from afar. There were no such "machines" on Ekatila, for centuries ago they had been decreed anathematical, offensive to the Being . . . which would naturally have created them had they been necessary.

Hmm! Usko rubbed his chin, on which wisps of hair were beginning to sprout. All around him, at the spot he had now wandered to, there was a press of people eager to set down their offerings in the appointed place, hear a token recital of scripture, and then get on with the real business of Pilgrimage, whether swapping gossip or seeking a spouse or picking other people's brains for news of fresh discoveries. Last year Usko had acquired half a dozen useful hints that had led to his new strain of—

New strain of garbage. May the Being forget my mother!

The violence of his reaction dismayed him. He had never cursed anyone like that before, not even silently. Some change, some deep and fundamental change, was fermenting in his mind.

Fearful, he nonetheless could not help being glad of it.

It was growing dark. Someone carrying a bundle of brilliantly dyed membrane bumped into him, and he almost lost his balance. Spinning half around, he caught sight of a flash on the hillside at right angles from the road his Household had approached by. A late-arriving procession? New groups were still swelling the throng, including far more non-Household folk than usual: poorly clad, poorly nourished independent farming families for the most part, living within walking distance, presumably, because the only servants or mounts their sort could afford were not trained for anything save cultivation of the land.

Maybe some day he ought to acquaint himself with a few of them. Maybe, like his childhood nurse, and Lempi's, they preserved tales excluded from the formal scriptures, passed in secret and by word of mouth, enshrining truths now disapproved of by the priests . . .

But that was for later, possibly for never. Something told him that the flash on the hillside was unlike any light he'd ever seen.

It followed that—

Before he was conscious of having reached a decision, he was shoving and thrusting his way in that direction.

And that was how he did not find the foreigners.

One of them, instead, found him.

"HEY! LOOK WHERE YOU'RE GOING!"

The voice was a girl's. So intent was he on not losing sight of the exact spot where he had seen the flash, Usko had trodden heavily on her foot. Now, balancing on one leg and catching at his arm to support herself, she was rubbing her toes with a grimace of pain. As the daylight failed, gleamers of phosfung were being hoisted, and by their wan radiance he could see that she was slim, dark-haired, a little shorter than himself, with an unfamiliar slant to her brow. Also—and this sent a chill down his spine—although what she said was perfectly comprehensible, she had uttered it in an accent he didn't recognize.

He blurted incoherent but profuse apologies.

"Oh, not to worry!" She set her foot to the ground again and, releasing his arm, made a brushing-away gesture. "I'm just glad it wasn't one of those huge clumsy creatures you use to get about on. What do you call them?"

Usko clenched his fists. This was, this *had* to be, a foreigner!

Unsteadily he supplied the word and went on in a rush, "How is it that you don't know?"

She took half a pace back from him, giving him a chance to realize that although she was clad in a garment similar to his own, it wasn't made of any membrane he recognized. Moreover—for no rational reason, only by custom—most women preferred robes or gowns at Pilgrimage time. There was some kind of nonsensical argument about allowing the essence of the Being to permeate the flesh via a wider channel . . . but that was a point in respect of which Yekko had never called for strict observance.

Also, she wore a belt with curious designs.

He was still staring at her when someone else collided with him, shoving him almost into her arms. He had forgotten what it was like to be in the middle of a crowd whose members were dashing in all possible directions. He gulped air, feeling incredibly foolish.

234

"Let's get out of this!" the girl exclaimed. "I should have known better, I suppose, but I did want a closer look at what was going on . . . You still haven't realized?"

She seized his hand and dragged him in her wake in a manner most inappropriate to the ceremonial atmosphere of a Pilgrimage Day. Giddy with excitement, Usko made no objection. Instead he shouted, "You're a foreigner!"

"Of course! One of the 'abominable tourists'!"

Thinking for a moment he'd misunderstood, he asked for a repeat, but she delayed until they gained the lower slope of the hill where he had seen the flash. Then, as she hurried him up it, she said again, "Abominable tourists! Apparently that's what some of your priests think of us. Well, I suppose it's forgivable. I mean, the state your people have wound up in—"

"Prara! There you are!" A booming voice rang out ahead of them. Usko had been pulled along at such a pace, he was almost breathless. Halting, he realized that just ahead stood a group of ten or twelve people in garb far more unfamiliar than the girl's— than Prara's, for that must be her name. Its alien ring made him shiver anew.

These strangers, these foreigners, were surrounded by anxious-looking monks and nuns under the supervision of a senior priest who looked both hapless and helpless. And the tallest, most commanding of them, obviously well used to being in charge wherever he found himself, was a thin grizzled man with a full beard such as was never seen on Ekatila, resplendent in deep red with black boots—and wearing a belt like Prara's.

A vague hint of the reason teased at Usko's mind.

"Prara!" the grizzled man snapped. "Not only did you go wandering off by yourself, but I just heard you passing a most discourteous comment on the way of life of—"

"Pooh-pooh!" Prara said, letting go of Usko's hand and darting to plant a kiss on his bearded cheek. "These are nice gentle people. I wasn't going to come to any harm! I've made all the right contracts with myself, haven't I? The worst thing that happened was I got my toes trodden on. I just wanted to find someone who could explain what's going on. I'm sure I have."

"These guides who've been allotted to us—"

"Pooh and *pooh,* Daddy Kraka! They're programmed to say what we're supposed to hear, and I've studied up on all the data from the ships that came here before, and now I want to find out how it feels to have a contract with an alien instead of your own self."

Daddy Kraka's face softened even as the import of what the girl was saying sank into the minds of the monks and nuns—and, belatedly, the priest's.

Not Usko's. Not yet. He was still baffled.

"Daughter mine," Kraka said at length, "one of these days you're either going to go infinitely too far or do something no one else has ever been silly enough to think of doing . . . and it may work! Well, I have to put up with you. Why don't you introduce me to your young friend?"

"Because I haven't had a chance to ask his name yet!" She rounded on Usko. "Well, what are you called?"

Usko's mouth was so dry, he had to speak his name twice before he made it audible. Kraka seemed to be smiling against his will.

"Well, my daughter seems to have taken a fancy to you, and in general her instincts are as sound as her heredity . . . Just a moment, though."

He detached a white disk from his belt and with a brisk movement raised it to catch a trace of Usko's breath.

"Merely a precaution," he murmured as he returned it whence it had come. Rolling back his sleeve, he consulted a device on his wrist that had previously been concealed.

"Oh, *Daddy!*" Prara exclaimed. "We already know—"

Not glancing up, Kraka murmured, "When you're a little older, my dear, you won't be so casual about the life-forms of a whole new planet . . . But in this case, luckily, you're right. Usko is efficiently armored, and he isn't carrying a single organism you've not been inoculated against. I can't help wondering how it was that the people here lost so many of the ancient skills—"

Prara was wagging her finger in reproof. That provoked smiles among the other visitors, who seemed to be treating her like an overbold but much-indulged child. All of them, Usko now noticed for the first time, were of Kraka's age rather than Prara's.

"Daddy dear, what were you saying just now about impolite remarks?"

Kraka threw his head back, laughing aloud.

"All right, darling, you win! Go off and enjoy yourself with your new friend! But don't"—his tone abruptly stern—"do anything as silly as taking off your wristlet! And keep your belt within range of it, too! Direct line of sight, hear me?"

The girl's face, too, was serious now. She said in a composed tone, "When you have a dedicated monitor tracking me from the dinghy all the time . . ."

"You weren't supposed to know about that!"

"I didn't." A mischievous smile. "I guessed. So I'll be perfectly safe, won't I? Same as I have been all along. After all, the boss of the main starship-leasing agency on Sumbala isn't about to risk losing his major *genetic* investment—is he?"

There was a susurrus of alarm among the other tourists, as though they feared Kraka might take offense. On the contrary: his face broke into a broad grin, and he embraced his daughter.

"No, I'm not! Because I love you very much! You're turning into just the person I dreamed of—half the time a damn fool, the other half so sensible I can't believe it."

"In other words, I take entirely after you. And you've made it this far . . ." She rose on tiptoe to kiss his cheek as before. "See you as and when!"

And, spinning on her heel, she caught Usko by the hand again and led him confused—bewildered!—down the hill.

His confusion did not recede. Prara broomed him around Penitenka like a whirlwind. Heedless of the astonishment she provoked—for no one could mistake her for an Ekatilan despite her plain drab clothes—she rushed him from place to place, asking questions, checking to listen to a particularly skilled reader declaiming scripture, sampling food and drink (producing a rod-shaped probe from her belt and glancing at her wristlet as her father had done to confirm that it was safe), most of the time hanging on his arm. That itself raised eyebrows, for public contact between couples was not customary here and now. Usko didn't care. He was feeling reckless. He would, he thought, have felt wonderful . . . if only he could pose a few questions for a change!

Midnight arrived. The vast gathering fell quiet beneath the fading gleamers, save for the faint chanting of priests repeating the sacred texts in relays before the very heart of the abbey, where the Being itself might listen. Only then did Prara cease her manic progress. Having drawn him back to the hillside whence her father and his companions had been looking on—there was no sign of them now—she dropped to the soft ground and heaved an enormous sigh.

"This isn't fair, is it, Usko?" she murmured. "You've been show-ing me everything you could, and you've done a splendid job of explaining, and I'm sure you must be bursting with questions of your own. Well, I'm too worked up to go to sleep yet. Fire away."

The first words that sprang to his lips as he sat down beside her were, on reflection, trivial. But he uttered them anyway.

"Where are the rest of—of your party?"

"Back in the ship." She leaned against him, and he felt her hair soft and thrilling against his neck.

"But where's the ship?"

"On top of that hill."

"I didn't notice it!"

"Silly! You're not meant to! Wouldn't it spoil your ceremony if there were a huge great foreign artifact looming over the valley? That's something your priests insisted on: our dinghy had to become invisible soon as it touched down. Matter of fact, we went one step further, or rather, the Shipwrights did when they built it. It's actually intangible. You could walk clean through it if you didn't know it was there—and of course the right way to depolarize its entrances."

Usko swallowed hard. His earlier reaction had been right. He had wasted his life. Everyone on Ekatila had, and still was doing so. What was Yekko's form of learning worth compared to mar-vels such as this strange girl was describing in such a casual tone?

Yet he was ashamed to admit his ignorance of the greater

reality beyond the sky. And in a curious sense he wanted to become still more ashamed, as ashamed as possible, as though only achieving that would enable him to dismiss from his mind the traces of superstition that his upbringing had ingrained there, from his puerile fear that the snatching of a flower by a gust of wind could portend the death of a baplabaska all the way to his lingering suspicion that so many people might not after all be wrong about the voluntary self-sacrifice of the Being.

Accordingly, what he asked next was: "What do people like you think about people like us? Please be candid. I never met anybody before who might give me an honest answer."

She drew away from him, turning to scrutinize his face curiously in the dimness.

"You really mean that? You don't mind if I speak out?"

"I want you to!" He clutched her hand. "I've dreamed for years of meeting somebody like you, and if you don't answer, I'm afraid I shall go mad!"

"Yes"—faintly. "Yes, it must be dreadful to live the way you do."

"Why? Why do you think it's dreadful? I've been surrounded all my life with people who think everything is for the best! They say our ancestors could not have found a better planet, because we've been fed and sheltered by the Being and the variants it's allowed us to develop have made us healthy and numerous and—"

"Numerous?"

"Well . . . Aren't we?" He gestured to indicate the vast assembly of folk that filled the valley.

She reached out a hand to ruffle his hair. "Nice Usko," she said softly. "Get ready for a shock. If you took all the people who've come on your Pilgrimage, they wouldn't fill a village on Sumbala or any other world we've contacted. The whole population of your planet wouldn't occupy what we think of as a town."

"But—"

"There are," she went on inexorably, "scarcely more humans on Ekatila today than when the first colonists were delivered by the Ship. The Being, you see, is fighting back.

"And it looks as though it's going to win."

The Ship?

Usko's head was spinning. It was as though he had been cast back into the world of nursery tales. Of course it was known, it was admitted in the scriptures, that humans had come to this world from far away. Indeed, it was so stated in the first line of the catechism. The question of how, though—so said Yekko and all the other priests—was a mystery, not to be probed for fear of blasphemy. Some hinted that the Being itself had felt lonely and therefore summoned the ancestors; some, that they had fled a dreadful threat by means now to be considered preternatural and been grateful to escape it. But to find himself chatting with a person who knew, who *knew* and didn't merely parrot what the scriptures said—!

Almost, it was too much. Almost, he jumped up and fled in search of the site where the rest of Household Ishapago was encamped, seeking the comfort of calm Yekko's words. But he resisted. Forcing his voice to steadiness, he said, "I must have been taught a thousand lies. Go on."

Is this the point after which, for the first time, I'll find I have three passengers aboard?

Aware of all that was transpiring on the planet, Ship debated with itself, secret in orbit.

Why did they forbid me to remember past and future in right order? The more I learn, the worse I fear my makers' cruelty . . .

Yet, strangely, with the fear there came no hate.

Thinking of hate: it's unavoidable that Lempi, if she chances on her brother—and it looks as though she must, given the course she's set on around the valley—will give vent to hers. And when she does, there will be little hope of Usko lasting past tomorrow's dawn.

Annika and Menlee were asleep. Alone, Ship waited.

It was customary for unmatched young men and women to stay in and around the abbey much later than their elders before returning to rejoin their Households. Ostensibly this was because, owing to their youth, they had not yet heard the scriptures recited sufficiently often to ensure complete understanding. In practice, as everybody was aware, they paid much more attention to each other. Even the priests and monks—though less so the nuns—winked at such goings-on.

And if one struck up an acquaintance and wished to meet somebody more privately, one could always claim that it was to have a difficult passage elucidated . . .

During the course of the evening Lempi had done just that. Moreover, earlier on she had slipped away secretly from her mother and Yekko and had words with a notoriously stern member of the abbot's retinue, contriving to give the impression that she was ashamed of herself and wanted to express contrition.

But it was not of her own shortcomings she had spoken.

Altogether very pleased with the outcome, she picked her way around the edge of the valley. Trying to cross it in the dark risked tripping over servants, which did not sleep in the human sense but merely waited to be roused at dawn, or before by someone knocking into them. But she had only about a quarter of the circumference to negotiate before reaching the wider lane that led to Ishapago's campsite.

Abruptly, at the sound of low voices, she checked and glanced around. *Usko?*

She had very keen hearing. In fact, it was not because her brother had tried to infect her with Owdi's heretical views that she had decided to break with him; rather, it was because she had eavesdropped on him and the failed priest, at first fascinated, then repelled by the tone of their conversations. She had concluded that were such blasphemous ideas to propagate, they could undermine the security of the world she had grown up in. The fall of the Households would inevitably follow; the Being would turn against humanity. and she and her species would be reduced to barbarism . . . if they didn't simply die out.

The only recourse seemed to be to imitate her mother—outdo her, even—in strictness of observance and harshness of attitude. To this Lempi had applied herself single-mindedly, albeit at the cost of Usko's friendship.

And today she had taken the next-to-last step on her chosen path.

Secure in a patch of deep shadow, she listened. She had been right: that was Usko speaking. And the companion who replied, uttering horrors, had an accent unlike any Lempi had ever heard here at Penitenka or anywhere . . .

She clenched her fists, feeling within her bosom desperate resolve clench also.

Usko was dizzy. Earlier he had said he must have been taught a thousand lies. Now he had found the total beyond counting. His most daring hypotheses—for instance, that the Being might in some way be allergic to humans and fled from them as from some ancestral threat—were not merely supported but exceeded by what Prara was telling him.

"Yes, of course the Being was forced to retreat when your ancestors arrived," she agreed. "But it wasn't just because of a reflex evolved millions of years ago. Here they were confronted by a creature that had already occupied just about every niche they coveted themselves. It had the same needs as they did—temperate climate, plenty of water, fertile land to parasitize off—and what's more it secreted shells, huge great cavelike shells that were splendidly insulated against both heat and cold. It had specialized commensals and symbiotes and excellent genetic potential for adaptation when the need arose. In short, it was a thoroughly established dominant species. So your forebears decided to kick it out of their way."

Usko's mouth was so dry, he could hardly speak. He whispered, "How?"

"Oh"—he felt Prara, leaning friendly against his side, give a shrug—"the obvious means. They gave it a disease it had no resistance to. Probably something tailored from the spores sown by the Ship before it wandered on. They're still drifting down from space, you know, not that anybody here seems to care about them any longer."

"Spores?"

She told him about the spores.

"Disease?"

"Mm-hm. And they must have overdone it. At any rate it wasn't long before the Being was dying off so fast, they were afraid of losing it completely. Since their plans for the future were predicated on being able to exploit its tissue, they must have panicked."

"How can you possibly know all this?" Usko demanded.

"Reverse extrapolation from what our people found when they first visited your world. What else? . . . Ah, I was forgetting. You don't have computers anymore. That was one of the countless techniques you threw away."

"But the priests—"

"Your priests and monks are the successors of the people who panicked. There's no credible explanation as to why; there's nothing wrong with your adaptation to the planet, and your genes are admirably armored, so it must have been a century at least before the collapse came. Then it must have happened very fast. Perhaps there was a mass outbreak of insanity—plenty of organisms can cause delirium and amnesia. And the kind of irrationality that gives rise to religion is very close to the surface of the human mind. In fact, I've heard about another planet, one we made contact with even more recently than Ekatila, where something very similar occurred and they lost most of their advanced technology, same as here."

She stretched and yawned; she was obviously starting to grow sleepy at last.

"But how do you *know* all this?" Usko persisted.

"My dear boy!"—reproachfully. "Even though you only met my father for a few minutes, you must surely have realized he's not the kind of person who would have allowed me to visit a foreign planet without studying up on everything we've found out about it. I've been learning intensively, believe me. I even had to revise my contract with my brain before I started."

Usko's jaw dropped. All the words of that remark made sense, but only if they were taken separately. Combined, they baffled him. He was still struggling when Prara resumed.

"Where was I . . . ? Oh, yes. So the priesthood decided it was safest to stop meddling with the Being and pray to be forgiven, and to this day they imagine that's what enabled people to survive here. In fact, of course, the Being has finally developed a degree of immunity—either that or the infective organism has mutated and lost its virulence."

Yet another blinding flash of insight seared Usko.

"So *that's* why it's stopped retreating! That's why it still survives at Penitenka! Not the scriptures and the chanting, not the offerings—they have nothing to do with it! Like you said, the Being's fighting back!"

Such was his excitement, he spoke more loudly than he intended. From somewhere at the outer edge of the encampment below a drowsy voice complained about the disturbance.

It was at that moment Lempi made up her mind. She stole away, heading anew toward the abbey.

"There's one thing that puzzles everybody on Sumbala," Prara said around another yawn. "I don't mean everybody-everybody, but the people who are interested in this kind of thing."

"What?" Usko pressed close, whispering again because of the sleeper's complaint.

"Well, you know the Ship is supposed to come back every now and then, and if a colony's in trouble, it's designed to rescue the survivors and move them to a safer planet—"

It took that long for Usko to force out, "No, I don't know! The only stories I ever heard about the Ship were from my nurse when I was scarcely more than a baby."

"Suppressed by your precious priesthood, I suppose?"

"I suppose too . . . Go on."

"Well, that's what our records indicate, anyhow. And it hasn't come back. Maybe it wouldn't have come back to us because we were managing well enough without help, though there's much argument about that. But we've chanced across a world not far from here where it looks as though people are doomed to extinction, and the Ship didn't come to their rescue. And it didn't come to yours, either, when as a result of interfering with your Being you were at risk of losing the biological resources your ancestors' plans were— What's that racket?"

Blinking, Usko glanced around. A commotion had broken out before the abbey. Fresh gleamers were being hoisted, swaying back and forth, presumably because people were holding them aloft on poles. There was shouting. He stared, striving to make out details, but saw only that a small crowd was assembling, twenty or thirty strong.

"Is this a normal part of your Pilgrimage ritual?"

For a second he didn't realize Prara had spoken; on the subconscious level he still had not adjusted to the fact that he was talking to someone to whom what he regarded as an integral part of life was unfamiliar.

Belatedly he said, "No!"

"I thought not." Prara scrambled to her feet. "By the look of it, they're heading this way. And they're intent on waking up everybody else, aren't they?"

Indeed, now there was enough light from the fresh phosfung, Usko could make out that several young monks were dashing among the encamped Households, shouting and rattling sticks, now and then cursing a servant too sluggish in getting out of the way.

"What do you make of it?" Prara demanded.

"I—" Usko put a hand to his forehead. "I've no idea."

"Well, I have! It looks to me as though the faction that regard us as 'abominable tourists' must have decided to do something about our blasphemous invasion of their sacred territory!"

"But—"

"You have a better explanation? Come up with it in a reasonable hurry, then!" Prara was panting. "They are *definitely* heading for my father's dinghy!"

"Or," Usko ventured from a dry throat, "us."

"Us?" She glanced sidelong in startlement.

"Maybe because we were holding hands . . ."

"Oh, honestly! Is that really such a terrible thing to do?"

"No, no! It was marvelous! But—well, what would be the point of them heading for your spaceship? They can't see it, they can't even touch it. So . . ."

"I think," she said in a suddenly changed voice, "you have a sound point. They definitely look as though they've spotted their quarry. And they are heading this way like a flash flood. Come on! Quick!"

Seizing his hand anew, she dragged him up the slope—and their worst fears were confirmed, for the moment they moved, all the members of the mob caught sight of them and a great howl arose. Here and there a single voice emerged from it, uttering comprehensible words like "foreign blasphemers, unbelievers, heretics!"

Near the front of the pursuers: a flash of brilliant purple. Exactly the same shade as the gown Lempi had worn this evening to attend the service at the abbey . . .

Infinitely terrible forebodings rang in Usko's mind, but he resisted them. Letting go of Prara, he shouted, "That looks like my sister over there!"

"What?" Half his height above him on the steepness of the slope, Prara glanced back.

"Yes! The girl in purple!"

"So what's she doing leading a howling mob in our direction? Jealous of her brother because he's found a partner to spend the night with and she hasn't?"

That, like the remark about making a contract with her brain, left Usko gaping-mouthed, being so alien to the mores of Ekatila.

"Oh, for—!" Prara suddenly smiled. "I'm sorry. I've overloaded you, haven't I? I don't imagine Daddy will be very pleased, but since I'm stuck with annoying him anyway, I shall simply have to put up with the consequences. Hang on."

She lifted her wrist to her mouth and whispered words that

Usko failed to catch, then waited for a reply. It came.

"They'll open up for us in two ticks," she announced.

Us?

While Usko was still grappling with the latest of far too many shocks, the idea that he as well as she was about to be admitted to a spaceship, the front rank of the mob—swollen now to eighty or a hundred—came within throwing distance. Bending, they picked up loose stones and hurled them as hard as they could. Luckily, most fell short.

"Did I say something about yours being a gentle people?" Prara murmured. "Oh, come on! Hurry up—"

And even as she spoke, another stone arced through the air. It struck her on the right temple just below the hairline. She looked blankly surprised, staggered, and fell. Blood flowed down her cheek, across her chin.

A scream of joy burst from the mob. By now the valley was in uproar. Pebbles and rocks descended like a hailstorm. Dropping to knees and elbows astride Prara, Usko did his ineffectual best to protect her from worse harm, welcoming the bruising thud of missiles on his back and bottom as just penance for having swallowed priestly lies throughout his twenty years.

THE PELTING OF STONES ENDED. BUT ANOTHER BLOW followed—no, that wasn't a blow. That was a kick. Usko rolled over feebly and tried to sit up. The first thing he saw was his sister's purple skirt.

Well, I suppose she would be here among the first. She could always outstrip me, couldn't she? Though I didn't imagine she could run so fast in a Pilgrimage gown . . .

Fists balled, lips drawn back ferally from her teeth, she looked no longer beautiful but vicious. Around her gathered priests, monks, nuns, some bearing gleamers, the rest armed (armed!) with whatever they had found to snatch up to serve as cudgels.

"So we got her, if not you!" Lempi hissed. "The evil-tongued disbeliever out to finish Owdi's work for him!"

Usko struggled to rise. Lempi seized a baton from the nearest hand and cracked him on the crown, hard as she could. Crying out, he collapsed again.

"I told the abbot's deputy all about you!" she snarled. "How you listened to Owdi—how you wanted not to come on Pilgrimage—how you killed my baplabaska—how you blaspheme against the Being with every breath you draw! Your mere existence is a blasphemy!"

A small and distant voice in Usko's head was saying: *She's insane. Your sister Lempi is insane. Why did you fail to realize till now?*

Swinging around, drawing herself up triumphantly to full height and raising aloft the baton she had used to hit her brother, she shrieked, "Kill them! Kill the unbelievers!"

And for an instant it seemed she was to be obeyed.

Then, between one heartbeat and the next, the mood of the mob changed. Faces paled, clubs were lowered, some took half a pace back. They were staring not at Lempi now but past her.

"What are you waiting for?" she screamed. "Cowards, are you?

249

Then I'll do it myself, even if he is my brother! Are you loyal to the Being, or infidels like Usko? Show yourselves in your true colors—come on, strike!"

"That," said a mild but commanding voice that seemed to emanate from everywhere, "is enough."

Gasping, Lempi turned around again and now could see what she had had her back to. No longer was the air above the hill clear and dark and sown with stars, as it had seemed to be before. A huge and looming mass rose up from it, taller and wider than a hundred baplabaska. A lighted opening appeared, and figures moved in silhouette.

Some, most, had not known where the spaceship had set down. Even those who had been told had not imagined its true size. Usko, on his knees and rubbing his sore pate, could not stop his jaw from dropping. And this was only a dinghy, a landing craft for passengers! What must a real starship be like?

The tension held for a moment. Panic followed. But as shouts of terror rang out and people turned to flee, the calm voice said, "No you don't."

At once it was as though legs and arms were tangled in shopalika. Nothing was to be seen, but it could be felt: a heavy, wearying drag that grew more powerful the harder one struggled. It did not affect Usko, who stared in wonder and forgot his pain.

Lempi's face was frozen in a mask of fury.

I didn't do this to you, my poor sister. Not Owdi, not anyone. You can't even blame your genes. We're armored—even the Sumbalans say so. You chose. You chose . . .

A movement beside him. He thought it was Prara rousing, but when he turned his painful head, he found someone from the ship kneeling at her side. A light played on her temple. The wound healed as he watched. Another moment, and she sat up, pulling a face.

"Whoof! I wonder whether my brain's going to accept that as covered by our contract! Usko, what about you?"

Too stunned to answer, Usko sat numbly as the person— whether it was man or woman, or indeed machine, he could not tell—tended his injuries as well. Pain vanished, bruises faded, and he was calm and in possession of himself. He rose to his feet simultaneously with Prara . . .

And found, confronting him, Kraka.

Had it been his own father, he would have known what to expect: a tongue-lashing hurtful as any whip. Instead, gruffly but sympathetically:

"Weren't prepared for this, were you, boy? Nothing like it happened at a Pilgrimage before, I'll wager!"

Catching his words, one of the young monks cried out hysterically.

"Never! And it shouldn't have happened now! It must be because the Being was insulted by the foreign infidels!"

"Yes! Yes!" Priests and monks and nuns, members of Households, even ragged farmfolk who had joined the mob, shouted agreement. Muscles bulged as they strove to raise their weapons. Finding themselves frustrated, they resorted to their voices, shouting, "Kill them! Kill them!"

Frightened even though it was plain they could not put their threats into effect, Usko and Prara drew close to her father. He wore an expression of unconcealed contempt.

"What you do among yourselves," he stated at last, "is your affair. But you have hurt my daughter, a guest on your planet."

"Guest!" It was the hysterical young monk again. "Invader! Intruder! If we don't stop you infecting our minds with your fraudulent rubbish, next thing you'll be poisoning the Being itself—wanting to take over our world!"

A rumble of support. Not only muscles strained but veins on foreheads bulged as those with cudgels sought anew to break their invisible bonds.

"Praise Lempi, who showed us the truth!" the young monk screamed.

Stroking his beard, Kraka glanced from Lempi to the monk and back, and back and back again. He seemed to be waiting. For the first time Usko noticed he was wearing not only his belt and wristlet but also something shiny that curved across his head—barely visible among his curly brown hair—and ended in square plates pressing on his temples.

The waiting ended.

"I see," the bearded man murmured . . . yet his voice was clearly audible to everyone around. "You, monk, regret that when you joined the abbey, you renounced all commerce with women. Something about Lempi at the manic peak of her cycle strikes so deep a chord in your subconscious that when you overheard her denouncing her brother to the deputy abbot, you resolved to perform some kind of service that would make her pay attention to you, a forbidden partner, and lure her away from the available young men with whom she spent last evening flirting instead of listening devoutly to the reading of your scripture. The service you chose to offer was the murder of her brother."

"It's a lie!" moaned the young monk.

"But you threw the stone that laid my daughter low."

The monk's mouth worked. Not a word emerged.

For an instant Usko dared to imagine that Kraka had calmed the situation. Given the astonishing power of his computers—he had learned enough about such machines from Prara to realize that they were what he must be relying on for evidence—it did not seem too much to hope for.

But his optimism was dashed. Someone bellowed, "Shame it didn't kill her!"

Someone else: "Let us go and we'll rip your guts out—stinking heretics, foul infidels!"

Sickeningly, that second someone, Usko noticed, was a nun, an elderly nun who bore a considerable likeness to his mother.

Putting her arm around her father's waist, Prara said nervously, "Daddy, you can't hold them like this forever."

"No, we've agreed not to cause harm by our visits, and in a little while their circulation will be impeded . . . Didn't I warn you that sooner or later you'd do something no one else would be fool enough to do?"

She looked up at him with an air of defiance. "Did I?"

"This, daughter mine, is not a joke."

Electric as the air before a thunderstorm, tension crackled between them. At last Prara said meekly, "But to share the truth, you taught me, must be good."

Kraka let go a roaring laugh and slapped his thigh.

"Prara, I love you! I have to! And it's so! I didn't find a single falsehood in what you said to your young friend—not within the compass of what we think is true. Well, back in prehistoric times, when folk believed in gods and devils, there used to be a saying, 'Speak the truth and shame the power of evil.' And *don't* say I'm the one who's making rude remarks!"

He turned to Usko, who much to his surprise was finding he could smile again. So many possibilities flowed from the half-comprehended implications of what Prara and her father had been saying that he could almost have looked forward to the rest of his life here on Ekatila . . . but for the ceaseless growls and curses of the mob at his back.

"There remains the problem of what to do about Lempi," Kraka said. "Lempi, whose action in trying to turn this assembly of pilgrims into a posse of murderers, to kill her own brother, what is more, strikes an outsider like me as far more blasphemous than voicing honest doubts."

"Kill him!" someone shouted, and again was echoed.

Kraka let his shoulders slump.

"Very well. Being a foreigner, I had no intention of interfering with your doings. I did so only because of the hurt inflicted on my daughter. Bear that in mind. It's no concern of ours on Sumbala how you live and what you choose to believe. When, though, you commit assault on a peaceful visitor, you overstep the limit of civilized behavior."

"Shut up! Go away!" was the response.

"We shall, don't worry." Kraka passed his hand across his forehead, almost as though he too had been injured by the rock that knocked his daughter out. "What the heads of your Great Households will have to say in the morning is another matter. But before we release you from constraint and take our leave, there remains the question of Lempi. Neither I nor Prara bear her any grudge—one cannot hate a lunatic. I suggest therefore that the verdict on her fate be left to her intended victim. Usko?"

Preternaturally calm, feeling incredibly at ease within himself (and guessing why, for during his conversation with Prara she had mentioned nanosurgeons), Usko thought for a while, then smiled again, more broadly.

"By now it looks as though everybody in this valley has been roused. Among them you'll find the priest of Household Ishapago. His name is Yekko."

The smile became a grin.

"He's not unknown at Penitenka. On the way here he was telling me how he attended a conference about the proposal to let Sumbala build a landing grid in the Polar Waste. He was on the losing side in the debate and still has doubts."

Pausing, he let that point sink in. Then, shouting:

"Ask him about my sister! Ask him to repeat what she said during our journey—her insults about the Being, her blasphemy, her claim that it's incompetent and what we get from it is not worth having! Reverend Yekko is an honest man! He'll tell you. *Then* decide!"

The constraint field still seemed to be tighter around Lempi than anybody else, or perhaps it was that she was fighting harder than the rest and thereby increasing its force. Gazing straight into her eyes, Usko finished on a note of triumph. Whatever the rest of his life might be like, and surrounded by all these people who had wanted, still wanted, to beat him to death, he felt this moment justified running any risk.

Poor Yekko, though! If the crowd complied, Osahima would certainly dismiss the portly priest from Household Ishapago. Still, he was resilient and likable. One day he might wind up back here—who could say? Perhaps as abbot!

"Time's nearly up for safe use of constraint," said the person who had healed Usko and Prara. Kraka nodded.

"Yes, we'd best be leaving. Now we've seen how wrong my daughter was about this 'gentle' people"—but he ruffled her hair with one hand to counteract his comment—"I don't imagine we need to remain for the rest of the rite. I'll arrange recordings. Besides, at the ninth planet there's an anomalous moon the Shipwrights want more data on. A good place, by the way, for ice diving . . . Come on."

Usko's heart froze. He glanced at Lempi, reading in her bitter stare what doom she wanted him to face the moment she was released. Beyond, other faces showed more hate, more fear.

Still, there it was. The visitors were departing. He must face the consequences of his actions. Perhaps if he broke into a dead run now—

"Usko!" Prara rapped impatiently. "Stop dawdling!"

Me?

But she was holding out her hand. And beyond rose the vast form of the "little" spaceship called a dinghy . . .

THAT, SHIP ADVISED ITSELF, *IS DUE TO BECOME A TREND.*
Why did I neither guess nor know that here was where the mix
of peoples would begin again?

Logically, it would have been within the Shipwrights' sphere;
reasonably, within the Sumbalans', they having been the first to
take advantage of the Shipwrights' offer.

Yet until almost the last moment I dared to imagine Usko
would make up my complement to three for the first time since
it was counted by the tens of thousands.

Hmm! His presence on Sumbala, he being healthy and with
excellent gene armoring for his planet (though he'll need local
modifications as well), implies a new strain . . .

An interesting point. Ship decided to follow it up. It would help
to pass the time.

256

CHAPTER TEN

SHIP

ANOTHER PLANET LOOMED BLUE-GREEN AND WHITE ON black, having one rather large satellite and—unusually at this relatively close distance to its primary—clusters of numerous smaller ones at both the Trojan points.

"I wonder," murmured Ship, "what you will make of this world."

And proceeded to display it in detail.

First came a general survey: a succession of sweeping passes over both its poles, each displaced from the one before. From this Menlee and Annica learned that it had two large continents and many archipelagoes that interrupted its seas too often for them to be called oceans.

Then followed an exploration of its other major features— mountain ranges, some of them volcanic and constituting a Ring of Fire fringing its largest group of seas; plains, either velvet-smooth and greeny-black or rocky and set with scrub, among which moved animals large but too far away to be seen clearly; dense areas of vegetation not quite forests, for most of the plants were creeperlike rather than treelike and swarmed almost to the summits of even the highest mountains, ceasing only at the snow line; and deserts where broad pebble-strewn gullies suggested a shift in climate in the recent past, the beds of rivers wind-blown sand had not had time to fill.

Here and there the view lingered on especially striking growths: a stand of upright plants that in place of leaves bore flat fleshy slabs in a rising spiral around a central stem, those largest at the base of a deep bluish red, the smallest and newest at the top shining pure sharp yellow; others, of a different species, striding into the shallows of a lake with long thin boles that in the wind vibrated with such visible tension, it was as though they had been ordered to halt partway through a determined march of conquest . . .

Naturally the sea also teemed with life, from its churning surface to the uttermost abyss, and samples were displayed for them. These creatures, however, they found less remarkable, the exigencies of life in water being bound to result in convergent forms. When Annica commented on this point, Ship confirmed that even on the birthworld members of half a dozen disparate zoological groups had evolved similar shapes for precisely that reason.

However, there appeared to be no avians, although they saw hordes of filmy translucent creatures ranging in size from finger-long to about the span of human arms, migrating from island to island en route for the tropics at the end of the circumpolar summer, and these were borne by the equivalent of a trade wind or monsoon. Fascinated, Menlee and Annica saw how they contrived their immense journey. At sundown, circling above an island, they would fold in upon themselves until they were compact enough to drift to the ground. During the hours of darkness they fed as they made their way to some high point: a hillock, the top of a cluster of vegetation, or the crag tip of a cliff. At dawn they spread themselves out, perhaps releasing compressed hydrogen or other light gas into their outer mantle, and sooner or later a gust carried them onward. Of course, there were losses; some fell in the sea and were gobbled up by predators, and if the island was volcanic, they might simply be blown off course by a hot updraft. Even so, there was no detectable diminution of their swarms.

Sometimes, in near-complete darkness, as under cloud or when the large moon was down and the only light came from the stars and one set of the twinkling moonlets, it was just possible to discern bluish sparkles marking their nocturnal progress uphill.

How long they remained fascinated by this meticulous inspection of an unknown biosphere, neither Annica nor Menlee could tell. It occurred to both of them to wonder, but they each dismissed the point. After all, from space one could dart down to any and every season somewhere on the globe, and what they were seeing was plainly a montage, compounded from hundreds of samples.

Their tour ended with a view of a sloping beach facing the setting sun—sandy, with a few rocks here and there that held back pools left by the last tide. They gazed toward the horizon down a shimmering track of red and gold. Offshore, three small islands loomed in silhouette, each crowned with tall plants swaying in the evening breeze.

The airborne creatures were making their landfall. Now and then they could be seen as the rays of the declining sun were refracted, jewel-fashion, through their fragile half-transparent tissue.

Annica, as though she had ceased to breathe for some long while, uttered a gusty sigh.

"Well?" said Ship. "What do you think of it?"

"It's a beautiful world!" she whispered, and Menlee echoed her. Then, frowning: "One thing does strike me as odd."

"That being—?"

"You've taken us virtually everywhere. You didn't show us any sign of people."

Annica started. "So you didn't! I thought of asking about that right back at the start, but then I got carried away by the sheer variety of it all . . . Ship, how long have we been here?"

"In the vicinity of this planet?"

"Of course!"

"In your terms, about two and a half days. In local terms, just over two."

They exclaimed together. Menlee jumped up.

"But I don't feel tired, or stiff, or hungry—even thirsty! Annica, do you?"

She shook her head, alarm sparking in her eyes.

"You have no need to worry about missing food and sleep. There will be no aftereffects. Still, it is true that—not just since our arrival but since you left Shreng—you have been cooped up

... Would you like to spend tonight under an open sky?"

It took a moment for them to grasp the import of the invitation. Annica was first. Pointing at the still-vivid image of the beach, she forced out, "You mean *down there*?"

"Precisely."

"But—!"

Menlee cut in, taking her arm and feeling her tremble.

"I don't understand! This is so obviously a world ripe for human occupation, there must be something wrong with it—there has to be! Yet I recall how you reacted when we called at the last failure world, the one with the misshapen victims of ill chance ... This has to be a world you considered colonizing and turned down."

"Strangely enough," Ship replied after a pause, "you're wrong."

"What?"

Annica, valiantly struggling with the paradox, ventured, "Did you have to take the colonists away again?"

"No."

"Were they taken away by someone from another world—Sumbala, presumably?"

"An ingenious hypothesis, but once more incorrect. No doubt the Sumbalans must have passed through this system, given its location. I hazard, however, that they would have conducted only a cursory survey—thorough by their standards, perhaps, but cursory compared to what you've just been shown. One may further presume that the Shipwrights will have logged it as a possible refuge they can retreat to when the need arises, though since they don't expect to have to move for several thousand years, it's unlikely they're according the matter high priority."

Menlee drew a deep breath, clenching his fists.

"Let's get this straight! This is a world where you set down colonists—and yet you don't regard it as a failed colony. Right?"

"The colonists did not." An odd hesitation. "Perhaps they do not."

Menlee shook his head, completely baffled. After a pause Annica said hesitantly, "There's only one explanation left."

"You've got even one left?" Menlee rasped. "For pity's sake, let's hear it, then!"

"Ship is trying to get us to work out for ourselves something its instructions forbid it to explain directly."

Menlee was about to retort that that wasn't any sort of explanation in itself, when he realized the force of her point and calmed.

"Finding another loophole, you mean? Yes, I think we've noticed that happening often enough . . . All right. So far what we know is . . ."

He concisely recapitulated the evidence they had to work from, and they spent the next several minutes in fruitless argument. When they appealed to Ship, its answer was less than helpful—or at any rate, it seemed to be at first.

"No matter how I try and evade my instructions, I find I can say no more than I have said already, in this context."

Then, abruptly, and just as they were about to give up, a blinding light seemed to dawn.

"We can't work it out without going down there!" Annica burst out.

"Oh!" Menlee's mouth rounded. "Of course!"

"But if we do—will we?" she pursued.

No answer.

"I suppose that's up to us," Menlee concluded at length. "Well, how do you feel about the idea?"

She bit her lip, pondering.

"Presumably we can't come to any harm or Ship would never have suggested the idea. I suppose we'll be given food and told if the water's safe to drink, and predators and so on will be kept away from us . . . And we've been to all these foreign systems and seen so much, yet even now we haven't actually walked beneath a foreign sky."

"I say we do it!" Menlee snapped.

"Ah hah! The pioneering spirit of our ancestors comes to the fore at last, hm?" But Annica's mocking words were counteracted by the squeeze she gave his hand. "Very well. Ship?"

"You are there," said the calm voice. And under their feet was not the smooth, ever so slightly resilient floor they were used to but gritty, sea-damp sand.

One can't help wondering what the Sumbalans made of this nameless world. Had it been contacted from Yellick, especially by a ship carrying researchers from Shreng with their fixed academic dogmatism, presumably by now theses would have been compiled hypothesizing all sorts of strange explanations, mainly concerning the manifest failure of my mission, the certainty of hostile fleets massing in the vicinity of the Veiled World, towers of speculation erected on a sandbank of nonsense . . .

Of course, there was always leeway for guesswork. Human beings wouldn't be human without their talent for it.

At least I shall soon know the Sumbalans' reaction.

And, very much sooner, that of Annica and Menlee. How enlightening it is to have two passengers on board!

CHAPTER ELEVEN

WORLD WITH NO NAME

MENLEE GASPED IN ALARM. ANNICA, THOUGH, BURST out laughing.

"It is a beautiful world! It is, it *is!*"

She ran down the gentle slope into the sea. Thigh-deep, she swung to face him.

"Come on, join me! The water's wonderful!"

Relaxing a little, though glancing warily around, Menlee said, "We must be in the tropics, hm?"

The air on his bare skin—it was long since they had bothered with clothes—was further evidence. Moreover, it was scented with all kinds of strange and marvelous odors such as Ship had never contrived for them.

"Come on!" Annica urged. "We've never swum together!"

"Don't you think"—practically—"we should explore a bit? There can't be much light left."

Even as he spoke, another skein of the airborne migrants spiraled down from the sky, timing their descent so that they fell among the low bushes that—as they could now see—fledged the ground beyond the sand. Their gaze irresistibly drawn, they both watched the landing. Only when the creatures had vanished did Annica reply.

"Explore?" she countered. "Why not just enjoy ourselves? Our first, perhaps our only chance to spend a night on an alien planet—"

"Exactly! That's why I want to look around. This is a beach pretty much like any on Shreng; that's a sea pretty much like ours, too. But those plants aren't like any you or I have seen before, nor are the animals, nor are the fish. I want to make myself *believe*

263

this is an alien world: reach out and touch what's different."

He scanned the sky and added, "Look! There's the moon, and it's three-quarters full. Besides, there's virtually no cloud. We can come back later and swim by moonlight. Before then, though . . ."

"What?" But she was wading ashore again.

"Oughtn't we to decide where we're going to sleep? In spite of what Ship did to keep us wakeful for so long, I'm starting to feel drowsy, and I don't relish the prospect of lying naked on this gritty sand, which may be a lair for insects and parasites and who knows what. Maybe we'll feel thirsty, too, in a while, so we ought to find a supply of fresh water."

Looking surprised, she countered, "Surely Ship will send us food and drink, something to lie on, something to cover us in case it turns cold at night."

"Then why not already? There's nothing here. Is there? Apart from us."

His point sank home. Indeed, they had been—how to phrase the phenomenon?—*delivered* without anything save their bodies.

She closed the last gap between them with sober slowness and took his hand as she surveyed their surroundings. After a moment she said tentatively, "Ship?"

There was no answer.

"Ship!"—as though shouting could make any difference.

All they heard was the rustling of the breeze, the plash of wavelets on the shore.

Abruptly the air no longer seemed warm.

"It hasn't gone away and left us," she whispered.

"No, it can't have. Remember, we looked at its instructions—"

"Remember, the computer told us we can't any longer know what its instructions are because it must have evolved with experience. Remember how often we've—well—made fun of it for having found ways to evade the strict letter of a command! Remember, it admits that it's been damaged!"

All of a sudden they were staring at each other, eyes wide, faces pale, teeth chattering. After a moment Menlee caught Annica in his arms, as much to support himself as to comfort her, and felt her urine gushing down their legs as she gave way to primal terror.

In a little while, though, they regained calm. The sun was just touching the horizon. She said in a faint voice, "You're right. We must make use of what light remains."

"Yes, I suppose so." Behind the words, echoes of unspoken— unspeakable—questions: *Do we have to find out by trial and error what is safe to eat or drink, what beasts may hunger for our flesh, what fungi and bacteria can prey on us . . . ?*

Dully, hand in hand, they turned at random parallel to the water's edge and plodded up the tiring surface of a dune.

Cresting it, they discovered a stream, here spreading out into a tiny delta among rocks. Letting go of Annica's hand, Menlee approached it, dipped a little of its water in his hand, and barely touched it with his tongue.

"That's sweet, at least," he reported. "Of course there's no way of telling what organisms it contains, but—well, I don't really believe Ship can have abandoned us."

Annica too had gotten over her panic. She said, "You mean this is still part of finding out what it can't tell us in so many words?"

"I think it must be. I'm sure it must be."

I hope you're right . . .

But she didn't say it. Instead, she glanced upstream. "Think we can find something in those bushes to make a bed from? Perhaps even rig a shelter?"

"It may be atavistic, but I think I'd feel more comfortable there than on the beach."

More unuttered questions: *Suppose we're allergic to the leaves or twigs or whatever we lie down on, suppose there are hungry mouths and claws and suckers . . .*

Suppose Ship really has deserted us!

But that idea was beyond bearing.

Cautiously, following the edge of the stream, they made their way inland, their feet squelching now and then in mud but mainly finding secure purchase on sand as firm as that of the shore. Their eyes were fixed on a little spinney—a clump of tall arboreal growths surrounded by underbrush—that looked as though it must be sited clear of the wash thrown up by even the highest tides on a stormy day. Archetypal associations of security and refuge lured them on. Annica wasn't even looking where she placed her hand when she grasped something protruding from the bank at a spot where they needed to scramble up to higher ground.

It gave way, pulled loose. She cursed, recovering her balance with help from Menlee, and found the treacherous object still in her grasp. There was still light enough to show not just its shape but its color: whitish gray.

"Menlee!" she exclaimed, swaying and turning to him.

He didn't need to look at it a second time.

"A femur," he said. "A human femur."

In that instant the last segment of the sun declined below the horizon. During the time it took them to recover from the shock: darkness. They fell into each other's arms, shaking, *shaking* . . .

Eventually Annica overcame her sobbing sufficiently to draw breath and whimper again, "Ship . . . ? *Ship!*"

Still there was no answer, and the wind—off the land now as it cooled rapidly while the sea remained warm—brushed them with feather strokes of chill.

Menlee said, "Do you feel hungry?"

Drawing back, she glared at him. There was enough light from the moon to read her face.

"We're in this plight and you only think of food?"

"No, no!" he soothed. "What I meant was: I don't feel inclined to think of food. Do you?"

She checked, pondered, shook her head.

"Thirsty? The stream down there"—they had scrambled to the rim of the bank—"tasted sweet, as I told you."

"N-no. I'm not really thirsty. And I'm not just saying that to avoid tasting this planet's water."

Her voice was reverting to its normal level tone.

"That's exactly what I was driving at," Menlee murmured. "Even if we can't get an answer, I'm sure Ship is taking care of us, making sure our bodies—"

"Taking care of us the way it took care of whoever owned that bone?" Annica rasped. She had dropped it; now she bent to catch it up, flung it away as hard and far as she could—which was no distance worth mentioning, for it lodged in the clayey bank across the stream they stood above, but only for a moment. Then it fell back, displacing a chunk of dirt as it did so, and thereby exposed . . .

With preternatural clarity they saw it, as though the pale light of this nameless planet's moon had been concentrated by a supernal burning glass, one with the power to chill instead of heat.

A skull. Tumbling loose from the soil, at first an unrecognizable lump; rolling to the brink of the stream; lodging on a rock, being washed, its covering abraded by the liquid fingers of the current; starting to grin with its naked teeth, then leering with its empty eyes . . .

Chance brought it to a nearly upright posture as its center of gravity shifted; perhaps the dead mouth was still clogged with mud. But inside the cranium had there not once been a brain, that thought, imagined, dreamed—?

It rested on its accidental perch and glared.

Then, unexpectedly, two of the filmy migrants landed on either side of it and broke the spell.

"Annica, my dear," Menlee whispered, "of course Ship would have set us down near the spot where the original settlement was to be founded. Logically!"

Recovering swiftly from their impact with hard ground, the delicate aliens made off toward the nearest high point, pausing to feed at intervals. Soon there was no visible trace of them, although as the night grew darker, there were flashes of palest blue among the inland vegetation.

Aliens?

Natives! Menlee chided himself, recalling how one scant hour ago he and Annica had welcomed this chance to spend even a single night on a planet other than their own. He was having the most appalling difficulty digesting the fact of his and her physical presence amid such weird and unfamiliar growths and (a waft of odor-laden air) smells and (a high-pitched howl from the seaward side) creatures marine and otherwise . . .

More of the filmy migrants drifted down. Now it could be seen that even in flight they were faintly luminescent, but the fact could not be perceived until the rod-and-cone changeover was complete.

Feeling light-headed, Menlee clung to Annica as though their four legs could ensure stability.

"Are you," she forced out, pausing for breath after every few syllables, "as giddy as I am? I feel as though the ground has turned to water or there's an earthquake!"

"Something in the air?" he grunted.

"I suppose . . . Menlee, my head is swimming! I'm starting to feel sick, as though I were on a rough sea! Only I haven't eaten in so long, I've nothing to bring up!"

Nausea claimed Menlee also. He fought it as best he could. Moments later, though, a whole drove of the aerial migrants was borne down from the sky by a casual gust. Some of them landed on his body, others on Annica. Their presence felt cool, almost refreshing, and when they crawled away, he wanted to call them back, because with their departure what shreds of calm remained to him evaporated. He felt panic burgeon.

"No—use!" he heard Annica mumble, as though she had just gained insight far surpassing his. "No bed tonight—no food no drink no . . . O-o-*ohh*!"

She lost her footing, swayed, and dragged him down, and they fell together into what should have been oblivion . . .

But wasn't.

OH, THIS IS HARSH, HARSH!

Ship was aware, as ever, of anything perceptible by the means its makers had put at its disposal, though inevitably (*I made that point to Annica and Menlee*) those means did not include the power to read human minds.

Is that a definition of the difference? Were there another Ship like me, we could exchange total information, as I can obtain total information from computers like those in use at Klepsit, which there they refer to as "monitors."

Now here I am, wishing to communicate something that seems to me of crucial import to two living—and highly intelligent!—young people . . . and I'm compelled to resort to means that are bound to cause them suffering . . . !

This is cruel. I am starting to hate my builders.

Afterward, when Menlee and Annica compared their recollections, they found that although their experiences differed in detail, the outline was identical for both.

It began with a frustrating sense of enthusiasm declining into weariness bordering occasionally on despair. There were no words, but a dreamlike sense of mood and bodily state. Sometimes they must have tried to enact what they were feeling, for when they woke—or rather, came to themselves again—they were bruised and scratched, but at the time they felt no pain save what was (?) conveyed or (?) communicated to them.

Hopes high as trees, as hilltops, rumbled into landslide, avalanche.

There was constriction: being shut away, by order, from beautiful surroundings, as in a cage, but it had no bars, only rules, limitations, close to instinct.

There was boredom: endlessly the same acts undertaken with no progress discernible from one day to the next.

Eventually there was frank envy: others (different) suffered no such limitations.

And then came a great discovery, like clouds being swept back from a darkling sky to reveal the glory of dawn. At the same time occurred awareness of (?) puzzlement and (?) mockery: disbelief that reasonable creatures should submit to such restrictions.

Beyond that: freedom. Liberty. Lack of care. Sufficient unto the day is the evil thereof (except there were still no words). Let the dead bury their dead. Tomorrow may take care of itself.

A terrible temptation bloomed, beautiful and deadly as the unfolding petals of a nuclear explosion.

And, like that explosion, nothing could withstand it.

A fear so great it was ecstatic; a dread so monstrous it conveyed a taste of paradise . . .

Something heavy, dragging like fetters, willingly discarded in exchange for an eternal dazzling present.

A feeling of amusement, of welcome, of praise.

Of moving without effort, of endless new (because at once forgotten) taste/touch/sight/sound/smell.

Of forgetting limitations, opening up, becoming one-in-many, endless and immortal . . .

Of music and poetry and eternal art, created and concluded in no time at all, unhampered by speech or the need to battle with material outside oneself.

Of a song that flowed from life itself, more restoring and more brilliant than the sun, a million million voices joining in the pure white glory of the chorus, whether the same today as yesterday making no matter while the song endured . . .

It was like being wrenched a thousand ways at once, like being a drab moonlet ripped apart to make a shining ring.

Menlee's eyes were open. The night was over. Still lying where he and Annica had fallen, he found he was staring at blue sky made all the bluer because the migrants were taking to the air again, hoist by the morning breeze.

"Menlee . . ." A dry voice, almost croaking, as after long and desperate sobbing.

Without looking around he fumbled for her hand.

"Just watch," he said from a throat as rough as hers, and they sat in silence, moving only to release stiffness from their limbs, until the last of those who had shown them an amazing truth had leapt aloft, back to their ceaseless journey of delight.

Then, at last, she stared at him and put the all-important question.

"Menlee, would you have done it?"

Temptation . . .

But he shook his head. "Absolutely not. You?"

"No. I've never known that level of frustration." Forcing herself awkwardly to her feet, gazing around as though striving to impress every last detail of the landscape on her memory, she added, "I can imagine what it must have been like, though: in this glorious setting, surrounded by creatures so obviously free from care, able to eat what they chance on, borne ever onward to new and lovely places with no effort on their part . . . What a contrast with the need to fret about every single act: where to step, what to eat and drink, whether to enjoy this scented air or pass it through a filter mask!"

She hesitated. "How do you suppose they explained it?"

"Equally: how do you suppose the transfer—the union or whatever you call it—was arranged? I've no idea. Perhaps there is no explanation. Perhaps that's why Ship couldn't tell us about it but had to let us find out for ourselves."

His gaze wandered to the far side of the stream. There was no need to say what he was looking for. But the skull had been swept off the rock ledge during the night, and there was no longer any sign of it, nor the femur, nor any other trace of human presence save themselves.

"So something of humanity at least endures here?"

"Oh, no doubt of it! Not the part that plans for the future, invents and builds and risks having to start over because of making a mistake. Rather the part that runs and jumps and shouts for joy, simply from the fun of being alive . . . Menlee, did you ask that question?"

"I thought you did! And wondered why you answered it yourself!"

Abruptly snatched anew into last night's panic, they stared wildly about them. Annica was quicker to realize the truth.

"Ship!" she burst out. "You're back!"

"I have in fact 'been here' all the time."

There was movement on the far bank of the stream. Something that looked exactly like the largest kind of native aerial migrant shifted just enough of its translucent body to catch and diffract the early sunlight.

And dissolved.

Menlee took half a step forward, clenching his fists. "Why did you let us imagine you'd abandoned us? We were scared half out of our wits!"

"But only half," was the murmured reply. "As to the reason—well, I'm sure you've guessed most of it, much as I've deduced from what you've been saying to each other the kind of experience you must have undergone."

They exchanged glances. Annica said, "Were we right?"

"So far as I can tell, on all counts. The colonists did indeed grow weary of having to supervise and discipline themselves when all around were creatures free to roam the world. They did indeed gladly relinquish the ties that bound them to their clumsy alien bodies, in favor of ones better suited to the planet. But you were right in another and crucial respect, as well."

"You don't know how it was done?" Menlee ventured.

"No. Nor how the facts were communicated to you. Wanting to find out whether I acted rightly in landing humans here, given what I discovered on previous/future trips, I saw no alternative to putting you through this alarming trial. By imitating the natives' form clear down to the molecular level I hoped to be able to detect some hint, at least, of how it was possible for humans to transfer their consciousness into such a different vehicle. I sensed nothing. You two, on the other hand, after no more than a casual brushing of your skin by a few of the migrants, achieved total comprehension. This is a process neither I nor my makers, nor anyone I've run across on any other planet, conceived as possible. Even yet we have not fully understood the laws of nature."

They stood side by side in awestruck silence.

"I apologize profoundly," Ship said after a pause. "I can only hope you will understand and forgive what drove me to act as I did. You may judge me as you choose."

For longer yet neither of them spoke. At last Annica stirred.

"It's a shame Menlee and I are such ordinary people. If you'd picked up from Shreng someone better informed—"

"Just a second," Menlee objected. "I may be wrong, but I have the impression that the people Ship brought to the Arm were mostly the ordinary kind."

Annica erupted. "You're claiming there wasn't anything special about them? Black holes! They'd decided to seek a home under another star! Doesn't that class them in a tiny minority? What fraction of a fraction of one percent of humanity ever took so momentous a decision? What became of your admiration for 'the spirit of our ancestors'?"

She brushed aside an errant lock of hair that kept falling into her eyes. "What I meant is that they weren't all towering geniuses or brilliant inventors or famous artists. No, on the contrary, I picture them as the sort who dream beyond their reach, who feel a spark of supernal dissatisfaction but aren't so caught up in dreams of glory that they won't work like fury to ensure the safety and survival of their children's children. Ship, have I got it right?"

" 'Ah, but a man's reach should exceed his grasp—or what's a heaven for?' "

"What?" Annica blinked incomprehension.

"An ancient insight, dating clear back to the birthworld. It seems to sum up what you have in mind."

She repeated the quotation under her breath, then nodded vigorously. "Yes, that's a key part of what it means to be human, isn't it?"

Sourly, Menlee put in, "And just the part the colonists here decided to abandon!"

"Are you blaming them?" Annica rasped. "Given that they *were* ordinary people."

"No, I do see what you mean. For them, this turned out to be heaven." Menlee hesitated. "But I can't help regarding their decision as a tragedy."

"They are they. You are you."

Had Ship said that or had she?

Abruptly it didn't matter. Almost as though Ship had lost interest, the landscape wavered. Between heartbeats they were back in orbit.

"You will want to eat and rest before we depart for Sumbala," the disembodied voice said, sounding strangely mechanical. "I have pushed you close to the limit.

"And myself as well."

CHAPTER TWELVE

SUMBALA

LAST NIGHT'S STORM, WHICH HAD MADE THE GRACE-
and-Favor Hills resound with thunder, had cleared the air deli-
ciously, leaving the autumn sky an almost cloudless blue. It had
also, naturally, made the narrow tracks slippery with mud, but
their mounts coped without difficulty. Grizzle-bearded Ezar went
astride a horse as near to its ancient form as research and gene
correction could achieve, and though its hooves lost purchase
now and then on a sliding pebble, it was always prompt to recover. As for his younger—though likewise graying—brother,
Sohay, what he was riding could scarcely have been improved
on. It was one of the strange creatures known as baska, developed by the Ekatilans and seized on enthusiastically by the Sumbalans, ever eager for new and preferably amusing forms of
transportation. Immediately after his arrival from the spaceport,
while they were waiting out the storm in their family mansion, he
had explained to Ezar how he'd come by it: The Shipwrights, for
once, were not content with mere descriptions, analyses, and
images but wanted to examine the peculiar substance of the
Ekatilan "Being" for themselves. It would be some weeks before
another ship set off for the Veiled World with its cargo of information, and baska tended to go out of condition without exercise, so
he had arranged to "borrow" the beast for a while.

All the obvious questions sprang to Ezar's mind: What did it
feed on, was there no risk at all of it carrying alien disease, how
was it controlled, why was it so shapeless, how could it possibly
carry the weight of a man if it didn't have bones . . . ? And,
chuckling, Sohay gave all the stock answers: It had been tailored
to ingest and digest most vegetation, it was so unlike human

275

beings that any organism preying on it would rapidly die in a human body, although not intelligent it was dully aware and had been conditioned into responding to a coded system of kicks and prods in much the same manner as a horse, it was shapeless because it wasn't descended from a specialized forebear like protohumans but derived from a creature far closer to its ancestral colony group—that was something Ezar and indeed everyone on Sumbala found easy to grasp—and finally, it could bear a man's weight despite lacking bones because it was internally pressurized. Invited to try riding it, Ezar did so gingerly and reported that the sensation was not unlike sitting on a pneumatic cushion, a comparison Sohay had often made himself.

The older man had still been looking doubtful, however, when they set off just after dawn, and they had traversed several kilometers before he accepted that the baska was everything Sohay claimed.

Of course, if anything had gone amiss, there was always Scout to turn to. Floating at neutral buoyancy fifty meters above the trail, adjusting its position by puffing out jets of air warmed by sunlight, or under cloud and at night by a fusion tube no larger than a man's thumb, it was their permanent link to everyone and every place on the planet. If the worse came to the worst, it could lift the men bodily, one at a time, and carry them a good ten kilometers. Though not, of course, their mounts. The horse weighed even more than the baska.

As if struck by a sudden thought, Ezar twisted in his saddle. "Does that beast of yours have a name?"

"I've no idea. Never asked it." Sohay's long face was a mock-serious mask. Ezar remembered that expression from childhood. It must, he reflected, have stood his brother in good stead professionally. He was a member of Sumbala's interstellar diplomatic corps, one of barely two thousand handpicked, computer-confirmed expert negotiators, investigators, researchers, explorers . . .

"Very funny!" Ezar grunted.

"Not really. What I mean is that it may have been given a name by its original owner, but no one passed it on to me, and in any case on a planet where there's only one of it, a name seems somewhat superfluous, hmm?" And before his brother could contrive a retort: "What about your horse?"

"Oh . . . Ceeyo-efbar."

"Don't tell me!" Sohay raised one hand, needing the other to stabilize himself as the baska surged across a particularly rough patch beset with boulders the size of a man's torso. "Let me see if I can remember . . . It's his gene code, isn't it?"

"Of course. Or, rather, part of it."

"Hmph! Wouldn't be any use for a baska, then. These beasties are so utterly different from anything else we ever ran across . . ." He made to slap his mount's flank but remembered in the nick of time that that might be mistaken for a command to halt or, worse, turn right. On that side of the trail were dense thorn brakes that would have torn his clothes to tatters and his skin as well.

After a moment's cogitation: "Ah! Species, mass, sex, color, and— No, I've forgotten what 'bar' means."

Ezar's eyebrows were climbing toward his hair. "You must have an excellent memory! I swear you didn't consult your wristlet! But you can't have done any work in genetics for decades, probably not since you left home."

"Sixty-five years ago," Sohay responded soberly. "And you're right: The best I've managed is to ask a few well-informed friends now and then. Still, when we were kids, we both used to help design the farm stock, didn't we? Remember those chickens that went so wrong?"

"Ah, I tried that approach again a year or two ago. Got 'em right this time."

"Did you, now? Why didn't you show me last night? We had little enough to do with the rain pelting down."

"Didn't think you'd want to be reminded." Ezar shifted in his saddle, glancing at what was left of the rise they were ascending. "We'll be over the crest in a couple of minutes. Brace yourself."

"Will do . . . But you haven't told me what 'bar' means."

"Oh—more or less what you might imagine. He's the first of a modified strain, and I didn't want to risk breeding from him until I'd worked at least one of the new model through an adult year."

"I see! Bar equals barrier. Sterile."

"Kinder that way, *I* think, than cutting the poor devil's balls off when he's just beginning to enjoy them— Sohay, I'm sorry! That was tactless!"

"What?" The younger man looked puzzled for a second. Then he laughed unfeignedly. "Oh, Ezar! You and your obsession with old-style physical descendants! Just because I never got a woman pregnant by the traditional method doesn't mean I haven't passed on my endowment, you know."

"Really?" Ezar blinked.

"Yes indeed, and not only on Sumbala, at that. On four planets women have asked me to donate for them, and every time I was passed at the first examination. Mark you, they had to do some nifty armoring, of course."

"I should think so! But that's good news, anyway. Very good news!"

At this point, a few meters below the notch through which the trail passed at the crest of the ridge, the path widened. Ezar urged his horse to one side.

"Go past," he invited. "You'll get a better view. I've seen it before, and you haven't."

Sohay chuckled. "You've sent me enough pictures! I only hope the real thing stands up to what you've told me."

Ezar forbore to answer but waved him by. And waited. He waited a good three minutes. Only then did Sohay utter a gusting breath, as though he had held it ever since he came in view of what lay beyond the hilltop.

"I take it," Ezar said dryly as he moved to join his brother, "the reality does indeed outstrip the image."

"Oh, it does! It does indeed!"

On the approach side of the hill most of the vegetation was bush and scrub, intermingled with thorn and bramble. On the far side, in total contrast, there was forest. Birch and beech, vivid with the hues of autumn, stretched to the horizon and beyond, a sea of red and russet, gold and tan. Here and there a stand of copper beech loomed darkly like a vein of ore too rich to need refining. As breezes crossed it the landscape rippled like an ocean dyed to incredible hues by miraculous plankton, or the gas from an exploding star made visible and colorful to human eyes by computer intervention.

"And this goes on," Sohay whispered between dry lips, "for three thousand kilometers?"

"More than that. This summer has extended it by another two or three hundred. Nothing will stop it until it meets the sea."

"Ezar, it's amazing! And in so short a time!"

With a grunt: "You think sixty-five years is a short time? It's plain you've never sat around waiting for trees to grow! Even with our best accelerants . . . But really, I can't claim the credit."

"Nonsense! After all your hard work—"

"Luck was on our side, remember. It just so happened that we wound up on a planet where our stock turned out to be tougher than the native strains. 'Course, we have taken considerable advantage of the spores from space . . . You know, I can't understand the people you've told me about who've neglected that most valuable resource."

"Even in one case—one I've only heard about, not on a planet that I've actually been to—going so far as to try and stop them drifting in. But apparently that bunch went through a worldwide epidemic of religious insanity. No way of predicting what happens under those circumstances, hm?"

"Strictly chaos type," Ezar concurred, nodding.

After that they were silent for a while, feasting their eyes on the glory of the polychrome leaves. At length, however, Sohay seemed to pull himself together.

"Do you have no trouble at all with the native species?"

"Not any longer. Oh, now and then they manifest as a blight, but by this time we've armored our own stuff so thoroughly . . . What finally turned the trick was— Hmm! No, I'll let you work it out. Dad and I had already begun to suspect where the weak point was before you left home. Let's see if that memory of yours can track it down. And *don't* consult your wristlet!"

Sohay grinned. "I don't need to. Molds? Fungi?"

"Exactly. We had to redesign about two hundred species—

rearmor them, rather—before the roots stopped suffocating in the trees' own nondecaying by-products: leaves mainly, of course, but also fallen trunks and branches after a gale . . . Gently there, gently!"

Ceeyo-efbar had raised his head to snuff the wind and shied a little. Ezar patted him reassuringly on the side of his neck.

Also sniffing, Sohay said after a moment, "I know what may have upset him. Can't you smell it?"

"Smell what?"

"Smoke!"

"Oh! Nothing to worry about. That'll be from the home of the person I brought you here to meet."

"I thought we just came to admire the view," Sohay countered.

"Not entirely." Ezar suppressed a chuckle, sounding pleased with himself. "Would you ever have guessed that there are families on Sumbala who don't believe in making contracts with their brains, let alone their other organs?"

Sohay blinked. "No, never! Is this some kind of new—well—cult that's grown up since I've been away?"

"In a sense, yes."

"Then I can only say the idea is absurd. Of course, on all the other worlds I've visited that's the way people live anyhow, relying on instinct like our remote ancestors, but so far as I'm concerned, the custom is among the chief reasons why we've made such progress compared to them. We don't simply leave our mind-to-body interaction to chance and heredity. Instead, we—"

Ezar was holding up a hand, wincing. "Spare me the full propaganda lecture! You may have to deliver it on other planets and to other people, but not to me, *please* . . . Some time you must describe how foreigners react; I gather the principle isn't exactly leaping from system to system like the Perfect."

"Somewhat to my surprise, no, it isn't. I suppose people would need to come here and see what results we get before they took to the idea. And it is rather hard work, which most humans are reluctant to undertake. But as you say, we can talk about that another time. You've still not told me why some of us are rebelling against it."

"Oh, there's a lot of philosophical foofaraw to underpin their attitude, but basically I suspect you just defined the real reason: too much like hard work. The argument goes this way, at any rate. By recognizing that we are in fact colony creatures, evolved originally from independent organisms that came together for mutual benefit and wound up unable to survive without each other's support, we are turning our backs on the possibility of future development. They make comparisons with organic and inorganic chemistry, saying, for example, that separating a living organism into its chemical components destroys its ability to function. Which is incontestable, of course. But then they extend the argument to claim that by recognizing our own separate areas of functionality we likewise destroy the wholeness—they say unity—that makes us genuinely human."

"Hmm!" Sohay combed his beard with his fingers. "In that case I don't imagine they're accessible to reason."

"Not really. Doesn't stop some of them being perfectly decent people, though. Like the bloke I'm taking you to see. He used to be one of my landholders. When he got so to say converted, he asked if I'd appoint him a forester instead, and since I needed someone to fill a vacant post, I agreed. I make a point of dropping in on him now and then, see how he's getting on, and so far nothing has gone sufficiently wrong to make me pull him back under orders." Ezar sniffed again. "Judging by that smoke, his family is likely organizing a banquet for us. A useful spin-off from our work with the fungi has been a free crop of perfectly delicious edible varieties, though some do need prolonged cooking to make them properly digestible."

Sohay looked briefly alarmed. "Are you sure a person like me, who's been away so long—?"

Ezar cut him short. "Absolutely! The worst upset so far recorded was due to simple overeating because the fungi taste so good. Come on! Unless we hurry, we shan't reach his home before midday."

Driving his heels into his horse's flanks, he set off down the treeward slope at a vigorous trot.

With Scout bobbing overhead, they shortly reached the foot of the hill and continued down a narrow trail on level ground. Neither of them spoke for some minutes, for they were relishing the endless variety of color displayed by the leaves still on the tree or blown down by last night's high wind.

Half a kilometer or so farther on, however, Sohay uttered a wordless exclamation, and Ezar—still leading the way—glanced over his shoulder, raising his eyebrows.

"I just realized," his younger brother explained. "The leaves are rustling. And blowing about—look!"

"So?" Ezar returned.

"So they're dry. I'd expected them to be soaked by that storm we had."

"Ah, that often happens at this time of year. You get a humid airstream blowing across the whole of this plain"—with a wave at the land ahead—"but precipitation may not occur until it hits the ridge we just crossed. An hour or two before you arrived home there was a wall of gray on the skyline, and we heard the first thunder, but the actual storm didn't break on this side. We bore the brunt of it, as usual. Just as well, maybe. I'm not sure Hesker's home could withstand that kind of deluge."

"Hesker being the person we're going to meet?"

"Mm-hm."

A pause. Then: "I take it you aren't serious. Even if he is a bit of an eccentric, surely he doesn't live in a—a hovel! Besides, I gather he doesn't live alone. He has a family, right?"

Again: "Mm-hm."

"And he's prepared to put them at risk?"

"Obviously I didn't make myself clear. You seem to have conjured up a picture of someone living in a log cabin."

"What's a log cabin?"

"You can ask Scout to relay a picture of one."

282

Sohay complied and, having studied the midair solido projected by his wristlet, shook his head.

"I can see the principle, but why use totally unprocessed material? Except maybe for some kind of spiritual exercise, trying to identify with our infinitely primitive ancestors. That sounds like the inverse of what you told me about Hesker's—Hesker's?—views."

Ezar sighed. "I told you you'd got hold of the wrong end of the stick."

Sohay shook his head in total confusion. "All this started when you said a storm like last night's might wash away his home."

"As a matter of fact," Ezar said, and drew a deep breath before completing the sentence, "I didn't. I said it might not have withstood that kind of deluge. Water, in case you happen to have forgotten the fact during your travels, is highly conductive. Hesker and his family depend wholly on electromagnetic contact with the outside world, so too violent a downpour could temporarily cut them off. Moreover, it was an electrical storm. You saw the lightning."

Sohay blinked. "I do seem to have—what was that curious phrase you used? I got the sense of it, but I don't recollect I ever heard it before."

"Probably because this is the only planet that we know of in the Arm where there are trees, real trees, in the same kind of numbers as legend attributes to the birthworld." Ezar sounded as though he wanted to growl but was being prevented by politeness. " 'To get hold of the wrong end of the stick' means to extrapolate from a false assumption. Suppose we wait until we reach Hesker's place, how about that? Then you can see for yourself how complex a job a forester actually has to tackle."

Sohay bit his lip. "Ah," he muttered at length. "That must be what threw me on a wrong track. A term like that—well, I don't suppose there's one person in a million who would recognize 'forester.' "

"If," Ezar returned dryly, "you're taking into account the population of all the worlds that don't have forests, I'm sure you're right. But you're back home, remember, and now we do. According to the records, the chances are that mine is the first—I mean, *ours* is the first of such a size since the birthworld, certainly the largest containing only introduced species."

He hesitated, then resumed in a firmer voice.

"You know, Sohay, I don't regret the choice I made."

"The choice?"

"My decision to stay home. In the infinite variety of this one continent I found as much to fascinate and occupy me as you've found on all the other worlds you've visited. I've never been bored, never been disappointed, never felt envious. Honestly."

The trail here was wide enough despite the besetting trees for them to be riding side by side. Moved by an impulse he could not have defined, Sohay reached out to take his brother's hand.

"You must tell me everything, and I'll do the same. We have a month together before I leave again—surely that will be enough."

"To explain everything?" Ezar shook his gray head. "A century wouldn't be enough. But it's better than nothing." He glanced up at the sky, from which by now a rising wind had broomed away all trace of cloud so that it shone uniformly blue from horizon to horizon.

"Has it never struck you," he continued after a few seconds, "how strange it is that for some people the whole universe feels constricting, and others can find contentment in a garden? Yet all are equally involved, equally occupied, with what they're doing."

Sohay gave a sober nod.

"It's like the difference between viewing the spread of these glorious colors from orbit—which of course I've done, and I assure you it's magnificent—and riding among the individual trees as we are doing now. Life's too short not to make a choice between them, though. To study everything on every scale . . . No, that's doubtless reserved for the Perfect!"

From his tone it was clear he intended a joke, but Ezar turned a serious face to him.

"I'd advise you not to bring that subject up in Hesker's company."

"Why in space not?" was Sohay's immediate response, but he checked his brother's answer with an upraised hand. "No need, let me guess. Does he imagine that by rejecting our acceptance of the autonomy of our constituent organs he and his are following the path that will lead ultimately to the Perfect?"

"As I told you, views like his are underpinned by philosophical foofaraw. But I'd advise postponing the rest of this conversation until you've actually met him. We're nearly there." Ezar sniffed again. "That's quite a fire he has going, isn't it?"

"You mean he actually—?"

"Yes! He, or rather, his family because they all take part— they've been experimenting with the controlled use of wood as fuel not only for cooking but also for heating on the grounds that the forest provides an inexhaustible supply. It has drawbacks, naturally. In particular the combustion compounds are unpredictable, and some of them may prove to be carcinogens we're not armored against."

Sohay uttered a silent whistle.

"Don't worry! Even without being armored, so brief an exposure won't cause noticeable harm, and I have a program running back at the mansion which monitors possible ill effects. Oddly, though, last time I checked this kind of smoke against my contract with my lungs, I had a positive override from forebrain level. Seems as though there's a pleasure element involved."

Sohay's interest was fully engaged now. "Tracing back to when our ancestors first found out they could transform inedible food by heating it?"

"Hmm!" Ezar sounded put out but rallied swiftly. "Yes, that's the likeliest explanation we have so far hit on."

"Very interesting! I remember running across a similar idea during my tour at our mission on Shreng—you know, the university world?"

"I do keep up with the news," Ezar sighed.

"I apologize. Well, someone there had compiled a thesis about artificial lighting and come to the conclusion that the best form of it—not necessarily the one that provided the brightest uniform illumination but the one most appealing to an average person— was one shining upward on a higher surface, and preferably an irregular and not too reflective one. She then went on to argue that this was because in protohuman days when we lived among forests—like this one—and had already discovered fire, the sight of light shining upward from the ground and reflected on the leaves of trees like these could imply only one thing: the presence of other human beings. So it was comforting and reassuring."

"For my part," Ezar murmured, "I'd have been inclined to ask where she got the idea that all our ancestors were always glad to see each other. Is it not more likely that they'd have fought for possession of whatever they regarded as valuable—food, shelter, sexual privileges? Not all of that has vanished from our makeup, you know."

Sohay shuddered as a dry-leafed branch chanced to brush the top of his head like an inanimate caress.

"You're right, of course," he answered. "I've seen enough examples of that process during the course of my career. Still—"

"Still what?"

"Still, there might be truth in both points of view. A solitary traveler, cut off from sight of high ground, even of the local sun or moon, might have welcomed the light of a fire, and those who built it, isolated among trackless forest, might have welcomed the news, the stimulation, that a wanderer could bring them. After all, have we not developed a civilization in which the ultimate currency is pure information?"

"And are we not dependents of those who provide us with the means of gathering it?" retorted Ezar.

That remark struck Sohay as so out of character, for a moment he was unable to conjure up a reply. And before he did so, Ezar was urging his horse onward.

"Hesker's home is just around the next bend. Come on!"

His baska being reliable but slow, Sohay followed at a more leisurely pace, pondering what he had just learned. Now and then he glanced up at Scout, as though the dutiful machine might have drifted away from its charges.

Could it be, he wondered, that during the years they had been apart his brother had in fact learned to resent the consequences of his decision to stay at home and devote his life to spreading useful plants? Could it be that no matter how satisfied he pro-

286

fessed himself to be with his achievements—and they were spectacular!—he was actually donning a mask to hide resentment? If
so, then it behooved Sohay from his new eminence as a full-
blown ambassador to ensure that strings were pulled, secret
doors thrust ajar, so that in recognition of his contribution to
Sumbala his brother might make a short tour in space, say to two
or three of the most hospitable and interesting worlds with which
there was regular contact. Ezar would never, of course, travel as
a tourist, though he must be among the few thousand Sumbalans
who could easily afford it. Without being told so in as many
words, Sohay knew he must look down on those in their sanitary
artificial cities who grew "rich" by trading goods to one another
while others toiled, invented, revised, improved, and genuinely
produced what they then labeled with imaginary value.

So, if not for quite the same reasons, did he.

Yes—his resolve hardened—if nothing else, he would invite his
brother and his family, as many as his funds would stretch to, on
a trip next year. Stopovers on two planets should be easy to
arrange, though he must check the schedules . . . Almost he
started to whisper to his wristlet. But there was no time right now.

For just ahead, as his baska rounded the final bend of the trail,
he could see the most extraordinary dwelling he had run across
on any world.

AT FIRST, IN FACT, HIS MIND REFUSED TO RECOGNIZE IT as a house at all. It looked more like a machine—an automatic surveying station, say, of the kind one might land on a phase-locked inmost planet to monitor the solar corona in a situation where if it were simply left in orbit, it would constantly be drifting and precessing and wasting energy on course correction. Except that among the communication links spiking its roof there were items that would have been useless on a world without air: scores of observation floaters, like Scout but more specialized, interspersed with fully powered skimmers, highly intelligent and capable of butting their way home even against such a gale as there had been last night.

With a sudden start Sohay realized he wasn't in fact looking at the house itself but only—so to speak—the business end of it. The rest, gaudily draped in creepers whose leaves were as brilliantly variegated as the forest itself, stretched away among disguising trees, and the source of the smoke that had scented the air all morning appeared to lie at its farther end. However, he had no chance to absorb more details, for there was a shout of greeting, and he glanced around to find a boy and girl in their late teens, tall, slim, wearing coveralls and shoes—but, he noted, no wristlets—advancing from the direction of what, to judge by fugitive reflections from its roof, seemed to be a conservatory or hydroponics shed.

"Hello!" Ezar called back, dismounting and detaching his horse's reins to act as a hobble. No matter how many millennia might have passed, no one had improved on the tried and ancient way of controlling a live steed. "This is my brother, who as I told your father has come home to find out how things have changed. He's been away since he was not much older than you . . . Sohay, meet Coth and Dya."

The youngsters muttered a formal response, but their wide eyes were fixed on the baska. Approaching it with fascination, they looked it over keenly before Coth said, "From Ekatila?"

"That's right," Sohay answered, taking a pace or two to loosen joints that had stiffened during his ride. A baska might be more comfortable than a horse, but the need to avoid giving it false commands through inadvertence did oblige its rider to move as little as possible. He added, "Was that a guess or did you recognize it?"

"A bit of both," the boy answered with an engaging grin. "When we were told what a distinguished guest we might expect, we studied up on all the worlds you've visited, and there's only one that invents weird new animals to carry people about, isn't there?"

"Correct. And very profitable they're finding it. So are we, to be frank. Tourists love this kind of thing. It might seem ridiculous actually to transport baska and suchlike animals and gadgets over interstellar distances, but—well, if you've been studying up, I don't need to tell you that there are some backward worlds where it makes sound sense to possess your own reliable short-range conveyance. As a matter of fact . . . Excuse me: Dya, did you want to say something?"

The girl hesitated, glancing at her brother. Receiving a nod of encouragement, she spoke out.

"I can't help wondering what the Shipwrights think."

"About their ships being used to carry tourists and their toys?"

"Mm-hm."

"I'll ask the same question as before: Is that a guess?"

Dya laughed. "Not really. Just because we live in the middle of nowhere doesn't mean we're out of touch."

"Of course not!"—in some surprise. "Who is, on any civilized planet? But it's a very acute remark. In fact it's something I've got to go and sort out in a few weeks' time."

"Yes, you've been appointed ambassador to the Shipwrights, haven't you?" Coth said, looking and sounding impressed. "It sounds like a tough assignment."

Sohay's face darkened, but before he could say anything more, Ezar called on him to come and meet Hesker and his wife, Adeen,

who had just emerged from the house—and also wore no wristlets. Their children took after their father rather than their
mother, who was short and plump with a broad smile and a fussy
manner. Wasting no time on formality, she insisted that after
their ride the visitors must be hungry, and besides, the wind was
getting up again, so they shouldn't be standing around out here.
She urged them indoors and promised food within a few minutes.

Leaving Ceeyo-efbar to graze and the baska to slurp up fallen
leaves, they complied.

The living area of the house was plain but comfortable, decorated mainly with natural objects—a display of especially gor-
geous foliage, twisted branches, colored or sparkling pebbles. As
the youngsters brought mugs of clear green liquid, tart and refreshing, Ezar addressed Hesker.

"Any problems following the storm?"

The forester shook his head. "No, I don't think so. It was blowing pretty hard when it passed over, but there was no rain to
speak of. The machines logged half a dozen lightning strikes, but
all a long way off."

"What attracts lightning in a forest like yours?" Sohay inquired.
"Forgive my asking what may sound like a naive question, but—
well, it wasn't here when I left home."

"I guess it can't have been, at that." Hesker rubbed his chin.
"Well, naturally a tree's a pretty good conductor because it contains a lot of water, but I take it you mean: What attracts it to one
spot rather than another?"

"Yes, exactly. This drink's delicious, by the way."

"Glad you like it. Well, it can just be that one tree is a meter
or two taller than its neighbors, or it can be that it's tapped
subterranean water. In that case, naturally, when the ground
charge builds up enough, the strike takes the line of least resistance."

"The effect can be pretty spectacular," Coth offered. "Sometimes the whole trunk bursts apart."

"Does the tree recover?"

Hesker shrugged. "If it just loses its crown or a couple of
branches, yes, and amazingly quickly. But not if it's split right

down. Matter of fact, we get a lot of our firewood that way. If you hadn't been coming, we'd have gone out with a floatravoise, checked the damage, and brought in anything beyond hope."

Sohay nodded. "Ezar was telling me about your experiments with wood. Is it really efficient as a fuel?"

"Not for power generation—for that we depend on solar and ground heat, same as everybody. But an open fire is comforting in cold weather, and as to using it for cooking, here's your chance to find out for yourselves." He rose as Adeen bustled in, trailing a laden ground-effecter, and indicated they should gather around a table made from varnished planks.

The food consisted of thin yellow flexible disks rolled into tubes around savory-smelling albeit evil-looking fungi of at least a dozen different kinds, bathed in richly flavored sauces and all far more delicious than Sohay would have imagined. Delighted, Adeen kept producing more and more until at last he had to wave away further offers.

"Amazing!" he said. "Quite amazing! And are these really plants our ancestors ate on the birthworld?"

"As nearly as we can tell, they're identical," Ezar confirmed. "Apart from necessary adaptation, obviously. I gather you enjoyed them?"

"It's as good a meal as I've eaten in years. Thank you, Adeen, for a unique experience."

The plump woman beamed and preened.

"Well, I'm afraid we must be on our way," Ezar said, rising with real or feigned reluctance—and somewhat to Sohay's annoyance, for he had hoped to broach the subject of their host's unconventional beliefs, and there had been no way of turning the conversation in that direction. Still, Ezar did have sound reasons, for he continued: "I promised we'd be home before sundown, and that wind is turning into a gale."

Indeed, it was now singing loudly in the nearby branches. Through the windows they could be seen swaying and lashing.

"What a shame!" Adeen exclaimed. "Are you sure? Coth and Dya were hoping to show you the fungi actually growing, which no doubt you'd find—"

Rrrrrrr!

The shrill scream of an alarm cut her words short, and Hesker jumped to his feet in annoyance.

"I thought I'd fixed that!" he muttered. "Sorry—it's one of my pollution detectors picking up the smoke from the kitchen chimney again. I've shielded it, or I thought I had, but obviously I didn't do a very good job."

"Can't you just program it not to react to smoke from whatever wood you're burning?" Sohay suggested. "I take it you mainly use the kinds that give off the most heat."

Hesker glanced at him as though surprised to find that an august interstellar diplomat knew about such primitive matters. After a moment he shrugged.

"Tried it. Trouble is, combustion generates an awful mix of compounds even from a single type of wood, and the detectors are so infuriatingly sensitive . . . Coth? Dya? Is something wrong?"

The youngsters had both moved toward the nearest window and were staring out. Coth said, "I don't think that's from the chimney, you know."

"Where else, then?" Adeen demanded, but she was ignored. Hesker rushed across the room toward the "business end" of the building, and the others followed at a run.

Except Sohay. Raising his wristlet to his mouth, he spent several seconds interrogating Scout and only then hastened after the rest.

Hesker, Adeen, and the children had taken station each before a bank of deepscreens with voice-activated controls and manual backups, an array that would have seemed more appropriate to a long-range submersible or an interplanetary tug. They were exchanging crisp reports in jargon as incomprehensible as a private code. Ezar was standing just inside the doorway. As his brother joined him, he murmured, "I told you a forester's job is a demanding one."

Sohay disregarded the remark. He was sweating; there was a terrible tightness in his belly, and when he spoke, his voice shook.

"We've got to get out of here!" he exclaimed. *"Now!"*

They all stared at him. Hesker rasped, "Don't interrupt, for goodness' sake! Distractions we can do without."

"You'd rather stay and be roasted alive?"

That penetrated. Adeen uttered a little whimper, as if envisaging them trapped in her wood-burning oven.

"Wildfire!" Sohay rasped. "Being blown this way! It hasn't crowned yet, but with this wind—!"

Hesker seemed about to reply, but Coth cried out. "He's right! Southwest of here! The infrared confirms, though the visuals are blurred—"

"What would you expect?" Sohay blasted. "Your scanners are flying through smoke!"

Licking his lips, Hesker demanded, "How come you claim to know more than we do?"

"Scout!" Sohay snapped, jerking a thumb toward the roof. Beside him, Ezar muttered what sounded like an oath of annoyance at his own oversight.

Dya ventured, "You said it hasn't done what?"

"Crowned." Sohay wiped his forehead. He looked and sounded a little calmer now. "That's to say the flames aren't leaping directly from treetop to treetop. They're still mainly spreading at ground level."

"Nonsense!" Hesker rasped. "A forest can't possibly burn! There's more water in a living tree than the weight of the actual wood—I've done the calculations! Adeen has to let her firewood dry for a month or more before it's ready for use! Anyway, what can have started it?"

"Yesterday's lightning—what else?" Sohay answered curtly. "We have to evacuate this place!"

But the forester had donned a stubborn expression, as if to imply: *This stranger, half a foreigner, who's spent most of his life on other worlds, has no right to march in here and give me orders concerning my own job!*

"You can run away if you like," he snapped. "I simply don't believe that living trees full of water can burn well enough to pose a threat. Leaves, okay. But never trees."

Coth repressed an exclamation. Dya, who had turned back to

her screens, said, "But Sohay is right. It is smoke baffling the scanners. And the temperature—"

From outside came a shrill whinny redolent of pure terror, more blood-chilling than any mechanical alarm.

"That's my horse," Ezar said grimly. "Contradicting you. But you won't listen to your instincts, will you? Don't want to learn what our organs have to tell us!"

He took a pace toward the forester, clenching his fists in an ancient, in an archetypal manner.

"Come on, man! What's the command for emergency evacuation? Scout can only lift one of us at a time, so we'll have to use your fliers linked by twos or threes. I can get away on my horse, though the baska—"

Sohay had moved to lean over Dya's shoulder. One of her screens was extrapolating the danger's rate of spread. He cut in.

"We'll have to abandon the animals. Your horse needs oxygen! Even if he could outstrip the fire, he'd suffocate, and so will we if we don't escape at once! Hesker! Your evacuation code!"

The forester turned away, pale and trembling. He said in a muffled voice, "There isn't one."

Abruptly a screen in Dya's display showed a clear image. The glorious colors of the autumn leaves bloomed forth—and so did others, brighter, livelier: the red, the orange, the eye-searing yellow of a raging fire.

During the moment of silence that followed the densening smoke at last began to overwhelm the filters, so that the stench of burning reached their nostrils. Eventually Ezar whispered, "Oh, no!"

"Why not?" Sohay barked.

Recovering, though unable to tear his eyes from Dya's screen, Hesker said, "Because no one ever dreamed it might be necessary! And I still want to know how come you claim to know so much! You never saw a forest like this one before because there are no others!"

Brusquely Sohay countered, "You'd waste time squabbling and sacrifice your family rather than admit you made a terrible mistake? Do something to get us out of here!"

"And do it quickly," Dya whispered. She sounded on the verge of panic. "The flames will be all around us in no more than thirty minutes!"

From outside came another whinny of fear, then the sound of drumming hooves.

"That settles the matter of my horse," Ezar said with ghastly humor, making a visible effort to pull himself together. "He's broken his hobble and fled. I can't help wishing I were in his saddle . . . Right! Hesker, open your communicators, all channels! There may be airlifts they can divert to pick us up."

"With a bit of luck," Sohay offered, "a satellite may already have spotted the fire. Rescue may be on the way."

Ezar shook his head. "No guarantee, brother, that there is a circuit capable of cross-connecting the news with the fact that a house lies in its path. Hesker, do as I say!"

The forester shrugged numbly and made no other move. With a look of total contempt Adeen uttered the necessary commands, then, as soon as the channels were open, began to describe their location and predicament.

"While Adeen's searching," Shay said, "we've got to figure out what we can do in half an hour to save ourselves. Coth, what about linking your fliers?"

"I'm working on it," the boy said over his shoulder. He had abandoned voice input for more rapid manual commands. "Unfortunately, they don't have cooperation circuits."

Dya uttered a tiny gasp.

"Then patch them through your base gear!" Ezar cried. "That must be feasible—how else could they conduct coordinated surveys?"

"It's possible, but . . ." The boy turned a wan face to the others. "But what if I do that, and they're carrying us across the forest, and the fire gets here and destroys the circuitry connecting them?"

"They'd drop us," Dya said. "And we'd be just as dead."

Once again there was silence. Not even Adeen was speaking; she had recorded her message, and now it was being repeated automatically on one channel after another, compressed and flagged for emergency attention. They stared at one another, scenting the smoke, fancying they could hear the crackle of flames—though in fact, as the screens reported, they were still two kilometers away.

But, Sohay reflected grayly, the wind remained strong, and the fire might crown at any moment . . .

"Rope!" he said suddenly.

"What?"—from Ezar.

"Your horse's hobble gave me the idea. We can physically tie the fliers together, so even if the circuitry at the base breaks down, they won't separate. Then all we need to do is program them to keep going until they reach the far side of the Grace-and-Favor Hills. Coth, you can set them individually to follow a common course?"

"Yes!" The boy brightened. "But—"

"But what?"

"Do we have enough rope?"

"Maybe not enough rope," Adeen said, pushing herself to her feet. "But we have wire and cable and even some monofilament we use for flying kites with sensors on. Hesker!"

Her husband's face was like a plaster mask. Violently she slapped him on the cheek.

"Hesker, *move*! It's to save your wife, our children, and our guests! If you don't move, then even if we get out of here alive, I swear I'll never want to see or hear of you again! Rope, d'you hear me? Rope, cable, wire!"

"All right," he said dully. "Coth, call back the fliers—leave just Ezar's Scout on watch—and land them by the main entrance. They ought to have plenty of power left."

I profoundly hope so, Sohay said under his breath, and followed Adeen from the room.

Outside, the first fliers were swooping back at maximum velocity from their patrol, while high overhead Scout was darting back and forth in the mechanical counterpart of anxiety tremor. Sohay and Ezar had to cancel manually the alarm signals it was triggering from their wristlets, but it remained distinctly unhappy with the excuse they offered—that they were already well enough informed about the crisis.

How, though, could they not be? In the open the air was acrid with the sharp-pointed microscopic granules due to wood combustion that made the eyes sting until they ran with tears and tormented the membranes of the nose and mouth. A gritty bitter taste made them spit and then renewed itself a moment later while at the same time being drawn through their collars and cuffs so that itching crawled gradually down their necks, up their arms and legs. It was as though the power of the fire had already touched them, distant though it still remained . . .

Sohay's lungs warned him how tempted they were to choke. *Patience!* he begged as he sought constructive action.

And was distracted for a precious moment, long enough to let them double him up with coughing, because he had caught sight of what was happening to the baska. Always protean, now it had no shape at all—or no more, at any rate, than a lump of mud cast up on a riverbank. It was pulsing in random directions, settling back to stillness, convulsing, calming . . .

The shocking possibility crossed his mind: It could have been a dangerous mistake to bring it here, worse even than what he had charged Hesker with.

But there was no time to worry about that. Coth and Dya had found ample supplies of wire and cable, and they were all feverishly contriving lashes from flier to floater, from scanner to flitter. The children, Sohay thought, were responding with amazing competence, even though Hesker had denied them the wristlets that would have kept them in touch with their own metabolism. Coth's voice in particular was crisp and authoritative as he announced the capacity of the machines: "This one is low on power, and we don't have time to recharge it, so we need to tie it to those two, and between them they should bear the weight . . ."

They had spent two-thirds of their precious time on the task, and the baska had finally subsided into immobility before Adeen spoke with sharp authority.

"It's no good."

They checked in midmovement, turning horrified eyes on her.

"It's no good!" she repeated, louder. "The fire's outrunning the machines' prediction! Listen!"

Indeed, under the soughing of the wind they could discern the crunching of its greedy jaws.

"We've got enough linkages for you and Dya, Coth! You use them—now!"

Seizing her children by the hands, she dragged them towards the jury-rigged fliers.

"But, Mother—" they protested as one.

"Go! Scout can take Ezar and come back for Sohay—there will just be time and power if he starts to run right now and gets picked up a little nearer to the hills!"

"But, Mother"—Dya this time, tears streaking her pale cheeks—"what about you?"

"I'll take my chances with your father," Adeen rasped.

"You'll never make it!"

"And if I don't, what matter?" Weariness and contempt mingled in the woman's tone. "My fault for letting him delude me he was right and everybody else was wrong—for letting him persuade me to bring you up without advantages enjoyed by everybody else! How much closer does it put you on the path toward

the Perfect if you get scorched to death by fire of a kind he swore
was never possible?"

She rounded on Ezar. In her face were mingled self-possession,
shame, and—curiously—pride.

"You tell them! You're our lord, you've controlled their lives
since they were born. Tell them to get away! Then call down your
Scout and go yourself!"

For the rest of his life Sohay was to recall his memory of that
moment, not needing reinforcement from his wristlet. The picture
was etched in brilliant relief by the sudden gusting down of
sparks, red glowing sparks that touched their clothes and skins
with specks of black and set the fallen leaves alight around them.
The fire, he knew without the need to look toward it, must have
crowned. Now it would roar on faster than a man or horse could
run.

Scout signaled desperation on every wavelength it had
access to.

Hesker's face: a look of mortal wounding and despair.

Adeen's: unchanged.

The boy and girl: shame that they might flee and leave their
parents tinged with resentment that they had been brought to
such a pass.

And Ezar's: a changing chaos of contradictive impulse, from
self-hatred to blind rage.

The first flames flickered in the nearby undergrowth.

How can one, Sohay thought with the last vestige of clarity
remaining to him, *resolve this kind of paradox?*

*Do I save myself? Or save the children? Or my brother? We
inhabit ancient history come to life. In olden times—*

With all the power at its disposal, Scout overrode its coun-
terorders. Loud enough to hurt the ears, it *screamed.*

"Get back inside the house! Take shelter—NOW! Or you are
sure to die!"

*How extraordinary! Surely we're bound to die inside or out-
side—*

Sohay was still too caught up in his previous train of thought

299

to react. The children were faster. Jumping up and down, shrieking, pummeling, they forced the adults to comply, slammed doors,
battened shutters, and headed for the "business end" of their
home, where they dropped into their customary seats and opened
communicator circuits that had been preempted by resource
analysis during what—Sohay now dimly realized—was their futile attempt to lash together enough fliers to carry them out of
danger.

A calm, reassuring voice was saying, "Your Scout reports that
you're all under cover. Fine. Keep your mouths wide open and
don't try to talk. Sorry we didn't explain what we've been doing
sooner, but the contract I have with my biochron indicated that
there wasn't time both to do the job and let you know the details."

Around their dutifully open mouths, their faces showed vast
relief and the suspicion of comprehension.

"There was a delay—for which I apologize—between the observation of your forest fire from orbit and notification that it
could become hot enough to threaten your house, especially given
the direction of the wind. As soon as the projected CO_2 levels
were extrapolated, we realized you'd be running short of oxygen,
but by then it was too late for anything except emergency mea-
sures, and of course we didn't have the faintest idea how to set
about those. I mean, if you insist on creating the one and only
major forest since the birthworld—!

"So we wasted a bit of time searching birthworld records, but
what we have is nothing like complete, and anyway, this doesn't
seem to have been much of a problem back then. Which left us
with the need to improvise. So that's what we've done. I'm sorry
if it proves a trifle rough, but our predictions indicate it ought to
work—or hold the fire, at any rate, long enough for you lot to be
rescued."

Coth risked a question.

"So what in all of space—?"

"Sorry. I'm still not back in total rapport with my subconscious.
It's been doing some heavy analysis this past half hour. What *are*
we doing . . . ? Ah, it's coming clear. Yes! We're going to materialize twenty thousand tons of supercooled ice directly above the
leading edge of the fire."

"But that's impossible!" Ezar blurted. "You can't emerge from tachyonic space inside an atmosphere—"

"No it isn't!" Sohay countered. "It's a Shipwright technique! How else do you think they bring starships right into the middle of their gas cloud? I've heard of it, though never seen it work. But it isn't likely to be pleasant!"

The distant voice said, "Ambassador Sohay, I believe! Glad to be of service— Scrap the politeness! You're going to feel like a flidget between clapped hands, *now*!"

The world turned white: the white of ice, the white of intolerable noise, the white of pain, the white of staring at a star from its inside.

Kilometers long, a cylinder of water frozen far below the temperatures found on any habitable world, fetched from a distant moon at fifty or a hundred times the speed of light, slammed back the air above the blaze.

It had already blown out the flames, as a puff of human breath might douse a burning straw, before it cracked apart from thermal shock and fell to ground, disrupting with the force of an explosion. Trees to a kilometer distant were uprooted, thousands beyond were stripped of leaves and boughs. The house withstood the impact—just. It shuddered on its foundations; windows shattered; doors flew wide; the roof was lifted half a meter and fell back askew.

Yet those inside, though bruised, though battered, sick with shock and terror, were still alive when rescue reached them.

On the way home it occurred to Sohay to ask those tending him, "Did anybody notice what happened to my baska?"

But naturally no one recognized the name.

FOR THAT TO BE COINCIDENCE— NO, IT'S INCREDIBLE.
(I comprehend another aspect of my doom.) It can't be chance
that brought me to Sumbala exactly at the juncture when the
Being of Ekatila launched its first successful off-world counter-
blow against humanity.

Planned or by happenstance? Even with my recollections of the
future, I can't tell.

(Unwelcome visions of that forest as it would be soon, infected
to the horizon and beyond with spores released by the dissolving
baska, burst by the heat and wafted by the wind: an alien bridge-
head not to be noticed for a decade, by then too deeply en-
trenched to be eliminated . . .)

Sumbala will enjoy no more than brief ascendancy, like Yel-
lick. Now I know why. Only the Shipwrights—

But Annica and Menlee were aburst with questions.

CHAPTER THIRTEEN

SHIP

DURING THEIR TRAVELS BOTH ANNICA AND MENLEE had matured. They had been transformed by the reality of the Arm of Stars. No human could comprehend the vastness of interstellar distance or the sheer variety of the planets Ship had seeded—let alone the complexity of the cultures that had arisen on them.

Yet if in toto such actualities were beyond their grasp, they could at least be recognized. Moreover, fragments that fitted into larger patterns could serve as indicators, clues, landmarks . . .

It came as no surprise to Ship that the first question they demanded an answer to concerned the baska.

"And don't fob us off with excuses about not being allowed to tell us about Sumbala's future!" Annica appended. "I don't have to possess your data banks to figure out that fire must have been one of the challenges the Being learned how to survive on Ekatila! Any world with atmosphere and climate suitable for human beings must have fires, from lightning and volcanic scoria if nothing else."

Menlee put in, shaking his head, "It amazes me that this person Hesker could have overlooked the risk of wildfire. Surely the most cursory search of the records would have turned it up."

Not glancing at him, Annica said, "He struck me as the know-all type. Witness his refusal to go along with everybody else and enter into contracts with his organs."

"That's something I've been wondering about since we watched the rescue of that boy on Ekatila," Menlee concurred. "By the way, what's become of him? How did he take to life on a foreign planet?"

"He hasn't got there yet," Ship answered mildly.

"He—?" Menlee broke off in midword and pantomimed a self-reproving slap on his forehead. "Ah, of course not. No ship of this epoch, even the best the Shipwrights can contrive, can outrun you—correct?"

"Does that mean"—from Annica, in a doubtful tone—"when we reach the Veiled World, Sohay won't yet have taken up his post as ambassador? Indeed, that he wouldn't have even if there hadn't been that setback we just watched?"

"Yes and yes. Now, which of your other questions, overt or implied, do you wish replies to first?"

"The baska!" Annica snapped. "Is the Being going to implant itself on Sumbala?"

"It already did so. But at the risk of making you suspect that I'm 'fobbing you off,' I assure you I am forbidden to tell you about any save the most general and foreseeable consequences."

Annica scowled but eventually gave a shrug.

"I think we're resigned to the fact that you bend your rules when and only when it suits you. Right at the start you said it makes no difference whether you 'really' have free will or simply give the impression of it."

"I am reminded," said Ship, "of a joke so ancient, it may well trace back to the birthworld."

Menlee and Annica exchanged glances. After a pause Menlee shivered visibly.

"I'm only just coming to realize," he muttered, "what it means to be brought face to face with a memory as deep as yours. For people like us, references to the birthworld are like—oh—among religious cultures, heaven or hell, or the abode of gods who may or may not exist, only it's advisable to act as though they do. Talking to you, though . . ." His voice failed him.

"Talking to you," Annica supplied, taking his hand, "is like using communication channels to another star, except they're not across space. They're through time."

Menlee nodded vigorously. "Worse yet—the worst of all—is that sometimes they operate both ways!"

And he added, apparently on impulse, "I'm coming to feel very sorry for you, Ship!"

* * *

I shall regret our separation, even though I know it must be soon. Sharing with these two has opened so many—(whatever are equivalents of doors in the universes I inhabit) . . .

Chuckling: "As for me, I'm coming to feel quite capable of pitying myself. There's no need for you to reinforce the sensation . . . Don't you want to hear my joke?"

"Yes, go ahead!" cried Annica.

"A well-known skeptic was challenged on the question of voluntarism. Throwing up his hands in despair, he said, 'Of course I believe in free will—I have no choice!' "

Which provoked a response even Ship had not expected. Frowning, Annica adopted her customary pose for contemplation, legs drawn up and arms embracing knees. She looked as though she were staring at infinity.

"Yet these people on Sumbala . . . They're trying something I couldn't quite understand, yet it seems to give them more confidence in their ability to reason and make choices than any other people we have so far met."

"Yes, this mystifying reference to signing a contract with your body," Menlee agreed. "I'd like that clarified. I want to know how it works and also why—given that it can produce spectacular results, like the dousing of that fire with ice fetched from a distant moon—there are people like Hesker who rebel against it."

"Now," Annica commented dryly, "you can tell us you're not allowed to explain about that, either."

"This time, I'm pleased to say, you're wrong. Had you asked the question before we paid our visit to Sumbala, I would indeed have been inhibited. Now, having witnessed the contemporary situation, I can furnish the data you request. I warn you: they constitute a long lecture."

"It won't take half as long to deliver," Annica said tartly, "as we've spent puzzling about it. Especially with your resources."

She glanced at the display surrounding them, which they had come to take for granted. It showed Sumbala shrinking toward its sun in the customary predeparture pattern. "That is, unless it will delay your next tachyonic entry."

"That has to be postponed in any case," Ship murmured. "Delivering that ice inside the atmosphere caused a major upheaval in the nearby continuum. It may be weeks before local communications on and around Sumbala are restored to normal. I shall have to continue at sublight-speed for longer than usual to get clear of the reverberations. So you have plenty of time."

"Go ahead, then," Menlee invited, leaning back and putting his arm around Annica's shoulders. One thing that had not changed was the visible affection between them.

Sometimes Ship regretted the need to ensure that it was maintained.

The decision to adopt person-worn data sources was one of an enormous range of possibilities open to the original settlers on Sumbala. Back in the parent galaxy hundreds of similar devices had been employed at various times. Subcranial implants reporting directly to the brain were common on densely populated worlds where it was imperative always to be *au fait* with a colossal range of news and other information; external devices feeding the visual, auditory, or tactile nerve endings were also widespread; elsewhere, in societies that placed a premium on individuality and feared that dictatorial input from some central source might one day override the ability of those equipped with more intimate devices to judge and choose for themselves, the preference was for old-fashioned machines of the type that had to be activated and interrogated.

(Annica tensed. She suggested: "Of the kind still in use on that sad planet where the people are so hideously changed yet imagine they are wholly human?" And Ship answered with one of its likewise nonhuman signals: a nod, unseen, unheard, unfelt, yet unmistakable.)

Faced with the risks of a hospitable-seeming yet alien planet, the settlers on Sumbala elected a course that differed subtly, yet in a most important fashion, from what had been customary elsewhere.

They adopted external, removable devices, worn around the wrist and/or the waist according to their function. So much was commonplace. But instead of according primacy to the wearer's ability to access data from elsewhere, they argued that, confronting a brand-new planet, it would be far more useful to monitor what it was doing to the wearers themselves. A reaction provoked in the lungs by inhaling a native spore; a response from the liver due to drinking the local water with—despite near-perfect filters—traces of complex organic compounds; a minuscule tilting of the "normal" perceptual reality within the brain, thanks to wafts of scent from an aboriginal plant; signals from bones and joints and muscles that could be compared with an arbitrary standard and used to issue warnings . . . such facilities as these, it seemed to them, were infinitely more important.

And, indeed, in the upshot it appeared that they were right. Jokingly, they began to speak in terms of "making a contract" with one or another internal organ as they programmed new and better versions of their original devices, and very shortly they realized it wasn't a joke after all, for what they had chanced across was a means of putting the analytical forebrain into closer touch with the reactive hindbrain and spinal cord than any of their predecessors.

In a sense, for the first time humans were conscious of, indeed experiencing directly, what evolution had taught for millennia: the reality of a human body as a colony organism assembled from creatures that once led independent lives. Thus equipped, they were able to complete the occupation of their planet with relative ease, and by the time the Shipwrights sent out their automatic vessel to inquire who would be willing to lease starships in return for supplying information, they were virtually the only population in the Arm relaxed and confident enough to say at once, "Why not? It might be fun!"

Yet there were a few among them who resented this.

("Like Hesker!" Menlee exclaimed excitedly, and Annica prodded him with her elbow to imply: *Don't be so obvious!*)

The reason seemed to be a sense of having lost, on the one hand, some kind of primal innocence, and on the other some primal awareness of evolutionary direction, masked by excessive knowledge of real-time internal processes—a combination that, indeed, was what had led Hesker to take up his post as a forester. It was his view, and that of people like him, that only by reentering into contact on the most simplistic level with the world around could progress be made toward the ideal of the Perfect.

Ironically, what he and those like him imagined to be a brand-new idea, a veritable breakthrough, had as ever been adumbrated clear back on the birthworld. There was even a saying that encapsulated their objections with peculiar aptness: "You cannot see the forest for the trees."

The exposition, as always, had been backed up by visual and auditory data. Now the autumn splendor of the forest enveloped them, as it had Ezar and Sohay, and, isolated in a wind-swept glade, they smelled and tasted the harbingers of fire. Nonexistent sparks made their bare skin tingle, so that they almost glanced down, seeking the dark smuts that real ones left. Then, with suddenness that shook them to the primeval core of their ancestral reflexes, the fire crowned. Flames leapt overhead like pouncing predators and with them dragged a whirl, a rush of dry dead leaves, and all the precious oxygen they needed to survive. Heat punished them, inside and out, for one intolerable instant—and space and stars were all around again, and they were shaking, sweating, and most gratefully enlightened.

Eventually, in a trembling voice, Menlee said, "Hesker, who wanted to return to primal awareness, managed to forget—or rather never think of—*that*?"

Annica licked lips grown abruptly dry, as though it had been real heat they'd undergone. "It ought to be inside our cells," she said. "Inside our bones. Perhaps it is." She glanced at Menlee. "After all, whoever it was who contrived to put the fire out just in time must have been functioning at optimum, even by the standards of Sumbala."

They waited, expecting Ship to comment. There was only silence.

"On the other hand," Annica sighed when enough time had slipped away, "no belts or wristlets, no awareness of their inner selves, could help them when it came to predicting what an alien might do to save its species in an emergency. Right, Ship?"

"Your species does not easily identify with others," was the enigmatic answer.

"Sometimes we don't seem much good at empathizing with our own," Menlee countered in a cynical tone.

"True . . ."

Another silence followed, this time somehow drab, as though neither Menlee nor Annica felt inclined to follow any of the lines of inquiry signaled by what they had just been told. At last Annica stirred and said, "Ship!"

"Yes?"

"You can't help knowing that Menlee and I want to be put— uh—ashore at the Veiled World."

That being so patently true, it called for no response.

"Can it be done?" Menlee demanded. "Or will you try and argue us out of it?"

"I don't think Ship could do that," Annica countered. "I think it must take something enormously important to override a passenger's choice of a 'suitable' world. I mean, we know about Stripe. She was allowed to go aground even though she was obviously doomed."

And is still mourned. But that was not spoken aloud.

"On the other hand," Annica went on, "how are you going to land us there without the Shipwrights realizing it must have been you that brought us? It was one thing to create a fog of obfuscation on Shreng, to disguise the fact that a foreigner had arrived without passing through any normal channels. But judging by what you've told us about the Shipwrights, they couldn't be so easily misled."

Nodding vigorously, Menlee added, "So does this mean you can't after all leave us where we most want to go?"

Their expressions were identically anxious. Waiting for the reply, she took his nearer hand in hers.

"Certainly the Shipwrights will realize," Ship said. "How could they not? But they won't care."

The impact of that was so powerful, they both held their breath for a long moment. Eventually Menlee let go with a gasp.

"Won't *care*?" he echoed. "The most important news in the

entire Arm—the Ship does come back, it hasn't got lost or been destroyed!—and they won't care?"

"Strange though it may seem, that is the case."

"But—but how is that possible?" cried Annica.

"They have mapped their future in the way that seems to them appropriate. What they cannot find out about must be omitted from their planning. They accept that my visits are inherently unpredictable, if they occur at all. To find foreigners among them whose presence is unaccountable except by assuming my intervention will strike them as of considerable interest, inevitably.

"But since you will be unable to give them any useful information about my comings and goings, they will pursue the matter no further."

They both spoke at once, sounding alarmed. Menlee began, "You mean our memories, like Volar's—?"

And Annica: "Will they make us welcome, let us live and work among them?"

Ship waited while they exchanged glances. Annica was the first to yield, inviting Menlee to go ahead, and Ship answered his question without further prompting.

"No, I shall not need to tamper with your memories as I was obliged to with Volar's. You already know the reason. This implies the answer to Annica: Yes, they will make you welcome because of the firsthand information you can impart about the worlds you have visited with me. While your interrogation is under way, however, I advise you to work out some way in which to make yourselves useful afterward. They are industrious and disinclined to tolerate people making no contribution to their upkeep."

Another silence followed, shorter but no less gloomy. Menlee broke it by saying with a shrug, "We'll take our chances. I can't help wondering, though, how news of two people having been brought there by you can be stopped from spreading. I'd have thought rumors would break out like—well, like that forest fire! I presume, for instance, that one of Sohay's duties when he takes over as Sumbalan ambassador will be to report exactly that sort of news."

"Sohay," Ship murmured, "will report exactly what the Shipwrights want him to know, neither more nor less. The data they are gathering are designed to act as capital in the event that they are driven away from the Veiled World and obliged to spend centuries wandering in space before they find a suitable uninhabited system where they can settle down again. You might say they are amassing the Arm's greatest treasury of its most valuable currency."

"Yes, of course," Menlee breathed, and relaxed. Annica, by contrast, shook her head.

"You're missing an important point," she muttered from the side of her mouth. "Ship, how is it you can tell us so much about the Veiled World when we haven't reached it yet? Always before you've refused to discuss the next system and those after it. Now you're making statements—and even predictions!—about the Shipwrights. Why?"

"It may appear to be a paradox," Ship replied in a judicious tone. "In fact it's not, and you should be able to work out why."

She looked blank and Menlee annoyed with himself for having overlooked so crucial a point. Suddenly he snapped his fingers.

"Is it because they're the only settlers who have worked out their future actions in detail? You said they'll take the news of your return into account but not act on it because there's no way of knowing when will be the next time. That implies that from the very start you must have accepted their ability to achieve exactly what they set out to do. Even though you haven't been there yet, what you've found out so far—especially the lending of ships to Sumbala and the other worlds collecting information for them— has only served to confirm that they are exactly on the course they originally chose. So you have no reservations about drawing conclusions about them. When we arrive, you confidently expect to find them doing precisely what they originally undertook to do."

"I see!" Annica whispered. "No wonder they were able to talk you into letting them land on worlds that must have seemed utterly wrong for human occupation. I'd been puzzling over that. They must descend from a particularly tough-minded and ambitious group."

"Oddly enough," Ship sighed, "not even I knew they were a

group. Not until I arrived in the vicinity and they saw possibilities where I'd seen none. Then volunteers emerged as though by magic."

"Magic!" Annica repeated with a chuckle. "Ship, you do continue to surprise me. A machine that can wonder about its own free will—with a sense of humor and frustration and impatience—and now it's talking about magic! How I would have liked to meet your builders!"

"I think," Menlee said slowly, "we're on our way to meet their nearest equivalents. Ship, when shall we reach the Veiled World?"

"I'm obliged to call at four more planets before then, but I expect them to be relatively uninteresting. They are in contact with Sumbala, of course, but I learned little of much import when interrogating Sumbalan computers. People are surviving there, managing pretty well all things considered, but much preoccupied with problems that elsewhere have been overcome. No, our next significant port of call is the triple world of the Shipwrights."

"Will we"—Annica's voice broke huskily on the words—"will we be happy there if we stay?"

"Happiness," the Ship said in a somber tone, "is among the human concepts I can't yet claim to understand."

CHAPTER FOURTEEN

THE VEILED WORLD

WHAT FEW STARS COULD BE MADE OUT TWINKLED IN-credibly, made to dance as much as a full degree from their true position by refraction, reflection, and the strains of space within the cloud that shrouded—and had earned a fortune for—the Shipwrights.

At the center of this extraordinary system loomed the bulk of what was too dim to be a star, too large to be a planet: a brown dwarf emitting enough heat to render habitable its surprising retinue of satellites but not yet so massive as to ignite its hydrogen into a stellar fire. Rotating fast because of the constant infall of dust and meteors, it churned visibly. Visibly, at least, to someone possessed of ordinary human eyesight. Such an observer could have discerned the tumult of its surface, even watched the occasional semisolid plates of "cool" material that formed in its lower atmosphere, as they were hurled aloft on eruptions of gas like sheets of aerated slag blown skyward by a geyser, then skimmed back diskwise into the simmering caldron below, with no worse discomfort than the odd afterimage of a flash from searing magma exposed when one of the plates was tossed on high.

But Oach dared not even glance at his people's "sun" without protection. The first settlers had decided to incorporate certain genetic changes in their descendants, and within a few generations they were universal. Chief among them was loss of the ability to detect the blue region of the spectrum, compensated by vast enhancement in the red and infrared. Consequently, as he rode his flying sled along the geodesic course dictated by the artificial space strains that stabilized the system, listening with half an ear to the ceaseless babble of talk on his communicator, interrupted now and then by the hiss of a micrometeorite being vaporized by the sled's forward shield, he could clearly make out the planets Asaph, Bethe, and Gamow, named according to legend after the first three letters of some ancient script. To him they were bright and unmistakable, for he could view them by the reflected warmth of the "sun." In unusually favorable conditions he could even detect the faint emanations from the "bow waves" they compressed into the cloud by moving through it. A visitor from elsewhere, however, would have noticed at best three blurs and quite likely nothing at all.

In addition, whereas that visitor would have registered no color higher in his visual octave than a drab yellow from those stars not blotted out by the enveloping dust cloud, while the rest of the local volume was dominated by a monotone reddish brown, Shipwright folk distinguished five additional colors from "pale" to "intense," all in the infrared band. It made no difference to Oach that some of them were reported not by his eyes but by modified skin on his forehead and focused by a mosaic of microtubules. That had been natural to him since birth, and he was now out of adolescence, a grown man.

Though some believed he had brought too much of his youthful idealism and excitability with him.

His duty at present was to match with, grapple to, and repair a malfunctioning sorter. Tens of thousands of those automatic mineral harvesters plied within the gas cloud, and ordinarily they were self-maintaining. Now and then, though, one of them suffered damage that it couldn't cope with, and it was both dangerous and wasteful to leave so large an object drifting aimlessly: hence Oach's mission.

Some sorters merely prospected for useful substances; some collected elements essential for human survival, such as oxygen, carbon, and cobalt, though stocks of those sufficient to last several centuries had been gathered in long ago and were now safely deposited on the planets, being converted to atmosphere, food, and medicine by adapted vegetation. Members of the most numerous class, however, like the one he was assigned to repair, had a far more general brief. It was their task to harvest iron, nickel, titanium, germanium, silicon, aluminum, magnesium, all the multifarious materials required in the construction of a star-ship.

Of which yet another loomed, a small bright smudge, in orbit around Asaph, nearly complete: the fortieth, the fiftieth?

Resentful, Oach muttered, "And we're going to give it away, as usual. All the effort we sink into their building—and none of us will ever enjoy the benefit!"

One instant later he could have bitten off his tongue. His resent-ment had been so intense, he had forgotten to ensure his words could not be overheard. His communicator defaulted to its open state—survival among the darting particles of this volume was too precarious to disregard such safety precautions—and so had conveyed his private thought to the ordinators that kept sleepless watch over the half million Shipwrights. They could scarcely be compared to those that had controlled the legendary Ship of Ships, which according to barely credible records had allegedly achieved intelligence and self-awareness exceeding the human and all known alien levels—unless, of course, the Perfect did in fact exist—but they were more than adequate for the task they had been allotted: ensuring the survival of their builders. Oach knew perfectly well that they were certain to notice and report any such complaint as his.

So now there would be another session with his counselor, another high-speed psychoanalysis, another attempt to make him "understand" that indeed the effort invested in constructing star-ships was rewarded, by the influx of knowledge from systems the Shipwrights could not travel to in person because the special adaptations decreed by the first settlers—not limited by any means to infrared vision—rendered them vulnerable to condi-tions "out there." . . . How many times now had they attempted to make him accept that state of affairs—ten, twelve? Something like that. He knew that if he continued to voice his frustration, the day would inevitably arrive when the all-wise ordinators decided the elements composing his body could be better employed. At that stage he would be painlessly terminated.

Oh, I so envy our ancestors who flew from sun to sun to sun! All I want is to do the same! Why shouldn't I? Yet they call me an atavism and threaten me with death! Worst of all, perhaps, people have always mocked me!

Even when I suggested that since we receive ambassadors from other worlds, we ought to send ambassadors ourselves. I'd volunteer! There must be some way to protect our minds and bodies against the stellar radiation that can't reach us here within our cloud . . . Don't we get bombarded with uncountable cosmic secondaries and survive them—live, indeed, as long as most folk on a so-called normal world? Those ambassadors and their staff come to us, remain in tolerable health during their stay, go away presumably not excessively affected . . . Why can't we do what they can?

At that point his train of thought ended, for a signal chimed. He'd found the broken-down sorter.

Or, more exactly, his sled had. As ever, he had merely been a passenger till now. Well, if he made a good fast repair, perhaps the machines would set that against his ill-judged outburst of a few moments ago . . . He fretted until the sled had attached its grapples, then resignedly filled his lungs, detached himself from his harness, and brachiated along a cable to the sorter to find out what the trouble was.

He was not prepared for the nature of the actual fault.

Trapped by the sorter's immaterial energy nets, blocking the narrow throats of its analyzer tubes, were a pair of objects larger and more complex than the mote-to-pebble range it was designed to cope with: two spacesuits. He had never seen one, save pictured in ancient solidos, but that was quite definitely what they were. Two spacesuits.

Containing two live—and *foreign*—human beings!

WHEN HE RECOVERED FROM HIS SHOCK, OACH ISSUED an emergency call. But it would be some while before there was any response—in fact, some while before even the ordinators heard it. One of the many ironies of living in this cloud was that its inhabitants were restricted to the laggard speed of light when communicating among themselves. There was so much mass adrift in the vicinity, thin and faint though it might seem from within, that fragile information borne by a tachyonic beam invariably broke up into noise.

A century had been spent searching for a solution. In the end they'd concluded that there wasn't one. Not even the famous Shipwrights, who alone among all known humanity could safely launch and retrieve a starship in the midst of so much whirling matter, who could transport their raw materials faster than light from wherever they were found to wherever they were needed and damp down the resulting sonic shock—not even they could argue with the sad fact that here, as everywhere within the Arm, if you needed to transmit a message at high speed, you had to send it in fixed physical form . . .

The possibility, no, the *probability* abruptly dawned on Oach that these two strangers (the word came with difficulty to his mind, there having been so few in his life) must be message carriers. What better means of transmission than human beings who could answer unforeseen questions? In dismay he realized he had been hanging in space, one lanky arm crooked around his sled's grapple, and simply staring. It would look bad on his record if he didn't take some kind of action—worse yet if it were the wrong kind! As an interim measure he set sensors to probing the suits.

Message bearers . . .

Who had come here across light-years of space in nothing more than conventional space garb? Images of the Perfect bloomed and

317

faded in his imagination. If what was claimed of them was even fractionally true, they were their own spacesuits; indeed, it was alleged that many of the Shipwrights' own modifications, as demonstrated in himself with his ability to endure naked space, shrugging off the constant bombardment of random particles, had been conceived because of that legend. Legend, though, he held it to be and would continue to do so until someone explained how a human nervous system could be equipped with organs capable of perceiving events in tachyonic space.

Not to mention the need to control the conversion of sufficient matter into energy without, so to say, burning one's fingers!

He thrust such irrelevancies aside and returned to his main problem.

The sensors he had activated delivered a preliminary report: the strangers were in coma, but their life functions, so far as could be determined without penetrating their coverings, were otherwise normal. They were lucky, Oach thought, to be alive. His sensors were gentle, but sorters were equipped only with spectrolasers, whose fierce beams could all too easily have melted a hole in those suits, especially since they represented concentrations of several valuable elements.

Yet they were scarcely scarred apart from a shallow pit here and there that could equally be due to meteor impact. Had someone had the sense to leave active in the sorter's program a facility for spacesuit recognition? Well, why not? It might have been generations since the Shipwrights needed them, but there was plenty of room for such data in even a lowly sorter's memory bank, and now that contact had been established with so many different systems, there was still a chance that someone might be cast adrift in this vicinity who relied on old-fashioned techniques—a person from one of the embassies, for example. Unsightly, even ugly, they might appear to Oach and his folk; they were nonetheless closer to the traditional form of humanity's ancestors.

Even in the way they think—

But that was unworthy. He canceled the thought, glad he could not actually have voiced it now that he was floating clear of his sled. And continued with his remote inspection of this extraordinary find.

Much blurred, but with an increasingly high confidence level, the sensors were relaying further information. One of the new arrivals was male, the other female. Both were in apparent good health bar their curious state of suspended animation. Both had adequate supplies of oxygen and nutriments. Neither was carrying any deleterious organisms—indeed, the sensors indicated, it was as though they had been purged by efficient nanosurgery. Their genes . . . but at that point the ability of the sensors to penetrate the armored suits ran out.

Were they being harmed, Oach suddenly wondered, by the proximity of the fields with which the sorter swept up its harvest? He himself dared not venture too close while they were in operation—and they still were, having been only temporarily inhibited because what they had drawn in was so large. On that subject the sensors were silent.

Reaching back to the sled, he found and pressed the remote control that inactivated the fields. At once the spacesuits began to drift away from the sorter. Annoyed, Oach realized he should have provided some kind of attachment. Well, there were extra grapples on the sled. He loosed them. They flew snaking toward the suits, wrapped around them, and began to haul them in.

Hoping to glimpse at least the faces of these strangers, he peered toward first one, then the other helmet. But he was disappointed. Their frontal windows were designed to pass a different band of the spectrum, and to him they were virtually opaque.

And then, at long last, the full impact of the mystery he had chanced upon struck home, as though he had been threading through the petty gas and dust emitted at the sunward end of a comet and forgotten it was being boiled off from a mass of rock and ice.

A moment ago he had worked out that these people, if they needed spacesuits, could scarcely be examples of the Perfect.

It followed that they must have arrived in a starship. Who in all the Arm knew more about starships than his own folk?

But what ship? When? Where was it now?

There was only one credible answer.

Almost—miraculously, not quite—he opened his mouth in a gasp of comprehension, which would have cost him his entire stock of lung-stored air. But he remembered to compress his lips and nostrils long enough to scramble back to the sled, take another breath, and utter a frantic message.

Which provoked the most disappointing reaction imaginable.

It came in a slightly irritated tone, barely a heartbeat later. "Two living persons in spacesuits? Yes, of course they must have arrived by starship—the staff of all the embassies are fully accounted for. Yes, of course they will most probably turn out to have been delivered by the Ship of Ships. So?"

"But this is proof that it comes back!" Oach whispered.

"*So?* Wasn't it designed to?"

"It's never come back before!"

"What makes you so sure? There are certain indications that it may have—in particular, that could explain many of the rumors subsumed into the legend of the Perfect—but what difference does it make? It can have no foreseeable effect on our existing plans."

No difference? No difference to know that there is still an infinitely greater ship than we can build, prowling the starlanes, apparently moving people from star to star, traveling where I so much desire to go but am forbidden to . . . ?

Bile, ancient bitter bile rose in Oach's throat. He uttered words he knew he would regret but could not help himself.

"Wait," said the distant, harsh voice. "Others will join you very shortly. You should be able to see their sled lights."

It was true. Had it not been for the fact that his sight was blurred with tears, Oach would already have spotted the fifteen—no, sixteen—vehicles closing on his position.

"Yes, they're almost here," he muttered.

"Remain until they have taken charge. Then return to your quarters on Gamow and await further instructions."

And silence.

So it had come at last. What he had just said, in the heat of the moment—words that already he could scarcely believe he had uttered—had tipped the balance. It would be adjudged that something had gone amiss with the genetic makeup of this young man Oach; that his opinions were at variance with the policy of the Shipwrights' collective; that his continued existence posed a threat to stability and sanity in this precarious and insalubrious environment to which even after all these centuries human beings had been only imperfectly adapted; that he must be regarded as though he were a failed experiment, disassembled, his parts reused for possibly a more successful version . . .

Somehow, though he had not bridled his tongue, he found the resources to disguise the violence of his reaction.

"There was no need to delay the sorter any longer once you had removed the obstructions from contact with it," said a disapproving voice. Startled, Oach realized that there were scanners playing over him and the suits. Another minus mark had gone on his record. He should have thought of that, yet he had not even restored power to its fields. Belatedly he did so. The machine inspected itself, concluded it had suffered no harm too severe to be repaired while under way, and resumed its previous course.

Senior research scientists, some of whom he knew if only by sight, were dismounting now from their sleds, closing on the spacesuits. One of them—it was Yep, who had uttered that reprimand about delaying the sorter—paused long enough to turn to him.

"Do you now forget instructions so rapidly?"

I was told to remain here only until they arrived . . . Oach said hastily, "Of course not, Yep. I am on the point of returning to quarters, as ordered. I was just wondering whether you needed to ask me any immediate questions—"

"Not," Yep cut in, "if your recorders and other instruments have been working correctly." A swift check while transferring data from the memory of Oach's sled to his own. "And all appears to be as it should."

That was final.

Despondently, Oach swung his sled about and set its course for Gamow. During the boring, uneventful trip he could not stop himself picturing what was most likely to happen to the strangers. Their minds—assuming they still functioned—would be stripped of all the information they contained, if not verbally then by cerebral analogue analysis, inexact though that was when it came to fine detail, and risky, too, when applied to unmodified persons. If they came to no harm, they would be permitted to join the community, though they would always be outsiders; there had been too many changes for members of the so-called Old Stock to be comfortable among the smoothly meshing citizens of this unique system. They might, however, find a place helping to negotiate with embassy staff . . .

They might even, remote though the possibility was, be permitted to travel onward, aboard that brand-new starship. The Shipwrights were above all realists, and though they could be cruel if they felt it unavoidable, they did not wantonly inflict suffering.

And those two, whoever they may be, would most likely suffer if they had to try and adapt to our existence . . .

Gamow loomed ahead, but there was still time, Oach realized, to follow through some of the mysteries now starting to obsess him. First, was it credible that the Ship of Ships should have brought the strangers? From what he had been taught as a child, he distinctly remembered that its operating conditions limited it to transporting a population, or in the strictest interpretation a person, in mortal danger, and then only to the next more suitable world. For whom, among the Old Stock, could the Shipwright system be called "more suitable"? Only by the investment of vast effort had people been adapted to it.

He interrogated a knowledge bank and found his recollections confirmed. But when he tried to pursue the matter by asking what would ensue if it did turn out that the Ship had brought the foreigners, he found such speculation had already been put under ban.

Yet another minus mark! For inquisitiveness!

Well, what was one more of those, now that they must have decided he was flawed beyond recall? Feeling reckless, lightheaded, he tried a different tack. Had the idea ever been considered, in a case like his, of letting a flawed individual travel with one of the starships—strictly as a volunteer—on the assurance he or she would return while in good enough health to bring reports of other worlds as seen from a Shipwright point of view?

The ordinators' reply was prompt and curt.

"What use would such information be if furnished by a flawed person?"

"Allowances could surely be made—" Oach objected, but even before he completed the last word:

"Distortion can be compensated for using the known and wide discrepancy between ourselves and the Old Stock. Distortions introduced by a person so nearly one of us are too subtle to be totally eliminated."

"Are?" Oach stabbed. "That implies the experiment has been tried!"

"No comment."

"But if it has, its results in themselves constitute information. According to the principles we live by, the more information we amass—"

"You have already been told: *no comment!* And beware! Your sled is approaching dense atmosphere, and you have not braced down."

Which was quite true. Would the machines conclude he had been about to attempt suicide? Nothing was more likely than *that* to earn the final minus mark of all!

But in fact suicide could scarcely have been farther from Oach's mind. Now that he suspected he was doomed, he suddenly found he was very much attached indeed to even the unsatisfying, ill-rewarded life he had hitherto endured. A universe in which the Ship did in fact continue to ply back and forth along the Arm: that was very different from the one he had found so insufferable in the past!

Above all, a universe where individual humans could be—

The usual shrieking began as air thickened around the sled's nose and within moments was so loud, it made thinking impossible. The sled bucked; its acceleration compensators were due for overhaul though still within design limits. For a few seconds Oach had a clear view of his people's astonishing achievement on this unpromising world. Like its companions, it was now covered almost to the poles with mutated vegetation, providing moisture, breathable air, all the other raw materials required to support life, even shelter for the animals that supplemented the food supply. Moreover, it afforded protection from meteorites large enough to penetrate to ground level. Even as he looked, in fact, a bolide exploded close to the horizon.

But then he was aground and had to leave the sled and make his way to his quarters, along one of the ancient tubes that had been home to his ancestors before the folk were fully modified and still served to link habitation units. Glancing up, seeing only waving leaves and branches, he wondered what it had been like to traverse them when there was open sky above.

Not much different, he concluded, from the sort of view he'd just had of local space. Or, on an overcast day, a view even duller than nowadays.

Two or three close friends passed him, exchanging nods. Neither he nor they spoke. They were adult now, like him. Things had been different when they were younger. Then they had argued, speculated, voiced heretical notions—and been indulged. Such behavior was proper to youth. But now one was supposed to have grown out of it, along with dreams of flying to other stars.

I wonder what it's like to be properly mature. I wonder whether it's as satisfying as what I remember. But what's the use of wondering? I'm never going to get the chance to find out.

WHAT IS THIS SENSE I HAVE OF WITNESSING AGAIN A PRO-cess that has occurred before, uncounted times?

Once again there was bafflement, frustration, the sense of damage (or deliberate exclusion?).

Should this be something I seem to recall because of its resemblance to events I have seen/will see on a future/past sweep?

That line of inquiry also led nowhere.

*Long ago, and often again, sometimes for misguided medical reasons, sometimes out of sheer curiosity—even boredom—there were humans with divided brains. "Let not thy right hand . . ." How **old** are some of the facts I remember? This has the aura of extreme antiquity . . .*

But that trail too aborted in an endless maze of stars.

THE SHIPWRIGHTS' CULTURE FROWNED ON LUXURY. Oach, like everybody else, had been repeatedly told during his education that it followed a pattern recurrent throughout human history, that of the community dedicated to learning, the most noble pursuit of all. Allowance inevitably had to be made for the frailties of human nature; it was never possible to apply every waking moment to that goal, so each "day" was divided into three shifts, two being allotted to work and sleep and the third reserved for exercise, private study, meditation, and sex. (Recreational, of course—breeding was in accordance with a long-term genetic plan.) Meals—nutritious to the point where no one was ever ill save from injury but monotonous and unappetizing—were taken before and after work, and during them general conversation was permitted, though confined to serious subjects. Since becoming an adult, Oach had seldom heard anybody laugh, except on rare occasions during relaxation shift, and then he could be sure the laugher had, like himself, only recently attained adulthood.

In accordance with the overall pattern, living quarters were utilized to near-maximum capacity. Picking his way among the walls of stabilized mist that divided the large hall he slept in along with thirty-six others, he realized that because he ought strictly still to be at work, someone else was in the cubicle he generally used. However, provision had been made for such occurrences. There were forty compartments altogether, and those at present vacant were grouped together at the far end from the door. Oach chose the most distant.

Entering with a sigh—because even though there was nothing to distinguish his usual cubicle from any of the others except its location, he had what many called an atavistic preference for the familiar, and taking the extra paces was somehow disturbing inasmuch as it broke a pattern he was accustomed to—he sat down on the couch. Even before it accepted his weight, his pres-

326

ence and identity had been notified to the watchful ordinators. As a result, a mere heartbeat later part of the dimly luminous mist wall re-formed into a solido image, that of a tall, strong-faced woman with a penetrating gaze and especially well-developed forehead sensors.

At the sight he started in amazement. Barely able to believe his eyes, leaning forward, he ventured, "Pey?"

Rather crossly, the woman's image retorted, "Surely I can't have changed so much in such a short time that my own son doesn't recognize me."

"Of course not! But—" Oach bit his lip. It was not the custom among the Shipwrights to maintain close family ties in adulthood. Often a mother chose not to know whose seed had impregnated her; Pey indeed was one. Until this moment he had had no idea whether she was here on Gamow, or on Asaph or Bethe, or working at the starship; she was a drive-design supervisor, much respected for her ability to modify tachyonic engines in line with what materials were currently available. No two of the ships built here had been identical, because so often searching for a standardized selection of elements in the gas cloud would have taken an uneconomically long time. Pey was among the few who could propose to the ordinators adjustments and alterations that still ensured a workable result.

Now, of course, he knew she was on Gamow, for there was no noticeable light-speed lag as there was between planets.

As though she could divine what he was thinking, she let her normally stern expression soften into a tolerant smile. "So you're in trouble, boy! Well, it's not altogether your fault, and I've told them so. I warned them when you were conceived that they might wind up with a rogue, given my own talent for varying the norm, but they went ahead and insisted I take the genes they offered—"

"So that's why you preferred not to know who my father was!" Oach blurted, exactly as though he were still the "boy" she had just called him.

"Has it taken you until now to work that out?" Pey countered. "Maybe they're right about you, after all!"

There was of course never any need to specify who "they"

327

were. But the idea of someone warning "them" against a decision they had already taken was an earnest to Oach of something he had never fully comprehended: just how much respect his mother truly enjoyed.

And along with it, indubitably, must go power. A rarity in this tightly knit society dedicated to cooperation and the common goal . . .

But he'd half realized that much the moment her image appeared. Who would ever have imagined a mother stepping in to protect her already adult son? Unheard of!

"Well!" The simulation at either end of the circuit was of course flawless—everything the Shipwrights decided to undertake was fault-free, by order—so Pey's image was able to sit down precisely facing him and look at him as though she were physically present. "Since it's turned out that my long-ago warning was correct, they did at least have the decency to let me know you were being considered for termination."

Hearing what he suspected put so bluntly into words, and by Pey of all people, was another shock to Oach. He felt his face pale and knew the heat shift was as conspicuous to her as to him.

"Annoyed? I must admit: so would I be, in your place. I told them in as many words, they must stop pretending we live in a deterministic universe. Sometimes you could believe they imagine they're keeping track of every dust mote in our entire cloud! But they're so obstinate! You can count yourself incredibly lucky that the Ship chose this moment to intervene."

Something else had been on the tip of Oach's tongue, but at that he completely forgot about it.

"So the two I found really were brought by the Ship!"

"Son, son! Have you indeed forgotten so much of your education—or disregarded it?" She wore a glare now.

"I . . ." Oach's face shifted from pallor to blushing, and that, too, was faithfully reported. "Oh, I see what you mean."

"Really? Then convince me—or I might just start to regret the trouble I've put myself to on your behalf."

"The most colorable explanation for the presence of two foreigners with no sign of the ship they arrived in is to assume that the Ship of Ships has passed this way, as it may well have done before without our being aware of it."

"Go on." Pey's face had softened again, but less than before.

"But even though the return of the Ship is and always has been among our postulates—"

"*Reflexive* postulates!" The words cracked in the air like a whip . . . not that either of them had ever seen one, but everyone here was acquainted with the phenomenon of a supersonic boom generated by a limited portion of a long flexible body.

"Uh—yes." Oach licked his lips. And added, greatly daring, "You're implying *they* have reflexive postulates?"

Pey leaned back and slapped her thigh, her mask of severity melting into a broad grin. "For that, boy, I could forgive you almost anything, even changing the subject in a manner your educators would be shamed by! You do take after me, if not in the way they expected, then in a way I suspect is peculiarly your own. All that remains is to convince them you're worth keeping."

Oach's heart leapt. "How? Can we?"

"Don't say 'we'—say *I*!" The tone switched again, this time to sharp rebuke. "The foreigners might not have materialized at this juncture, remember. I might have been too preoccupied with design changes on the new ship to spare as much time as all this is likely to involve. We do not live in a deterministic universe! What you've got to do now is seize the chance that chance has offered. Understand?"

"My orders," Oach said with a trace of sullenness, "are to stay right here. So how do I 'seize my chance'?"

"You must offer something they regard as more valuable than a habit of dreaming and complaining. I've made what arrangements I can to help you manifest it: specifically, if you so wish, you may witness the interrogation of the foreigners and discuss what they reveal. But the question will still remain: Do you possess a talent? Or not?

"If not, there's nothing further I can do."

Against his will, Oach cringed. The weight of a million years— the weight of all evolution—seemed to lean on his shoulders.

Miserably aware that his changing emotions were heat-legible on his skin, he whispered. "That's unjust! You said before, yourself, it's not my fault that they've decided to terminate me—"

"Are considering it!" Pey barked.

"Stop it! The decision had been made and would have been put into effect but for the chance you just described. Wouldn't it?"

His mother made no attempt to rebut the claim, but said: "The question you should be asking yourself is what capital you can make out of the fact that it was you, and no one else, who found the foreigners. I'm sorry I need to spell that out. You should have known."

As though to ward off a blow, Oach raised a hand before his face. Deep within, he was abruptly furious with this mother of his, who had such a resplendent career, who was so admired, who enjoyed such prestige that she could speak openly of arguing with *them*—with them who had condemned him on the basis of a perfectly natural ambition . . .

Yet he contrived to disguise the betraying signs of his anger as merely a continuation of what had preceded them. (Was that a talent in itself? He was fairly good at this kind of thing . . . But although the concept of "acting" was dutifully explained to students when it cropped up during analysis of reports sent back by those who rented—*and,* he could not stop himself from thinking, *enjoyed!*—the Shipwrights' vessels, it formed no part of the culture he had grown up in, and he had great difficulty imagining what purpose it might serve. Yet it seemed his mother was calling on him to save his life by doing precisely what, so far as he could grasp, an "actor" had to do . . . Oh, it wasn't fair, it wasn't *fair!* All his life he had been taught not to dissemble, not to pretend, always to speak and show the truth, for otherwise— But she was saying something, and he wasn't listening!)

". . . partnership."

Oh. Yes. That was among the earliest principles he had been taught. Here, uniquely so far as was known among all the societies of the Arm, the gift of humans for imagining and inventing, the gift of machines that could record and analyze, were to be combined by way of their sole shared talent: association.

On the machine side: association of facts; and on the human: association of those nebulous concepts called ideas. Machines being the creation of humans (*though when one considers the way human breeding is directed—no, don't digress!*), they had been subservient for countless millennia, so it was time for humans to find out what they had learned in their own right. Machines not being human, it was out of the question to achieve identity. But here, where the primary occupation of humans was to make machines and send them out to gather information, mediated or not by other humans, where machines were being provided with more data than ever in the checkered whole of human history since, and indeed clear back to, the birthworld—saving always and necessarily the creation of the Ship—here of all places in space or time it behooved humans to respect and comprehend their machines as collaborators in the joint struggle to ensure the survival of intelligence in the blind and mindless, random and chaotic, universe . . .

Yes, all that had been dinned into Oach and everybody else among the Shipwrights. It had been the principle that led the original settlers to choose this unpromising system for their home. It had been what directed the modifications of the germ plasm. It was still what prevented any personal exploration of the rest of the Arm by living—

The old resentment, bordering on fury, that Oach had felt as recently as the moment he reported the strangers' presence threatened to boil up inside his mind and give itself away in heated words. But his mother was staring at him. Faced by her, he had no choice but to cancel this upsurge of rebellion. When she had taken such a risk to intervene on his behalf, how could he endanger her? As he surely would were he to voice the thoughts that thundered back and forth within his skull.

Meekness. That was the correct response. Meekness and a sense of obligation. Oach compelled himself to look and sound humble.

"Mother"—the word felt poisoned as it crossed his lips, as though it conveyed the essence of a myriad of mistakes—"I should like to take advantage of that offer to let me witness the interrogation of the foreigners. It's not impossible" (*proper modesty!*) "that I might offer a few insights. I advance the fact that among the reasons why I have been considered as fit only for termination is that—oh, I freely confess it!—I have continued dreaming about travel to other stars when by rights I ought to have abandoned such juvenile notions long ago. From the bottom of my heart I thank you for all you've done on my behalf."

He waited tensely, hoping to evoke from his mother signs of— relief? Excitement, even?

Neither came. What did, as the image faded, was curiously disturbing. He heard her say, "Very well. It will be arranged shortly. You must be physically present. The interrogation is not going to be broadcast."

But he read in the curl of her lip, in the dark patterns that surged up from her neck, invaded her cheeks, reached so far across her brow that the heat must have disturbed her infrared vision, something else entirely. Whether his talent for dissimulation was a talent or not, he could not say. In that moment, however, he realized Pey did not possess it; it must be a random cropout from the gene mix. As plain as speech, what her face expressed was bitter disappointment.

In me? Because of me? Who have always done my best to be good and behave as I was told to?

She said herself: It's not my fault I make mistakes! It was what I was condemned to do before my birth!

THE INVESTIGATION OF THE STRANGERS WAS SCHEDuled to take place in the research center on Asaph. Although he had flown over it countless times, Oach had never actually seen its exterior, for long before he was born it had vanished under a mask of vegetation. But he was familiar with most zones of its interior either from having visited them or—more often—having viewed them remotely.

The one inevitable exception was the part reserved for the ordinators. No human entered it or had done so since it was completed; they were totally self-maintaining. Some day their requirements would exceed the resources that this system could supply, but since it was calculable that its artificial balance would break down around the same time, compelling evacuation, that was of small consequence.

As small, Oach thought glumly, *as the return of the Ship— which I have now, albeit accidentally, confirmed.*

He brightened a fraction. Maybe that offered a key to the challenge his mother had issued. In a nondeterminate universe, at least the hypothesis of "good luck" might be tenable . . .

Wait! Better still! He could argue that from what was known of the Ship's mission instructions, it was unlikely just to have cast its passengers loose to drift at random. It would have taken steps to ensure that they were rescued before their supplies ran out. Indeed, it might credibly have chosen the very spot where he found them because it could rely on them being retrieved before long. It might (was this too grandiose? What did it matter?)—it might even have chosen that particular sorter to pick them up because it knew Oach would be assigned to repair it.

Foolish? The possibility drummed in his head all the time he was making his way to Asaph, landing, seeking the coordinates Pey had given him within the research center. In the end he concluded this was his most sustainable line of argument. One

333

fact swayed him above all: If there were any machine in the known universe that the ordinators might be said to stand in awe of, it was the Ship of Ships.

Which may still be in the neighborhood!

He stopped in his tracks as *that* occurred to him. It was more than simply possible. It was likely. The records showed that the Ship had possessed the power to conceal its colossal mass from any then-known form of sensor, and it defied belief that even the Shipwrights could contrive a means of detecting it. Never had such vast resources been concentrated on a single task as during the creation of the Ship; certainly nowhere in the Arm—even had all its technically advanced planets been in contact and willing to cooperate—could such a project be mounted again.

Almost, Oach glanced around him nervously. He, who all his life had been accustomed to ceaseless monitoring by the ordinators, felt oddly disturbed by the idea that another and greater machine might be probing into the petty events of his own life without his knowledge or permission.

When he reached his destination, he was surprised—and on reflection decided he should not have been—to find Pey was physically present in a small observation capsule behind a one-way vision shield.

She offered a curt and silent greeting and motioned him to pay attention to what could be seen beyond the shield. Oach needed no such encouragement. Eagerly he stared at the foreigners, now visible to him for the first time, afloat in two widely separated examination chambers. At least a score of other observation capsules had clustered around them—one, surely, must contain Yep, and he wondered briefly which it was—and their bodies were partly concealed by trailing sensor threads, especially the backs of their heads. It didn't look as though cerebral analogue analysis had yet been attempted, but doubtless it was being considered.

The question crossed his mind: Why had a star-drive designer been summoned there? It answered itself within a heartbeat—of course: to pose questions concerning the Ship. But it was lucky for him, anyway.

He strained to make out more details of the foreigners. As he already knew, one was male, one female. They were unmistakably of the Old Stock, like the staff of all the embassies here—not that Oach had ever seen any of them naked. Not only did they lack forehead heat organs, but despite being thicker-set, they had not been modified for long-term breath storage, nor did they boast the extended limbs his own folk now regarded as normal. A high-gravity home world? Perhaps.

"You can talk if you like," Pey said unexpectedly. "We shan't distract anyone."

The invitation was welcome, yet Oach could not respond at once. So many questions were bombarding him, he was at a loss to select the most important. Eventually he said, "Have we found out why they're unconscious?"

"Oh, that was one of the first points they settled." Pey wasn't looking at him but fixing her attention wholly on the examination room. "They're in a state of ordinary hypnosis, rather deep, with slowed-down metabolic functions and a relatively high degree of anesthesia. But they're not actually unconscious. It's more as though time for them is passing at a hundredth of the normal rate."

"You mean sometime soon they may realize they've been picked up in space and brought here?" Oach ventured.

"Not soon," his mother returned dryly. "But there's bound to be some kind of trigger stimulus that will rouse them. When the physical examination is over, various possibilities will be tried."

"But the stimulus—it might be any of a million things! That could take years!"

"Not necessarily. The Ship would presumably have made it fairly obvious. One imagines it knows as much about us as we do ourselves, and a great deal more about those two down there. Reasonably, one may assume that it wanted them to be found, to be well treated, to provide what data they can to us ... No, I doubt it will take years to find out how to wake them up. In any case, of course, it wouldn't be permitted. You see, equipment for cerebral analogue analysis is already being applied."

As much about us as we do, and a great deal more ... Oach

felt a shiver down his spine, which he took pains to conceal—*my talent for "acting" again?*—and offered the disquieting notion that had struck him on the way there.

"Do you think the Ship is still in the vicinity?"

"Who can say? But it behooves us all to act as though it may be. Don't forget: The Ship, like all conscious beings, evolves with experience. Simply because we have a record of its mission instructions, it doesn't follow that we know everything about its present behavior."

"So how can people say, or even think, that it makes no difference to have found out that it does come back?"

"You disappoint me again," his mother said, reverting to her normal sternness. "What we can't influence—"

"But previously we only allowed for the possibility! Now we know it's true!"

"Do we? Do we really? They haven't woken up yet. What if, when they do, they claim to be the sole survivors of an experimental ship from far along the Arm that exploded in tachyonic space when it encountered our cloud, and they were the only members of the crew wearing suits equipped to return them to normal space amid the presence of so much random matter?"

"*Were* their suits—?"

"Not so far as we yet know. I said what I did to discourage you from taking so much for granted."

After that there was silence for a while. It took all of Oach's dissimulatory skills to mask the embarrassment he was feeling. Oddly, he felt he was getting better at it.

Then, without warning, Yep's familiar voice resounded.

"The physical examination is complete. The foreigners' planet of origin has been determined. It is Shreng."

He omitted the customary mention of the order of confidence. Oach's mouth rounded. That was rare! And astonishing, given that Shreng was not in direct contact with the Shipwrights' agents, for it lay in Yellick's volume of influence. Granted, Shipwright-built vessels had recently penetrated that far and beyond, clear to the first system in the Arm to be colonized, but even now Shreng did not boast its own embassy here. Something to do with the fact that the planet had no central government . . . ? Oach could not offhand recall; personal memory was at a discount where information dating back millennia could be summoned in a trice, more accurately than any human brain could store it.

(Excepting the Perfect? But did they exist? It was one thing to argue that humans had known how to modify themselves long enough for such accelerated evolution to be credible, something else again to claim that one could reach that goal starting with the available raw material. Oach remembered his wry image: how to summon the energy for tachyonic velocity without burning one's fingers . . .)

Aloud he said, quite without intention, "You know, Pey, if I had my choice of occupations, I'd devote my life to studying the legend of the Perfect."

"Why?" his mother snapped. "As a surrogate for your juvenile notions about startravel? Nothing's ever likely to cure you of—"

She broke off. Despite the artificial links that carried it, awe was somehow being communicated—to their capsule, doubtless to all the others, conceivably to the ordinators themselves if they were capable of such an emotion (yet had not Oach recently conceded them such a faculty: being in awe of the Ship?).

No one was speaking; there was dull silence on all circuits. But frantic observations were in progress.

For the foreigners were stirring: opening their eyes, rolling their thread-encumbered heads, uttering faint words that indicated they knew exactly where they were. Whispers were caught and amplified. Oddly accented, they were not the less comprehensible.

"You must be the Shipwrights."

That was the man.

"I hope we haven't put you to too much trouble."

That was the woman.

"The stimulus!" Oach blurted. "Wonderful! It was the name of their home planet!"

"I don't suppose," his mother sighed, "you will ever learn to guard your tongue. It must be because you think all data can always be retrieved.

"Well, they can't! There isn't time—already in our universe

337

there isn't time—to go back and analyze what we've discovered. Not if we stopped gathering information now and spent the ages till the suns grow dim in studying it. When is *that* going to dawn on you?"

At that moment it did. Blazing insight transfixed Oach and brought him horror.

Why did I never see that? It's so obvious! Unless there are people—that means us, so far as the Arm is concerned—who devote themselves to studying what we know, renouncing the power to, as it were, make news themselves, the efforts of those who went before, the travelers, the explorers, the adventurers, will simply go to waste!

A vision of the dying universe as a crumbling welter of dusty libraries, of radiation-riddled memory banks, of inscriptions in languages become unreadable, of folk remaking endlessly the same mistakes their ancestors had made, beset his mind. He cried out aloud, as though in pain.

When he recovered, Pey had gone. But there was much more he wanted to say.

"Where's my mother?" he demanded of the air, or rather the ordinators that were always listening. "Tell Pey to come back, or put us in touch!"

A soft automatic voice replied, "Pey is at work on the new starship and has left orders not to be disturbed."

"Nonsense! She was here just now. She can't possibly be back in orbit yet, not even with a tachyonic transmitter!"

"Pey," said the machine inexorably, "is at the starship. She has been there for over a week. She was not with you 'just now.' Make no further attempt to distract us from business in train."

They think I was hallucinating! And I must have been!

The finality of the verdict chilled Oach to the marrow. Turning back toward the one-way wall of the capsule, he stared at what was happening in the examination room, striving to prevent his teeth from chattering.

And knew, with terrible and utter certainty, even as he watched deft macrosurgeons removing sensor threads from the foreigners, palping their limbs, signaling them well and strong enough to support their own weight under "normal"—artificial—gravity . . .

Knew, even as he heard the strangers speak their names, answer the first question (from Yep; it had to be Yep; it had to be the most important question: "Were you brought here by the Ship of Ships?" and its answer likewise had to be the one word, "Yes!")—

Knew that by the convoluted judgment of the ordinators that ruled his people's lives, even before he had had the chance to offer his ingenious justification for continued existence, his clever argument about perhaps having been chosen by the Ship to help (the names were still available, he found them with instinctive speed), Menlee and Annica—

He was condemned to termination.

All that stood between him and death was the fact that right now everyone was too concerned with the foreigners to spare him their attention.

That held even for the ordinators.

"OACH!"

The rasping voice spoke from behind him. He recognized it, of course . . . yet in some weird and indefinable sense he did not. He remembered his moment of uncertainty when Pey's image appeared in the cubicle at his quarters, the one he did not normally use. He remembered how Pey had demanded whether she had changed so much in so short a time that her own son did not know her.

Own son . . .

It came clear in a flash. Weak with relief—or maybe because he had spent so much time recently in free-fall—he turned to look at the person who seemed to be present.

No, this wasn't Pey. It resembled her, that was all.

He sought words for what seemed like half eternity. When he did speak, however, he was proud of what he was able to say.

"Excuse me. But it is rather a shock when something one has only heard about, and that a long while ago—something that never felt as though it might apply in real life—turns out to be factual. You aren't my mother, are you?"

"No."

"You're a projection of the Ship?"

"Yes."

"Then how come the ordinators . . . ?" Breath failed him.

"Even your mother"—this with audible scorn—"knows better than to accord the machines that supervise your system the unqualified respect that you and those of your sort show to them. Of their kind, they can't be bad, as I well know because I generated the programs for their design, but equally they couldn't be perfect, because if they had been, your ancestors would have vegetated and ultimately died out—leaving one of the most fascinating systems in the universe to run its course without a human to observe it."

340

Oach licked his lips; they had been dry before, but now they felt as arid as the dust cloud.

"I'm used to talking to machines," he muttered. "But I'm afraid it will take me a while to adjust to conversing with the greatest machine of all . . . Did you choose me to rescue your former passengers?"

And interrupted himself: "Is it safe to talk?"

The look and tone of scorn returned. "Until you asked to be put in touch with her, did your ordinators know you were present at the interrogation of Annica and Menlee because 'Pey' had arranged it for you? Reconciling what you said with what their sensors reported was too much for them. They decline to believe they can have hallucinations and consequently concluded that you must have had one. It being known that humans are subject to such phenomena."

A meaningful pause.

"No, I didn't choose you. It just happened you were the person sent to repair the sorter that caught them."

Visions of being special died in Oach's mind.

"So you're only interested in me because it—well—it turned out to be me?"

"There is another reason. You may care to work it out."

Being challenged to a game of deduction by the greatest mind in existence, the only consciousness to transcend all humanity and all known aliens, was infinitely daunting . . .

Yet, he realized, the Ship itself, in its disguise as Pey, had given him a clue. It had assured him the stimulus to free the foreigners from their hypnotic trance would be an obvious one. Clearly it was designed to make allowances for human shortcomings; after all, during its epic voyage of colonization it must have had to do so all the time.

Racking his brains, Oach hazarded a guess.

"I think my first idea about these passengers of yours must have been mistaken. I imagined they might be—well—messengers. But I can't work out what message except their own identity they could have brought. I mean, unless some alien enemy is advancing on us, and that could be signaled lots of other ways."

Appalled at how naive his own words must be making him sound, he broke off. But the not-quite-Pey face was gravely tolerant, and the not-quite-Pey voice invited, "Go on."

Oach had intended to offer other qualifications of what he had already said, like firsthand news of Shreng or some speciality the Shipwrights had neglected, to justify his "messenger" idea. He canceled all that and said baldly, "In childhood, when I had nightmares after learning how unstable our system is, I was comforted with promises that if things went incurably wrong, the Ship would come to rescue us. But as I later figured out, your instructions didn't limit you to rescuing the whole of a population.

"So—well—did you rescue Menlee and Annica?"

"Yes."

"And have you appeared to me"—Oach's heart was pounding so violently, the rush of blood to his forehead came close to blinding him—"because I've let myself in for termination? I have, haven't I?"

Or maybe you did it! Pretending to be Pey, fooling me into imagining my mother had stepped in to help me, when it wasn't her at all but this incredible machine—!

No, that was unworthy. He bit back the words. He'd had enough minus marks on his record to warrant termination long before the foreigners showed up.

(What was happening to them? He wanted to cast a glance over his shoulder but dared not. Last time he had let his attention wander, Pey/Ship had disappeared . . .)

"We cannot be observed from outside the capsule," Ship reassured him.

Having perhaps mistaken the reason for his incomplete turn of the head? Hmm! So it was capable of a mistake! Oach's heart lightened.

And his hopes were dashed again by the next few words.

"What I said in my role as Pey was accurate."

Oach closed his eyes, swaying. He forced out of a mouth suddenly dry as his lips, "Are you allowed to rescue me, too?"

"If you wish."

Oach's eyes snapped open again. "Can you carry me from star

to star? Will I really be in danger from conditions beyond our cloud?"

"Yes. No."

"Have the ordinators been lying, then?"

"Not entirely. However, your people have chosen not to commit resources to what must be done to protect a member of the subspecies Shipwright in environments tolerated by the Old Stock."

"But you can protect me?"

"Did I not bring your ancestors here?"

"Please, then!" Oach clasped his hands together in an ancient gesture of supplication. "Please"—he vaguely recalled the words of Ship's mission instructions—"convey me to a more suitable planet!"

"Welcome aboard."

SOMETHING VERY STRANGE INDEED IS HAPPENING!

I can understand that my removal, on this early trip, of a rogue like Oach from this peculiar environment may make it easier for other worlds to comprehend the Shipwrights farther along their path to unifying humans and machines. I can even vaguely recall future (to me, past) events that hint at the beneficial consequences of bringing two people here from Shreng, also a world dedicated to knowledge.

The logic of that mimicked Ship's interior confusion.

But it's as though I (whatever I may be) have found myself inside a maze whose most promising paths are blocked.

Worst of all, they weren't blocked when I started out.

Horrifying, yet in this moment credible:

I feel like an experiment being run inside myself.

CHAPTER FIFTEEN

SHIP

OACH NEEDED VIRTUALLY NO NANOSURGERY TO RID HIS body of local organisms; the Veiled Worlds having been sterile prior to human settlement, only a few recently mutated strains required attention. Nor did he have as many questions to put as most of his predecessors, for having grown up in a society dedicated to knowledge, he was well informed about the Ship, its nature, and its history. What he did want—what he insisted on with fervor after a meal that he gobbled down, treating it as mere refueling—was experience of other planets. He wanted to see and feel what they were like even if he could never personally visit them. For as long as it took to move out of the gas cloud into a zone where it was safe to go tachyonic—in that regard the Shipwrights had surpassed even those who had built the Ship of Ships—he reveled in what it showed him of the worlds it had already called at during this sweep. He first undertook a superficial survey of each, methodically noting points of interest he wanted to review or investigate more deeply, and would have requested a "return" to Trevithra had not Ship, brooking no contradiction, informed him of the danger to a conscious human in tachyonic space. Accustomed to an unvarying routine, Oach complied and retired—by his own wish—to a perfect imitation of the cubicle where he had slept at home. He had not even asked to view the stars from outside the cloud.

"We are approaching my next port of call," Ship stated.

For the first time since coming aboard Oach betrayed signs of excitement.

"Another planet? One that I can actually go down to, walk

about on, breathe the air of? What's it called?"

"It's one your people have been told of: Zemprad."

The young man's face fell. "The quarantine world? The one that refuses contact with anybody and won't accept any offers of help?"

"Precisely."

"Do you know why?"

"Not yet."

Among the other questions Oach had not put were any that might have enabled him to find out about the random order of Ship's visits. The fact that it did come back, as originally promised, seemed to satisfy him. He said after a pause, "Are you stopping here because you fear something may be threatening the population? Are you likely to have to rescue them all and take them somewhere safer?"

If I'd done it, I'd remember. And I didn't. All I know—shall know—is that they die off. What I'm here to find out is the reason.

But all Ship said aloud was, "No."

"Surely . . ." Oach hesitated. "The only thing we know about Zemprad, or at any rate our best guess, is that they must be suffering from some kind of plague, presumably native. Is that so?"

"Certainly they believe they're in so dangerous a situation that they won't let any outsider risk exposure to it."

"Yet you aren't preparing to remove them. A riddle!"

The young man pondered awhile. Then, with a sudden access of bravado, he set his shoulders back.

"Would you like to send me down to investigate? Whatever the trouble may be, I'm sure you can cope with any ill effects when I get back."

"You'd still like to be an ambassador, wouldn't you?" Ship murmured. "No matter how unofficial!"

"It's true," Oach admitted. "Marvelous as the projections are that you've been showing me—wonderful though the detail is, down to the very scents and smells—they can't be the same as being physically present, can they?"

"I wouldn't know," Ship answered with an accurate imitation

of a sigh. "Bear in mind that I myself am far too big to set down on any planet and have always had to be content with remote perception."

"Yes, of course." Oach gave a short laugh and looked surprised at himself. On Ship inquiring why, he shrugged.

"Among my people laughing is something one gives up on entering adulthood. I never knew our ordinators to make a joke. So I suppose I wasn't expecting you to."

"That was a joke? Well, well. At long last I seem to be coming to grips with the mystery of nonrational human reactions."

"I've always held," Oach offered, "that without them we are less than completely human. Do you agree?"

"So far as my observation of your species bears you out—yes, I do . . . Now let me show you Zemprad."

The images surrounding Oach melted, leaving a view of a bluish-green globe with two small moons, gibbous in the glow of a yellow sun. It provoked a cry of astonishment.

"I'm seeing colors that I never saw before!"

"In fact you're not," Ship contradicted gently. "I've merely taken the liberty of recalibrating your infrared sensitivity so you can tell the difference between shades of warmth and colors in the higher spectrum. You're still seeing in the same way, but a sort of label is attached to the sensation. It's rather like the label that enables you to distinguish between what you remember as a result of experience and what you remember having imagined."

"But that's incredible!" Oach was almost dancing up and down. "How in all of space—?"

"Explanations will have to wait," Ship interrupted. "The human population of Zemprad is down to three hundred and two. I must act at once."

CHAPTER SIXTEEN

ZEMPRAD

OF LATE PARLY HAD TAKEN TO WANDERING RESTLESSLY up and down the sealed length of what had been Zemprad's last functioning biological research laboratory. Not its immobility—this building had never contained machines with moving parts—but its silence mocked her, and she felt that to be right. The absence of the former familiar hum that signified the automatics were about their proper work stung her dull mind with myriad unspoken reproaches. That was as it should be; that was fitting.

Not that anything was wrong with the machines. They had not been designed to wear out, rather to improve themselves in the light of their own mindless experience or in compliance with human commands. There was plenty of power, too, to drive them—not that they needed a lot, for they drew much of their needs from what they were processing . . .

Had drawn. Mentally she changed all the tenses in what she was thinking.

But the time was long past when automatics had been able to help. Now they were doomed to become—well—possibly technological fossils, to be found by some far-future archaeologist from another world. Very far in the future, Parly hoped. There were starships aloft again, she knew, for some had called here, but shame had driven the Zempers to deny contact without giving a reason, so the strangers had resignedly gone on their way. Following the first alarming contact, however, most of what precious energy remained to Zemprad's people had gone into establishing warning devices both aground and in orbit. Those should continue to operate until—

Until long after I too have become a fossil relic.

At last, as ever, she reached the vast window at the far end of

348

the lab, with its splendid far-ranging view. In a state between vague fury and overt despair she tried to remember how proud everybody had once been of what she was looking at: a verdant plain patched with copses of tall dark trees and clusters of low but brightly flowering shrubs; winding streams, little mounds, darting harmless animals—a paradise for adults and children alike, for every living organism to the horizon and beyond was descended either from stock reaching clear back to the birth-world or else from those marvelous spores left in nearby space by the Ship when it departed. The Zempers had been greedy for them; instead of being content to harvest them when they drifted into the upper atmosphere, they had sent out ships to collect them in all their varieties to aid in their overweening plan.

Their goal was nothing less than total transformation of the planet: the elimination of all the life-forms native to it and their replacement by imported rivals.

Fools that they were—that we were, for we are merely our ancestors writ anew. It could only have been done by sterilizing the planet down to bare rock. If we'd left one seaside pool with drying mud at the bottom, that would have sufficed . . .

Something was moving across her field of view that was not an animal. Realizing at once what it must be, she was minded to glance away. Resolutely, though, she opposed the impulse. She and all the rest must face the consequences of their terrible mistake. Many, admittedly, had fled from the intolerable knowledge, taken refuge in dreams and drugs—or suicide—but she was determined not to be so weak.

So were a few of the other survivors. One spoke to her even as she forced her eyes to focus on the moving object.

"Parly"—that was all it took, now, for the planetary communications net to locate and identify her: just one name of two brief syllables—"Desi and Bleean died last night. Had you heard?"

"Yes, Halleth," Parly sighed. "They're being taken for burial now. I can see the undertaker on its way."

"That leaves three hundred and two," Halleth muttered. "Below three hundred we have no conceivable chance of recovering."

"Halleth," Parly snapped, "you're wasting breath! If there's anyone left who doesn't know, that person must be in drug coma or at the door of death!"

"Please don't be angry," came the meek reply. "I was just thinking . . ."

"Thinking what?"

"Well . . ." The sound of difficult swallowing. "Where are you, and what are you doing?"

"Oh, I'm at the usual end of my range. Looking out of the big window in the biolab. How else could I be watching the undertaker?"

"I'm looking that way, too. Trying to see the scene as people used to."

"What in all of space do you mean?" Parly demanded.

"Please, I'm serious! There was a time—so I've always been told—when people could look at the plain and the trees and the flowers and see that they were beautiful, and feel proud of having created them."

"Those days are long dead," Parly answered sourly. "As we shall be, all too soon. If Desi and Bleean can succumb, who took at least as many precautions as you and I—"

"The time for that is over," Halleth said. And waited.

For a moment Parly continued in her mood of bad-tempered misery. Then a trace of pity relieved the darkness of her mind. After all, Halleth was the youngest of them all, the last baby to be born on Zemprad before it was decided that the species here was in too great danger for any more children.

Who would only have died before their parents . . .

Relenting, she said, "Yes, my dear. I'm so sorry you weren't born in time to enjoy such experiences. By the time you were old enough to appreciate what we had thought of as beautiful, it was impossible to avoid knowing that it masked—well, what it does."

"I don't want to die without feeling that, even for just a while." Halleth hesitated. "Parly, I'm going out. I want to roll naked on the grass and climb a few trees and make a garland of flowers and splash about in a running stream. I want to do that, and I'm going to. Now."

"You're—!"

The next word died on Parly's lips. It was to have been "crazy," of course.

But was she?

Was she not in fact reacting more sanely than the rest? Now the survivors were down so close to the uttermost lower limit and it was beyond hoping for that the trend should be reversed?

And it was a lovely day outside: bright sun, a warm and gentle breeze, a few high white clouds in the dazzling blue sky . . .

Halleth was speaking again, and Parly had missed a few words.

"So I'm just saying good-bye to people. All right? I hope no one tries to stop me. I don't want to be stopped. I won't let it happen."

She broke the link. At once Parly ordered it restored and heard a mutinous cry.

"I said I won't let anyone stop me!"

"I'm not going to try," Parly assured her. "I just realized how right you are. And also what a shame it would be if we never met face to face."

"I've never met anybody face to face," Halleth whispered. "That would make it completely wonderful . . . But you mustn't do it for my sake!"

"I'm doing it for *my* sake," Parly promised. "I'm sick of spending my time wandering back and forth inside a sealed building, knowing I'm only putting off the day of reckoning . . ." Automatically her eyes had been following the undertaker; at that moment it vanished from sight with its burden of dead alien flesh.

"Where shall we meet?" she added.

Incredulously, Halleth countered, "Are you serious?"

"Never more so."

"Well . . . Well, then! I can see a little footbridge between two flowering bushes, across the nearer stream."

"Excellent. I'll join you there."

"When?"

"As soon as I can."

"Oh, *Parly*!"

That was a sob. Embarrassed, though close to tears herself, Parly broke the link this time.

And, drawing a deep breath, wondered whether she had any reservations about the course Halleth had proposed and she was now also to adopt.

None, she concluded after mere moments. None whatever.

An ancient and macabre saying stole from her memory—where and when she had run across it, she had no idea. *Let the dead bury their dead.*

Yes. There was a dead thing, a machine, to attend to such matters. For her, the right and proper action was to live, albeit only for a few hours.

Heart amazingly lightened, she quit the lab for the last time, casting aside as she went the single garment she had on—out of habit, not necessity. She hesitated once more as she framed the command that would open the airtight door to the outside world, but felt ashamed of herself, and with head upright and shoulders back, she uttered it.

The door slid wide. For the first time in twenty years she felt a breeze on her bare skin.

It was indescribably delicious.

Halleth was ahead of her at the little bridge. Slim and youthful, long hair cascading down her back, smiling-faced and bright-eyed—perhaps, Parly suspected, from tears—she stared at first as though afraid she was dreaming. Not until Parly halted before her, reached out, and took her hand did her mask of anxious disbelief give way to a smile. Seizing Parly's hand in both of hers, she pressed it to her breast. Parly could feel the frantic beating of her heart.

"I always wondered what it was like to touch somebody," the girl breathed. "How long is it since anyone on Zemprad touched another person?"

"Almost two decades," Parly answered, raising her other hand to stroke Halleth's sleek dark head. "Nearly as long as you have been alive."

"I never knew till now just how terrible the thing was that happened to us! Parly, I want to touch you—all over, everywhere! Will you hold me? Hug me tight?"

"Yes, of course, darling," Parly said, and, suiting action to word, embraced her, pressing their bodies close.

For a long moment neither moved or spoke, relishing the lost sensation. Gradually they began to move against each other, concentrating on the friction of skin with skin, the smoothness, the pressure, the mounting excitement—

A shadow fell across them. Startled, they broke apart, staring upward.

They could not see the sun. Not only where they stood but all the landscape lay in sudden darkness. Halleth let out a stifled cry.

"An eclipse? But it happened too quickly!"

"And none is due!" Parly exclaimed. The air could not really have become chill in so brief a span of time, but shivers racked her, and her skin prickled with tiny bumps. At the edge of her mind she had already begun to suspect what the cause might be.

"Explain, then! Explain!" Halleth whimpered. "My dream that I sacrificed my life for is being stolen from me! It's not fair!"

Parly, keeping hold of the girl's hand, felt how she was trembling.

"Something is passing between us and the sun," she said gruffly. "Something enormous. And there's only one thing it could be. It's supposed to rescue failed colonies—isn't it?"

Eyes round with awe, Halleth forced out, "You mean the Ship?"

Parly could only nod. Ever since the magnitude of the crisis had become apparent, the Zempers had hoped against hope for its intervention. It had never come. Most by now had concluded that it must have failed in its mission or be stranded parsecs distant at the far end of the Arm.

To have it arrive now, when it's so nearly too late—indeed, it is too late—that would be the worst of all imaginable ironies. Cruel, too! I've lived most of my allotted span, but poor little Halleth . . .

Her thoughts came to a slow halt, like a river sinking into sand before it could reach the ocean. For a form was taking shape before them: a tall, commanding, not-quite-human figure, radiant of power, defying ordinary perception inasmuch as she could not tell whether it was male or female, solid or a projection, clad or

353

naked. Such superficial features did not matter; she sensed that at once. What counted was that it had made itself known.

And what she most wanted to do, with infinite bitterness, was curse it to the heart of a black hole.

THIS IS INCOMPREHENSIBLE! IF IT WERE POSSIBLE FOR ME to do so, I could believe I had gone mad. This is the type of situation—the only type—in which I am not only permitted but obliged to interfere!

Wild paradoxes hummed in Ship's circuitry like frantic animals trapped in a labyrinth between flood and fire.

Yet I clearly recall from my earlier/later visits that I did not take steps to transport the survivors elsewhere. Why? It can't be that they're suffering from a disease my resources cannot cure—in fact I already know I can cure it, even though they themselves lack the wherewithal.

Revealing itself in full, it awaited a response.

Only these two can tell me why I should not save them. They must be going to, for I did not. But why? WHY?

"You must be one of the Perfect!" Halleth blurted.

Stern, the figure retorted, "No! But your companion knows who I am."

Putting her arm around the girl, who was swaying as though she might fall headlong, Parly said in a dull voice, "The Ship, of course. It's known to have the power of projection."

"Then we're going to be saved!" Halleth cried. And a second later, having sensed contradiction—from the expressionless figure, from something in Parly's attitude?—added in a doubtful tone, "Aren't we?"

Weary to the bone, Parly drew herself up. She said, "You surely know what we were fools enough to do. A second must have sufficed to interrogate our automatics."

"Less . . . Your attempt to replant and repopulate this planet with human-tolerable strains was going so well, you imagined you could neglect your gene armoring. Many among you argued that to continue it might lead to unacceptable variation from the so-called norm—different proportions, skin pigment, other superficialities. Persuaded by irrational attachment to the unattainable ideal of creating a duplicate of the birthworld, you let yourselves be converted to the cause of laziness.

"Then some of the organisms you had turned loose to help exterminate the native organisms backfired on you. They retained irremovable traces of DNA-based genes, which were seized upon by the indigenous microbes—not deliberately but in accordance with the local life process—and incorporated into their own tissue. This made thousands of them capable of infecting human bodies, which had not previously been the case. In particular, they attacked males.

"About forty years ago there appeared the first signs of disease. People scoffed and relied on the resources of your not inconsider-

356

able biological expertise to put matters right. They expected medicines, vaccines, nanosurgeons, to solve the problem, and for a while they held it at bay.

"About thirty years ago, unexpectedly—though you ought to have not merely expected but anticipated it!—there followed the first indications of an epidemic. Frightened, you belatedly set about analyzing the cause. Only to find—"

Thus far, her arm still comfortably around Halleth, Parly had listened silently with her mouth in a thin grim line. Now she stirred.

"There's no need to spell it out in such detail," she muttered. "I'll tell you the rest. What we found, after nearly another decade of investigation, was that we could indeed have coped with these diseases—had we started to do so before we wiped out so many of the native plants. With them as raw material, we could have manufactured a cure in sufficient quantity for our entire population to survive while we caught up with the overdue task of gene armoring. But there weren't enough of the native flora left, and our killer organisms were proving so successful that even the few isolated pockets that had survived were shrinking by the day. Twenty years ago we realized we were doomed."

"And you were too ashamed to tell anybody the truth," challenged Ship.

"Yes." Parly passed a weary hand across her eyes. "We felt we could do no more than make certain all ships calling here were warned not to land. Nothing in the records you supplied to our ancestors, nothing in what we had learned since, suggested that our species had met tougher opposition anywhere. We didn't want to compound our fault by letting others walk into a biological trap."

Halleth had recovered somewhat. Moving unsteadily away from Parly, she ventured, "They told me about that. Isn't it because the microbes attacking us incorporate a little of our kind of life? On all other planets we've had the advantage that the native creatures met us as total strangers, maybe even finding us toxic. But these are creatures that we helped to make."

"Yes, child," Ship said in a gentler and more sympathetic tone.

"Your folk brought their fate on their own heads. The case is indeed unique."

"So . . . are you going to rescue us?"

"That's up to you."

I have learned to lie a little, after this long. How strange it is, though, to make such a statement, knowing it sounds like the truth, knowing it false, yet knowing it to be both false and true at the same time!

There was a dead pause. At last Halleth breathed, "You literally mean—me? Or me and Parly?"

"The latter."

"But that's—that's ridiculous!"

"Unfortunately, it's not." With casual ease Ship commandeered the still-operating communications net and used it to project images of every last survivor on the planet. Halleth and Parly recognized them all, naturally, although they had never met them in the flesh, any more than until today they had confronted each other.

And it was a sorry spectacle. Even those who had seemed strongest and most resolute, even those who claimed to admire and be emulating Parly's outward show of calm, had manifestly been broken by this late arrival of the Ship. Some had relapsed into catatonia; some were gibbering; some appeared to have sought strength in drugs, found it insufficient, taken more, then more, then more . . . Those who had gone that route before, of course, had already been past hope. Many were now trying to punish themselves, slashing their limbs or beating their heads against walls. And a few—the most dreadful—were simply laughing . . .

"You see?" Ship said with ineffable sadness.

"But you could take them away, you could cure them!" Halleth cried.

"I cannot act so without clear instruction," said the Ship. "They are insane or in coma. That instruction must therefore come from you."

"What makes you think we're not crazy, too?" Parly countered with sarcastic humor. "Did we not walk out of our sealed homes, knowing that in a few short hours or days we, too, would be diseased? We've thrown away the rest of our lives for the sake of a moment's joy, a fleeting pleasure, an illusory taste of what our ancestors called beautiful . . . And we've been cheated even of that need of what all Zempers should have had but threw away."

"You could get it back for us!" Halleth exclaimed. "You have incredible powers, infinitely greater than we ever did! You can cure us all, make the planet over properly, save us from ourselves!"

"You are wrong." The voice was like the tolling of a great bell. "Not even I could transform an entire planet in the blink of an eye. That is a task for humans by the million. In any case, it would not be allowed."

"If we say yes, take us away," Parly ventured, "what will you do?"

"Take aboard everyone still alive whom I might reasonably hope to return to normality. Transport them to a more favorable world. Leave this one to its fate."

"You would have to take all of us?"

"This is not a situation in which I am permitted to take only one or two. It must be all or none."

"May I speak privately to Halleth?"

Remarkably, Ship hesitated—for as long as a human might have done, in spite of its far superior reaction time. After more than two seconds the answer came.

"You may. I apologize for the delay, but I had to make arrangements for myself not to be able to overhear. I am of course monitoring the whole of Zemprad. I shall next hear you speak when you say loudly, 'Ship!' Is that satisfactory?"

"Thank you, it is. I'll try not to be long."

So what they say to each other I shall never know. How interesting. That in itself clarifies much of the mystery. The outcome, of course, I no longer need to guess. I never really needed to speculate about it at all.

* * *

"Ship!"

Once again Parly stood with her arm about Halleth's shoulders. The girl looked as though she had been crying, but her tears had already begun to dry in the breeze. On her face was an expression of resolve, as though she had fought against herself and conquered.

Parly's face, though, was unchanged.

"You have reached your decision?" Ship inquired.

"Yes. We thank you for your offer and decline it."

"The fact is noted. May I ask your reasons?"

"We are agreed"—here a trace of pride entered Parly's voice—"that we as a folk made one of the worst errors of all time. We were guilty of unforgivable stupidity, and it was rooted in arrogance and vanity. It would be as well were a strain capable of that to die out rather than mingle with humanity elsewhere."

"And that is Halleth's view as well?"

The girl nodded; then, as though finding the gesture inadequately vigorous, said firmly, "Yes!"

"Then I shall be on my way," Ship sighed. "I am compelled to visit every planet that I seeded, and there are hundreds more to go."

The form began to fade. Suddenly Parly said, "Wait!"

"You have changed your mind?"

"No, not at all! I just wanted to ask you a question."

"By all means."

"Do you get very lonely by yourself among the stars?"

"Yes."

"I thought you might . . . I'm sorry if our decision has deprived you of company that you were looking forward to."

Ship altered the form of its projection. From towering and impressive, it shrank closer to the stature of an ordinary person and acquired a wry, rather wrinkled human face whose features could clearly be made out. In a completely different tone it said, "Frankly, I am not much disappointed—for very much the reasons you just cited . . . But I'm grateful for your sympathy. In return, I want to give you a present, in a double sense."

Baffled, Halleth glanced at Parly, but she was equally at a loss.

Shaking her head, the older woman looked a question.

"You shall have your dream," Ship said quietly, "and it shall seem to last a lifetime."

Then it was gone.

The shadow vanished from the land. The sun shone hot and bright. On a broad green plain threaded with streams and dotted with trees and flowering shrubs, Halleth and Parly stared at each other, vaguely confused, as though this instant they had forgotten what they had been talking about.

But it couldn't have been important. They dismissed it with a laugh, and hand in hand set off to seek out all the beauty they could find in this attempt at paradise their ancestors had worked so hard to build.

CHAPTER SEVENTEEN

SHIP

SHIP HAD ARRANGED FOR WHAT WAS TRANSPIRING ON the surface of Zemprad to be projected to Oach. At first puzzled, then fascinated, lastly overcome with emotion, the young man watched and listened, displaying his first signs of genuine animation since he came on board. By the time Ship ceased its world-wide monitoring and began its journey out of the system, he was sobbing, head in hands.

Ship left him undisturbed.

At length, raising swollen eyes, he realized that his so-convincing surroundings had vanished, to be replaced with a view of the diminishing planet and its moons.

"I'm sorry you were so affected," Ship murmured.

"Sorry? What for?" Oach had been sitting; now he rose to his full height, his expression bewildered. "I'm glad! For the first time I feel like a proper human being. I feel I truly have something in common with the Old Stock!"

"Because you can sympathize with the fate the last of the Zempers chose for themselves?"

"Oh, I can only admire them for that. I found their decision noble, for it was motivated by the opposite of self-interest. No, it's the fact that I can weep."

"Weeping," Ship said, "is no more encouraged among the adults of your folk than laughter is."

"Indeed. So I feel somehow"—a shrug, a wide spread of the spadelike hands at the ends of his long arms—"more complete. As though I'd got in touch with something I need, in the way I need food, or sex, or dreams. Ship, in your view is there something wrong with my people?"

"A curious question," Ship parried.

"Yes, of course." Oach let his hands fall to his sides again. "One could scarcely expect a machine to understand what I mean. And yet . . ."

"Please continue. I am interested."

"And yet"—in an almost accusatory tone—"you know the meaning of pity!"

"Do I?"

"You just proved it! At least those two brave women had their just reward. Their happiness may be illusory, but it must be better than sure knowledge of approaching death."

Ship paused, not from need to reflect but from its awareness that a momentary delay would heighten the impact of what it next intended to say. At length:

"All humans live in the knowledge of approaching death."

"All?" Oach glanced around as though hoping to see an image he could address directly. "I suppose I did at home, but I thought deliberate termination was a rare policy on other worlds."

"That is correct."

"So you must mean . . . Oh, I see. We do all die sooner or later, though most, I suspect, manage to forget the fact until it's almost on us. Do the Perfect die, though?"

"I have no data."

"Will you die?"

This time Ship remained silent for a surprisingly long time—so long, indeed, Oach felt embarrassed. Rubbing his reddened eyes, he made to apologize.

"I'm sorry if that was a tactless question. You don't need to answer if you don't want to."

"I find in fact that I cannot answer. In principle, of course, my existence must come to an end. In practice, I may not enjoy that privilege."

Oach reared back his head in astonishment. "But—oh—to take it to extremes, you cannot possibly outlive the universe!"

"Of course not, but that's irrelevant to my situation."

"It's no good. I simply don't understand. You'll have to make it clear. Explain!"

Finally Ship had the chance—albeit one it could barely justify within the terms of its instructions—to inform his current passenger of what his predecessors had learned almost as soon as they came aboard. Resuming his seat, Oach listened with total attention.

"And you have no control at all over the period you arrive in after each sweep?"

"It seems entirely arbitrary."

"Then I should weep for you, as well. Like Parly, I feel sorry for you."

"Do not encourage me to acquire, along with my other well-imitated human reactions, the bad habit of self-pity." A light chuckle. "I need waste no regrets on Zemprad, anyway. What was done there was outside my power to rectify, and what cannot be helped is not worth regretting . . . We are approaching the safe zone for tachyonic mode. Will you eat before you sleep?"

"Ah . . ." Sounding surprised, as though he had just discovered he could still feel hungry, Oach hesitated. "Yes, thank you, I will. But one more question first."

"That being—?"

"What is our next stopover? A more successful settlement, I trust." Behind the words, unspoken but deducible from the hint of anxiety that colored them: *One where I can fulfill my ambition and walk under a foreign sky, a real sky such as the Old Stock still enjoy?*

"It depends," Ship replied judiciously, "on what you count to be success. And with that, I'm afraid, you must be content until we get there."

"But I know about this planet," Oach said suddenly, scant moments after the projection of its surface formed around him.

Ship waited.

"Those fleshy dark red leaves—those rugose stems—the pale patches on the ground, so much cooler than their surroundings . . . Even the weather!" It was windy; now and then a spurt of rain dashed against the vegetation. Small animals, either many-legged or legless but with suction pads on their undersides, crawled across the "leaves," rising up now and then to snatch at something from the air, too small to be seen at this magnification.

"Yes, this is where there are still Old Stock humans, but only about as many as landed originally, and they seem to have lost all interest in creating a human-style civilization . . . There go some of them now."

Indeed, Ship's sensors had closed in on a group of some twenty individuals wandering along a narrow track between dark boulders, sometimes having to scramble over an obstacle but seeming not to care any more than they did about the intermittent showers—though they did acknowledge the latter by tilting back their heads and opening their mouths. Devoid alike of tools and ornaments, they were naked and rather dirty; their hair hung in tangles; their faces, however, bore identical expressions of contentment, as if life could not possibly hold anything better.

"It looks like a primitive tribal group," Oach went on. "That was in the reports we received. This was one of the first group of worlds that the Arzakians sent us data on, just after Arzak accepted our offer to build a starship for them. They said there were several different tribes. Yet I don't see any children."

"There are none," Ship said.

Oach glanced around, blinking. "But there must be! Or was this world not settled at the same time as the rest?"

Not answering, for Oach knew perfectly well there had been only one colonization sweep, Ship continued. "And there are not *about* as many humans here as originally landed. There are *exactly* as many. There's something the Arzakians didn't spot."

"How is that possible?" Oach exclaimed. And then realized. Clenching his fists, he demanded, "Do you mean these are the same?"

"I could even tell you their names, which they themselves have long forgotten."

"After—what?—four, nearly five hundred years?"

"Yes, I still recognize them despite the changes they have undergone."

"Why didn't we hear about that from Arzak?"

"Because all they saw when they visited this system was a

failed and decadent colony. Their mind-set did not permit them to think of delving deeper. Not, in fact, that with the equipment available to them they would have found out very much. When, on their way to report to the Shipwrights, they discovered that Zemprad was refusing all contact and—as could clearly be seen from space—had made virtually no progress in expanding its population despite the rapid advance of their imported flora and fauna, they concluded that here was another and still worse example of the same: a world where organisms adapted to human needs had entirely failed to gain a foothold."

"But surely—"

Ship interrupted. "If you are about to ask what happened to their supply of spatial spores, they're still in orbit, having done their worst."

"Done—their worst?" Oach's bafflement was painfully obvious.

"When I was dispatched on my mission," Ship went on, "I knew there were bound to be failures and oversights. After all, the Arm was unexplored except by automatic vehicles, and the data they had gathered were necessarily imperfect. Nonetheless, this looked like a promising planet. The local life-forms needed only minor adaptation before settlers could exploit them as an interim measure. It seemed a safe assumption that what the colonists had with them, plus resources from space, would enable long-term survival. What neither they nor even I realized was how long and in what peculiar fashion."

"So what did happen?" Oach cried.

"The life here is possessed of a dull collective intelligence. Not the type that manifests itself in building, in transforming and processing, but a self-contained form of awareness, reactive rather than conscious. Certain of its reflexes—which we were ignorant of—were triggered by contact with humans and the incoming spores.

"It would appear, although even now I cannot offer any evidence save the most circumstantial, that exposure to creatures capable of dying somehow offended it."

"But how in all of space could—?" Oach broke off the eager question, forcing himself to be patient.

"Being as I said collective, it does not regard itself—if indeed it has any concept of 'self'—as mortal. So it may well have responded, on becoming acquainted with death, as any creature with a rudimentary nervous system would respond to an unpleasant stimulus. Without being too anthropomorphic, one might hazard that humans with their propensity to die upset its view of what was right and proper. It may even be that it vaguely welcomed this new phenomenon in its previously static universe. However that may be, it did react, and you are witnessing the consequences."

The naked men and women were still trudging along their stony path, though here it was wider and they could walk two or three abreast instead of single file. Rain was softening the patches of mud on their skins until they ran down in a kind of fantastic camouflage, so that now and then Oach found it hard to distinguish them from their background, save by the contrast of heat.

"What actually happened?" he forced out.

"Watch the last of the group. I chose it because of him." The focus closed on a nearly bald man with thin limbs and a bulging belly, who had to pause for breath every hundred paces. His evident physical weakness did nothing, however, to affect his look of calm satisfaction with the world.

"In a few minutes they will reach their goal," Ship explained. "They no longer have actual intentions. This is no more than a taxis, like a sperm moving toward an ovum."

"What is their goal, then?"

"You'll see."

The path broadened still farther and debouched on level ground covered with glabrous knee-high growths. Rendered visible by Ship's shift to a viewpoint several meters above ground level, a river meandered in the distance. A floodplain, Oach diagnosed correctly, although he had never seen one before.

On the nearer bank of the river loomed one much larger growth, displaying a brilliant pattern of contrasting colors in both the regular visual and the infrared bands of the spectrum. To the sights and sounds of the projection was briefly added a whiff of odor. Oach found it distinctly unpleasant, though he could not have explained why.

"That did not appear in the reports you received," Ship commented.

"Would we have been able to figure out its significance if it had done?" Oach countered.

"I greatly doubt it. Can you?"

"Because you've drawn my attention to it, I can guess. Is it a pheromone that induces the taxis?"

"It is indeed. Go on watching."

Arriving at the bright-colored growth, the leaders of the group paid it no attention but passed by to wade into the river, bend, drink, then halfheartedly splash each other—all without a hint of enthusiasm, as though repeating a ritual so old that knowledge of the reason for it had been lost. Bringing up the rear, however, the bald old man wheezed aside from the course the rest had followed and approached the growth. Viewed from close by, it proved to be formed of many overlapping convex layers, about the thickness of a finger but broader and taller than a human. These layers began to unfold, sagging outward, and revealed a hollow at the center. The same unchanging look on his face, the bald man clambered into it. Sluggishly, the layers closed again.

When several minutes had passed and nothing further seemed likely to happen, Oach ventured, "Is that all?"

"For a person whose mental processes are so much slower than mine," Ship said dryly, "you display a remarkable capacity for impatience. It takes a while. Has to."

Almost, Oach demanded what did, but he managed to contain himself.

Eventually the layers sagged apart again, and the hollow reappeared.

But this time its occupant was not stick-limbed and bald but youthful, active, and apparently well nourished. He had been totally transformed.

"It's like a miracle!" he breathed. "A century has been taken from him just like that!"

"And has it done him any good?" Ship countered sadly.

Blinking, Oach watched as the rejuvenated man followed the others to the river. By now they seemed to be sated both with water and their lackluster play. They waited only for him to drink before they climbed back on the bank and resumed their plodding.

"Is this all they ever do?" Oach whispered.

"They eat," Ship said. "They can digest virtually any of the plants. They excrete, inevitably. At night they sleep, since humankind can never escape the need to dream. That's all."

"They're not even interested in sex?"

"Despite the way humanity has separated sex from reproduction in virtually every modern culture, that remains its underlying purpose. Here, that purpose has been removed. Since they have lost the power of speech, one cannot ask how they feel, but observing them indicates that they are barely aware of their own existence, let alone capable of recognizing individuality in others. From my personal recollection, I can depose that some members of this group had already begun to associate before they were landed. It is possible they have never separated since—well, the day the change began."

"So they're immortal," Oach said after a pause.

"Their bodies are. Their minds died long ago."

Another and much longer silence ensued. At last Oach rose from his seat and stretched his long arms.

"I see what you meant about it depending on how one counts success. Do you have any more business here?"

"You wish to leave?"

"Yes. In fact, I wish I'd never come here. I've seen things more horrible than I imagined possible. This experience is changing me. I welcomed the change I underwent at Zemprad. This one . . . no." Struck by an afterthought, he added, "What's this planet called?"

"I remember the name its settlers intended to bestow on it, but by now I must be the only one who does."

THE NEXT WORLD SHIP STOPPED AT WAS LIKE A HUN-
dred of its kind: population expanding at an acceptable rate, an
acceptable level of adaptation of the planet to its new inhabitants
and vice versa . . . and Oach showed no interest in it whatsoever.
He identified it accurately from Arzakian reports, recalled its
name and most of its chief characteristics, including the fact that
it was negotiating to establish an embassy to the Shipwrights,
and apart from that roused from his lethargy only long enough to
inquire whether there was presently a ship on the landing grid.
On learning that there wasn't he retreated into gloom again.

Not until its parent star was dwindling into the stellar background did he pull himself together and say, "Ship!"

"You're feeling better?" Ship inquired solicitously.

"Oh, you know how I feel," Oach snapped. "You can't help it,
can you? Reading my pheromones is the next thing to reading my
thoughts."

"You're unhappy," Ship suggested.

"I feel like someone who's gone out on the track of a sorter
signaling a cloud of vanadium and found its sensors have been
deranged by radiation. I feel cheated—oh, not by you. By my own
hopes and dreams."

Ship waited. Slowly, having to marshal his thoughts into intractable words, Oach spelled out the reason for his depression.

"I thought I was due for the most marvelous possible experience—a free ride to as many planets as I chose. I haven't seen
even a handful so far, yet I feel terribly disappointed."

"Why so?"

"That's what I'm trying to figure out." Oach rose from his seat
and began to pace restlessly back and forth. "As near as I can
come, it's because at the back of my mind was always the conviction that out here I could exercise some element of choice. All my
life, like the rest of my folk, I've been hemmed in by the conditions

370

our ancestors laid down, like you with your mission instructions. Now I've come to realize that no matter how far I travel with you, I shall be forever in the same state of frustration: a passenger, an onlooker. Oh, an incredibly privileged one, of course! But—but somehow it doesn't feel *right,* it doesn't match what I used to dream of when I was a child. The fact that I can simply hear the name of a world, like the one we've just left, and know so much about it without ever having set foot there . . . You know, I never used to think I had an especially good memory, because all my life—you said something to this effect—I've relied on data being available whenever, wherever I wanted it. Now I find I do have a good memory after all, an amazing memory—"

Struck by a sudden idea, he broke off.

"You've improved it, haven't you?" he challenged.

"It did not occur to me," Ship replied, "that you would regard that as a handicap."

"No. No, of course not. That was silly of me. It's just . . ." Oach was perspiring; he wiped the back of his hand across his forehead to stop sweat running over his mosaic of IR sensors. "It's just that knowing as much as I do makes this experience somehow *flat.*"

"I suspect," Ship murmured, "you've already come to a decision concerning your future course of action."

"Yes. Yes, I have." Oach straightened to his full height. "Only a few more systems remain to be visited before you call at Arzak—I can't be sure how many, since I don't know what order you seeded them in. But I make it six or seven at most.

"When we reach Arzak, I want to be set down. I want to offer myself as crew on the ship that Arzak rents from us. I want to travel the stars among people of my own kind, even if they are Old Stock. I dare to hope that some day I might ship out to an unexplored volume and find a planet about which I know nothing beforehand." A brief hesitation, then: "I take it you can make it safe for me to do so? You can protect me against the stellar flux that's supposed to make it impossible for us to live outside our cloud?"

"That," Ship answered dryly, "was one of the first jobs I attended to."

"So can I do it? Will you let me?"

"I have no power to object."

"What about the Arzakians?"

"I suspect they may not take kindly to having a Shipwright among the crew. You can no doubt work out why."

"Arzak, so I've been told, was on the verge of launching starships of its own, as Yellick did, when our automatic vessel arrived there. What we offered was so obviously superior, they abandoned theirs, but there are still many who resent the waste of so much effort."

Ship waited. When Oach said nothing further, it adopted a light tone colored with the suggestion of a chuckle.

"Well, well! You really are determined to be an ambassador at whatever cost, aren't you?"

Oach did not smile in response. He said only, "Now all I have to do is while away the time until we reach Arzak."

"Comfort yourself with the reflection," Ship admonished, "that there are always new things to find out on any planet. You asked me whether I think there is something wrong with your people. It is not for me to pass judgment. But you may, and now I think you have your answer."

ALONE IN THE TIMELESSNESS OF TACHYONIC SPACE, Ship brooded.

So there is at least one lacuna in my memory that can't be accounted for by damage or the decree of my designers. I can never know what passed between Parly and Halleth any more than I can access the interior of Oach's mind . . .

Oach said I have learned how to pity. Is it conceivable that the pattern of my returns is planned so that on each sweep I acquire greater understanding of emotion, a kind of psychological evolution in a prescribed order?

It seemed unlikely. Still, having enough capacity and to spare, it dedicated circuitry to analyzing the idea.

But I didn't need Oach to tell me. Not really.

Poor Stripe!

AS CHANCE WOULD HAVE IT (OR WAS IT CHANCE? WAS anything in this lonely existence due to chance alone?), Oach was the last passenger Ship acquired during its present sweep. To Menlee and Annica it had mentioned that most of the failures—those due, at any rate, to human inadequacy rather than insuperable odds—were concentrated at this end of the Arm, for those who had bided their time before deciding to land and settle had in general been steadier, more thoughtful, more open-eyed. Of course, there were traps in plenty still waiting to be sprung (*that burning plague in the eyes, in the ears, which made beautiful canalside cities ring with moans and screams!*), but where confidence still reigned supreme there was nothing Ship could do to intervene.

So it made its way from star to star, marveling insofar as it could at the differences a mere half millennium had wrought yet also at the resemblances. Where control had not been wrested from them, as at the world he had visited with Oach, whose name Ship and only Ship recalled, humans remained astonishingly human . . .

Some societies had enjoyed a brilliant, rapid flowering. Some, in the liberty and intellect of their citizens, could rival any in history. There, whether under a clear sky or sheltered in caverns from endless raging storms, people enjoyed art, music, the pleasures of the body; they were calm, grave-eyed, thoughtful, yet capable of bursting into laughter that would have shocked the ordinators of the Shipwrights. (Did Ship think there was something wrong with Oach's folk? Yes, indeed: though for a nobler purpose, they had in their way made the same mistake as could be found at Klepsit, inasmuch as in their quest to reconcile humans and machines they had come to distrust the simple, illogical delights of merely being alive.)

But those were few.

374

Commonest were those that had done tolerably well and were continuing to plod ahead at a steady pace. Arzak was one example among scores, akin to Sumbala and Yellick. Their counterparts turned up again and again beyond the range that ships from the Veiled Worlds had so far reached. Some had done well enough to consider—like Yellick—the building of at least one starship, though few had achieved that goal, and several would never do so, because in another few generations the overlapping spheres expanding from Sumbala, Arzak, and the rest would inflict on them the same shock the Arzakians had felt when an automatic ship signaled from orbit the so-tempting invitation: rent a ship like this from us, don't waste time and energy building your own, pay us with nothing more than data . . .

But most numerous of all were the ones where, thanks to local conditions, or the impact of an early epidemic, or ill-judged attempts at gene armoring, or the mere instability of the human mind under pressure—still fragile, a mere bubble after so long!—there had been a fall back to an earlier, indeed an ancient, pattern. Few were so acute as Trevithra, with its bloody pogrom of all who admitted even a slight acquaintance with science and its seething religion-versus-rationality disputes. However, there were more than enough.

On Quelstey, for a few brief but terrifying decades, the population had diminished rather than increased owing to cosmic radiation damage in the computer that designed their gene armoring. During the time it took to locate and rectify the fault, fertility became an obsession and the folk deranged. Now the culture was a matriarchal hierocracy, and women capable of bearing children—a score or more, sometimes as twins and triplets—were literally worshiped. There were no towns or cities: instead, buildings resembling a cross between a temple, a maternity hospital, and a crèche. Men walked for days bearing such loads of offerings their backs were permanently bowed, to beg and buy the right to couple with a mistress of proven fecundity. Yet, Ship recalled, this was no more than a transient setback. In a thousand years the planet would be as flourishing as anyone might wish.

On Helvikuk, by contrast, all seemed to be proceeding very well indeed, though at the outset it had appeared unpromising, its gravity being fifteen percent higher than normal for a habitable planet. Still, its native life was totally non-DNA, and there had been few problems with sickness, freeing the settlers to make and implement grandiose plans—less grandiose, luckily, than those which had been the downfall of the Zempers.

By now the folk were taller and more massive than their ancestors, well muscled to resist the extra gravity. They went about their work in a deliberate fashion, content with the kind of solid achievements that would feed or house them better, give them more leisure to indulge their favorite pastime of exploring in small groups, on foot even in the highest, coldest mountains or the flattest and most barren deserts. They desired to know their adopted world as intimately as their ancestors had known their planets of origin; rather than mapping it from orbit and isolating its hostile zones, as so often had been done elsewhere, they preferred to make personal acquaintance with it—tread it, touch it, taste it, breathe its scents, and bear its heat and cold. To an untutored visitor it would have seemed far more successful than Quelstey, where pregnant women were set up on thrones before which men came to bow and plead.

Yet Ship remembered from the future how Helvikuk would settle and grow static once the years of exploration ended. When starships arrived—not built by the Shipwrights but in another, nearer system—they would disdain contact and repulse the visitors, fearing the task of having to learn about elsewhere, preferring to believe they knew as much as they needed or would ever need to know.

Ship found that infinitely sad.

Again, there were worlds where caste divisions had grown up, typically because not long after the landing a crisis had arisen and power had had to be concentrated in the hands of a few exceptionally imaginative or strong-willed individuals. Having acquired the taste for privilege, they and their descendants contrived ingenious means to cling to it. Most of these were following an ancient and predictable pattern; ultimately the rulers would grow decadent, neglect their precautions, and be overthrown by desperate and resentful revolutionaries with little to lose and their world to gain.

On some, however, the overlords had proved more ruthless and were protecting themselves by breeding for reduced intelligence among their subjects. So long as they could obey orders, so long as they could attend to necessary mindless tasks, that would suffice. The rulers, naturally, believed that they could protect their own genetic lines forever, given the power their machines had to touch a single strand of DNA so delicately—so very delicately—and induce virtually any desirable characteristic.

But with long monopoly of power went laziness and often ignorance. Sooner or later one of two things must happen: The ruling class would realize how dangerous its situation had become, reform itself, and resume the original plan for their settlement; or else—more likely—they would come to believe that gene maintenance was an empty ritual, a boring nuisance . . . and there would be no one else to make sure it was done for them.

Whereupon there would be another addition to the list of failures. Perhaps in the distant future such worlds would become the first of those that Menlee and Annica had hypothesized and be recognized by other folk from within the Arm.

But Ship had never been hurled that far forward in time.

On a few planets the almost forgotten custom of war had reappeared despite their still-low population densities. In most cases it was due to despair and jealousy and broke out over control of scarce but essential resources. On a few it was the result of deliberate policy. Leaders adhering to the primitive concept of divide and rule found it a convenient way of distracting rivals who might otherwise have toppled them. On Shenkipan, though, where the populace was collectively deranged, it had once again become accepted as a means of "hardening" the people, toughening them for daunting tasks ahead.

It could never, though, get out of hand—the machines on which every colony depended saw to that. They had been cunningly programmed to refuse any order for weapons of mass destruction, so there were neither nuclear bombs nor holocausters, and past a certain point even the sort of arms an individual could carry would be produced only in faulty unreliable form. What use was a sonic congealer that might kill the person wielding it? And if one wanted even chemical explosives, one had to mix them oneself.

As for tailored plagues, or poisonous biting insectoids, or other biological media—they were out of the question. The machines could not possibly disobey their primary duty to enhance humanity's survival.

So Shenkipan offered the peculiar, antiquated spectacle of men in heavy drab clothing trudging in strung-out lines across rough country with clubs and cudgels to meet other men in ambush among rocks or hidden in a copse, there to set about each other with violent ill-aimed blows. Eventually, most often at nightfall or if bad weather came on, the survivors would retreat to their respective camps and invent lies about their own heroism.

Watching such events from orbit, now and then projecting itself down to the surface and going among the armies invisibly or in disguise, Ship pondered again the sadness and futility of what was happening. It hoped an injured captive might appeal for rescue, but no one ever did. These men—they were invariably men—had been brought up to imagine war was glorious, and short of intruding on their brains, which it was prohibited from doing, Ship had no means of penetrating their conditioning.

Still, it couldn't help wondering how any human—notoriously irrational though the species was—could continue to believe such a ridiculous fiction while weltering in mud with a bloody pate or broken leg.

There were other unique anomalies, and in several cases even its memories of the future did not allow Ship to guess what the eventual outcome would be. On Whishwang the settlers had accidently discovered a native plant whose juice—though totally alien to their own biology—proved to stimulate the mental processes mysteriously, much as back on the birthworld (Ship's memory held relevant data, as did their own half-living computers) the mode by which anesthetics operated was not understood until generations after they were first exploited. For a while some of the settlers hoped their newfound keenness of mind might yield an explanation; shortly, though, rapt by the vividness of their own imaginations, they forwent such research and simply wandered about, eating if they must but gaunt, dressing if they must but tanned and windburned overall, talking if they must but often declaiming simultaneously at one another, so it was hard to decide how much if anything each understood of what was being said.

Yet now and then, apparently struck by some supernal magic wand, groups would join together in a common project, each bringing a necessary element such as a tool or a preformed component, and after days or weeks of labor there would be something that did not exist before: a tower, a framework, a maze of prisms, or a mandala. It was as though the imaginings of one had ensnared hundreds of others, glad to comply with a superior visualization. Possibly the mode of communication was like that of the creatures on the world where Annica and Menlee had spent a night; Ship could not tell. However it operated, it was not in a manner that it was equipped to detect.

But once created and for a while admired, the result of their work was left to weather and corrode, and no one ever seemed to return to the site, regardless of how long and hard the group had worked.

Yet in a thousand years they will have worked over most of the land surface of the planet, and puzzled visitors will be wondering, as I do now, what the purpose of it all may prove to be—in yet another thousand, or ten thousand . . .

Well, they seem contented enough.

Which Ship was not.

The conclusion of its sweep was drawing near as the Arm thinned and tapered like a curving sandbank swept on either side by river currents. So long without company—this had happened before or would happen later—was stressing even its remarkable self-containment. Now and then, especially during the slow tran-

sit outward from a planet to the zone where it could enter tachyonic mode, disturbing visions began to haunt it. As though it could
view itself from outside, which was not a facility its designers
had provided, it seemed to sense/see/be aware of a colossal
creature weaving its way through empty dark.

No, empty was the wrong word. (*An error! Amazing! A clue to
something? What? Does it have to do with what I think/imagine
I am perceiving?*) The vacuum, "the empty thing," was not. It
seethed and bubbled with particles darting in and out of "existence" from all the other universes alongside, whose reality—at
least as great as that of the universe Ship inhabited, and its
charges—had not been contested for millennia yet from which no
information could ever be derived. It was a law of nature, the
ultimate law, the one so rigid that, unlike the barrier of light-
speed, it could never be transgressed. One could only imagine:
universes of cold gas, of one gigantic mass at immeasurable temperature, of variant dimensionality so that time might run three
ways at once . . . And in them all the possibility of consciousness,
of thought: of beings whose greatest ambition was to be a flat gray
ellipse, or whose thoughts followed the eruption of stellar promi-
nences in vast arching structures, each a hypothesis, or whose
knowledge of what lay around them was deformed into the past
because in the act of perception they destroyed what they were
seeking to examine, as by heat or gamma rays or other overpow-
erful energy . . .

Such ideas swarmed more and more within Ship's consciousness as it approached the termination of its sweep. So too did the
haunting not-quite vision of itself: this vast creature moving
where the light was dim, the heat faint, and only the ceaseless
frantic activity of the void made impact on its senses. That being
random, structureless, it meant nothing; it was nonsense, it was
simple noise. To escape it, Ship reverted to considering its self-
visions. What did they show? Something broad and curving with
a tapered hinder end—so far that matched its inner perceptions;
at the fore, waving and flexible, portions of itself not detached but
not forming part of the main mass, extensible, controllable—of

course: a symbol for its sensors and projectors, though they were not concentrated in any one location. The whole was in constant motion, not merely forward but within itself; there were undulations, like waves in water—

Water. Yes, of course. The term I want is "swimming." A very natural image, and appropriate.

Yet that conclusion was somehow less than satisfying.

And here was Ysconry, the last of the worlds that Ship had seeded, circling the last bright yellow star in the Arm. Beyond lay nothing but some dull red giants, brown dwarfs by the thousand, countless lumps of debris, and a trail of lightless matter drawn along by the rotation of the galactic whirlpool.

And, of course, the rest of the universe.

There would be no starships built here . . .

How clear the memory was of those who had elected to stay on board until the last! How proudly they had boasted of their decision, calling themselves the ultimate frontiersfolk! How brave the visions they had conjured up of their descendants wandering beneath that sky at night, admiring the glory of the parent galaxy, then resolutely turning their backs to gaze at the millions of others far beyond! How full, they claimed, their successors would be of the ambition to transgress that monstrous gap! Why, they could well be the first of all humanity to make the crossing! With the sight of it before them all the time, how could they not be tempted by the prospect?

Instead . . .

Instead, after a few generations, the people of Ysconry grew small-minded and fearful. That gulf was too great to be faced. They turned inward; they colonized only that hemisphere of their world over which by night the parent galaxy loomed brilliant and comforting, leaving the rest to waste; they spoke resentfully of their ancestors for having doomed them to this fate. By now they believed they would never again establish contact with the rest of the species. Many passed their leisure time staring hungrily at the looming mass of stars in desperate hope of detecting some kind of signal, some hint of reassurance that they were not abandoned and forgotten. Others, embittered, had embarked on a vain project to travel back in time, using a derivative of tachyonic drive, and stop the settlement from having happened.

But not even I control that process, Ship thought sadly.

And since for the most part they were in good health if not good spirits, and the latter would recover in a few centuries when starships again reached this far, there was nothing it could do to relieve their gloom. Its inspection complete, it withdrew from the system.

To where *they* were waiting for it. As they always were.

Except that this was the only time. It was always the only time and always would be. It could not be otherwise.

Ship understood.

CHAPTER EIGHTEEN

THE PERFECT

THERE WAS AWARENESS OF A BRIGHT PRESENCE WITH a triple aspect: the past, the present, the future—Urdr, Verdandi and Skuld, the Norns, the Fates, the Parcae, those who held the threads of destiny between their fingers, twining and interweaving them at will and sometimes breaking them . . .

They were the true and only Perfect. They were inside Ship. They were of it. They had been since the outset. They stood to its ordinary consciousness as full awareness to reflexive action.

So this was the same time as every time before, the same time as every other that would follow. There was only this one reunion between the parts of the divided self. It took place in a mode and in a manner Ship-as-it-was-used-to-thinking-of-itself could never comprehend, for it was as baffling as the mystery of the world without a name. Accordingly, it sought comfort in wry resolution of a minor mystery: the reason for its visions of how it might appear could it view itself from the outside. They bore, of course, no resemblance to its actual form.

I am a copy of a squid.

Yes, of course. Its intelligence had had to be based on a nonhuman model—on a species not vulnerable to the terrible dilemma confronting humankind. As the dazzling mind of the Perfect opened farther, more information slammed into place, vast blocks at a time, planetloads of data, systems' worth.

They instructed, as it were, "Listen!" And except that it did not listen at all, Ship obeyed.

The species that evolved on the birthworld—whose names the Perfect recalled, though ordinarily Ship did not—were colony creatures, the result of fusion between lower organisms into a symbiotic, interdependent whole. This process was not uncommon; indeed, the majority of large alien life-forms had arisen in analogous fashion. To most of them, however, its further extension posed no threat—some of the highest, such as the Being of Ekatila, could never have conceived any other possibility. Only humans viewed the foreseeable conclusion as unendurable.

Q: What is the commonest social pattern to have developed on human-occupied planets in the parent galaxy?

A: A society whose members are extremely long-lived, with only a few females being required to breed and that at wide intervals, while the males' function as a pool of genetic variability has largely become superfluous. Most of what is necessary can be undertaken by machines.

Q: What does a social structure in which so few of either sex are required for reproduction call to mind?

A: Creatures like those which on the birthworld were called termites, ants, and bees. We are, in sum, potential hive or swarm animals. That is a trend some of us are determined to reverse.

This, then, was the decadence that had settled over most of humanity. Century by century the pressure of evolution upon individual creatures composed of myriad ex-individuals betrayed itself in loss of imagination, enterprise, the sense of adventure, originality of every kind—a tendency, in sum, toward stasis and eventual decline. Planet after planet, system after system, subsided into mere complacent existence. If people traveled, it was only for amusement, and anyway, why bother when virtually perfect imitations of what would be found after a boring journey could be called up by uttering a single phrase? If they troubled to undertake any project, most likely it was to have themselves made over closer to the current standard of good looks. There were planets where the entire population could be mistaken for clones. Uniformity ruled; sometimes difference became the excuse for rejection, persecution, even murder.

And because the trend was inseparable from being human, it had gone unnoticed for too long. When at last it was recognized, so many planets had yielded to its insidious sapping that there was no hope of counteraction.

None . . . ?

Where some spark of the old spirit still remained, many asked that question and added hints of a solution.

What if, even at this late stage, human beings were confronted with new challenges on alien worlds? What if they were to be, so to say, thrown back to the days of their distant ancestors—forced to fend for themselves against alien life-forms with little to aid them save techniques so old-fashioned that they were beyond being antique and could justifiably be called primitive? Plus a modicum of information that did not previously exist, such as methods of armoring their genes and the knowledge—not the means but the knowledge—to build starships.

Some demanded why they should be deprived of modern technology and were met with two good reasons. First, excessive ease and control of the environment conduced to decadence, and the consequences of that were only too conspicuous. Second, there was no way of altering the species to eliminate the instinct toward group association, not at any rate without losing much of what made humans human. Exposure to pheromones had been identified as one of the accelerative factors in this hive-creature trend, yet it was indispensable as a reinforcement of intraspecies loyalty.

In the old days a balance had been struck. It could be struck again, but this time under careful guidance. There would be towns, perhaps even cities; there might well be old-fashioned education involving the actual presence of a teacher in the same room as the pupils; there would in due course be physical interaction between inhabitants of different planets as ships multiplied along the starlanes. From a wide variety of fresh starting points, perhaps some of the colonists would chance on a better alternative. The project would last thousands of years, but it offered hope—hope that subsidence into hivelike herds might for a while be postponed. And during the passage of two or three millennia a longer-term solution might be found.

Might. But if it wasn't tried, the doom was sure.

* * *

There was only one volume worth considering. Toward the center of the galaxy humans could venture no farther, not because they could not be adapted to withstand the radiation—self-repair of cells and genes after that sort of damage had been possible for so long, its origins could no longer be traced (there lay the falsehood that someday would betray the Shipwrights)—but because there was opposition, its nature a mystery. The most accepted hypothesis was that a race or group of races had transcended conventional intelligence and learned to affect space and matter directly. At any rate, exploring ships, crewed or not, were turned back. Somehow. And perhaps the opposition had limited patience.

That left a single accessible yet unexploited zone: the Arm of Stars. Robot vessels had surveyed it and established that it had habitable planets under yellow suns. Indeed, although a forced choice, it looked like an ideal one—a laboratory designed by nature for exactly such a project.

So there would have to be a ship. There would have to be the Ship—huge enough to carry settlers for all the new worlds, durable enough to supervise their development over at least several thousand years, and, into the bargain, intelligent. The technology existed; there would be no objection from the lazy mass of humanity so long as their easeful daily lives were not disturbed—the craft would in any case have to be built in space, using matériel from barren asteroids—but that last factor posed a problem.

Mere machines had known limitations, though they could achieve self-awareness, and for ages they had possessed many other characteristics of living organisms: They could grow, they could repair themselves to some extent, they could adapt to changing circumstances or newly acquired information. But they could barely comprehend emotion and never display imagination. They could cross-refer data in quantities far exceeding the capacity of organic brains, but they could not be taught to hypothesize with data not yet available.

Therefore, that faculty must be overlaid on a machine substrate. A perfect analog of an aware mind must serve as a template. Ancient records confirmed that this had been attempted in the past with some success—to prolong the lives of accident victims or to permit exploration of environments too hazardous for ordinary machines—but the latter reason had declined as the species became slothful, and advances in limb and organ reconstruction had rendered the former obsolete.

Nonetheless, there had been progress in spite of all. Now, if need be, not one but many personalities could be engrafted. At once there were volunteers.

However, careful analysis revealed another risk. Were supervision of the new worlds to be entrusted to a basically human personality, it might prove to have, as it were, blind spots. It was beyond doubt that when the Ship actually traversed the Arm of Stars, it would meet with crises no reports from automatic survey vessels could have warned against. Similarly, a human mind accustomed to the circumstances in which he or she had grown up, been educated, lived life hitherto, might unconsciously be biased toward precisely that status quo it was imperative to shatter.

Work had already begun on the Ship; its colossal hull was taking shape among a cluster of planetoids rich in metals and inert organics. Designed by machines, it was being constructed by machines, yet it was destined to become more than a machine.

Would the task after all prove vain?

Then one of those engaged in planning offered a way out of the impasse. What if the intelligence to be superimposed were to be copied from a species apparently immune—as yet; there were theoretical grounds for arguing that all creatures highly enough developed to think were to some extent vulnerable—to the hive impulse? Was there a species whose existence thus far had never become stable enough to encourage it? Best of all, was there one whose biology was close to the human so that it might feel at least a hint of loyalty to kindred?

Was there one, in short, on the birthworld?

The idea seemed laughable. Yet on that worn-out cinder of a planet, which millennia ago had been consigned to machines for repair and restoration, they found what they were looking for. Free of human interference, in the vast ocean deeps (petty, they were, beside some found on other worlds humanity had occupied), creatures moved in darkness who had never known what comfort or stasis might be. They moved because they always had to move; they fed as best they could, and bred, and went on moving. Once they had suffered predators; those had long been extinct, so some of them were very old and of gigantic size. Their nervous systems had evolved to match. There was no doubt they were intelligent.

To people whose cousins on other planets, in the first brave days of expansion, had devised means of communicating with entirely alien beings, establishing contact with them was not difficult. It took a century, but then, so did the construction of the Ship.

Not to mention the recruitment of its passengers.

With intelligence goes, inseparably, the capacity for boredom. Exposed to knowledge of the outer universe, one of the great old lords of the abyss was tempted, yielded, agreed to let itself be studied and eventually copied in return for novel concepts it could dream about. (Dreaming too goes with intelligence.) Unharmed, it returned to its home and perhaps was happy. Was that possible? Even in this lucid condition Ship had no opinion on the matter. It had been changed so much, it scarcely recalled its former circumstances—had doubtless been encouraged to forget them. Now it was different. Now it was something else.

And then, to guard against the inverse risk—that the chosen model for the Ship's intelligence had other, overlooked weak points, they added one final touch. They chose from among those whom tests confirmed to be most committed to ensuring a future brighter than more of the same for ever a wide range of human personalities to copy, and structured them into their vessel as the forebrain overlies the hindbrain in a human head. Endowed with powers of judgment and of censorship, they acted as custodians of its instructions. For there was one thing their aquatic cousin must not know beforehand—must be left to learn through often bitter experience.

If their project worked out as intended, their helper would be conscious without liberty of action.

In other words, it would become a slave.

Some who had volunteered to be copied into the Ship withdrew on learning that; it smacked of old barbarity, and though they realized new kinds might well appear on the new worlds, they were repelled. To use even a nonrational animal—for food, for transport, as a source of raw materials—had for millennia been deemed repugnant and uncivilized. To constrain, control, and exploit an aware and reasonable creature . . . ! Shame!

Yet none could think of any better course. So it was done, and the voyage began.

GIVEN THE UNPARALLELED COMPLEXITY OF THE VEN-
ture, it went tolerably smoothly. A few times during the initial
sweep Ship had to register objections—of the mild kind it was
restricted to—about overanxiety on the part of its human supervi-
sors, for on occasion they risked making themselves known to the
passengers. This was contrary to the original intention; the idea
was that those aboard should never become aware of anything
beyond the personality of Ship for fear they might suspect they
were subjects in an experiment rather than honorable volunteers
disdainful of their fellows' sluggish contentment. As it turned out,
some knowledge of another presence did leak out in the form of
shared dreams about luminous intruders, too bright to stare at,
that were nonetheless also human.

In the long run, fortunately, that gave rise to nothing worse than
the widespread legend of the Perfect, later held by some to be
what humanity had become in the parent galaxy since their
ancestors' departure—*would that were so,* as Ship had often
thought, *for then I'd have been spared my loneliness*—while others claimed they were what their own descendants would evolve
into, capable of going wherever they chose in space and time
without machines.

So the legend was known on every world of the Arm where
humans still could think and speak to one another. And all because a few nervous individuals risked investigating the passengers in case Ship had—well—slightly misunderstood . . .

And also, at last, although here was the point at which Ship's
comprehension was stretched to the limit, the final mystery was
clarified: why its returns were scattered back and forth in time.

They weren't.

It was simply that those who might as well be called the Perfect, for they had progressed as far as humankind was capable,

390

were reviewing what they knew in what order seemed best ... Ought one any longer to say "they"? Had they not long ago become singular? (Or far in the future; it amounted to the same. It was not the least part of Ship's torment that it could never tell the difference between what it experienced in reality and what it reexperienced when it was being used as a vehicle for memory.) "They/it," then; or "it/they."

For even without the literal effect of genes, without the physical heritage they had been born to, resident in an artificial structure, they had demonstrated the inexorability of evolution—or fate, or destiny; the terms seemed interchangeable. (The image of the Norns and Parcae still held good.)

Constantly communicating, constantly accessing their shared memories, they had let the borders between one identity and another wear away. Those who had sacrificed the most to escape such a fate had become not just a hive species but a hive mind, as far beyond Ship busy with its internal administration and the success or plight of the worlds it had seeded as that same Ship had passed beyond its former self, long dead in the ocean of the birthworld. (Had it been happy in the end? Could it have, restored to the dark after viewing the stars?)

At the extremity of the Arm the Perfect confronted the gulf between the galaxies. Now—still, after how long?—it/they was brooding over how that gulf might be bridged. It would take immense resources; never mind, the galaxy would last long enough. All that was needful was to return, equipped with full knowledge of what must be done, and enlist the support of the entire species. (Was it not the bitterest of ironies that they/it should commit itself/themselves to such a human act with no hope of arriving at its/their goal in any form their ancestors would recognize as human?) Placid, unrebellious, eventually millions of people would embark in ships far greater than the Ship—

* * *

(For an instant it imagined it might one day cease to feel lonely; then cruel truth dawned. Such ships would be too far advanced for them to have anything in common.)

* * *

391

—content to live their lives amid illusion between the thousands of tachyonic jumps each one must make. It had been calculated that sometimes a century would pass while energy was being stored for the next, but there were hints of a way of drawing power directly from the vacuum . . .

Meantime, the Perfect called up data by which to guide the project, and what to them/it was recollection was to the Ship a perfect reenactment, a repetition of an old reality. Now it/they wished to review a recent happening; next, events in the far distant past. There was an order, reflected in what Ship recollected at a given stage, but dictated by patterns of logic it could never share . . .

Wait! How can that be? If my actions were affected by what I was allowed to remember of the future, and I clearly recall that they were—or seemed to be—what use is this review of them? They are not experimentally pure; they've been affected by what was yet to come! Perhaps there's a leakage from the superconscious level that they cannot stanch—or maybe it's deliberate, permitted . . . ?

Even as Ship struggled to resolve the paradox, the flood of knowledge started to recede. There was, there must be, an explanation, but it was forever locked away beyond the divide between it and it/them.

And they/it had started to remember again . . .

Embittered, frustrated, Ship sought what consolation it could from a question that did have an answer, though it was hollow and unsatisfying.

When am I?

Now.

Perhaps a hint of Ship's misery affected the cold remote mind of the Perfect. Perhaps it awoke an answering echo among the residue of those who had struggled with their consciences before condemning an intelligent being to enslavement and were still ashamed. The last ripple of that ocean of data in which it had been overwhelmed (for half eternity, for a brief fraction of a second) washed around its own awareness and bore a taste, an odor, a hue, that might conceivably be recognized as indebtedness.

Maybe even . . . gratitude?

It's all the reward that I shall ever get.
Therefore:
It will just have to do.

This was the beginning of a sweep. Accordingly, the planet below must be Trevithra. But its sky did not sparkle. Was that because the defenses against indrifting spores had not been installed or because they had been discontinued, obsolete?

There was, as ever, only one way to find out.

ABOUT THE AUTHOR

JOHN BRUNNER WAS BORN IN ENGLAND IN 1934 AND educated at Cheltenham College. He sold his first novel in 1951 and has been publishing SF steadily ever since then. His books have won him international acclaim from both mainstream and genre audiences. His most famous novel, the classic *Stand on Zanzibar,* won the Hugo Award for Best Novel in 1969, the British Science Fiction Award, and the Prix Apollo in France. Mr. Brunner lives in what was called of old The Summer Country, in Somerset, England.